ANOTHER CHANCE AT LOVE

"Can't you at least take a leave and try it?" Christopher asked. "Take a chance on me?"

"Can't you at least come to San Diego and explore the possibilities there?" Kirstin asked back.

"I can't, not yet, if ever. I have to be honest with you."

"See, we do need time and distance to test our feelings. If what we have is true and strong, things will work out for us; we'll find a fair compromise. Let's do as we planned while we continue to explore and deepen our relationship."

"If you leave, I'll lose you. You'll find a better man, a whole man, one who can give you what I can't, and you'll forget about me."

"You're the only man I want Christopher."

"Swear it, Kirstin. Swear you won't stop loving me."

Kirstin brought her lips to Christopher's. "I swear it, Christopher. I swear I won't stop loving you because no other man has made me feel as you do . . ."

JANELLE TAYLOR

TAKING CHANCES

ZEBRA BOOKS
KENSINGTON PUBLISHING CORP.

ZEBRA BOOKS are published by

Kensington Publishing Corp.
475 Park Avenue South
New York, NY 10016

First Printing: August, 1993

Printed in the United States of America

One

Kirstin Lowrey gradually regained consciousness. A physician's face hovered within inches of hers, close enough for Kirstin to feel his breath tickling her cheeks and to smell his cologne. As he checked her eyes with a tiny flashlight and felt the pulse point in her throat, her still dazed mind surrendered to a seductive dream of playing doctor with Mel Gibson. *Such beautiful green eyes . . . So handsome . . . Old Spice . . . Climb up here with me and —*

"She's coming out of it, John." The man in the white medical coat leaned closer to her. "Can you hear me? Can you tell me your name?"

"Kirstin Lowrey."

"How many fingers am I holding up?"

"Two. Now three," she added when he raised another. She felt queasy, weak. She looked around in confusion. She noticed an IV in her left arm. She was on an examination table in a

7

doctor's office but didn't know how she had gotten there. She realized she wasn't dreaming and the handsome man with the sexy five o'clock shadow wasn't Mel Gibson, though there was quite a strong resemblance. "Where am I? What happened? Who are you?"

As he took her blood pressure the stranger replied, "You were driving erratically and ran off the road; damaged your car badly." Motioning to the other man with a nod and glance, he said, "This is Captain John Two Fists from the local police. He thought you were drunk or on drugs. You passed out before he could get any information, so he checked your car and purse for identification and clues to your problem."

While adjusting the IV flow to a slower pace, he continued. "John found a medical alert card, but he didn't have any liquid sugar to use. Neither did you, Mrs. Lowrey. I'm Doctor Christopher Harrison. Since I was closer than the High Plains Hospital and you seemed in bad shape, John brought you to the office on my ranch. You're lucky you didn't kill yourself or injure another driver. You need to be more careful with your diabetes." He saw her sea-blue eyes widen in distress, then her thick lashes lower in shame. Reactions, he thought in bitterness, she *should* be feeling after imperiling the safety of others with her carelessness behind the wheel. "I'm giving you glucose, so relax and let it take effect."

Kirstin was disquieted by the physician's cool

green gaze, scolding tone, and grim expression. She closed the gap in her shirt after he removed his stethoscope and straightened. She spoke quietly as he focused his piercing gaze on her again. "The accident is pretty much a blur. When I left Amarillo, I thought I could make it to Roswell for lunch and Carlsbad for dinner. But there were miles of road construction and I was held up for hours."

She took a deep breath and exhaled, aware of her rapid heartbeat and trembling. "I remember dodging barricade barrels and feeling strange, but I don't know why I didn't pull over, unless there wasn't a safe spot. I've never experienced anything weird like that. I recall a rough bump, being jostled around, and the policeman asking me questions; then, everything went black. Will I be all right?"

As he nodded, Christopher's keen gaze took in her designer jeans and red western shirt which were rumpled and damp, partly due to her symptoms and partly to his own dislike of air-conditioning. A diamond-cluster ring on the hand that adjusted her clothing sparkled beneath the bright examination lights. Each time he leaned close, she exuded a provocative smell that evoked thoughts of a summer breeze wafting over wildflowers, a scent he found pleasing, as was her voice. According to her driver's license, she'd be forty-six on August fifteenth, but she could easily pass for mid-thirties. It was clear to him that she

9

took extra care with her appearance and figure because both were topnotch. Her hair was the color of ripened wheat like his uncle used to grow on this land before he inherited it and her blue eyes were wide and expressive. A real looker, he concluded. He realized it must seem as if he was inspecting her and he looked away, reluctant to let her see how attractive he found her.

"You're lucky John was the one to come by. He was heading back to Clovis from Elida. At a different time, Mrs. Lowrey, you could have lain there too long without help to avoid complications, or maybe even to survive. Somebody dangerous could have taken advantage of your unconscious state. You could have been robbed or kidnapped, your car stolen, and you dumped in the desert. That's happened before on lonely stretches of road."

Kirstin was horrified by the jeopardy in which she had placed herself.

He stopped at the stricken look in her eyes. His heart softened a little. It wasn't her fault he was in a bad mood after receiving that tormenting letter from his ex-wife. He shouldn't take out his anger and frustration on a patient, even a reckless one. "You must have gunned the gas pedal in your confusion, because John said you suddenly took off into nowhere at top speed; you crashed through the barrels and plowed into the sand. Your car's undriveable, so he's having it towed to the Nissan dealer in Clovis, unless you prefer another shop and mechanic."

She shook her head as she kept her alarmed gaze glued to his.

"In case you remember your meeting with John, I told him that being belligerent and uncooperative are common symptoms of your illness."

Kirstin recalled parts of an embarrassing confrontation. She explained to the officer that she had found out about her diabetes and took some educational classes on it only six weeks ago. "I don't usually have problems, but I guess I was careless," she admitted. "When I realized I had run out of snacks, I was already caught up in the road construction and there was no place to buy more. I had glucose tablets and I thought I had ample time to reach Roswell to eat. You don't have to worry, Captain Two Fists, I won't let this happen again. And I'm sorry I was rude; that isn't like me."

The half-Apache lawman smiled and said, "I'm sure you've learned a valuable lesson today, Mrs. Lowrey."

Kirstin liked the warmth in his dark-brown eyes and comforting smile. "I promise you I did, John." She turned to the other man, "How am I doing, Doctor Harrison? What's the treatment and prognosis?"

Christopher was impressed by her manners and attitude. "John called me while you were en route and I got in touch with your doctor; her name and number were in your kit. She faxed me cop-

11

ies of your records and info on your problem. I used a medical program on my computer system to call up diabetes and hypoglycemic attacks so I'd know the best way to treat your condition. I've had experience with this before, a long time ago. I put an ampule of D50-W in the drip to get glucose into you fast. I don't have any treatment kits or shots because I don't have any diabetic patients, but I'll start stocking Glutose and Glycagon for emergencies. Don't worry, Mrs. Lowrey, we got to you soon enough so you'll be fine. That is, if you take proper care of yourself."

Kirstin imagined how furious Steve was going to be when or if he learned about all this, as if she didn't have enough problems with him already. Worse, she could lose her new job if her employer learned about her diabetes, and it might be difficult to find another, as too many companies still discriminated against people with disabilities and diseases, despite laws to protect them. It was hard enough to be an older female in the work force without adding a medical problem. She had to keep her condition a secret until she learned how to deal with it and proved herself at the Medico. "As I said, Doctor, I usually do take good care of myself. Be assured, this was an accident that won't be repeated."

Christopher noticed her tension and assumed she was peeved by his scolding. Though she had deserved a tongue-lashing, she sounded and looked sorry, and seemed determined not to allow it to happen again. *Have empathy, Chris. She's probably scared, hurting, and worried just like you were after your accident.* "I tried the Augusta number listed on your ID but an operator said it was disconnected. I also phoned Katie Lowrey, the person listed to notify in case of an emergency; an answering machine said she was out and would return my call later. Is there anyone else I should phone? Your husband or parents?"

"My parents are deceased. And I'm a widow. Katie is my daughter. She lives and works in Los Angeles. I'm in the process of moving from Augusta to San Diego. I was sightseeing along the way and got snared by your road repairs."

"Next time, every time, be prepared for emergencies. That's why they're called emergencies, Mrs. Lowrey, they're unforseen. I'll continue the drip for a while longer, but you need to get food inside you. Milk, fruit, and peanut butter sandwich all right with you? That's what you need under these conditions."

"Yes, fine." She watched him leave the room and heard another door close in the adjoining one. She looked at the policeman and smiled. "Thank you again for the rescue. I could have been in deep trouble if you hadn't . . ." Her eyes filled with tears. She dabbed their corners with a tissue the captain handed to her. Thank heaven she hadn't been so out of her mind that she'd pulled the revolver friends had insisted she bring along for protection. In her crazy state, she might

13

have shot him, killed him . . .

"Chris will do all he can to get you well fast. You can trust him, Mrs. Lowrey. I've known him since we were kids. His uncle was a good man, too; did lots of doctoring on the Mescalero Reservation southwest of here; that's where I was born and raised." John kept talking while she got her tears under control. "While I was attending ENMU in Portales, I worked here. During Chris's visits, we became close friends, *ch'uunes* as we Apaches say." He chuckled and leaned against the wall. "I was glad when he moved here three years ago and took over after his uncle died and left him this ranch and practice. Older folks especially like a healer who treats them like a person, not a number or chart. Even makes house calls. And he doesn't charge an arm 'n' leg like those big-city doctors. 'Course, he doesn't have to."

The implication in John's last statement was clear: Harrison had money. Kirstin prayed he wasn't just a rich country boy playing doctor. She accepted another tissue to wipe away the last of her tears, as she did not want to be bawling like a child when the handsome physician returned. She was grateful John was kind and friendly and understanding. He reminded her of a gentle giant, though he was shorter than his tall friend.

"That's right, no need to cry. Chris will take good care of you. Before you know it, you'll be on your way again. 'Course I hope you stay long enough to see some of our beautiful state. You were heading for Carlsbad?"

"Yes, to visit the caverns, then White Sands. I haven't seen much of the United States, so I was really looking forward to my trip. This accident could certainly wreck my plans. Does my car look bad?" She wondered if she could cover damages without reporting them to the insurance company. Only if it wasn't expensive. She didn't want to dig too deeply into her dwindled savings, as the money David had left her had barely covered his debts, Katie's college, and Katie's move to California.

"It didn't look good to me, Mrs. Lowrey. You can check —"

John stopped as Christopher returned with a plate containing small glass of milk, a pear, and a sandwich. He set it down, helped Kirstin sit up, and waited for her to steady herself before releasing his hold on her forearm and passing her the plate with his right hand. In case she became dizzy, he remained close as he looked at his long-time friend and said, "It could be hours before Mrs. Lowrey fully recovers physically and mentally, John, and I'll need to watch for rebound hyperglycemia. Why don't you head on to the office? I'll give you a call and a full report later."

"Suits me, Chris. I have work to do before five. You know Maria, she gets on her high horse if I'm too late for supper." He chuckled, then looked at Kirstin. "Doc Harrison will take good care of you, Mrs. Lowrey. You can handle the problem

15

with your car when you're feeling better. It'll be in good hands with Joe Bob. He's a good mechanic, honest and reasonable."

"Thank you, Captain Two Fists. You've been most kind. Will I get a ticket for reckless driving or something?" How, Kirstin fretted, could she keep this incident a secret if it went on her record and in her work file?

"No need to write it up. I'm sure you'll be more careful in the future."

Relieved and grateful, Kirstin smiled and thanked him.

Christopher made certain she was clear-headed and sitting with her back against the wall for support before he walked outside with John and chatted for a few minutes while she ate. When he returned and she finished her food, he put aside the plate and told her to lie down and relax. "Let's see if we can figure out what went wrong so it won't happen again."

Kirstin rested one arm across her stomach and tried not to stare at him as she said, "I haven't had any serious problems until now, not since Dr. Cooper got my treatment plan regulated. I guess my brain was clouded today."

"Probably because you were sitting for hours and were relaxed, until the road construction delayed you and stressed you. Are you sure you would recognize a low coming on? You could have hypoglycemic unawareness. That causes some patients to ignore or misread the symptoms.

If you have a fear of lows and imagine symptoms but find none when you check your blood-sugar level, that can cause you to unconsciously ignore real symptoms."

"So far that hasn't happened," she replied, alarmed about the possibility of developing a new complication. "I had some lows at first, so my doctor reduced the amount of medication I was taking; that should be on the records she faxed you." He nodded. "I didn't have any warning symptoms that I noticed. I've been in good control for weeks, holding near-normal levels."

"That's good and bad, Mrs. Lowrey. Near-normal-control doesn't allow much flexibility. The slightest change in your meals, activities, or moods can mess up your balance. You know that proper exercise and diet are as much a part of your prescription as your pills or shots are, don't you?" She nodded, wide-eyed with concern. "Diabetes changes your lifestyle, rules your routine, or it *should* if you want to stay healthy, not to mention *alive*. You can over-do as easily as under-do any part of your triangle. Did you do any vigorous exercise or have too much to drink last night? Both of those things can cause adverse reactions hours later, or even the following day."

"I used a treadmill at the hotel and had one glass of wine with dinner as instructed, Doctor Harrison. My blood sugar was fine before and after I exercised. I thought I had my schedule worked out perfectly for today's travel, but I didn't count on running out of snacks in this deserted area or on being delayed. I also noticed my emergency Coke was a sugarfree-diet one that the store clerk gave me by mistake. I was going to restock my supplies at my next stop in Roswell. As you can see, I didn't make it there."

While looking at a paper in his right hand, he asked in a casual tone, "What is your meal schedule?"

"Breakfast at eight, lunch at twelve, snack at three-thirty, dinner at six, and snack at nine to ten. I have forty-two carbos with one optional protein and fat at breakfast; sixty-two carbos, one protein, and one optional fat at lunch; one carbo for snack; sixty-six carbos, two to three proteins, and two optional fats at dinner; and one carbo and an optional alcoholic drink as a snack. I also have a free-foods and drinks list."

"That's what your doctor's instructions say, so no problem there."

Had he been testing her? There was no need; she had memorized those required quantities of carbohydrates, proteins, and fats, and always ate properly and on schedule. "I changed my car clock to local time, but kept my watch on Georgia time to prevent mistakes."

As he observed her for mood changes and reactions, he asked, "Did you correct it when you crossed the New Mexico line this morning?"

"Yes, at Texico when I stopped at the welcome center to pick up tourist brochures on Carlsbad

18

and White Sands. According to my watch, I should have eaten lunch at twelve. When I left Portales, I had ample time to reach Roswell, but got delayed, as you know."

"In your dazed state, you must have been looking at your car clock, because John brought you here at one forty-five Georgia time. Still, that's fast acting for such severe hypoglycemia; there must be another cause for it. Perhaps you've gotten in such good control that your oral medication might still be too strong. You definitely didn't eat right and eat on time and weren't prepared for any problems. Have you lost a lot of weight?"

"Not recently. About ten pounds last year when I started working out at the gym a few times a week with friends. Doctor Cooper stressed the importance of maintaining proper weight to help fight this thing." For some reason, Kirstin couldn't bring herself to call diabetes a *disease*. She preferred to think of it more like an illness or ailment that must be treated daily. To her medically trained mind, *Disease* sounded dangerous and insidious, debilitating. She was determined not to allow the "condition" to ruin her life, spoil her fresh start. She had too much lost time to make up for and lots of living to do.

"I saw on your medical record that there's a family history of diabetes on your paternal side."

"Yes, so I shouldn't have been surprised when I was diagnosed, but I still was. Despite it being in our family, I didn't know much about it. I do now."

He kept reading. "Family history, over forty, two large babies . . . It's apparent that being overweight, having high blood pressure, or being African or Hispanic or Native American weren't factors for you."

Kirstin watched him as he studied her records. "You know a lot about diabetes, Doctor Harrison. Did you get all this information from Doctor Cooper and your computer program?"

He glanced at her, half-smiled at the compliment, then focused his gaze back on the pages. "Some, mostly refresher stuff. My college roommate and best friend was diabetic, but he was on insulin shots. At least once or twice a year, no matter how good he was, he wound up in the hospital for insulin reaction, severe hyperglycemia. I'm sure Doctor Cooper told you that some diabetics have inexplicable sudden highs and lows or complications."

"Yes, but I was doing everything I could to prevent them."

He reminded, "Except following your meal schedule and being prepared for emergencies. You weren't wearing a medical alert bracelet either."

"I signed up for Medic Alert but I hadn't received the bracelet before I left. If they've notified me by mail, I missed the letter during my move. I normally keep glucose tablets within reach, but I must have put them away while I was disoriented."

"Before traveling, you should have purchased one of those inexpensive bracelets from a drugstore. You should never be without medical ID and treatment tablets. It's best to keep them in your pocket in case you don't have your purse with you when trouble strikes. Weren't you told that?"

Kirstin nodded and her cheeks reddened. She wished he would stop treating her like a child who had misbehaved. Yet, he—along with Officer Two Fists—had saved her life, so she knew she should be polite and grateful. "You're right; I admit I was careless this time. I suppose I had a lot on my mind. I'm sorry."

As Christopher checked her pulse and blood pressure again, he said, "I apologize if it sounds as if I've been giving you a scolding, Mrs. Lowrey, but what you did could have been dangerous for others."

"Thank you, Doctor Harrison, and you're right to fuss at me. I was stupid." Kirstin watched him fumble with the equipment, as if he were suddenly all thumbs. She wondered if she was making him as nervous as he was making her. He hadn't struck her as a man who would be uneasy or insecure around women. He looked to be around her own age, with mussed sable hair that fell over his forehead but was trimmed in a neat style, short like men were wearing again these days. His brows were straight and close to his dark-green eyes, giving them a hooded appearance that hinted at playfulness and mystery. His nose was straight, smaller and narrower than most men's but suited to his features. There were shallow lines across his forehead, and tiny creases fanned near his eyes. He hadn't shaved, but her arrival might have interrupted his morning routine. She wondered if he were married, divorced, or widowed. No doubt, if he was unattached, he had no trouble getting dates and probably had to fight women off with a stick. Good looks, money, status, education, and manners: Christopher Harrison had a hefty share of them.

"We all make stupid mistakes, Mrs. Lowrey. Some are just more dangerous and costly to us than others. You're lucky you can correct yours."

"And I was told chivalry was dead," she murmured as she experienced an unsettling warmth at his touch. "Perhaps you westerners are different from city men, nicer, more polite. Where I work, most men don't even open a door or move a chair for a woman. I wonder where all the southern gentlemen went?"

Obviously amused, he put away his instruments and supplies and inquired, "You said you were moving?"

She noted the change of subject. "Yes, to San Diego."

To move in with someone? To get married? "Moving for family or work?" he inquired aloud without

22

meaning to do so.

Kirstin looked up at him and said, "For work."

"What kind of work do you do, Mrs. Lowrey?"

"You can call me Kirstin. Medical research technologist for Medico of America. I'm transferring from Augusta to San Diego. They closed their Georgia branch and asked me to move to the head complex in California."

He gazed at her as respect—and envy—filled him. His patient was clearly quite intelligent and skilled, as Medico—he knew—only hired the best. That she'd been asked to relocate for them spoke even more highly of her talents. "Which field of research are you in?"

"Mostly pharmacology and physiology."

"What exactly is your job at Medico?"

"I do specimen surgery, treatment, dissection, and autopsies myself, or I assist with them. I run chemical tests, blood and tissue samples, chart and analyze data, observe new techniques and procedures, act as liaison with other researchers and drug firms, and handle experiments, either alone or with my boss. I assume I'll have the same duties in San Diego; that's what I was told. I hope it's true because I love my work."

Christopher grasped the excitement and pride in her expression and voice. That's how he had felt about his past career before . . . "Where did you train?" he asked. She was the first woman in ages to arouse his interest. He wanted to learn more about her. He felt enlivened, stimulated.

23

They had a great deal in common.

"I graduated from the University of Georgia. I studied and worked in pharmacology, physiology, and endocrinology for a few years at the Medical College of Georgia in Augusta before I resigned to have a third child. David wanted . . ." She paused. "I've been with Medico in private research for a year."

"You hide your age well; that's a lot to accomplish for a woman who appears so young," he remarked.

Kirstin felt a rush of heat race over her at his compliment. "I was a college freshman at seventeen. I received my technologist's degree and apprenticed between my second and third child. My chart probably told you I'm forty-five, at least until August fifteenth. How old are you?" she asked before thinking she shouldn't have.

"Forty-nine for a few more months. The big five-O coming up."

"Where did *you* study and train?"

"Harvard and Johns Hopkins. I practiced in New York City, Chicago, and Dallas, then wound up in Baltimore. I retired four years ago and moved here three years ago, but I got dragged into a part-time country practice."

His smile and mellow manner disarmed her. She wanted to know more about this man. "*Dragged* into? How so?"

"There are a lot of farmers and ranchers close by who are too busy during the day for making

24

doctor's appointments, and Clovis is a long ride for them when they have chores to do, especially in busy seasons like spring and fall. Many of them don't like big and noisy hospitals and offices or being herded through examinations like cattle. Plus, some have farming accidents that have to be treated quickly. Had a few myself when I was learning the ropes around here. The locals got used to my uncle's personal attention and treatment, so they forced me to become his replacement. I tried my best to refuse them, but they wouldn't let me. How can you turn your back on people who need you so much they won't take no for an answer? So much for early retirement." He grinned. "I don't have a nurse because I'm not that busy and I don't have regular hours."

Retire at forty-nine? No, she corrected, at *forty-five*. Yet, he must be dedicated and love medicine to have allowed people to persuade him to reopen the practice "The lady at the welcome station said this state is the fifth largest in the U.S., but metro Atlanta has a larger population than New Mexico. Isn't this area rather deserted for a man with such credentials?" she questioned, then blushed as she realized he may have had personal reasons for an early retirement.

"Nope. I like New Mexico. Clean air, blue skies, open spaces, uncomplicated existence, friendly folks, easy living. No more chasing planes or rushing to work on countless patients a day or living in overcrowded and dangerous cities. Once in a while, I play veterinarian for friends whose finances are tight or when the vet isn't in. I've even had to take a few emergency stitches. But let's get back to you," he said abruptly, unwilling to reveal any more about himself. There was no need to expose his troubles, and he didn't want to evoke pity.

Kirstin noticed his sudden withdrawal but said nothing. Perhaps he thought their conversation was getting too personal.

"Do you have any friends or family in this area?"

"No, why?"

"By the time you recover fully later today, Mrs. Lowrey, it'll be too late to continue your trip. You also need to be watched for rebound hyperglycemia; high blood sugar often follows severe hypoglycemia. You should be regulated before you continue, especially since you're traveling alone. If you can stay around a few days, I'll use Dr. Cooper's notes to get your diet, medication, and exercise balanced; get the old triangle repaired. While you're unstable and experiencing difficulty, you shouldn't be alone in a hotel room, either. You're welcome to stay at the ranch tonight, so I can keep an eye on you for side effects. Better still, why not stay for the next few days and give us plenty of time to make certain you're okay? I have a guest room I use for disabled patients or those I need to observe a while longer." It seemed only logical, not to mention hospitable, to invite her to stay over since she was a stranger in the area, and had no one to watch over her at a motel. Her problem really didn't require hospitalization; besides, he found her rather fascinating and an excellent medical challenge. "Remember your car needs repairs and that could take days, longer if parts have to be ordered. The Nissan dealership where they towed your car is in Clovis, over thirty miles away. If you'd rather not stay at the ranch, Mrs. Lowrey, you should check into the High Plains Hospital in Clovis for observation and treatment."

"Stay here . . . with you? But . . ." she started to argue, then halted in confusion.

"But, what? I am a doctor, Mrs. Lowrey, and I do—as I said—have patients stay over sometimes. You'll be quite safe. No need to worry. I'll be a perfect gentleman."

Why, Kirstin wondered, was her mouth suddenly dry, her gaze too wide, her heart racing? He wasn't coming on to her or suggesting she sleep with him! Why was she feeling so silly? "Won't that be an imposition, Doctor Harrison? Surely your wife will object to your lodging a female patient."

"I'm not married, Mrs. Lowrey. There's no one here except a foreman who lives in a house a few miles away and two part-time ranch hands who come over three times a week to do chores for me. I have a housekeeper who cooks and cleans for me, but Helen's away on a family emergency; her husband is my foreman. Their daughter is having a baby."

Kirstin was tense and silent. They would be . . . alone. Miles from the nearest town and neighbor, if she recalled the area correctly. Was he trustworthy? Was this proper? Safe? Necessary?

Christopher grinned and suggested, "You can repay my hospitality by helping out with the cooking and cleaning while Helen's gone. I'm not useless around the house and kitchen, but I admit I get out of those chores anytime I can. So you see, I have an ulterior motive." He chuckled. Her hesitation intrigued him. Was she, he mused, a liberated woman who didn't want to depend on a man for anything, afraid of him and the secluded setting. Or was she being coy? Whatever, she would be safe with him. Although she was beautiful and tempting, matters had to remain professional between them.

Kirstin pondered her options. Should she stay with a stranger? But what else could she do? The local authorities did know she was here. John might even check on her because of the traffic accident. She worried that if she went to a hospital, Medico would be informed and her new job might be put in jeopardy. If she'd known she was a diabetic a year, or even three months ago, she night not have gotten the position and transfer. She needed to handle this matter discreetly and she had to get her health under control before reaching San Diego. Once she proved herself at

Medico she would reveal her condition, as it could be dangerous not to do so.

Perhaps she should stay at the ranch. Christopher seemed like a gentleman, and a compassionate and skilled doctor. He was charming, a little mysterious, and had a boyish smile she liked. There was something in his gaze and voice that said he was trustworthy . . . unless he was a good con artist. Staying with this handsome stranger for a while would provide a little excitement and adventure in her life, an interesting tale to relate to her friends; it would certainly be different than anything she had done before. If she didn't like the situation by morning, she could go to a motel while her car was being repaired and he could treat her during daylight visits.

Kirstin thought about her reaction to her would-be host. His husky voice sent tingles over her, feelings she hadn't experienced in a long time. Actually, ones she hadn't ever felt before, even with David. How strange for a woman her age — a mother, grandmother, and widow to boot — to be thinking and feeling as she was, like a teenager with out-of-control hormones! She could remember thinking as a young girl that forty-five was old, over the hill. Of course, Steve would have a royal fit if he learned of any of this. Well, he would just have to accept the fact that the accident wasn't her fault, and "Chris" wasn't a threat. She met his gaze squarely and said, "If you're dangerous, Doctor Harrison, the local police wouldn't have left me alone with you." If she gave him no opening or reason to make a pass at her, the arrangement should be fine for a short time.

"It's my hospitality or the Clovis High Plains Hospital because, as I told you, a motel alone would be too risky in your condition. Rest assured I have no romantic interest in my female patients. You said you were from Augusta, so you can tell me all about the Master's Golf Tournament; it starts this week."

Kirstin permitted his second statement to pass unchallenged. Still, it rankled that he thought she was flirting with him, or that he'd find it necessary to warn her not to do so. "Naturally I'll pay for any hospitality and medical treatment I receive, Doctor Harrison, if you don't mind putting up with me for a day or so." He needn't worry; she wasn't interested in marriage at this point in her life and might never be again, not after David, and not even if Chris did have her hormones going wild. She had worked hard to become a medical technologist at the prestigious Medico of America. She was excited about relocating across the country. She had independence and a golden opportunity and was ready to enjoy life and her career to the fullest. She wanted to spread her wings and fly. Sure, it was a little scary to pull up roots and move so far from where she'd been born and reared and lived half of her life. Everything in California would be new and different, but she would have Katie nearby to help her adjust. And Steve . . .

Christopher observed her hesitation. Perhaps she was worried about what her boyfriend might think of the set-up. She needn't concern herself, as she would be—could be—nothing more than a patient to him, a short medical diversion and challenge. "This might be the perfect opportunity and time for you to accept and face the risks of damaging your body; then, maybe you'll learn to take better care of it."

"I don't take chances with my life and health. It just happened."

He admired the way her blue eyes sparkled and her cheeks flushed as she rose to her defense. "Calm down, Mrs. Lowrey. It could be a natural mistake; that's what we need to find out. Besides, I can use company and help for a while. After all, country doctors don't get many beautiful and charming patients. It'll give me a break from a dull season. I'll be the perfect host. I'll have you in A-1 condition before you leave my ranch."

Was he flirting with her? Was it crazy to stay here? Yet, she warmed to his compliment and stirring voice, his flattering attention that gave her feminine ego a needed boost. *This could be fun and interesting, Kirstin, a real adventure. It could give you a chance to enjoy spending time with a man, maybe even make a new friend. You're an adult; you know how to behave yourself. Be brave. Go for it, as your children would say. And, who knows, maybe a little innocent*

31

hanky panky wouldn't be bad for a change!

"Do you always take so long to make a decision?" he teased.

"If I didn't know better, Doctor, I'd believe you're enjoying having a guinea pig to work on. Maybe you're running low on your monthly patient quota," she jested as her body responded from head to foot to the sensual sound of his voice.

"Absolutely, Mrs. Lowrey. I don't get many captive patients to practice on these days," he quipped, then chuckled to show he was jesting. "Why don't you prick your finger so I can check your blood sugar and make certain you're taking a sufficient sample to measure. Here's your kit. John brought along your things; he didn't want them to get stolen from the car before the towers reached it. He put your suitcases inside the house. Let me disconnect that IV. first; it's finished its work."

Taking care not to hurt her or to make the diminished dexterity in his left hand obvious, Christopher removed the needle from her arm and placed a Band-Aid over the insertion point. There was a little bruising and bleeding there, but they would pass. He handed her a Diapac with her equipment.

Kirstin set the monitor beside her, pressed the on button, and inserted a test strip when the instrument was ready for use. She winced as she lanced a finger and squeezed it until a small drop of blood formed. She placed the liquid red dot on the white circle and waited for the automatic readout.

Christopher said, "Your technique is fine." She sent him a tiny smile. He scanned her from head to toe as she did the task. Her tawny hair was parted off center and curled to fall just below her shoulders in a casual style that flattered her face. During his initial examination, he had touched those flaxen locks and found them soft and silky. Her eye color reminded him of a stormy blue sea. Her complexion told him she was very careful about exposing her skin to the sun. A firm figure that her casual outfit did not conceal said she either exercised a great deal or was an avid sportswoman and dieter, as she had hinted at earlier. Her medium-length nails were manicured and covered with clear polish. She wore little makeup but looked as if she needed none to enhance her natural beauty. Now that her striking features were relaxed, he realized there was a sensual softness to them that reminded him of Michelle Pfeiffer in the movie he had seen the other night. Why was she traveling alone? "You said you're sightseeing along the way?"

"I haven't seen much of the United States, so I was taking advantage of my month off to explore all I could along the way. There's so much to see in America. I suppose you've been to Carlsbad and White Sands many times."

"Only once each. I'm pretty much a homebody."

He lifted the vial of test strips and toyed with it as a deep torment gnawed at him. Living here was all right, but it wasn't what he wanted, what he needed. He damned the twist of fate that had stolen his life from him. He wished he hadn't received that letter today — it had brought back the pain of his loss and put him in a foul mood. The past was over and he had to accept his circumstances, his exile. He had to come to grips with himself, and find personal and professional fulfillment here, if possible. That's what he'd been trying to do for four bitter years. Though it was a worthy position, he hadn't sacrificed, studied, and trained to become a country doctor. He'd had a brilliant, lucrative, and satisfying surgical career snatched from him by a love-crazed and scorned woman. That added to his ex-wife's betrayal, made it surprising he could even trust any female!

Kirstin wondered if she detected resentment in his last statement. He had drifted into a broody silence that tugged at her heart. Perhaps his wife had left him or died and he was still suffering. A loss, whether by death or divorce, always hurt. Some cases she knew hurt more than others and caused terrible damage to those left behind. David had . . . *Get off it, Kirstin, the past is over and you're doing great.* "The brochures looked wonderful. I can hardly wait to visit both places, if I have enough time after I handle my problems here. Captain Two Fists said my car is in bad shape. I hope they can repair it quickly. And inexpensively," she mumbled before thinking how that might sound to him.

"Don't you have insurance? A person can find himself in a terrible bind without sufficient coverage."

"Yes, but I'd rather not report this. Do you know what I mean?"

"Higher premiums or a possible cancellation or added stipulation?" he surmised. She nodded, but looked as if she meant more. Maybe there was another reason not to report it; maybe she already had black marks on her insurance and traffic record. "Joe Bob Bridges is one of the best mechanics I've ever known. Your car couldn't be in better hands. We'll call him tomorrow to check on it . . . Let's see what your reading is." He lifted the monitor, but it had automatically shut off during their distraction. He pressed the on button, then the memory control to get the last reading. His gaze widened in surprise.

At his reaction, Kirstin panicked. "What's wrong? Is it that bad? Is my blood sugar too high—or too low?"

Christopher lifted the vial, read the code number, then checked the one on the monitor. "Did you open this bottle today?"

"Yes. What's the matter? Has it expired? Am I out of control?"

"You didn't change your monitor code to match the vial code; you've been getting false readings since you began using these test strips. That could partially explain why you didn't realize you were on a downward spiral. It's reading much higher than it actually is. Let's test again."

With shaky hands, Kirstin changed the monitor code and repeated the procedure. That done, she and Christopher smiled and relaxed. Before he could scold her again, she said, "I know — another careless error. I've never done that before, Doctor Harrison. I'm usually so careful." She knew why she had made the mistake: that distressing talk with her youngest daughter this morning about Steve, who was demanding that Katie tell him how and where to reach her so he could take advantage of her again. After she was settled in her new apartment and job, she had to settle matters with Steve. They couldn't go on as they had been doing for the past year.

"That answers one of our questions, but not all of them. We still have to get you balanced and prevent swings." He decided she had something preying on her mind, something to do with a man probably. A woman like Kirstin Lowrey didn't sit home many nights, he assumed, unless she wanted to. Perhaps she was moving across country to make a fresh start, as he'd been forced to do, far away from the pains and demands of a lost past.

With her legs and bare feet dangling over the side of the table and trying to conceal her apprehension, Kirstin inquired, "What now?"

"I think you should lie down and take a nap, or

at least stay quiet and still and rest. This has been stressful for you, and you don't need stress to send your blood sugar skyrocketing. Doctor's order, Mrs. Lowrey: sleep."

Kirstin didn't argue. She lay down and watched as he flung a blue sheet over her lower body. He was so gentle and caring at that moment, and it felt good to have him tending her. Her gaze followed him out the door and her ears heard the second one close again, then a click. She wasn't frightened, as he'd said he was locking it to prevent her from being disturbed by another patient or visitor, and she could turn the bolt from inside if she needed to get out. But she didn't want to get up or to leave. She just wanted to relax, to get well, to have everything be all right again. She was in capable hands and charming company, so why not enjoy both? She was tired, and surprisingly drowsy. She closed her eyes and let her body relax. If she had flown, driven I-20, or done as Steve almost demanded, she wouldn't have met Christopher Harrison. And this alarming incident with her diabetes might not have happened; Steve would be certain to point that out when she revealed it to him, if she ever did . . .

Two

As Kirstin stretched and yawned, she realized she was in a strange place, and rose with haste. Simultaneously, she recalled where she was and why, and saw Dr. Christopher Harrison sitting nearby watching her.

"How do you feel?" he asked as he stood and approached her.

"Fine, just didn't know where I was for a minute." She untangled herself from the sheet and tossed it aside. She straightened her clothing and fingercombed her hair. She assumed she looked a rumpled mess, and wished that weren't true.

"I sneaked in to make sure you didn't have another attack while you were sleeping. But you seem fine . . .Does anyone live with you?"

"What?" Why, she fretted, would he ask such a personal question?

Christopher witnessed her reaction and suspected she must have misunderstood his meaning. "People who live alone don't have anybody to check on them during the night to see if they have warning symptoms while they're asleep. Do you ever wake up feeling strange or with headaches? And do you have to get up during the night to drink water or use the bathroom?"

His last few words embarrassed her for a moment, but then she reminded herself he was a doctor, hers for a while, and that the question was a necessary one. "No to both medical questions, and I do live alone. I have since my husband was killed in a traffic accident fifteen months ago. My children are grown; two are married and gone, one living overseas and one in Denver, and my single daughter lives and works in Los Angeles." She felt awkward about her silly reaction and hurried past it to ask, "Should I check my blood again?"

"I was about to ask you to do that."

After she completed the test, both smiled in relief at the good result.

"Ready to eat?" he asked.

"What time is it?" She glanced around for a wall clock.

"Heading toward six. You didn't nap long. I skipped lunch, so I'm starved. You should join me. You need to get on a new eating schedule. Crossing so many time zones has contributed to your being off balance. Since you'll be living out here, It's best to adjust to California time."

A hungry Kirstin agreed, "I am ready to eat, thank you."

"Here are your shoes. I removed them earlier."

Kirstin slipped them on and smiled.

"Take it slow; you don't want to have another accident. If you feel the slightest bit weak or dizzy, tell me immediately." Christopher assisted her down from the worn leather table and held on to her hand until he was certain her head was clear and her balance was steady.

Kirstin felt his left hand at her waist. The right one that was holding hers was large and warm, and sparked feelings of pleasure, as did his closeness and scent. This man was intelligent and hard-working; it seemed apparent from his callused hands and muscular physique that his money and profession didn't prevent him from laboring alongside his hired men. Yet, it struck her as odd for a wealthy and talented doctor to be doing menial ranch chores and running such a small practice in the near desert.

When he made an abrupt halt before opening the door, she bumped into him. "Sorry, Doc, but you have to warn me of sudden stops and turns; my driving is off today." He joined her laughter, and she enjoyed its sound.

Now that she was standing next to him, she could see he was quite tall — over six feet for certain. His body was well taken care of; her left hand had touched his firm back as she sought her balance, and slipped away from a narrow and firm waist. She noticed he'd shaved during her nap and changed clothes. *Trying to impress me, Doc, or simply completing the morning tasks I interrupted?* Curiosity flooded Kirstin, the most she'd experienced about a man since her teenage years. She was impressed by the care he obviously took with both his appearance and his health. David also had taken care of his looks but only out of vanity.

Christopher glanced at his patient before leading her out of the small building he used as an office. For a minute, he wished he hadn't asked her to stay at his home; she evoked such crazy thoughts and a fiery heat in his loins, and this was an age of outrageous lawsuits, justified and unjustified. Besides, only a dedicated career woman would relocate across the country. He was lonely and miserable enough without making it worse by allowing her to get to him, only to leave him. There might be good reasons why she wasn't married again, or at least living with someone. For all he knew, she could be an embittered woman who was carrying around emotional baggage he didn't want to help tote or unpack. It would be best to get her healed and gone as fast as possible. A sexy but independent woman like Kirstin Lowrey could be big trouble, and he didn't need any more problems in his life. Yet . . .

As Christopher guided Kirstin across a well-kept yard and into a large and airy kitchen, she realized—in the short time she'd been with him—how different he seemed from her deceased husband. He exuded self-assurance, strength, and pride. Again she wondered why he had left doctoring and big-city life for small-town ranching? Well, almost left it; he did have a tiny practice. Why wasn't he married? Was he recently divorced or widowed? Did he have a girlfriend? Was he gay? She didn't think so, not that it was any of her business. Had he been forced out of medicine in one state only to seek a new start in another?

Get a grip on it, Kirstin; this is only a professional arrangement. You don't have to know everything about him or understand him; you never did those things with David and look how that affected you. Strong men—and Christopher's one of them—demand full control of everything and everyone around them, and a woman gets lost in that kind of relationship. Don't even consider starting anything with this tempting stranger.

Kirstin was surprised to find the kitchen neat, as he'd said he wasn't much on cleaning and that his housekeeper was gone. Of course, the woman could have left town just this morning. David had never lifted a finger to help at home and didn't think a man should either do or help with such chores. Yet David had expected "his" home, yard, wife, and children to be at their peak at all times, and she had complied to the best of her ability.

Christopher noticed how her inquisitive gaze scanned the room and he was relieved he'd straightened up while she was napping. He pulled out a chair and said, "Sit at the table while I check the fridge to see what I have to tempt your taste buds."

She remained standing to ask, "Can I help with anything?"

"No need. You might get weak and have another attack. Just relax tonight, and tomorrow, too. You can impress me Thursday with your culinary skills. Helen keeps the freezer well stocked, so feel free to raid it. In the two weeks she's been gone, I've been starving for a real meal."

"You haven't even asked if I can cook. Simply because I'm a woman doesn't mean I'm skilled or experienced in that area."

Christopher sent her a look of playful mischief. "Can you cook and do housework? Or did you accept my offer under false pretenses?"

Kirstin laughed at his expression and tone. "You assumed I could do both when you made our bargain. Not to worry, Doctor, I can cook and clean well enough to honor my part of our deal."

"A woman with confidence and honesty; I like

that. If you want to freshen up, there's a bathroom around the corner, on the left." He'd also done a quick and sufficient job of cleaning it. His knew his bedroom and bath were still disaster areas, but she wouldn't be seeing those two rooms.

Kirstin followed the direction of his nod to wash her hands. As she looked in the mirror to fingercomb and fluff her hair, she mused, *What on earth are you doing here alone with a sexy stranger who makes you feel so crazy? You don't need complications in your new life.* Maybe she was intrigued by Christopher Harrison because he was so different from David Lowrey and from other men she'd met. Her husband had been good-looking and charming, but he hadn't been on a par with her host. Unlike the easygoing rancher, David had been a workaholic who was determined to be prosperous and never felt he attained the heights he wanted and seemed to need. He had taken care of everyone's needs—financially and emotionally—except those of his family; he'd let them suffer before and after his death.

She hadn't realized how much David had controlled her until he was gone and she was left in charge. She had cared for her invalid mother and borne the brunt of raising their three children. She had helped with three grandchildren as much as possible. Now, she could do as she pleased and when she pleased, almost. She hadn't planned on having trouble with Steve and her health. If she wanted to attain her goals and be happy — and she did — she must give both matters prompt attention.

As she stared at her reflection, Kirstin wished she had her purse so she could freshen her makeup and cologne. She wasn't a total wreck, but she could look better with a few repairs. David would have gone bonkers if he'd seen her looking like this. Image had been so damned important to him. He had insisted she be up and dressed — full makeup and all — before rousing the children from bed, and remain her "best" until retiring for the night, even while doing house- or yardwork or tending the children. If he came home without warning and found her mussed, he made her stop what she was doing to "repair" herself. From the beginning of their marriage and especially after she left work, he had trained her with cleverness and persistence; he had done his task so well — formed her "habits" and colored her opinions — that she hadn't realized what had taken place until it was almost too late to change.

David wasn't the only man she'd known like that. In the old days, a southern girl was taught to be a lady and to look her best at all times; she was expected to marry, have children, be a homemaker, to put her family's needs and desires above her own and to have the highest morals. She was fortunate she had gotten to attend college and to train for a job she loved; all women, she now felt, should be prepared to support themselves. She considered herself a liberated female, but it had taken David's death to enlighten her.

Her two closest friends kept saying she should go out on dates, with the intention of finding another man with whom to settle down. Even they, much as she loved them, believed a woman needed a man in her life to be fulfilled. But she had learned the vast difference between being alone and being lonely, in being dependent and being a partner, in being a person of her own and a man's shadow. After spending fifteen months in freedom, a second marriage was not appealing yet. Nor had romance been enticing so far. To be honest, she had lost interest in sex long ago when David began treating it as part of his job and her as an employee. The time came when he always seemed to be gone, either in body or spirit. She had given up trying to regain his attention in and out of bed. "Tricks" and suggestions in advice books and on television programs failed to work on him; her attempts and defeats began to make her feel silly, awkward, undesirable, and even wanton on occasion. She had settled into limbo and concentrated on her home, children, grandchildren, and invalid mother.

Then her mother died, her oldest daughter and family moved overseas, David was killed in a car wreck, her son and family were transferred to Denver, and Katie — admittedly the apple of her eye — quit the local college and moved to Los Angeles to begin a career. She didn't want to move in with or too near any of her children as they had lives of their own and also needed privacy. Once she'd overcome the fear and shock of David's death, she'd known what she wanted: to return to medical research, to have her own friends, and to enjoy her family and the rest of her life. Then today, she had met a man who evoked feelings she didn't know she had or could experience, and she was afraid to explore them.

If Elaine and Betty could see you now, alone with a man like him . . . She could imagine what they would advise: go after him if only for a good time. They would stress how hard it was to find a good, free man these days. But the sexy doctor might not be available, or interested. If he were, she could become just as swallowed up by and lost in him as she had been with David, something she didn't want to endure again. *Get well and get out, and behave yourself until you're gone.*

Kirstin returned to the kitchen and sat down at the table.

Christopher glanced at her, but she was looking the other way. She had been gone a long time and he wondered if she was nervous in his home and regretting her decision. "Ham sandwiches, carrots, fruit, and milk all right with you?" he asked, having already taken those items from the refrigerator. "It covers your meal plan according to Dr. Cooper's fax."

"Sounds marvelous. You sure I can't help? It feels so strange to be waited on like this, especially by a man."

That statement told Christopher it was a new experience for her, and it pleased him. He hadn't done much of it in the past, but he'd heard and read that women liked being pampered. In an odd way, it felt good to him, too, with Kirstin. "Just relax and I'll serve you this time. Later you can wait on me," he said with undisguised humor.

She allowed her gaze to wander over him from the rear while he worked at the counter. He was wearing well-worn cowboy boots. His faded jeans were snug and his long-sleeved blue shirt was fitted, both garments tight enough to evince an excellent physique that spread a curious warmth over her again. There was only a smidgen of silver at his temples, and she decided it would be a long time before his black hair turned gray. Her own tresses were a glorious tawny hue, thanks to her beautician and a bottle of magic. She liked this modern style Amy had suggested, almost forced her to try, she recalled with a smile. It did, as promised, make her look younger and more attractive. So did the cosmetic makeover and wardrobe changes her friends in Augusta had persuaded her to splurge on last year.

Splurge . . . David would have had a fit if she had "wasted" money on her desires if he hadn't suggested the changes himself. How nice it was not to account to him, or to anyone, about how and where she spent her money. While he was alive, she'd received an "allowance." After his death, it had taken her time — plus a few pains and fears — to learn how to handle money, as he'd never allowed her to do so during their marriage. At first, she had felt dumb, helpless, intimidated, and bitter; those feelings had lessened or passed with knowledge and practice — and some alarming mistakes she'd managed to correct with Steve's advice. Katie had been the biggest help and comfort to her while she learned about budgets and bank statements and insurance forms — starting fresh. She and Katie both liked the changes in her appearance and personality. Those changes had given her the confidence she needed when she returned to work. The subject of dating had come up, and her youngest child wanted her to go out and have fun but hadn't pressed the scary issue, as things and times had changed drastically since Kirstin was young. *If you met Dr. Christopher*

Harrison, Katie, my girl, you might urge me to—

Kirstin became aware that she was sitting there "as silent as a bump on a log," as her grandfather used to say. "Did you ever think your duties would include this?" she inquired, laughing to calm herself. Being waited on by a man—this man—was pleasing and stimulating. David would never have played nursemaid or lifted a finger, even in an emergency. He would have hired someone to tend her, as she had tended her invalid mother. That was the only time Kirstin could recall putting her foot down on any matter. David had wanted to place the elderly woman in a nursing home but Kirstin had flatly refused. Still, he hadn't allowed her mother to move in, only live in an adjoining "mother-in-law suite" he intended to turn into a game room after the woman died.

"I've had to spoon-feed a patient or two, so I'm qualified and experienced in TLC. You want mayo or mustard on your sandwich?"

"Very light mayo, please," she replied, settling back in the chair. *You're mighty nice on all the senses, Doc. I imagine you're a good date. Dating.* That had been a scary education after twenty-four years of marriage and having dated only David during college. Since his death, she had gone out with men she had met at or through work or been introduced to by friends. She had found most of the episodes unpleasant. Too

50

many men came with the complications of difficult ex-wives and resentful children, or with emotional ties to ex-mates or ex-girlfriends, or men with children—often troubled teenagers—who only wanted a wife and mother replacement. Some became too serious or too demanding too quickly, or were only out to make an "easy score" with a "lonely widow." Only a rare few hadn't fallen into those categories, and they hadn't interested her. Also there was the danger of all kinds of sexually transmitted diseases in modern relationships.

Sex. Why was that on her mind? She considered it all right for other unattached adults her age to do as they pleased but had told herself she was too old for wild and impulsive romps in bed. In fact, she couldn't imagine even getting undressed in front of a date, never mind having sex with one. It gave her the jitters to even think of putting herself in that situation. She certainly hadn't gotten to know any man well enough to consent to an intimate relationship, nor could she have a one-night stand, though the man nearby was enough to entice a woman to give it serious consideration. She wasn't ashamed of her body; she had a good one, but there was something scary about getting naked before a male.

It had been awkward to awaken to find her shirt unbuttoned and spread and a stranger's fingers grazing her bosom as he checked her heartbeat. She wasn't inexperienced in sex; nor was she ignorant about the different ways of making love. Katie, her friends, magazine articles, and television shows had revealed plenty since the so-called "female sexual revolution" had begun. At times, she'd been red-faced and openmouthed, astonished by what she heard or read. Maybe she was just old-fashioned to the point of believing one usually got married first or at least had to possess deep feelings for someone before sleeping with him. No, she wasn't ready for a casual liaison. She didn't want to have that intrusion in her new life or want to raise someone else's family. Besides, she was still fertile and was off the pill since David's death; pregnancy after forty-five would not suit her at all. Bearing another child, perhaps while remaining single, was an alarming thought. Accidents happened even with the best of precautions. Look at what had happened with Katie. Kirstin moved her fingers over the Band-Aid on her inner elbow and sighed in dreamy but troubled thought.

Christopher stole a glance at her but she didn't notice, as she was in a world of her own, and in an odd way he felt shut out, disappointed. He looked at his hands as they prepared lunch for two and admitted why he hadn't wanted her to assist with the task: she would find out about his problem and might be consumed with pity or think less of him before she could get to know him. He despised having people feel sorry for him. After a year of surgeries and therapies on the left and three years of practice with the other, he had learned to use his right hand but he was not as skilled with it as he had been with his left, and nowhere deft enough to remain in his beloved surgical career. He couldn't fully close the left hand and, because of the diminished dexterity and partial loss of feeling, he had to be cautious when handling things especially those with a thickness of less than an inch. If Kirstin had noticed his fumblings, she hadn't asked any questions, or she was too polite to do so even if she had added two and two to get four. He half-turned and looked at her to find her still rubbing the bandage. "Does it hurt? I'm not the best with shots and IV's. Nurses usually did those chores for me."

She smiled and said, "It's fine. The Band-Aid just itches and binds a little when I bend my arm. You were very gentle, Christopher, so don't worry. I was just thinking about my condition and what happened today. Sometimes diabetes makes even simple or everyday things difficult or impossible or frustrating."

Those were feelings he understood and endured daily. He liked the soft and romantic way she spoke his name. But he put those thoughts aside and focused on her needs as a patient. "Explain," he coaxed.

Kirstin had never bared her deepest feelings about her "condition." She didn't want to worry Katie, her physician, or her friends. Here was someone who would understand, provide help — and someone she'd never see again to have to worry over his pity. "Sometimes I get annoyed at having to always be conscious of food and the clock and over exerting myself. I have to remind myself I can't grab a snack even if I'm hungry unless it's on that yucky free-list or that I have to stop what I'm doing if it's refueling time, or check every item that enters my mouth for sugar and fat. I can't exercise even five minutes longer or finish a sport if my blood sugar crashes."

She glanced down at her hands. "My fingers get sore from so many lances a day and if I'm careless I get blood on my clothes and things. I can't go to certain restaurants because they don't have the food I need, even if I use the exchange system. If I ask waiters, 'Are you sure that has no sugar; I'm diabetic,' or I have a hypoglycemic attack, they look at me as if I'm contagious or a freak. I just don't want to be treated differently from anyone else." Kirstin suddenly fretted that she sounded like a whiner, filled with self-pity. "I've only known about this condition for six weeks. I'll eventually adjust to its demands; I have to. My grandfather and aunt did. Seven million other diabetics do."

"They have no choice if they want to stay healthy and survive. You're lucky it can be treated and controlled. Some problems can't; they can totally ruin your life. You'll do fine, Kirstin Lowrey. You're intelligent and determined. It'll get easier."

Will it? Can anybody, except another person in my condition or a similar one, truly understand what it's like to lose control of one's life? "Do you have a phone?" she inquired to change the topic.

He laughed. "Naturally. I don't live that far from civilization. A fax, computer, satellite dish, and all the modern conveniences." Did she, he wondered, need to call someone special? He tried to master his curiosity.

"I meant, may I use your phone? I'll reverse the charges. I should let my daughter in Los Angeles know what happened. I don't want her to worry about me after she finds your message on her answering machine."

"You can call after we eat. The food's ready and you need to get back on schedule or risk losing all our progress. You right- or left-handed?"

"Mostly right, but I use both."

"Most people do." He placed utensils and napkin to her right.

"I meant, I do as much with the left one. Animal surgery and such. It calls for two steady, deft hands." That meant she couldn't afford to get shaky and confused in the lab from low sugar bouts, or she could get cut with an infectious scalpel or stick herself with a syringe containing a dangerous chemical or spill a radioactive tracer. *I need a cure, but there isn't one, not yet. Maybe one day, Kirstin, with research.*

If anyone knew her last statement was true, Christopher did. "You do much surgery?" Not trusting his weakened left hand, he set down her plate, then also fetched her glass with the right one. To distract her from the curious task, he teased, "Think you can manage or should I feed you?"

She laughed, too. "I'm sure I can manage by myself." *But, my, your offer is appealing!*

He sat opposite her to eat his meal. "Well?"

Assuming he referred to the food, she replied, "It's delicious. Thanks, Doctor Harrison. You're a good cook," she joked.

"The name's Christopher, *Mrs. Lowrey.*" She laughed, and the sound mellowed him. "You always eat that slowly and take such tiny bites?"

"You should know it's best for the digestion, Doctor. And the name's Kirstin." He laughed with her now and his eyes sparkled.

"I always wait until I'm ravenous, then I can't eat fast enough. Guess it comes from years of

56

eating in a rush and now eating alone and having no reason to linger. Helen's a great cook, but she doesn't take her meals with me."

"You should practice slowing down even when you're alone. It's a great time to relax and think. You're retired; that's what it's about, no more hurrying." She sipped her milk and eyed him over the rim of the glass. The way their gazes locked and searched the other's for a moment caused her to squirm and lower her lashes, and to pray her cheeks wouldn't flush.

"If you prefer something else to drink, I'll see what I have. I'm afraid I don't buy diet drinks or snacks. I'll get you some tomorrow."

"I almost always drink milk at all my meals. It's required, so thank goodness it's a favorite of mine. I rarely do an exchange with it. Of course, I love buttermilk, too," she informed him for some inexplicable reason.

He grinned. "*You* like buttermilk? Isn't that odd for a city girl?"

Delaying her next bite, she said, "I was born and partly reared in the country, the boondocks to be accurate. You know, so far back in the sticks that running water and electricity didn't exist for years."

"You're teasing me," he accused as his gaze scanned her sophisticated appearance once more.

"Not at all. I remember doing homework by

oil lanterns, carrying water from a distant well, hauling in firewood, and emptying chamber pots. Don't tell me you've never experienced such character-building chores? That's what my grandfather called them."

"You're pulling my leg, Kirstin. You aren't that old," he replied with a broader grin.

"I'm not kidding, Christopher, I swear. I'm from the country, miles outside of a small Georgia town. My grandfather was a farmer. We lived with my grandparents until my father became an insurance salesman in Augusta and we moved there. I remember Gramps plowing his garden with a stubborn mule named Bill and chickens chasing me, especially an ornery rooster he had that petrified me. We used to keep milk in a cold spring not far from the house. I can close my eyes and still picture that wooden outhouse with sunflowers growing around it and peanuts spread out atop it to dry. I've even picked cotton and plucked potato bugs. Of course, you've probably never been poor, so you wouldn't know about such rustic conditions."

There was an inquisitive tone to her voice. Was she checking out his financial status as his ex-wife had done years ago before setting out to use him before dumping him so cruelly? He pushed aside those bitter memories. "You're wrong, Kirstin; I was born and reared poor. I worked my way through college and med school. I work as hard on this ranch as any hired man. I can remember the days of oil lanterns, wood fires, and outdoor johns. But we had a dependable windmill to draw water. Between having a few patients and ranching, I do fine. Of course, some of my patients don't have the money to pay me; that's how I got some of my calves and colts."

"Just like in the old days when patients paid with poultry and crops. How fascinating, like having a continuing piece of history."

"I get some chickens, too, but Helen takes care of them for me." *And you're what's fascinating, woman, and a pleasant surprise.*

"Evidently you love this area or you wouldn't have come back home."

"This wasn't my home. It belonged to my uncle and aunt. The medical practice was his, too. They both died a few years back and I inherited it. Frank, my foreman, Helen's husband, ran it for me until I moved here. He and Helen worked for Uncle Chester, too. I was born and reared near Dallas. My Texas twang just softened a little while I was practicing back East."

"Do you raise mostly cattle or horses?"

"Both. Uncle Chester raised wheat—that's the number-one local crop—and some cattle when he wasn't doctoring, but I'm not a farmer. I only raise enough grain to feed my stock in the winter. As I told you, when I retired here, I didn't intend to become a country doctor. The locals pressed me into it. I suppose you prefer the big city now. San Diego."

"I don't know, but a person has to live where her work is."

"Would you live in the country again if Medico was there?"

An odd question . . . "Certainly. But big companies bring people and progress. It wouldn't remain deserted country very long. They are too few places like this left; you wouldn't want this one spoiled."

Spoiled like Laura had been before her betrayal and their divorce . . . "I don't care for anything that's spoiled or more trouble than it's worth."

Kirstin reached for her glass and knocked it over. Milk raced across the table toward Christopher, who jumped up to avoid the white flood and sent his chair clattering to the linoleum floor. Kirstin's face went scarlet. She stammered, "I . . . I'm terribly sorry."

"Don't worry about it," he told her, grabbing a dishcloth to mop up the mess. He rinsed it several times and finally had the table and floor clean. "More milk?" he offered as he reached for her slippery glass.

"Yes, thank you. I promise not to spill that,

too." Kirstin had been taken off guard by the chilliness in his tone and gaze at his previous remark. He hadn't been talking about this area—more like about a person, an enemy.

"It's no big deal if you do, Kirstin. You don't have to be embarrassed; it was an accident. You're probably still a little shaky." He'd had plenty of mishaps with his disabled hand. He got herself some more milk and they finished their meal in silence.

Christopher stood. "I'll get this cleared away. You rest."

"Can I at least wash the dishes?" she asked, unused to inactivity.

"I'll take care of them. You go into the living room and relax. You need to conserve your energy today while your blood sugar is still fluctuating."

He took the dishes to the sink in several trips. He didn't roll up his sleeves and expose the revealing scars on his left wrist. As he rinsed the dishes and put them in the dishwasher, he realized she hadn't moved from her seat.

At his questioning look she prompted, "Where is the living room?"

"I forgot you don't know your way around my house. Bear with me, Kirstin; I seem to have misplaced my manners. I'll show you."

"You've been most generous and patient, Christopher. I'm sorry to be such a bother. I promise to repay your kindness."

"Don't cry, Kirstin; the weakness and all the emotional strain will pass."

Her nerves were touchy, her emotions were in a turmoil, and her voice was quivery, but she wasn't about to cry as he presumed. Yet, she scolded in a soft tone, "That's easy for you to say. You don't know what I'm feeling and how this mess could ruin my life." The moment those words were out of her mouth, she wanted to recall them. *What's wrong with you, Kirstin?* She was normally in control of her feelings and, for a year now, master of her life. But she had not been prepared for an experience like this—neither the accident nor Dr. Christopher Harrison.

"I do understand what you're experiencing, but you'll have to learn to adjust to things you can't change. I'll help any way I can. Getting upset won't help; it only plays havoc with your blood sugar level."

"You're right. I'm sorry I'm being silly and cranky. Maybe I'm just tired; I haven't slept much the last few nights."

"I'll take you to the guest room if you want to turn in now."

"I never get to sleep early unless I'm sick. Crossing time zones has my body clock out of kilter, too. How long before it settles down again?"

"Three days to a week. Accept your new limitations, Kirstin. Fighting them doesn't help."

Something in his sad look and tone said he was referring to more than her condition, and her heart went out to him. She didn't have a right to probe, so she didn't. She wondered if she had evoked bad memories. "I hate to sound repetitious, Christopher, but I'm sorry again. I'm not usually rude to strangers, especially nice ones like you. If you don't mind, I'll sit in the living room and try to relax."

He smiled and led her there. Without thinking to ask her preference, Christopher chose music he thought she would enjoy hearing from the collection lying atop his stereo. He switched on the CD player and inserted five discs to play at random. He closed the panel, pressed a few buttons, and the sultry voice of Barbra Streisand filled the room. He adjusted the volume, set aside the plastic cases, and turned on lamps to prepare for dusk.

As he did those tasks, Kirstin sat on a sofa with overstuffed loose cushions at its back, rolled arms, and many accent pillows scattered along its length. It was old but not frayed or stained, nor were the two matching chairs nearby. The chairs had an oval table between them; one chair had a low ottoman before it. The room wasn't formal but it *was* large; it had a country air that implied the ex-big-city physician hadn't changed anything or much since inheriting it from his elderly kin. On the dark wood square end tables, she noticed the homemade scarves that reminded Kirstin of her grandmother's prized pieces of crochet. Three stained-glass lamps on the tables looked hand-blown, hand-painted, and antiquish. It was a nice and cozy room, but she had the feeling he rarely used it.

Christopher turned and asked, "How's that?"

"Soft music and lighting to soothe the savage breast?" slipped out.

He chuckled and grinned. "I have ranch chores to do, if you don't mind my leaving you alone for a while?"

"Certainly not. I'll try not to interfere with your normal routine. I'll sit right here and be a good girl for a change." *Heavens, Kirstin, you sound like an enamored teenager and a brazen flirt.*

He studied her with growing interest. She was certainly different from the other women he knew. Without a doubt, this was a nerve-wracking episode for her. There was no harm in showing a little extra kindness and attention. After all, she was brightening his day and mood more than the three lamps did to this room. Already he was looking forward to spending the next few days with her. It seemed as if she was going to be a nice break in his routine. "If you need anything, I'll be back in an hour or two. Make yourself at home. If I'm gone longer, don't forget your snack. Search the kitchen for whatever you need."

"Thank you." *But I'm not a child or that distracted by you.* Kirstin could almost hear "Liar, liar, your pants are on fire" fill her ears,

After he left, Kirstin tried to relax as she studied the surroundings in more detail. A large and old family Bible was on the coffee table. She started to peek inside to see if anything was recorded about her host but didn't because he might return and think she was being a snoop. The lace panel beneath corded-back ivory drapes allowed her to see it wasn't dark outside, but she didn't know how much time evening chores required.

She twisted and looked upward to view a painting over the sofa; it was a forest scene at dawn with deer drinking from a stream as fog lifted. She glanced at recessed decorative shelves on both sides of the fireplace which was covered by a glass-and-brass screen. She saw exquisite porcelain flowers and birds similar to her small collection by Lenox, older pieces that implied they had belonged to his aunt. There were books, figurines, and bric-a-brac, many pieces with a western flavor. What caught her attention the most were family pictures displayed in frames of assorted sizes and types. She wanted to get a closer look but would do it another time in case he returned without warning.

Kirstin listened to music for a while, but it failed to calm her. Perhaps her tense mood was an aftereffect of her medical disaster. Or was she uneasy about being in an unfamiliar man's home at night, with bedtime looming before her? She went to the bathroom, fetched a glass of water from the kitchen, then curled up on the sofa again. She closed her eyes and listened to experts crooning love songs. She walked to the CD player and scanned the disc cases atop it — Barbra Streisand, Kenny Rogers, Air Supply, The Bee Gees, Neil Diamond — to find that his taste in past and current music matched hers. The same was true of the videotaped movies there.

Maybe, she told herself, this was a dream. How could she be trapped in a ranch house in the middle of nowhere with a stranger with whom she had so much in common? A man whose voice and manner compelled her to envision wild fantasies and crave to make them realities? It was crazy. Ridiculous. Hazardous. She knew so little about him and had a life of her own elsewhere but was drawn to him like a metal to a magnet. Didn't such things only happen in movies and books?

Some of those romance novels flashed before her mind's eye: heroines captivated in heart and sometimes in body by mysterious and sensual heroes, men like Christopher Harrison. She could envision him as a pirate standing spread-legged on the deck of a tall-masted ship, a cutlass in one hand and the other wrapped around her waist. *Get a grip, Kirstin. Real men aren't like novel or film heroes. David wasn't, and neither were any of those saps you've met since he died. Christopher probably isn't one, either. He—*

She shrieked, jumped, and clasped a hand over her racing heart as those dreamy reflections were shattered by a loud noise. "Heavens, you scared the life out of me! Why did you do that?"

Three

"And why on earth are you talking to a telephone like an idiot?" The ringer, she decided, must be set on high to be heard outside. She hoped it was Katie returning Christopher's call. "Hello."

"Who is this?"

"Kirstin Lowrey."

"Is this Doctor Harrison's residence?"

"Yes, but he's out doing chores. Would you like to leave a message?"

"Who are you? Where's Helen? Why are you answering Chris's phone?"

"I'm a patient of his. Helen's out of town. Is there a message?"

"What kind of patient? What are you doing in his house if he's not there?"

"I beg your pardon?"

"I asked what kind of patient you are and why you're in his house."

"Do you want to leave Christopher a message or call back later?"

"Christopher? Christopher! No message! I'll call back!"

The female caller slammed the receiver into its cradle. Kirstin was baffled and startled by the woman's actions. Even a girlfriend had no reason or right to be rude to a patient. Kirstin realized that perhaps she shouldn't have answered the phone. If it had been an emergency, she couldn't have located him anyway. She was surprised at herself for forgetting to call her youngest daughter, and dialed the number.

As Kirstin was about to hang up, the girl answered, breathless.

"Katie, it's me."

"Hi, Mom. I was racing in and out. How's it going?" she asked, still panting from her rush. "I didn't think you would call tonight. I'm glad you did. I wanted to make sure you were all right after our talk this morning. I hope you didn't let Steve's crap upset you. He can be such a fool at times."

Kirstin didn't want to talk about the Steve matter again today, so she asked, "You haven't checked your messages tonight?"

"No, why? Is something wrong, Mom? Your voice sounds odd."

"I'm fine, Katie, but I had an accident. I—"

"Accident! Are you hurt? What happened?

Where are you? Do you need me to fly out to-night?"

"Not exactly that kind of accident, honey. It's a problem with my diabetes, but not to worry. The doctor says I have to stay here a few days to get regulated. Fact is, Katie, your old mom is stranded at his ranch in eastern New Mexico. I'm staying . . . in his guest room."

There was a short silence; then, Katie asked, "Say what, Mom?"

"The trouble happened near his ranch. He has an office next to his house. Doctor Harrison is very smart and skilled—a graduate of Harvard and Johns Hopkins, no less—so I have confidence in him. Besides, the hospital and hotels are in Clovis, thirty-something miles away. The policeman who stopped to help me brought me here because it was closer and he thought I was in worse shape than I actually was. He assured me it was safe to stay here, and I've been given no reason by the good doctor to doubt his word. I also need a few car repairs." Kirstin explained the incident in detail to one of the few people who knew the truth about her medical condition. In her opinion, no one knew her better or was closer to her or loved her more than Katie.

"He's right. You're lucky you weren't injured. It's best to get this fixed before you head out again. Do you need anything? What's the address there?"

"I don't know. I'll have to get it and call you back tomorrow. I didn't think to ask Christopher before he left and he's out doing chores."

"Christopher?" Katie echoed in a merry tone. "What's going on over there, Mom?" she teased.

"Kathryn Lowrey, behave yourself. This is purely professional. He's letting me stay here while he straightens me out; it's not a serious enough matter to require hospitalization. He's already been in touch with Doctor Cooper, and he's experienced with diabetics. He's been a perfect gentleman, worrywart. He's kind and considerate and compassionate."

"I didn't hear a wife mentioned amidst all those compliments."

"He isn't married."

"Has he ever *been* married?"

"I didn't ask. His private life is none of my business, only his medical skills. But he does have a housekeeper, foreman, and two workers."

"Are they staying in the house with you two?"

"Do employees normally live with their bosses?"

"Is that a yes or a no, Mom?"

"Actually the housekeeper is away for a while. I'm supposed to trade cooking and cleaning for his hospitality and medical services."

"Um-m-m huh . . . Make sure that's all you trade," the girl jested.

"Katie!" Kirstin shrieked, then laughed. "It's a good bargain, since I want to keep this matter concealed from Medico until I prove myself at the new complex. Besides, if this incident is reported to my health and car insurance anytime soon, I won't be able to afford either policy, if they don't drop me like a hot skillet. I know how sneaky and unfair some insurance companies and policies are. I overheard your father and his friends scheming plenty of times about how to get rid of high-risk people. As soon as I have this thing under control, I'll tell the right people."

They had discussed the possible repercussions on her mother's job and her whole life, so Katie understood. "How old is he? What does he look like?"

"I'm a big girl, Katie. I can take care of myself. Don't worry."

"Evading my questions, Mom? That makes me suspicious."

"Katie, you sneak! He's forty-nine and, yes, nosy, he's handsome and charming. Right now, I'm sitting alone and listening to music."

"Until he finishes his cowboy chores. Then, cozy and romantic."

"I'm too old for 'cozy and romantic.' "

"No, you're not. I keep telling you, Mom, you're gorgeous and good company. Any man would be lucky to get his hands on you. Put some romance and adventure in your life. Try it, you might like it."

"Katie, I'm a grandmother, a widow, and we're strangers."

"So? What's wrong with fun and romance? You deserve them and you're on vacation. I'm not saying to be impulsive or wild, just have some great times with a nice and safe man. He is, isn't he?"

"Yes, but I can't talk anymore, Katie. I don't want him to return and hear me discussing him like this with my nineteen-year-old daughter. Did the furniture arrive on schedule?"

"Yes, and it's locked up safely. You handle things there and I'll take care of things here. You're sure you're all right, Mom?"

"I'll be fine, I promise. How is the new commercial going?"

"Terrific." Katie couldn't suppress the hope that her mother was attracted to this mysterious doctor. She had been giving advice in a jesting tone and manner but deep down she wanted her mother to get over her fear of dating and to find someone special. She didn't want Kirstin to be alone for the rest of her life, which could happen after her experience with her cold and demanding father. Especially if her mother didn't do something brave to get a real love life going. "I'll go down to your place this weekend and do a little straightening. I know you're going to be thrilled with the apartment I found you. When I met the movers, I had them put the boxes you need to unpack and sort first in the extra bedroom. If I'm gone when you call in the morning, just leave a message on my machine."

Love and pride flowed through Kirstin for the girl on whom she could depend. She and Katie had always been close, and had grown even closer during the last fifteen months. They could be open and honest with each other — something both cherished. She knew Katie was only being half serious but . . . "Thanks for the help, honey, and I'll try to act the liberated and mature woman."

Katie laughed. "Sure you don't want me to come check on you?"

Amidst laughter, Kirstin asked, "Isn't it still true that three's a crowd? I'll call tomorrow. Bye, honey."

"Bye, Mom. Don't do anything I wouldn't do, and be careful."

"Kathryn Lowrey, behave yourself."

"I try, Mom, but it's impossible sometimes. Love you. Bye."

"Bye, honey."

Kirstin removed her shoes and curled her legs on the sofa. She rested her head on a soft pillow and closed her eyes. She hummed along with Air Supply on the CD player and allowed sensuous fantasies to return and flourish. Daydreaming never harmed anyone, she told herself, but that was all she would do where the mysterious doctor was concerned.

About thirty minutes later, the phone rang again. She was about to get up to answer it when Christopher called out from the doorway, "I've got it, Kirstin." He lifted the receiver. "Doctor Harrison . . . What?"

He was quiet for a time, then told someone, "A patient . . . I can't make it; she needs watching and treating . . . No, and it's late anyway."

Kirstin was about to say he didn't have to stay home because of her, but she remained silent. She couldn't help but overhear his side of the conversation, apparently with the snippy woman who had called earlier.

"I see . . . Sounds fine . . . Doesn't matter to me . . . I can't talk now . . . I wouldn't advise that," he warned in a tone she thought frosty. "I'm hanging up. I have my patient and chores to tend. Bye."

He turned to Kirstin. "I'd appreciate it if you don't answer my phone while you're here, Mrs. Lowrey. You needn't trouble yourself. I have an answering machine and a medical service that picks up after the fourth ring."

His voice and expression were unsettling. "I'm sorry if I did something wrong, Doctor Harrison. A woman phoned, but wouldn't leave her name or a message. I suppose that was her calling back. I only answered earlier because I thought it might be Katie returning your call and I didn't want her to worry. I called and explained everything to her. I don't know your address, so I'm to phone her with it tomorrow."

He wondered if she had talked to anyone in addition to her daughter, perhaps the man in her life? "Why do you need my address? You want someone to come after you? Did you change your mind about me treating you or staying here?"

"No, Katie wanted to know where I am in case I need to be reached. She's handling deliveries for my new apartment and running errands for me until I reach San Diego."

"I'll give it to you when you phone her tomorrow, or I can talk to her myself. She might want to ask me questions about your condition."

"Thank you, Doctor Harrison," she said, matching his formality. "I won't answer the phone again," she promised, assuming that was the source of his anger. *What did I do, anger a jealous sweetie by being caught here alone with you?*

She propped an elbow on the end of the sofa and rested her chin on it, staring at the braided rug on a hardwood floor that could use dust-mopping. The music changed to lively tunes by the original Bee Gees. She felt uncomfortable in the loud emotional silence that followed her vow.

She didn't want to look his way, but wondered what he was doing.

He was staring at her profile and asking himself why he was peeved because she took Carla's call. Kirstin probably assumed it was a sweetheart who was furious to find another woman there. No doubt Carla had been rude. So be it, because he wasn't going to explain anything to either woman. Kirstin was only a patient, and Carla had been an occasional date. *Had been,* he stressed to himself and wished Carla could get it through her thick skull he didn't want to see her again. He was sorry he had ever asked her out; now, she pestered him like a mosquito. So far, no matter what he said or did, Carla couldn't comprehend that it was over and he couldn't stand her. He had been as clear and polite as he could be, but it appeared as if he was going to have to get nasty to get his point across. He wasn't interested in being her date at a barbecue at her father's ranch on Saturday, or in ever seeing her again.

Christopher grinned when a bold idea came to mind. What better way, he mused, to discourage Carla than to show up with a ravishing blue-eyed blonde on his arm and to have a great time? He frowned as he realized Kirstin would probably be gone in a few days, especially if he kept acting as he did moments ago. He hadn't rushed through his evening chores and his usual

chat with Frank Graham just so he could behave like a total ass! She had him thinking and
acting like a schoolboy on his first date! Lordy,
he hadn't felt this excited about a woman in
ages, if ever. Of course, he had to get Kirstin
well before she could leave . . .

He asked, "Would you like to take a walk?
Get some fresh air and see a beautiful sunset?
New Mexico is famous for its twilight colors."

She was tempted to refuse, but noticed his
mood had altered. "Yes, thank you. You can
tell me about your ranch and state. This might
be all I see of it if I have to rush to San Diego
after you're finished with me."

As her last few words danced mischievously
across his mind, he held the door open for her
to go outside. "Watch your step, Kirstin; there's
a slight drop-down to the porch," he cautioned.
"It's always tripping up people; I'll have to think
of a way to change it one day. I don't want anybody falling and suing the pants off me."

Kirstin laughed to let him know his attempts
at humor and subtle apology had worked. She
waited a minute while he went back inside to
fetch something. He offered his hand and she
accepted it as he cautioned her again to be careful as they ascended several steps to the ground.

Afterward, they strolled toward the corral.
The brown brick house was large and T-shaped.
The yards displayed a few large bushes and sev-

eral varieties of western plants, but there were few tall trees. She noticed a satellite dish, a swimming pool, several mercury-vapor lights on poles, a pump house, his office, a shed, endless fencing, and several barns. There was a circular driveway with a grassy teardrop center where a blue Jeep Wagoneer was parked. The house sat about seven hundred feet off the main road and was surrounded by verdant but desertlike vegetation, some plants a darker green than others with splashes of yellow or tan here and there. As far as she could see in any direction—and it almost seemed as if the horizon and flat land went on forever—only telephone poles, scrubs, and weeds seemed to jut from the high plains landscape. It exuded an impression of barren wilderness, as if they were the only two people in the area, or even perhaps on earth. The sky was blue with an occasional wispy cloud, but dusk and sunset were approaching. A few cars and trucks traveled the highway and vanished from sight before others came into view.

Kirstin wondered how a busy, big-city doctor had adjusted so well to such a deserted place. At the corral, she listened to horses neigh and watched them prance as if showing off for their master. Christopher hadn't released her left hand, and she made no attempt to pull it from his light grasp. She enjoyed and needed his strength and security.

"What kind of horses do you raise?" Kirstin inquired. She hoped her voice and body didn't expose the trembling she felt from head to foot. It seemed absurd to feel this crazy way but she couldn't help it.

Christopher watched her from the corner of his eye and wished he knew what made her frown and sigh in what seemed like annoyance at herself. "Morgans, Appaloosas, and a variety of others. Do you ride?"

"I haven't in a long time, but I know how. I can't wait to see your Appaloosas; they're favorites of mine. How many do you own?"

"About ten. They're in the north pasture tonight; some have foals. Perhaps we can go riding before you leave."

"I would love it. Tell me about your ranch," she encouraged.

He suggested they walk a while. He guided her around obstacles of prickly bushes and clumps of thick vegetation. "If we get on the other side of the barns, in the open, we'll have a better view of the sunset."

As they headed that way, his left arm rounded her waist to lead her past piles of dried and fresh horse droppings. Dodging one manure heap, she stumbled and he steadied her balance. She squeezed his right hand and grasped his left one as it came forward to offer additional aid. As soon as she was in control, he released both hands. She instantly missed his touch; it seemed as if he had withdrawn it with an odd abruptness. She liked holding hands and being him, but maybe physical contact was too personal, especially if he had a girlfriend. "I'm not usually so clumsy."

"Are you experiencing any weakness or strange feelings?"

"No," she replied. *If emotions don't count*, her mind added.

"If you do feel funny, I brought along candy for an emergency." He patted his shirt pocket and the cellophane wrappings made a noise.

Uh oh, Kirstin, you forgot your glucose tablets. Another lecture about carelessness is sure to follow. But it didn't, to her pleasure.

He described his ranch and the surrounding area. It was interesting, but her mind wandered at his nearness and engulfing voice. She wondered how it would feel to snuggle against his hard body and to kiss him, to throw caution and inhibitions to the wind. *Are you nuts, Kirstin? Behave yourself!*

Christopher talked about the two closest towns, the area's crops, the importance of irrigation, and seasons of the rancher and farmer. He didn't know why he was chattering away about such things that were probably boring to a city girl, except that talking was one way to keep her near him.

81

He kept stealing glances at her. Desire gnawed at him, but he wasn't one to be ruled by demanding loins. In three days, she would leave. That wasn't enough time to get to know her or to begin . . . *Get off it, Chris; you're being stupid.*

Kirstin gradually learned the Rocking-H Ranch consisted of one hundred and ninety acres of good grazing land, two "tanks"—the western word for ponds—over fifty head of cattle, and thirty horses. Some areas were used to raise winter feed for his stock and the rest was pastureland. Frank Graham was his foreman and right hand. Besides Frank, there were two other men who worked the ranch part-time. He told her about Helen, his housekeeper, and the Graham family.

Heady scents of grasses and wildflowers drifted into her nostrils as a mild breeze played over the landscape. Surprisingly the fresh air was warm, not insufferably hot as she had imagined New Mexico and this part of the West would be. He explained that low humidity in the high plains area made it seem cooler than it was. For a visit, she was intrigued by the serenity and wild beauty of this marvelous place. Yet, she couldn't imagine living here—or Christopher Harrison retiring here. Was there an unknown reason why he had done so? Arms crossing her chest, Kirstin cupped her elbows as she gazed at the sunset in full glory.

"Getting chilly?"

"No." Her gaze remained glued to the horizon where vivid red, pink, gold, and purple kissed a shadowy earth. She noticed several windmills silhouetted against the colorful skyline. As her eyes roved the heavens, they found a quarter moon and sprinkling of stars in the darkest layer. "It's so breathtaking, so beautiful. You can see so far."

"That's because of a lack of obstructions and city lights. I have control switches on my mercury vapor poles so I can enjoy the nights better."

She realized he was wearing a long-sleeved shirt. Was he cold-natured? she wondered. It felt so warm and blissful to her.

For a while, they observed the setting sun without talking. When it was gone and only fading colors remained, dusk closed in on them. Both realized it was a provocatively romantic setting, and a heavy silence ensued.

Christopher finally stretched and said, "It'll be dark soon and we don't want you to stumble, so we'd best get back to the house."

As they headed in that direction, she asked, "What time is it? I don't have my watch, I must have left it in the bathroom when I washed my hands for dinner." The thought of impending bedtime in the secluded house alone with the handsome man made her nervous.

"Nine thirty-six. Sleepy? I suppose you must be after a long drive and all the trouble."

"I am a little tired. Don't let me interfere with the your routine."

You already have, thank goodness. "I put your bags in the guest room. Need any other help settling in?"

"No. You've been most generous and helpful, Christopher. Thanks."

He smiled in appreciation of her compliments. "You need to test your blood sugar again, and don't forget your snack before turning in."

"Thanks for the reminders," she said as they entered the house.

Christopher wondered what was left to do until bedtime and grinned as his imagination raced wild and free as an escaped stallion. "Would you like to watch TV? It's my usual wind-down trick while I read at the same time."

"Mine, too. That sounds fine for about an hour. First, I'll follow my doctor's orders. I'll do my test, then join you."

"We'll prepare a snack after we see how much fuel you need."

While Kirstin did her task at the kitchen counter, he straightened the den where the television was located. Christopher joined her and asked for the results of the test.

Kirstin frowned as she replied, "Seventy-four."

"That calls for a peanut-butter sandwich, milk, and juice to carry you to breakfast," he said as he fetched the items needed, one at a time. "You can take them to the den and eat while you relax and watch TV."

When she asked if he wanted anything, he shook his head, but took a cola from the refrigerator. Kirstin made a sandwich, poured the two liquids, drank her juice, and cleaned up afterward. With plate in one hand and glass of milk in the other, she followed him down the hall. She sat on one end of a short sofa while he took a recliner nearby. He lifted the remote control and located a program that was agreeable to both, a sitcom.

Kirstin ate the snack with eyes locked on the screen. Every so often, they laughed together at some funny line. A commercial came on about the Master's Golf Tournament in Augusta. She asked if he played golf.

"Not anymore. I stay pretty busy with the ranch and my practice." He lifted his drink and took a few swallows to wash down the bitterness that seemed to rise as a tangible taste in his mouth.

Kirstin noticed how he glanced at his left hand and rolled it on the chair's arm, and how his voice altered. She thought his reaction odd but didn't question his answer. "Do you always watch the Master's?"

He glanced at her. "Most of it. I've attended several in the past. It's a beauty of a course, one of the best in the world, but I've never played it."

"You've been to Augusta?"

"Three times for the tournament, a few times on medical business at MCG or local hospitals. Did you always attend?"

"Most of them. David had clients who had to be entertained, and the Master's is a special treat because tickets are so hard to come by. Finding gold can be easier than finding Master's tickets. He was on the list for years. They dropped his name when he died; you can't pass along your annual tickets to your family. My son misses going. He's an avid golfer, like his father was." Kirstin wished she hadn't mentioned her deceased husband. She didn't want to think about David tonight. Not here, not with Chri—

"You said you have three children, all of them grown?"

"Yes, a son and two daughters. I also have three grandchildren, all boys, one set of twins. What about you?"

"One daughter. She's married and lives in Oregon. No grandchildren. They want to get firmly established before having kids."

Kirstin wanted to ask about his wife—a divorce or death?—but didn't because he held si-

lent on that matter. He had been to her home-
town many times. Perhaps they had stood
within feet of each other at the tournament or
sat at side-by-side tables in a restaurant. If they
had met during those visits, would he have affected her the way he affected her now? Would
she have been tempted to give up an unhappy
existence with David to—*Don't even think such
wanton things!* she cautioned herself

The news and weather came on and they only
half-listened to it. Sensual currents pervaded the
wood-paneled room as they realized they would
soon be sleeping in adjoining rooms alone and
far from other people.

Kirstin's tension increased. "I'll put away these
dishes," she remarked and stood, needing to put
space between them for a little while.

"Just leave them in the sink until morning.
You don't need to overexert yourself anymore
tonight. I'll show you to your room," he suggested, assuming she was ready to get to bed
and away from him.

She followed him into the hall, where she listened and observed as he gave a verbal tour of
the house to familiarize her with the location of
everything. "If you need something or have another problem tonight, sing out; I'm next door.
Do you usually sleep late or rise early?"

"Why?" she asked, her mouth suddenly dry
and her pulse racing.

"I'm up at dawn for chores. I eat around eight. But if you want to sleep in and rest, I'll wait until later and join you in the kitchen."

"I'm usually up by six-thirty to be at work by eight. I can't skip breakfast and my specimens don't care much for tardiness. They insist on their food and shots by eight-fifteen sharp. I was never much for eating a breakfast of more than coffee and toast until I developed this condition."

"You're a caffeine junkie, like me? Need morning coffee to get going?"

"Afraid so. Now, it's cereal, fruit, and milk, too. Or the equivalent."

"A woman after my own heart." He chuckled, then said, "I'll warn you now, I'm a grouch until I've had at least one cup. Coffee will be ready when you rise. If I'm not here, just look for whatever you need. See you at eight. Good-night, Kirstin. If you have any trouble, just yell; I'm a light sleeper."

"I'll put some glucose tablets next to the bed. I'll be fine. Thanks."

"You've already done more than fine for yourself."

"What do you mean?"

"Medico. You must be very proud of yourself."

"I am. It was a long, hard road to get there, but I made it."

88

"Ever think of going into another line of work?"

"Heavens, no. I love research. I can't imagine not doing it."

"I know what you mean. Goodnight. See you tomorrow."

Kirstin wondered if he had stopped talking and left so hurriedly for a particular reason. She closed the door and approached the bed, where he had placed her suitcases. She put her things in drawers and into the closet, as if planning to stay a long time. She grinned as she unpacked a black nightgown and a bottle of Night Magic cologne her friends had given her, along with sexy advice on how to use them. She trailed fingers over the lace-and-satin garment and envisioned herself in it.

Kirstin closed the drawer and commanded herself to cease her silly fantasies. She entered the bathroom and tended to her teeth, hair, and skin. She changed into a modest gown, dropped her slippers by the bed, and tossed a matching robe over a chair, in case they were needed during the night.

She placed David's expensive luggage in a corner; it had been too attractive to dispose of with his other possessions. She climbed into bed and turned off the lamp. She was glad the pillow was the kind she liked, and realized she was tired and sleepy.

She snuggled into the inviting bed and relaxed. She could hardly believe where she was and what she was doing there. She tried to fall asleep but she kept thinking of Christopher Harrison in the next room. She admired his mixture of gentleness and strength, found them irresistible. Never had she met a man who had captivated so—not even David Lowrey had made her feel as the doctor did.

At last, sleep claimed her for a few hours.

Kirstin sensed a presence and opened her eyes. She was glad she didn't scream or jerk upward. A nightlight in the hallway and open door revealed Christopher's form not far away. She knew he couldn't see her face in the darkness. She struggled to remain still and to keep her breathing normal so he wouldn't know she was awake. What, she fretted, did he want? Would he try anything? Had she been foolish to accept his invitation? Was she in danger of being attacked?

Four

Kirstin remained motionless and silent as she watched Christopher stare at her supposedly sleeping form. She wished she could see his face, his expression, and know what he was thinking. In a few minutes, he crept from the room and closed the door. She made certain she did not send out an audible sigh of relief, as she sensed him lingering outside the room. Her heart pounded and her pulse raced; she tried to calm herself. Recalling how he had sneaked into the office this afternoon to check on her during her nap, she decided that was the motive for his nocturnal visit. That conclusion relaxed and pleased her, warmed her. She scolded herself for letting her imagination run wild.

Kirstin stretched and yawned as fantasies about him returned. He was so kind, considerate, and compassionate. David would have slept through the night without a thought — or perhaps a care — to her unstable condition. No doubt her deceased husband would have been vexed by her health problem and considered it a defect that could interfere with his life. David had wanted everything and everybody around him to be perfect, or at least be trouble-free. She couldn't explain even to herself why she had put up with a man's demands and selfishness, lived as his doormat, and near-slave as so many southern women of her generation did. But Christopher Harrison seemed different, refreshingly and delightfully unique.

What was the secluded physician really like? How was it possible to find a stranger so overwhelmingly attractive? How could just sitting with him and watching television be this exciting? How could simply holding his hand or brushing against him or looking at him create such blissful sensations, such daring ideas? Surely she wasn't considering an affair with him . . . Affair? That was a terrible word to describe a few days of physical and emotional enrichment. She didn't know why that temptation panicked her; she wasn't a virgin, nor an inexperienced and vulnerable teenager. For heaven's sake, she had been married for over twenty years, and she'd dated other men since David's death. Yet, none of them had been sexually appealing. She'd wondered if she'd become frigid because of David's lack of interest; now her reaction to Christopher proved that wasn't true. She responded to even his light touches, his glances, his voice, his incredible green eyes. All of those things stirred her. Should she—could she—do anything about it? As a wealthy and handsome doctor, surely he had plenty of beautiful young, women after him. Perhaps he was involved with the spitfire who'd called him twice, or even with several women. Kirstin asked herself if it made more or less sense to respond to a man she would never see again, one whose appeal was so powerful that it alarmed her.

Much as she tried to control and ignore them, instinctive and repressed longings called out to her to seize what she wanted. She tossed and turned as she wondered what it would be like to kiss him, to make love to him. She wouldn't be so brazen as to throw herself at him. But if he tried to seduce her, did she dare yield to the first overture he made?

In the next room, Christopher was uncomfortable too. Kirstin was the most provocative and refreshing female he'd met in years, maybe in his lifetime, if she was what she seemed. He knew women could be cunning. They couldn't seem to take a relationship slow and easy and just have fun. Most had marriage in mind. But wasn't that currently true of him? His loins flamed at the thought of Kirstin lying beneath him.

What would she do if he made a pass at her? He was a physician; she, his patient. The intimate situation reeked of temptation and trouble. Too many doctors had been sued for sexual offenses, some, he knew, over misunderstandings where the female had seemed inviting or consenting. It wasn't wise to have Kirstin or any female patient alone with him. Why hadn't he patched her up and sent her to the Clovis hospital to be under another doctor's care, one who was a specialist in diabetes?

He knew why. After spending most of the day with her, he hadn't wanted her to leave so soon. He cautioned himself to tread gingerly in this unpredictable situation.

The troubled man rolled to his stomach and thought about the many women he'd bedded in an effort to recover his male pride after what his ex-wife had done to him. He hadn't forgotten or forgiven Laura's humiliating treachery. But he'd settled down before his accident four years ago and behaved himself since then.

At last, both Kirstin and Christopher slept fitfully.

* * *

There was a tap at Kirstin's door. She sat up. "Yes?"

"You awake?" a mellow voice asked from the other side.

"What time is it?" There was no clock in the room and she hadn't retrieved her watch from the hall bathroom last night but brilliant sunlight beamed against the shades at the two windows.

He didn't open the door as he answered in a raised voice, "Nine o'clock. You need to check your blood and get some food in you soon, Kirstin."

She threw back the covers, sat up, and waited for her senses to clear before rising. "You're right. I can't believe I slept so late." No doubt because she'd been unable to fall back to sleep for hours after his nocturnal visit.

Christopher leaned against the door jamb and stared at the barrier. "You were exhausted from yesterday's events. I peeked in on you several times during the night and you seemed fine. Any problems?"

Kirstin was delighted to hear his explanation. "None, and thanks for checking on me. This area is as silent as a tomb. I got used to highway noises near hotels keeping me awake or disturbing me countless times a night."

95

"It doesn't take long to get used to the peace and quiet here."

"You've been quiet as a mouse this morning, or did you sleep late, too?"

"I've been up and on the range since six. You ready for a caffeine fix?" he inquired in a mock cowboy drawl. "I've already had two."

"I'd like to shower and dress first. Be there in fifteen minutes."

"No woman gets dressed that fast. I'll be in my office checking with my answering service," he told her, then left, whistling a country tune.

Kirstin checked her blood-sugar level, frowned, and chewed a glucose tablet to get her to breakfast. She didn't want to join her host as she was, but any exertion would take her level too low. She showered and brushed her teeth, then donned a pair jeans, a shirt, and tennis shoes. She applied makeup and cologne lightly to enhance her appearance but not enough of them to boldly reveal she was doing so. She straightened the bathroom and bedroom and headed for the kitchen. "My coffee still hot?"

Christopher turned, grinned, and let his gaze walk over her. "I don't believe it, sixteen minutes from start to finish. You're amazing, woman."

She could light up a dark room with the

glow she was experiencing from his words and look. "I take that as a compliment. I know I was a pain in the . . . rump yesterday for you and Captain Two Fists."

"I've had my share of worse pains," the doctor murmured. "This way," he motioned, taking her hand and seating her. He poured a cup of coffee and turned to ask, "How do you take it?"

"Two sweeteners, no cream," Kirstin replied, feeling wonderful.

"You're lucky Helen uses Equal or I wouldn't have any." He set the cup before her then fetched a spoon and two packets of the sweetener. "Careful, it's hot."

"Thanks, Christopher. I've never had better service. You joining me?"

"Thanks, but I've had my fill. You want some toast and eggs and bacon?"

"Don't bother with cooking," she declined, although she was hungry for a big and hot breakfast for a change. It must be the fresh air, she decided.

Before she could ask if he had cereal, he chuckled and, motioning with his sable head at the stove, he said, "I'm good on this range, too. Bacon . . . scrambled eggs . . . toast . . ." he tempted with a grin.

"Coffee and cereal are fine," she responded. "But I'm game to try your cooking skills. If they match your doctoring ones, it'll be a real treat."

"Did you test your blood?"

"Seventy-six . . . Yes, I know. I took a glucose tablet immediately."

"Wise woman. You could have eaten before you bathed and dressed."

"I know" was all she replied. *Please don't lecture me today.*

Within minutes, he had meat sizzling in the microwave and the table set. "I insist my patients eat right, and a hearty breakfast doesn't hurt on occasion. Fried or scrambled, ma'am?" he asked.

His expression was amusing, as was the towel he draped over his left wrist like a waiter. She laughed. "You're too much, Christopher Harrison. Scrambled, well done. Toast, just before burning. Bacon, crisp."

When the food was ready, he placed it before her. "Are you strong enough to do this alone or shall I feed you?" he jested, feeling cheerful and calm.

"I'm sure I can manage. Thank goodness I'll be well in a few days and on my way; service like this could find me ten pounds overweight within a week."

He stiffened at her first statement, then laughed and relaxed at her reason. He teased, "You do look a little scrawny, Mrs. Lowrey.

Maybe I should keep you here longer and fatten you up like I do my prize cattle."

"Don't you dare, Christopher Harrison!" she shrieked playfully.

"Got someone watching your figure? Perhaps several men?"

"Not with my permission," she informed him deliberately.

"Then there's no reason you can't eat well for a change."

"I do eat right, Doc. I take good care of myself. Don't I look healthy?"

"Maybe I should examine you before I answer," he quipped with a roguish grin. "When was your last thorough physical?"

Kirstin experienced that rush of heat once more at the thought of him examining her. "Just what kind of doctor are you, Christopher?"

"General practitioner, but I majored in surgery." He cursed his blunder when she perked up

"Surgery? Do you practice at the Clovis hospital?"

"I don't operate anymore. Gave it up years ago. I don't even take stitches unless it's an absolute emergency. How are the eggs and bacon?"

"Delicious. Why did you give up surgery? Didn't you like it? Don't you miss it?"

"Retired, remember? Eat, woman. I have more chores to do. Leave the table. I'll clean up later. Just take it easy today. See you later, Kirstin."

He was gone before she could swallow her coffee and speak. He rushed outside, in desperate need of fresh air and solitude. Flexing the disabled hand and pounding it into his other one, he cursed the accident that had ended his career. He had finally regained use of the hand but not enough to return to his beloved field. He had taught for a year while undergoing repair work and therapy, but had tired of the pity and "That's a shame" comments. He had come here to practice where these people needed him and didn't know about his troubles. Occasionally he did a few stitches after accidents, but it wasn't the same as performing daily operations that saved countless lives.

Why, he raged, wouldn't this infernal bitterness and emptiness cease? He felt like an impotent man who couldn't make love but still suffered from an overwhelming desire for sex! If the ability was gone, why couldn't the desire die, too? He stalked to the barn and resaddled his favorite horse. He rode fast and hard, as if real demons pursued him.

Kirstin was bewildered and worried by his odd behavior. Why would a surgeon "retire" to

100

a .small practice in general medicine in such a secluded area? Why had he terminated their pleasant talk when she asked why he'd quit? Something didn't add up.

She grimaced as dismaying speculations stormed her mind. He might be ill . . . He might have been kicked out for reasons of ethics or incompetence . . . He might have confronted a personal tragedy in the operating room that left him incapable of continuing. He could be blaming himself for the death or maiming of a special patient, perhaps his "missing" wife or a child. The possibilities were endless. He didn't want to discuss it, so for certain, the reason was a raw spot, a revealing wound. Whatever happened, she had no right to meddle. Unless, she refuted, the reason could affect—endanger—her treatment or survival. *Get well and get out,* she warned herself.

Her appetite lost, Kirstin still finished her food: it was necessary for her health. As she rinsed dishes and placed them in the dishwasher, she noticed his untouched meal next to the stove. She dumped his chilled food in the disposal and wiped the table and counter tops.

As she worked, Kirstin couldn't get Christopher off her mind. He had given her only good impressions of him and his skills, and she didn't believe she had misjudged them. There must be a logical reason behind his secrecy and evasiveness. Whatever was wrong with him, it was painful and private. She had realized he always used his right hand and carried items one at a time and that he always wore long-sleeved shirts. Maybe he was concealing physical as well as emotional scars. He had admitted he'd had accidents while working the ranch, so perhaps he had lost his operating ability after moving here and suffering one.

After finishing in the kitchen, Kirstin found a dust mop and some cloths to use on the floors and furniture in the living room and den, doing chores to keep her moody and mysterious host off her mind. While cleaning the hall bathroom, Kirstin retrieved her watch and placed it in the bedroom. Before she'd completed her task, Christopher returned

He leaned against the bathroom door jamb, relieved she hadn't taken flight while he was gone. Of course, he realized, she didn't have transportation. But, if she was frightened or desperate enough, she could have phoned a cab or called John. "What are you doing? You're supposed to be resting and recovering."

"Keeping my end of our bargain, Doc," she said with a smile as she attempted to sound calm and genial.

"You don't really have to do my house chores; that was a joke."

"A trick to get a guinea pig to practice on?" she quipped. She was relieved he was sounding and acting nice, genuine, again.

"Guilty as charged," he replied with a sexy grin. "It's lunchtime. Do your test while I get things ready in the kitchen. I'm starved. I should have eaten that second breakfast with you, but I have to watch my weight, too."

"Shouldn't we all?" she replied, and laughed to let him get away with the white lie, if it was one. He could be telling the truth. Perhaps he had planned to join her with a second helping but then the conversation had gone awry.

Everything was ready when she came into the kitchen. With a look of apology, she said, "My reading was sixty-seven." That put her below the 70-120 norm and close to a low blood sugar range.

"So, you'll promise to relax this afternoon while I run errands with Frank, right? Read, or watch TV, or nap. No more overdoing."

"I promise to be a good girl while you're gone."

"In the morning, reduce your medication by half, then test more frequently for a while to see if that's the problem?"

"Yes, sir," she agreed, dreading the additional tests.

"I started a chart on you. I want everything

recorded. I'll send copies to Doctor Cooper and to your new physician in San Diego. Have you chosen one there? Did Cooper make a recommendation?"

"Yes, and I already have an appointment set up with him."

"Give me his name before you leave and I'll speak with him, let him know the facts before you see him for the first time."

"Thanks, Christopher. You're a big help. I wish I could repay you properly for your many kindnesses. In this condition, I'm not much good."

"Don't think that way, Kirstin. It doesn't help; only depresses you and has ill effects on your health and mood." He should know.

Kirstin noticed how sad he looked. Her heart went out to him. As with her, he wasn't perfect. He had problems, worries, frustrations, and fears. He had a vulnerable streak that made him more appealing—human—than David could ever have been. That knowledge drew her closer to him. *What's tormenting you, Christopher? Talking about it might help, like talking to you helps me cope with my condition.* She ate in silence, as did he.

When they finished, he suggested that she sit in the den while he cleaned up. "No arguments, woman; you promised."

"Is it all right if I phone my daughter and

give her your address?"

"The phone's on the wall over there. I'll give her a report if you like."

"That will be nice; it will make Katie feel better. Thanks."

Kirstin placed the call. "Katie, it's Mom."

Christopher listened to her side of the brief conversation: "Yes, I'm doing fine . . . Doctor Harrison is lowering my medication and making sure I eat and exercise right . . . I'll be here a few more days or until I'm in control." He liked that statement and continued to listen. "He's going to speak with you to give you his address and medical opinion. Here he is now. I'll talk to you again before he hangs up."

"Hello, Miss Lowrey, Doctor Harrison here. Your mother's doing fine. With proper treatment and care, I don't foresee any complications."

Katie asked questions and liked the answers the physician gave. Impressed by his compassionate voice and competent manner, she thanked him for his care and told him to call if her mother needed anything. As she jotted down his address, she wished she could visit and meet him in person, but she didn't want to risk destroying a potentially romantic setting or shortening her mother's stay at the ranch. When Christopher gave Kirstin back the receiver, Katie didn't tell her about the talk she'd had with Steve this morning or his accusations about Kirstin's "selfishness" that would only upset her at a time when she needed to stay calm and to concentrate only on her health. Nor would she mention the stern lecture she had given Steve about Kirstin deserving happiness and her own life. She had even told Steve he only thought about himself and wasn't being fair with his latest demand. She wasn't about to reveal Kirstin's whereabouts to him and allow him to intrude on her. With luck and courage, perhaps her mother would come out of this mess with a new love.

"You take care, Mom, and I'll speak with you again Friday. Bye."

"Bye, honey, and congratulations on the movie part."

"Movie part?" Christopher echoed after she hung up the phone.

"Katie's a model and aspiring actress. She's done several magazine and TV commercials. She just landed a small role in a CBS movie-of-the-week that's being filmed in July. I'm so proud of her. She's done well on her own, but I've missed her terribly in the seven months she's been gone."

Christopher finished loading the dishwasher and turned it on. "How did she get into modeling and acting?" He leaned against the counter and observed Kirstin as she remained in the doorway.

"She took local classes and did shows at malls and stores. One of the TV stations hired her to do a few commercials for them. A scout from Los Angeles was in town, saw them, and tracked her down. He signed her up before he left, then called within a week with several auditions. She got the jobs and things have been rolling ever since."

"That was good luck and great timing. We can all use plenty of both. What about your other children? What do they do?"

"Sandi and her husband have lived overseas for a year, with two to go. Cliff is an oil expert; foreign companies pay handsomely for men with his knowledge. It was an excellent opportunity to earn a small fortune for three years' work, so he accepted. It seems like a good experience for them, and they love it, but I miss them and my grandson; he's eighteen months old. Of course, he'll return before he's too old to be a stranger to his grandmother."

"Your son?" he prompted when she didn't continue.

"Steve's a banker in Denver. He and Louise have twin boys almost two years old. They're expecting their third child in six months. He transferred from a local bank in early February."

"So there was no family or any ties left in

107

Augusta to hold you there?"

Ties? As in sweetheart? "None. As I told you yesterday, my parents are dead. What about your daughter?" *What about your wife?*

Christopher noticed how her expression and voice appeared strained as she spoke of her son; he suspected there was a problem there. It also seemed odd that while traveling across the country she didn't visit him. "Peggy's twenty-four. She and Phil live in Oregon, as I told you. Been there three years and have no plans to move. He's in the lumber business and she's in environmental work. They don't have any kids yet."

"Those two careers sound as if they could conflict on occasion if they aren't careful."

"That's how they met, butting heads over a project. But they love each other too much to let anything or anyone come between them."

"That's smart; love is too rare and special to spoil with selfish demands." *Shut up, woman, or you'll sound ridiculous.*

"You're right. But too many people don't realize that truth in this day of two-career families," he added with a frown. "You were lucky you didn't have to reject a transfer because your husband had a career in Augusta. It's obvious you love research and working for Medico."

"I do." Kirstin wondered if that was one of

Christopher's problems, a wife who wouldn't move here because she had a career elsewhere. Could she ever give up research to live in the secluded high plains of New Mexico? Did he resent liberated women and want only a housewife at his side? Maybe he had the same ideas and needs as David Lowrey. Maybe he believed a woman's place was at home, with or without children. Maybe he was still trying to get back an estranged and stubborn wife, or was looking for a comfortable replacement, one he could dominate?

Following a short silence, Christopher asked, "Where did your parents come up with the name Kirstin? It's unusual and pretty."

"Thanks. My father's middle name was Curtis and my mother's, Christine. If they had used their first names, I'd be called Jimmary."

He chuckled as she laughed. He enjoyed the mellow and genuine tone of the sound. He liked her smile and admirable character traits. He liked her appearance, it was normal to be first attracted to someone's good looks and sunny personality. She was attractive and slim, and had a super figure, especially for a woman of forty-five who'd given birth to three children. The few wrinkles on her face were barely visible tiny crow's-feet near the eyes and shallow creases from nose to mouth. Her complexion was smooth and radiant. She was educated, well mannered; the men she'd dated must have been impressed by her and must have enjoyed her company and conversation as much as he did.

He wanted to get to know her, to get better acquainted with the special woman he perceived her to be. He was relieved she hadn't questioned his behavior this morning. He didn't want to explain yet and risk sounding like a bitter and pathetic coward who'd exiled himself here to hide from the truth and pain. When and if they got closer, he'd confide in her. "You should be careful when you play with your grandchildren; they can eat up your blood sugar fast at that active age. And make certain they aren't sick when you're around them because you can't risk exposing yourself to illness; it's rougher on diabetics. You could lose all the progress you've made and even wind up on insulin."

"I know. I kept them at Christmas, New Year's, and in February during their move. To be honest, they wore me out. They can be a handful. 'Terrible Two's, it's called, and the twins have it bad right now. I hope to be in control before I keep them again."

"Just make certain you keep glucose tablets in your pocket and stay alert for sudden and rapid lows. Do you want me to call Steve and explain?"

"No," she replied in a hurry and blushed in guilt. "Actually, my son doesn't know about my condition. He was so busy with the move and new job that I didn't want to worry him. I'll tell him later. I'm not being irresponsible, Christopher; he recently had a physical for the transfer so I know he hasn't inherited my condition. Medico doesn't know about it, either. I hope you won't have to tell them before I can prove myself there and explain." She trusted him with a few of her secrets with the hope he would do the same with her. "Is that wrong of me, Christopher, to wait just a short time before risking problems there?"

"I understand, Kirstin, and I can't disagree. I won't report you. Any defect, no matter how small, can ruin a brilliant career. Some people don't seem to comprehend that certain disabilities can be controlled. Just make sure you watch yourself carefully. A lab accident would expose you fast; then, they'd lose trust and confidence in you."

"Thanks, Christopher, and I'll handle the matter as soon as possible."

"Is the need for secrecy the reason you didn't visit the grandkids?"

She was surprised he asked such a personal question, since he was being evasive himself. "Yes, and it's a good thing I wasn't babysitting the twins when this trouble came up." She

111

wouldn't reveal that not keeping them had caused another kind of trouble with Steve.

"You're right. But don't worry; we'll have you in top shape before you leave. By the time you see them again, you'll be prepared for any emergency."

"Are you eager to have grandchildren?" she asked to take the focus off her to learn his opinions on women.

"Yep, but Peggy isn't being cooperative. She loves her job and freedom too much. Phil wants her to quit and get pregnant, but she—" A car horn blew again. "Company," he remarked. "Be back in a minute." He headed for the front door.

Kirstin went to the den window and peeked outside to see if the visitor might be the woman who had called yesterday. It was Captain John Two Fists. The Indian officer bordered on being ruggedly handsome, his long black hair secured in a pony tail at the nape of his neck. Though nearing fifty, his dark skin had few wrinkles and creases. As she watched the two men, she observed their easy rapport. They smiled, chatted, and laughed as they leaned negligently against the officer's patrol car.

Car! She hadn't checked on it this morning. After her host returned, she would remind him they should do so. The extent of damage and length of repairs would determine how long she stayed after her diabetic situation was handled. She allowed her gaze to wander over Christopher Harrison's face and body. She knew what her friend Elaine would say about this situation — go after him!

She hadn't learned the truth with her earlier ploy of grandchildren; he had answered amidst chuckles, as if teasing. *I like your sense of humor and charm, Doc, and your integrity. You haven't made a pass yet. Maybe you won't, and maybe that's best for both of us.*

Kirstin rushed to the sofa when she saw Christopher returning and turned on the television with the remote control. She glanced up when he halted in the doorway.

"John came by to see how you're doing. He said to say hello for him. He checked on your car before driving out. Parts have to be ordered. Your catalytic converter is shot. One fender, door, and your hood are crumpled. The right sideview mirror and parking light are broken. The bumper's a mess. One tire was lost, and you bent a rim. Along with a few other things."

"My heavens! All that by going off the road?"

"Afraid so. It was a rough drop-off with lots of obstacles. You struck them all hard and fast when you gunned the gas pedal."

"But this Joe Bob Bridges you mentioned can fix everything?"

"Yes, but he has another vehicle to finish before he can get to yours. Should take a week or less to get it back. Joe Bob said it'll cost about eighteen to twenty-three hundred dollars." When her blue gaze widened even more, he explained, "Parts for a Nissan LE Fastback don't come cheap, and you have plenty to be replaced or repaired." He saw her frown in dismay. "There's such a large span in the estimate because he won't know the total labor charge until he's finished. He told John that some parts slide in easy and quick and others can give trouble. Once he gets started, he'll know if there's any hidden trouble he missed. That okay with you?"

Kirstin was shocked to learn how bad her accident had been. She was lucky she hadn't been injured badly. *Seat belts work, thank God.*

Christopher misread her thoughtful silence. "If you'd like to get a second opinion and estimate, there's no problem, Kirstin. If you plan to use your insurance, they might require two or more estimates."

"No, that's fine. I hope you thanked Captain Two Fists for me."

"I did. You can trust Joe Bob, Kirstin."

"I'll accept your word on his honesty and abilities."

"My guest room doesn't have any reservations waiting so you can stay as long as it takes to get your car back." He intentionally did not add, *unless you'd prefer to move to a hotel.* He didn't want to put that idea into her head or make her think he was suggesting she leave once she was well.

"I don't want to put you out for such a long time, Christopher."

"It's no bother, and I can observe you and treat you better here."

"Then I'll stay if you say it's all right."

"It is, Kirstin. Do you want me to phone Joe Bob and tell him to order the parts, or do you want to contact your insurance company first?"

"I'll try to pay it out-of-pocket. I've already filed against my insurance twice in the last year; another claim might ruin me."

"You've had two other wrecks in this car? For the same reason?"

"Heavens, no. I let Steve borrow it and he had a mishap. Then, I let his wife use it and she had one. Both were minor accidents and no one was injured. Since I didn't have any strikes against me and they both did, I took the blame to keep their insurance from rising."

He wanted to ask why Steve hadn't paid out-of-pocket himself for those other claims, but didn't. "John says she's a beauty, a sporty red model. A Fastback is a lotta power and speed to control, isn't it?"

"Yes, but I didn't exactly choose it. When Sandi and Cliff left America, they coaxed me into taking their car. It was only a few months old, and mine was giving me trouble. I loved it. I sold my mini-van and jumped on their offer. The Aztec red color and its sleek design were what stole my heart. Steve calls it my 'extravagant and foolish sports car,' but I don't care and I'm keeping it." *Damn, Kirstin, why not just expose the entire mess between you and Steve!* "It's fun to drive."

He caught her slip. "And gets you lots of male attention," he teased.

"That isn't why I wanted it. It gives a feeling of free — Why don't you call Joe Bob now before we forget?"

He also let her second slip pass as if he hadn't noticed either one. "Will do, ma'am. Then I'm heading into town with Frank on business."

"Ask if he needs a deposit. I can send him a check with you."

"Will do," he responded again. He wondered if paying cash would be a strain on her finances. Probably not or she wouldn't have taken on such a pricey car, even if it did sound as if she'd needed the spirit booster for enjoying "free —"dom . . .

After he completed the call, Christopher left with his foreman.

Kirstin made herself comfortable in the den, reading magazines and watching television. She hoped it would take many days for the car repairs. Was it wicked to feel delighted by this romantic setup? There had been so little love and romance, not to mention good sex, in her marriage. Was it wanton to have the desire to experience a heaping taste of all of those things? She was getting older every day and life could be snatched away in the blink of an eye; she didn't want to miss any chance for joy and enrichment. The excitement and anticipation of a romantic interlude made her feel younger and more alive, desirable. Yet she couldn't just jump into bed with him. She had to get to know him and get closer to him before she could do anything like that. But time was short and this opportunity would vanish soon. What to do, she fretted, if the occasion presented itself?

She gave in to the urge to phone her best friend in Augusta. "Elaine, it's me. I was hoping to catch you at home before you went to work."

"I start at MCG next week. It sounds like a terrific job. Lordy, I miss Medico. You're fortunate you could up and move with them. Are you there yet?"

"No, I'm in New Mexico." Kirstin explained what had happened to Elaine.

"You lucky woman. Single and gorgeous, wealthy and charming, too. What a delicious find! Why not enjoy a fling? What better chance to have a passionate and uncomplicated affair? Let him sweep you off your feet for a while."

"I couldn't."

"Why not? There's nothing wrong with a little fun and romance. The flame might not be burning right now, but the pilot light's still on. He's nice and sexy, isn't he?"

"Yes, but . . ."

"I thought so; I can hear it in your voice. Go for it, Kirstin; your ego can use a boost. You deserve to do something wild and wicked, and this might be your perfect chance."

"I can't believe you're encouraging me to sleep with a near stranger."

"Time is limited, old girl, and so is this opportunity. Once you reach San Diego, you'll have to protect the old reputation. Have some real fun and romance for heaven's sake! Days alone with a gorgeous doctor . . . He sounds like my kind of man. If you're chicken, send him my way. Just kidding! Put those going-away gifts to good use while you're there; I would."

"Stop teasing me, Elaine. This is serious. I never expected to find a dreamy man along

118

the road, and there isn't enough time to see how compatible we are. I've never been so confused in my life."

"What's the problem, silly; jump his bones every chance you get."

"That's easy for you to say, my liberated friend. You've been divorced and dating for years. I'm new at this. Heavens, how things have changed since my high school and college days."

"Just take the leap, Kirstin. Don't think, just do it. You'll be glad. Nothing makes a woman feel more confident and desirable than good loving from a good man. It's not as if you're married, and you weren't happy when you were. Right?"

Happily married? "I thought so in the beginning; I tried to keep that illusion alive for the kids' and my parents' sakes. For mine, too, so I wouldn't realize how miserable I really was. If divorce ever entered my mind, it was as an unconscious thought. I believed a marriage involving children shouldn't be dissolved simply because of . . . 'diminished desire,' as it's called. For me to rip apart my family and home would have required something drastic such as an extramarital affair, or clear-cut abuse. If David was ever unfaithful, he took that secret to his grave." *Others, too.* "He was never physically mean, Elaine. He just made me his emotional

119

prisoner; he did it so cunningly that I failed to understand my situation."

"That happens to us women more than we realize or care to admit."

"I confess I allowed it to happen and refused to deal with it because of the children and my parents. I really believed I loved David when we got married. But after I quit work and had our third child, which turned out to be an unplanned blessing, he just took over my life. I lived with him, bore his children, and buried him. I lived under his thumb, and Kirstin Darnell ceased to exist. The odd thing is that David's image seems to get dimmer each week, as if it's a vanishing mirage. Sometimes, it's as if he never existed, as if my current life is the only reality. Does that sound crazy? Am I going off the deep end?"

"No, it's human nature. It's the way the mind and heart heal our wounds so we can go on with our lives. Look at it this way; the old Kirstin has returned from a premature grave and is even better and more alive than she was before David. She's free, new, and growing like a spring weed."

"You're right, Elaine, but to think of enduring another emotional and physical winter frightens me and makes me want to hold back from any man, even one who seems perfect for me. Losing David was difficult. I was so

120

dependent on him, so ignorant in so many areas. I missed him so much. I pushed myself to the point of near physical and emotional exhaustion while I learned to run my own life."

"So, you deserve a break, some fun and happiness. Go for them with the sexy doctor."

"What if I fall hard for him? That would complicate matters."

"Only if he doesn't fall for you, too. Even if he doesn't, look at what you'll gain: valuable experience you need to deal with men. Practice, woman! Pretend it's an experiment; throw in all the right chemicals, select the best specimen, run it through the centrifuge, and see what comes out. Love is a science, old girl, you have to study it and practice it to get good at it. Don't always be an observer of life, Kirstin, be a participant. Take control of the situation. It's perfect."

"Steve would have a fit if he knew where I was and what I'm doing."

"Forget about Steve. Do something for yourself for a change. Lordy, Kirstin, don't let him continue to make you feel guilty or take advantage of you. How much more do you owe him? You raised him and were there every time he needed you. You kept his kids three times in the last few months and on countless weekends and gobs of other nights before he left town. One kid is enough work and responsibility, but he has *two*, both of whom are rambunctious. You don't need that energy drain, especially now."

"Sometimes I wish he'd had one baby at a time so I could give all my attention to them separately. They'll be more fun when they're older and potty trained and I can take them places without worrying about diapers, feeding, and naps. Steve and Louise let them get away with anything; that's why they're so hard to handle. Those tantrums are awful. Usually grandchildren act better for their grannies than for their parents. Steve's don't."

"I know; mine are getting worse all the time. These modern parents are for the birds sometimes. They spoil their kids, then want grandparents to beg to keep them so they can have a break. A relaxing cruise in the tropics, wasn't it?"

"Yes, and Steve said they couldn't go if I didn't babysit. This just isn't a good time for me, not with moving and the diabetes. Steve thinks I shouldn't have other interests, that my grandchildren should be my life, like my own kids were my life for over twenty years. He doesn't understand his children aren't my responsibility, nor that not wanting to keep them at the drop of a hat doesn't mean I don't love them. I *do* love them. I do want to spend time

122

with them. Just not now. Besides *wanting* to work, I *have* to work to support myself. I can't be a full-time grannie or come running every time he calls. I've been honest and open with him about my feelings but he sees this one refusal as a betrayal and selfishness. I've kept them plenty of times when I was too tired, when I had to cancel my own plans. He even gets angry when I tell him I can't take time off from work to do him a favor. I have bills and my retirement to think about. I'm almost forty-six. Besides, at any moment, a diabetic complication could force me to quit work. If it did, I couldn't afford my medical bills and support on my savings and insurance. It would be a while before Medicare kicked in, and Social Security isn't enough to live on these days. What does Steve expect of me? I can't risk my health and job by being at his beck and call every day. Life can be so frustrating."

"Yes, it can be, especially if we're unwilling to take chances when they're dropped in our laps. Steve's the one who's selfish, Kirstin, not you."

"Then why do I feel so guilty about refusing him?"

"Because you're a good person and a good parent."

"Learning to be a good grandmother is as

hard as learning to be a good parent was. I wish there was a list of instructions that came with the birth of a child to tell a woman what the right thing to do is. I was a good mother and wife, Elaine, but now I want to do something for *me*. I want to relax, go places, have money to spend, enjoy my job, maybe do volunteer work to meet new people. My life centered around my home and family, their needs and schedules; now Steve expects me to do the same with his children. He's been calling Katie to find out where I am because he still hopes he can coerce me into racing to Denver so he and Louise can leave next week. I bet a month's salary he hasn't made other arrangements because he believes I'll show up as always. If I'm ever going to break this cycle, I can't go. He has to get out of the habit of using me, and that's what it is, whether or not he realizes it or admits it. I'm not going to call him until I reach San Diego. After I explain about my diabetes, maybe . . ."

"Don't count on it, Kirstin. I know Steve well, remember? I've been there when he tried to manipulate you, pull those guilt trips of his. He's been so possessive since David died. You've been terrific to him, more generous than most parents. I'm glad you put your foot down this time; I would have been disappointed if you hadn't. Lordy, he's had more fun and time off in the last few months than you have in over twenty years! Think of all the good times you've missed just to give him a night or a weekend off."

"I can see his point this time. Louise is pregnant and this will be their last chance to travel for a while. He says they want time alone for romance."

"Don't you dare weaken! I'll bet my first month's salary that he'll call as soon as the baby's born and want you to keep all *three* of them so they can get away before digging in to raise them. Nip it now or it'll be trouble later."

"I suppose you're right."

"I am right. It's not like he can't afford to hire a sitter. I'm sure he can get recommendations from his new friends, or staff, or neighbors. Remember, Kirstin, he didn't even offer to pay for your plane ticket or to have your car shipped to California if you agreed to fly out to babysit. He certainly has more money than you do. And to tell you that you can 'rest up' and vacation while you're chasing after those two boys is a bunch of bull."

"Maybe I should have stopped by to visit on my way to San Diego."

"And give him the perfect opportunity to wear you down? You couldn't have gotten out of it gracefully, and you know it. If he doesn't want to use a new sitter, Louise has sisters and a mother who don't work; they can exchange favors for once. You always put your family first; it's your turn to be first now. It's past time for Steve to realize and accept the fact you're a person, too, one who deserves and has earned the right to a life of her own. After all, you aren't rejecting or abandoning them; it's just one measly refusal. Besides old girl, if you were in Denver, you wouldn't have met the handsome doctor. It's fate, Kirstin, so don't fight it or beat yourself over the head."

They chatted a while longer about work and other friends.

"Have fun and stop worrying, you lucky dog."

"I'll try. Thanks for the pep talk, Elaine. I needed it."

"That's what best friends are for. Take care of yourself. And give me a full report after you reach San Diego—if you ever do." Elaine laughed. "Bye."

Kirstin hung up the receiver and went to test her blood and fetch a snack. She was tempted to do a few chores and to begin dinner but she had promised Christopher she would relax all afternoon.

Relax? How can you relax when you have important decisions to make? Decisions, Kirstin? How can you have a choice to make when Christopher hasn't

126

even made the slightest overture? And he probably won't, you nitwit. But if he does make a move, how are you going to respond? Like a scared virgin? A love-starved fiend? You had better decide before the occasion arises or you'll ruin a promising friendship. Maybe you have to give him a hint you're interested and receptive. But if you do, you'd better be prepared to follow through. Think, because he'll be home soon. What's it to be, Kirstin?

Five

Christopher returned about four o'clock. She saw the foreman get into a pickup truck and drive away. Her host began carrying in groceries and placing sacks on the kitchen counter. Kirstin joined him and offered to help. He suggested she put away the purchases while he finished unloading.

She was amazed by the quality of his selections, not to mention that he'd gone shopping in the first place. David had never even wanted to stop by a curb market to pick up something she needed or had forgotten. Since she had "all day to get things done," why, he would ask in annoyance, should he spend his "precious time and energy doing your job after a hard day at the office?" After a few such episodes, she'd done without an item rather than ask him to pick it up on his way home, which had no doubt been his intention.

Christopher said, "I forgot to ask you to make a list before I left, so I hope I got everything you'll need. If not, I'll fetch it tomorrow."

Kirstin glanced over the sugar-free snacks, cereal, and drinks. He had also selected fresh fruit, meats, and vegetables, even skim milk and a few low-fat items. "I couldn't have done a better job myself, Christopher. Thanks." She laughed. "But you have enough food to last a month."

"Better to be prepared since we can't tell how long your treatment and car repairs will take." *Especially if I decide to slow them down.*

"I have to be at work on May fourth, less than a month from today."

"I'm afraid I can't allow you to leave until all of this is eaten," he teased. "Besides, I don't know how to cook half of it."

He opened another package. "Scales for weighing and measuring; correct amounts are crucial to your control. If you depend on guesstimates, portions tend to creep upward without your noticing it."

"You're right. I usually weigh and measure every three to four days to make certain my eyeballing stays accurate. Thank you for being so kind and thoughtful. I really should pay you for my meals and board; this is an extra expenditure for you."

He noticed her eyes were damp and her

voice thick with emotion. Her reaction and gratitude touched him deeply. "Guests don't normally reimburse their hosts for meals and room."

"But I'm a patient—a burden, an intrusion."

"Patient and new friend, Kirstin, neither of those other two. Besides, you'll be whipping up some tasty treats for me in a few days as repayment."

Begin cooking for him in a *few days?* She was supposed to *stay* only a few days. "Fair enough," she replied with newfound courage.

"This is for you, too. It should protect you until the one from Medic Alert arrives. Wear it at all times until you get yours."

Kirstin halted her task to accept the gift he handed her, a medical alert bracelet designed for diabetics. She stared at it in surprise and pleasure. "That's thoughtful and generous, Christopher. Thank you again."

"It's just a cheapie, but it might save your life in another emergency."

The metal bracelet was more precious than a gold one to her because he had thought of it and bought it out of the kindness of his heart. Just as he had done with the food and scales. "You're an amazing man, Doctor Christopher Harrison," she murmured aloud without meaning to do so. "This is one of the nicest things anyone has ever done for me."

"Isn't there an old saying that goes something like, It's easy to be nice to nice people?"

"You're nice people," she said with a smile and misty eyes.

He was vexed he couldn't help her put the bracelet on, what with its difficult catch, but his left hand didn't have the dexterity. He watched her work with the tricky closing until she succeeded. She held up her arm, admired the silver-plated bracelet with its red caduceus, then sent him a bright smile.

Her blue eyes locked with his green ones and they gazed at each other. He wanted to lean over and kiss her but controlled that urge. They had known each other for less than two days. He didn't want to scare her and send her running for cover, perhaps even screaming accusations about him. For some reason, he was as charged up as a new battery. And she seemed to be sending him signals she was, too, but he might be mistaken. *Wait and see, Chris.*

Kirstin wished that he would kiss her. She wanted him to, but she also wanted—needed—to go slow with him. *Oh, Elaine, you shouldn't have planted such wicked thoughts in my head. Your dear friend doesn't have the vaguest idea what to do with them. Stop thinking such crazy thoughts or you'll complicate your life,* she ordered. *Sex and secret affairs should be the last things on your mind. You have enough problems to deal with without adding*

131

such foolishness to the list.

Thankfully something—someone—intruded at that moment. A horn blew, causing Kirstin and Christopher to jump, as the kitchen door was open and the vehicle wasn't far from it. Both glanced in that direction, looked back at each other, grinned, then laughed.

"Here's my patient. You relax until I'm finished with him."

Saved by a timely interruption, her confused mind announced.

Kirstin needed fresh air and distraction. She strolled outside, walked to a free-standing swing, and sat down. Despite the loud squeaks and groans the swing emitted, she swayed back and forth until a menacing growl from behind reached her ears. She froze as the ominous throaty rumble came again, this time nearer. With caution, she looked over her shoulder to find a huge black dog inching toward her. The animal's teeth were bared and saliva dripped from his drooling mouth. She realized, if she jumped up and ran, he might come after her. And she saw no close place to leap out of his reach. "Christopher! Christopher, hurry!"

The office door flew open in seconds. "Git, Ranger!" he shouted at the dog, who belonged to his patient Henry. The doberman tucked his tail and raced around the house. Christopher hurried to her, sat down beside her, and pulled

132

her into his arms. She was pale and shaking. "It's all right, Kirstin. He's gone. I don't know why he threatened you; he's usually very gentle."

Her heart pounded and she trembled. Her breathing was erratic. She buried her head against his chest as the terror subsided. She had to struggle hard not to burst into hysterical sobs.

"He's gone. You're safe," he whispered, holding her against him.

"I was petrified. I just knew he was going to attack any minute."

"He isn't a bad dog. I doubt he would have bitten you. 'Course you might have had to hang around for a few weeks to see if he had rabies."

To calm down, she jested, "You sound disappointed he didn't bite me. Did you sic him on me to force me to be your guinea pig longer?"

"Not a bad idea. Let me see if I can find him and get him to—"

"Don't you dare! You have no idea how frightening that was! Some vacation I'm having," she muttered.

"At least you're lucky enough to get stranded here. It isn't all bad."

Henry came outside and asked if something was wrong.

"Ranger scared her. He was growling at her.

Listen to me, Kirstin; go inside until I finish with Henry. You're safe now."

"I'm sorry, ma'am. Ranger don't usually do things like that."

"The swing squeaks badly and probably scared him." Christopher said. "Everything's all right, Henry. Just go back in the office; I'll be there shortly."

Henry apologized again, then obeyed his doctor. Christopher pulled Kirstin to her feet and took her to the kitchen door. "Will you be all right?"

"I'm fine, again thanks to you."

"Check your sugar level; that experience might have sent it soaring."

"Yes, Doc."

Christopher returned in an hour, and Kirstin told him she'd placed a call to a friend this afternoon with her telephone charge number.

"She worried about you?" he asked to discover the friend's sex.

"Yes. We've been best friends for over a year and we worked together."

"Did she warn you of the perils of staying here alone with a bachelor? Did she want to race over and rescue you?"

His chuckle warmed Kirstin. "She was more interested in checking out my mystery doctor.

Elaine's quite a flirt, but a harmless one."

He ignored the evocative word "mystery" for now. "You painted a glowing picture of me?"

Kirstin was surprised by his playful query. "How could I do otherwise?" She recalled how she had described him: Jungle-green eyes and lush black hair. Six feet two and weight slightly over two hundred, all lean muscle. No visible scars or beard. Strong features and smooth flesh, except for slight stubble by late afternoon. Lots of male hormones. He's anything but ordinary.

Kirstin realized she was staring at him and breathing funny. And he was staring back with a come-hither invitation in those hypnotic eyes. "What time do we eat supper?" she asked. She felt awkward after their earlier contact—they'd almost been snuggling in the swing. Why was she trembling and tingling like a school girl? *Heavens, Kirstin, you're a grown woman!*

"How do grilled hamburgers sound? Tempt your taste buds any?"

"Um-m-m-m," she murmured in anticipation. "At least I can help tonight. I won't drain my energy banks making patties."

"Meat in the fridge. Plate in the cabinet behind you. Cloth to your left in the drawer. Need anything else?"

"You're good company, Christopher. I couldn't ask for a better host, or a better place to get stranded."

"And I couldn't ask for a better guest or patient. Let's see . . . Rolls, mustard, ketchup, pickles, chips, lettuce, tomato, cheese . . . Carrots, milk, and fruit for you. Starch, protein, veg, fruit, milk: that has your requirements met. What else do we need?" he asked as his gaze scanned the refrigerator shelves.

Both were delighted when the other didn't mention onions.

"You like big burgers, Doc?"

He grinned. "Nice big ones for me. Two to three ounces for you, remember?"

"Of course." She prepared a sample and asked, "How's this?"

"Perfect," he responded as he allowed his gaze to travel over her.

Kirstin sensed he wasn't referring to the beef patty and almost thanked him for the subtle compliment. "Great," she said instead.

Once the table was set, Kirstin went outside with him. She sat on the steps while he whistled and worked at the nearby grill. Soon, the teasing aroma of hamburgers filled their nostrils. When they were almost ready, he told her to take a seat at the table, and a few minutes later, he joined her.

"How do you like your hamburger?" he asked. "What can I pass you?"

"The works."

"Don't want to miss anything, huh? An adventuress at heart?"

Kirstin was feeling deliriously carefree. "Sometimes. A person doesn't know what's she's missing unless she's willing to try new things." *Oh, my, was that too risqué?* she fretted.

He chuckled. "What if the old things are better than new ones?"

"What better way to learn than by comparison shopping?"

"This is an awfully deep discussion of the simple hamburger."

"Nothing in life is simple anymore. Challenges keep people alive and thinking. Don't you agree?"

He shrugged. "Sometimes. When did you tell your daughter and friend you'd get to San Diego?"

"I didn't give Katie a date. I said I'd call in a few days to give her better information. Once you fix the old bod and my car's repaired, I'll let her know something definite. You ready to ship me out already? A real pill, am I?"

"Not at all. In fact, company's fun for a change. And as you said, we all need challenges to enliven us and keep the gray cells functioning."

"How often do you get to see your daughter?"

"We talk on the phone every week. Sometimes she acts more like the parent than I do and checks on me if I don't report in on schedule."

"She worries about you?"

"Don't all kids when you're separated from them?"

"You're right. How long have you lived alone here?"

"Three years, if you don't count Frank and Helen."

She noticed how he ignored talking about his wife.

"Try this to see if your taste matches mine," he coaxed after putting a plate before her.

"What would you like to drink, Doc? I forgot to ask."

"A Classic Coke full of nasty caffeine and lots of sugar . . . and a nice dash of Old Grandad. I'll get it." As he prepared the drink, he said, "I'm off duty, unless there's an emergency." He glanced down at the amber liquid. "The perfect companion to this pièce de résistance. Wish it wasn't on your list of no-no's. I have wine, red and white, but it's best if you eat first."

"Milk's fine, and necessary I know. My favorite drink was Wild Turkey in Classic Coke. I miss it. Somehow, diet colas don't taste the same. A spicy Coke sounds divine tonight, but

I'll be good and drink my milk."

"Then I won't have to worry about you getting tipsy and taking advantage of me," he joked, another thirst craving to be appeased.

"You're quite safe with me. Besides, I never get tipsy. David said a lady . . ." The moment she said that, she was sorry.

He stopped sipping to ask, "A lady what?"

It was silly not to answer. "Always keeps her wits and manners about her." He laughed as she flushed. Truth was, David never wanted her or the kids to do anything that might embarrass him or cost him a client. It was shocking to see the real David more clearly each day . . .

"What if I get tipsy and take advantage of my lovely patient?" Using a terrible but comical French accent, he murmured, "You are trapped in a secluded rendezvous with a captivated man, *ma petite*."

"Professional ethics, Doc, remember?" she jested in return as her heart pounded wildly at his seductive tone, sexy smile, and insinuation.

He chuckled and grinned. "What if I lack those, Mrs. Lowrey?"

"You're teasing a helpless victim," she scolded with a laugh.

For an instant, he locked gazes with her as if to ask, Am I? "Of course I am," he responded before focusing on his food and drink.

They ate in heavily seductive silence, unsure of what to say next. Afterward, she rinsed the dishes while he placed them inside the dishwasher; each was keenly aware of how nice it was to work together. When the kitchen was clean, he suggested they take a walk to settle their dinner.

They ended up at the swing and they sat down, close to each other in its narrowness. The gentle swaying of the suspended seat was tranquilizing, despite the noise of the grating chain and aging wood. His arm rested along the back and brushed her shoulder, she was aware of the touch of his muscular thigh against her leg.

Three jets zoomed overhead and both looked upward.

"They're from Cannon Air Force Base, six miles west of Clovis," Christopher explained. "About ten percent of the town's population works there. Melrose, twenty miles northeast of here, has a firing range the fighters and bombers use. It doesn't even have to be a quiet day to hear them practicing."

"Twenty miles isn't far for something traveling that fast. Have you ever feared they'd overshoot their target range, or whatever it's called?"

"Nope. The 27th Tactical Fighter Wing is one of the best worldwide. Since you're stuck here, I'll have to show you around. There's plenty to see in all directions."

He told her more about the area and his ranch and about some of his neighbors. His deep voice lulled her into blissful serenity. How peaceful it was here with him, she thought. She didn't want to think of leaving soon. When she had traveled with David, it had been for business only. To do things with Christopher would be fun and interesting, enlightening.

"Do you have any chores this evening?"

"Frank's taking care of everything. He's a good man. He constantly tells me if I ever want to sell out, to give him first shot at the place. I can't blame him; the ranch is a beauty and has good resources."

"Would you ever think of moving away? Back to a large city?"

"Nope; this is the best place for me, the *only* place for me."

When he didn't elaborate, she didn't probe.

After enjoying the sunset, they went back to the house and watched television in the den and chatted about current events and the program in progress.

He mentioned that his daughter Peggy had wanted to become a model like Katie, but she'd been too short and plump to follow her teenage dream. Then, she had gotten involved in environmental issues in college.

141

"Peggy and Katie would be good friends if they met; they have similar interests. Katie's done several TV spots on environmental issues. Certain advertisers think she has an athletic, outdoor, all-American look."

"Does she look like you?"

"A little, but I think she looks like the actress Meg Ryan more."

"She's lucky; appearances are important in her career. But sometimes looks are too important to some people. It's dangerous and foolish what some females do in search of perfection, or what society labels as perfection. Before you scold me, I realize some men are just as guilty of jumping on that carousel, but it's mainly females who become anorexia nervosa and bulimia victims. I've repaired stomach ruptures and esophagus tears and—You get the picture. I'm glad Peggy didn't want to be a model that badly. She's a beautiful woman now, a perfect size for her height."

"Sometimes looks can be as much of a burden as a blessing. Exceptional beauty and other charms cause some people to treat their owner differently, out of jealousy or a misconception about an inflated ego."

"Do yours ever give you such problems?"

She stared at him. "Mine?"

He laughed at her reaction. "Yes, yours. Have you had to fight off men?"

"Sometimes men flirt, but only because I'm a woman and single, not because I'm a raving beauty with abundant charms."

"You're wrong, Kirstin; you underestimate yourself."

She laughed, then blushed. "Are you flirting with me, Doctor?"

"Naturally. A smart man never passes up a golden opportunity."

"Thank you for the compliment. But I would think a man like you has more trouble in that area than I would, especially with there being more widows and female divorcees our age."

"Not in this area, thank goodness."

"Ah ha, so you prefer to remain a carefree bachelor."

"Unless somebody special and unique comes along unexpectedly."

Is that a hint, Doc? Do I hope so? "I know what you mean."

"It's getting late. Better eat your snack and test your blood."

Conversation getting too scary for you, Doc? "You're right. Want anything?" When he grinned, she added, "From the kitchen?"

"I'm fine, thanks."

Later, curled in bed, Kirstin tried not to think about Christopher and their verbal dances around each other.

* * *

143

Following breakfast, Christopher left to do chores. Kirstin cleaned the kitchen and straightened the den, then she tested her blood, found the glucose level too low for her to exercise, and ate two tablets to raise it. She went to the room where Christopher had a mini-gym set up and used the treadmill. As she finished, she heard a persistent horn blowing, then the doorbell ringing. She hurried toward the kitchen door and opened it. She looked out, and when she saw a delivery truck leaving, she rushed outside and tried to flag down the driver, but he didn't see her waves or hear her shouts.

Kirstin started back inside to shower and change from the sweaty exercise clothes before Christopher arrived for lunch. At the same time, she saw and heard a rattlesnake. With caution, and her gaze glued to the viper, she inched backward toward the porch. Her vision blurred and her head whirled in dizziness. She was weak, nauseous, shaky, clammy — symptoms she recognized: hypoglycemia. "Don't you dare pass out," she ordered herself, "Get inside." She was just clearheaded enough to know she didn't want the physician to find her unconscious, without emergency tablets in her pocket as ordered, and with a snakebite. When the creature hissed and sprang, she screamed and turned to run but entangled her feet and tripped.

Kirstin's hands floundered about in an attempt to break her fall. Covering her face with one hand, she scrambled up the steps and sat on the floor, dizzy and hurting. She glanced at the viper, who remained coiled and shaking his rattle in warning. Surely, she hoped, she was out of his reach and he wasn't able to climb steps. Her nose had taken the worst of the fall by striking the top step. She felt sticky liquid on her hand and lips, then realized blood was pouring from her nostrils. She yanked the shirttail from her jeans and held it up to staunch the flow. Crimson fluid saturated it and eased between her fingers. She felt it rolling down her arm.

"You clumsy ninny!" she chastised herself. She didn't want to use a dishcloth for a bloody nose; nor did she want to risk dripping it over the carpet by heading for the bathroom. *Kitchen! Paper towel!* her dazed mind ordered through a near fog and her body obeyed the message. She was struggling to stand up on weak legs and was leaning over the sink when Christopher arrived.

He hurried to her. "What happened?" he asked, seizing her chin and lifting her head to check her out.

Kirstin jerked away, quickly lowered it, and replaced the paper towel. Mumbling through

145

it, she told him what had occurred. "Just a bloody nose; it isn't broken," she panted, hardly able to breathe or keep her wits. "Hand me more paper towels."

He grabbed a dishcloth and wet it, then mopped the blood from her arm and hands and cheek. He pushed away the saturated paper and pressed the cloth tightly to her nostrils. "Lean your head back and keep pressure on it."

Disoriented and close to tears, she seized it and snapped, "I can do it myself! I'm not a child! You'll get it on you!"

He let her have the cloth and fetched another and wet it. "Here, wash your face and hands. Your shirt is ruined, maybe your jeans, too. Better get them off and let me wash them in cold water right now."

"I'm slightly occupied, Doctor Harrison. Don't worry about them." She removed the cloth to see if the bleeding had stopped or slowed; it hadn't. Her nose was sore and her head was spinning. She didn't know if she wanted to throw up or faint or cry like a baby.

"Let me do that," he insisted and took the cloth. "I may have to cauterize any broken vessels with silver nitrate. I'll check it later."

She allowed him to tend the injury, too confused and weak to argue anymore. At last, the bleeding halted. When she asked for a tissue to blow her nose, he refused, telling her it would start the bleeding again.

Christopher noted the glazed look in her blue eyes and the paleness of her complexion. He detected her trembling and odd breathing. In the tension of the moment, he had overlooked her other symptoms. "Where are your tablets? You're having a low blood sugar attack." When she appeared to have trouble responding, he poured some orange juice and helped her drink it by holding the glass to her lips. He sat her down and fetched the glucose tablets from her room, then hovered over her while she chewed them. "What brought this on, Kirstin?"

She explained with lowered lashes and a guilty expression.

"You shouldn't exercise vigorously this soon with me out of the house. And I warned you to keep the tablets with you at all times. What if I hadn't returned in time to treat you? You could have passed out."

Still gripped by aftereffects of the attack, she snapped, "It was the damned snake's fault! And that delivery man's! I had tablets on the treadmill in case I needed them. Look, if you don't believe me."

"That isn't good enough, woman! You weren't at the treadmill when trouble struck. You can't take chances like this, Kirstin."

"All right, all right! Stop fussing at me! It

was a mistake."

"Such a mistake could have caused you to faint right on top of that rattler. You have to learn to be careful, to take this disease seriously."

Heavens, how she hated that word. "I do take it seriously. Don't you think I know how dangerous it can be? It practically controls my entire life."

Christopher knew her moodiness and terse replies weren't her fault; but her carelessness was. Besides, he was sounding more like a scared lover than a concerned doctor. He wasn't worried about her suing him. He was worried about her continued recklessness. He admonished himself for leaving her alone for hours. Even normal activities could be dangerous for her in this unbalanced state. "Sit here while I see if the rattler's still around. Don't get up, understand? Just relax and recover."

Feeling better, she said, "Yes, sir, and I'm sorry for being a pain."

"I understand." At times when he had been under pressure following his accident, he had behaved worse. He took a pistol from a cabinet and went outside, smiling to himself as she shouted after him to be careful. To his surprise, the snake was still occupying its chosen spot. Christopher took aim and fired several shots, striking the creature each time. He left it lying there for a vulture to dine on. He rejoined Kirstin, who looked a mess.

"Did you get him?"

"Yep. I'm an A-1 shot, an ex-quail hunter." *Even right-handed.*

"Do you have them crawling around the yard all the time?"

"Not many, not often."

"I certainly won't step outside alone again."

"You don't have snakes where you used to live?"

"No."

"What about when you were growing up in the country?"

"Not even then. I've only seen a couple, little green ones and a king snake or two, nonpoisonous and gentle. We always had dogs and they keep them away from houses. Why don't you have a dog?"

"I did but—"

She noticed a frown as he paused. "He died?"

"No, someone took him. I didn't want to get another one."

Kirstin didn't know if "took him" meant stolen or lost by divorce.

He grasped her hand, pulled her to her feet, and guided her down the hall. "Get out of those clothes and hand them to me. I'm going to wash them right now or they'll be ruined.

Besides, you've got blood all over you. Go change, but take your glucose level first and pop another tablet or two if necessary. I'll have lunch ready by the time you finish." He decided it was best to take command of this situation.

"Did I make a mess?" she asked, glancing toward the kitchen.

"Only on yourself," he white-lied, recalling the blood smeared on the screen and back doors, and all over the kitchen. "You better shower off so you can eat. You have blood on your neck and chest." He would clean everything up while she was taking a bath and changing clothes so she wouldn't be embarrassed when she saw the results of her carelessness.

"Okay," Kirstin agreed as she submitted to his masterful air and permitted him to lead her into the guest bath. "I won't dilly-dally."

He chuckled and closed the door while she stripped. Standing to the side, she opened it a crack to pass the jeans and shirt to him, forgetting about the mirror that revealed her shapely figure to him. "From the looks of this shirt, what goes under it is probably soaked and stained, too, Kirstin. Hand it out; I've seen women's underwear before."

She flushed, then unsnapped the bra, and passed it out to him. He might be a doctor, but she didn't think of him in that light at this moment! But he was being helpful, so a refusal seemed silly and overly modest. If he asked for her panties, though, she might scold him! He didn't.

But he did ask, "Want me to hand you more clothes?"

"I can get them later. Just pass me my robe on the bed, please."

He did so, gaining a pleasant view of her almost naked body through the crack. His groin tightened in his jeans. If she could see the results of her appeal on him, she might be shocked! She closed the door and locked it. He chuckled to himself when he heard the telltale click.

Kirstin monitored her blood sugar and found it all right. She showered, then dried herself. Unaware that Christopher hadn't closed the bedroom door, she walked to the dresser to get fresh garments. She dropped the damp towel to the floor and slipped into panties and jeans, then a bra and shirt.

Having come to make sure she wasn't having trouble Christopher halted at the doorway as she released the towel. He couldn't seem to move for a moment as he stared at her. Kirstin was wrong if she didn't believe she was beautiful and charming. She was very much a woman, a mighty tempting one. But he shouldn't be playing the peeping Tom. Before he sneaked away to prevent being seen, he gaped at the necklace she was wearing. The wedding band she had removed from her finger was suspended from a gold chain around her neck! Why? She could have placed it in her suitcase, a drawer, her purse, or on the dresser or nightstand. Why wear it? He frowned.

Kirstin scooped up the towel and went to straighten the bathroom. Standing in front of the mirror, she finger-tossed her loosely curled hair; the delicately pointed bangs across her forehead were scrunched with gel to add thickness. She entered the kitchen and saw Christopher waiting at the table, lunch ready. "Are you sure I didn't make a mess in here?" she fretted.

"Not a drop of blood in sight. You better sit down and eat. We don't want your glucose crashing." He stared at her for a short time as she eyed the clean kitchen and the food, trying to figure her out. As he ate, he fumed that she wasn't available after all; she was still pining over that lost husband.

"I'm sorry about my behavior earlier; I'm sure it was atrocious. If I don't stop being a pain, you'll be shipping me off to the Clovis hospital."

Hellfire, Chris! What did you expect, your dream girl to stroll in one spring afternoon and fall into bed

152

with you! She isn't to blame because you've mistaken her politeness and gratitude for a mutual attraction. "And give up the best guinea pig I've had in ages?" he teased as he tried to lighten the gloomy situation.

"That might be wise, Doc. I'm a walking disaster," she quipped as she lifted her sandwich and began to eat. She couldn't put her finger on it, but something about him was different since he'd returned to the house.

"It isn't that bad. I shouldn't have left you alone for so long; it's really my fault you tangled with that step. I should have realized you aren't stable."

"Stable" had an odd sound to it. What, she fretted, was wrong? "If you want to get rid of me soon, you'd better make sure I don't have another accident," she teased to test his new mood. "My nose is sore, but I don't need any stitches."

. Thank goodness, because I couldn't do the delicate sewing needed on a beautiful face like yours to prevent scars. Harry Stoker could. Just ask Laura about his magical hands! "A small scratch, nothing serious. It'll be touchy for a few days."

"Is it swollen?" she questioned, but knew it wasn't, as she'd checked.

He laughed, the sound of it different, not genuine and cheerful as before.

"Just like a woman to fret about her looks.

153

No, Kirstin, you look fine."

"I *am* a woman, Doc. Shouldn't I behave like one?"

"That you are, Kirstin."

Kirstin's mind questioned the hint of resentment she picked up from him. To see what he would say, when she finished chewing, she told him, "At least with me around, you have one patient to keep you busy." Today's episode was another accident, but maybe she was too much trouble for him. *Don't misread his kindness as* —

"I have several others today, Kirstin," he said between bites. "Think you can sit quietly in the den and avoid any mishaps while I see them?" he asked as he leaned back in his chair, finished with his meal. He watched her as he took long swallows of his beverage.

"I'll do my level best, Doc." She was concerned when he didn't crack even a tiny smile at her humor. She eyed him over the rim of her glass of milk as she sipped it, then watched him put his dishes in the sink and leave after saying he'd see her later.

Kirstin finished eating and loaded the dishwasher. She put on a beef roast and beans for supper, then went to the den and read a magazine, a medical journal. Between articles, her gaze scanned the room. She got up to look at the family pictures, books, keepsakes, and other possessions that appeared to have belonged to his family. He said he had been living there for three years but he hadn't made the house his, not yet. She wondered why he hadn't replaced their belongings with his own. Except for medical journals with his name on their mailing labels and his presence in family pictures, Christopher's essence wasn't in this room, in the house. She was tempted to check out his bedroom and bathroom but thought it unwise.

It was obvious he did not return to the house between patients. She hoped he wasn't avoiding her. She peeked at the roast and beans that were creating wonderful smells. She remembered her clothes and removed them from the washer. The jeans and bra were fine, but the shirt was stained on the tail. She tossed them all into the dryer, then went to watch television, her mood bored and edgy.

At four, she did a blood test and ate a snack, relieved the glucose level was fine once more. She watched more television.

When she went to stir the beans again, Christopher entered the kitchen and glanced at her. She saw him sniff the air and smile in pleasure.

"If that aroma is any indication of your skills, I'll be stuffed tonight."

"I hope you like it."

"Anything I don't have to prepare will be wonderful. Thanks." He leaned negligently against the counter near the stove where she worked.

She replaced the top on the bean pot and turned to face him. "Why don't you have a nurse or an assistant? You obviously see more patients than I assumed you did. Isn't it dangerous to treat females without a nurse present as a witness? Don't you worry about lawsuits from false charges or misunderstandings?"

As he shook his head, he thought, *Lordy, this place looks and feels good with you in it.* It was going to feel empty and lonely when she departed, something he tried to ignore. "You applying for the job?"

"I doubt I'm qualified. But I bet it would be an interesting position."

What are you looking for, Kirstin Lowrey? he pondered. He came over to her at the sink after she washed her hands. He took her right hand and looked at it, then the left one.

"What are you doing?" she questioned. When he didn't release one hand, she made no attempt to pull it free.

Out for a distracting ride with me, woman? "Look like strong, steady hands to me. A trained medical technologist with a background in science, chemistry, and animal surgery . . . Sounds like you're more than qualified to me."

"Think you can afford to entice me away from Medico? They pay well."

His green gaze dove into hers as if it was a pool of blue water. His left hand lifted to caress one cheek with the backs of his fingers. "How much are you worth, *Mrs.* Lowrey?" he questioned in a voice gone husky.

Her brain echoed the word he had stressed. She stared into his eyes and she moistened dry lips. "Why did you say 'Mrs.' like that, like an insult?" she inquired; she guessed he was making a point.

"This," he remarked, pressing the gold band into her chest.

"Ouch!" she squealed and jerked backward. She was confused. "You know I'm a widow. Do you think I lied about it? You think I'm married?"

"In a morbid way. You are still wearing his wedding band."

Could that be what had him acting so strangely? "Yes, it's a wedding band. It was my mother's. I wear it on a chain as a remembrance of my parents. On occasion, I wear it on my finger to ward off wolves."

"Like me?"

Kirstin was pleased he was annoyed at the thought she was still attached to David. "No."

"Look, I was out of place earlier. I'm sorry. I thought . . ."

"My husband is dead, Doctor Harrison. I'd rather not discuss my past life or David just now, if you don't mind."

"I'm sorry about your loss, Kirstin. I had no right to pry."

"You needn't be sorry; you didn't know him." *Neither did I.*

"But I know *you.* As your doctor, I have to be just as concerned about your mental health as your physical condition; they go hand in hand."

He had evaded the real answer and she probed it before getting more interested in him. "Why were you angry about a mistaken assumption?"

"You know why."

"I do?" she queried in a skeptical tone. "You verbally attack a patient because you suspect she's concealed her marital status from you? That doesn't make sense to me."

"Doesn't it, Kirstin?" he refuted as he caressed her cheek.

Make him clarify it. "How so, Christopher?"

"Like this," he replied, pulled her into his arms, and kissed her.

Their contact almost crackled with electricity. When he leaned back and looked down at her parted lips and startled expression, he asked, "Does that answer your question, Mrs. Lowrey?"

She sighed lightly and then laughed. "That's some bedside manner, Doctor Harrison. Do you treat all of your female patients like this?"

"Do you always tempt every man who sees you to desire you beyond his self-control?" he retorted with a playful grin. "Perhaps I should send Doctor Cooper a thank-you note for dropping you into my lap."

She smiled. "Perhaps we both should."

Following that remark, he almost kissed her again. "I'm really sorry about what I said earlier. Even the best doctors make mistakes, Kirstin."

"Do they?" She suspected he meant his statement in more than one light and she wanted to know what it was.

"I'm afraid so. I've certainly made my share of them." He frowned and wished he'd sidetracked the disturbing topic.

"Like what, Doctor Harrison?" She caressed his cheek and gazed into his eyes to distract and disarm him as she sought the reason for the chip on his shoulder. She wondered if he would respond and be honest.

Six

Christopher didn't want to spoil the moment, their beginning, with bitter confessions about his ex-wife and his disabled hand. Later. Soon. But not now. "I believe the doctor is the one to ask questions. Perhaps you should fill me in on everything about you," he coaxed.

Kirstin knew he was asking about things he didn't want to reveal about himself first. Somehow she also couldn't open her past life to him, not yet. "I think you know all a doctor needs to know about a temporary patient."

"What if I ask, man to woman?"

She swallowed and turned her face from him. "Don't you think it selfish you want to know about me when you refuse to talk about yourself?"

He tensed. "Perhaps you're right, Kirstin. Besides, we have plenty of time while you're here to get better acquainted at a pace comfortable for both of us. We're both new at this sort of thing, so let's move slow. For now, it's enough to know we're attracted to each other. Isn't that right?" After she nodded and smiled, Christopher took her face between his hands and kissed her with heady thoroughness.

Kirstin surrendered to his lips and embrace, placing her arms around him. She savored the contact as his mouth seared hers. She felt as if she were melting into him as his lips traveled to her ears and over her face. David had never kissed like this, even at the beginning of their romance. It was wild and wonderful with Christopher; it made her tremble.

"You've been getting to me like crazy, Kirstin," he confessed.

Her hands wandered up and down the rippling muscles of his back. He was a man of many facets; strong, yet heart-stirringly gentle. He had so many marvelous qualities. His mouth and arms felt good to her aching body. Maybe she would take Elaine's advice . . .

He kissed her again, his body throbbing to possess her then and there on the kitchen floor. He was about to pick her up and carry her into his room when the oven buzzer sounded and startled them apart. His voice was tight with emotion when he told her, "I think dinner is ready. You get things on the table; I have a quick chore to do in my of-

161

fice." He needed to check his answering machine and service to make sure there wouldn't be any interruptions later if things got cozy between them.

He was gone before she could agree or protest. Her breathing was ragged; her body vibrated with unspent passion and frustration. What lousy timing! If things had kept going like that, she knew she would have surrendered to him. Her nerves were on edge! Was she nuts? Maybe. Would she actually make love to a man she didn't know? Yes, him.

The phone rang twice. Soon Christopher entered the house in a rush, muttering. "Kirstin, I've got an emergency. Go ahead and eat without me. I don't know how long this will take. I'm sorry."

"I'll be fine, Christopher. Drive carefully."

"I might be gone all night. Lock the doors. And don't forget your tests and snacks. And no exercising."

I haven't lost my wits completely. "I'll be good; I promise."

He walked to her. "Don't open this door for anyone; you hear me?"

"I promise. I'll be an angel while you're gone."

Just so you aren't one when I get back. We have some unfinished business. He pulled her into his arms and covered her mouth with his.

When he released her, she was dizzy and limp, and highly aroused.

"You tempt a doctor to forget all patients except a mighty special one."

"I hope so, Doctor Harrison." She savored another kiss before he locked up and left.

She sat down at the table until she was steady, then ate dinner, all the while wishing he was with her. How fast she was becoming accustomed to him and loving his company! With David, it had reached a point where she was glad he was out of town or had late or weekend meetings. *Please don't be anything like he was,* she silently implored. *His secrets were stunning and painful to me. I hope yours aren't.*

She sat on the den sofa and watched the Master's Golf Tournament recap of the opening day. She had never cared much for golf, but if Christopher liked it, she should learn more about it for conversation.

At one in the morning, he still hadn't come home. Kirstin went to bed, worried. She was asleep when he arrived near three o'clock.

Christopher opened the door to Kirstin's bedroom. He stood there a moment just gazing at her as she lay sleeping. Damn, how he wanted and needed her, in more than a physical way! The thought of waking up each

163

morning with her curled against him made his hunger for her increase. The thought of spending each day with her caused his lonely heart to sing. He had collected his emotions, put them in a jar, screwed the lid on tight, and refused to open it even a crack. He had believed — and feared — he'd never set them free again. And now, after enduring so much pain and torment, there still might exist a chance for happiness, a special woman who could be trusted with his heart and soul. He hadn't known Kirstin Lowrey long enough for her to work magic on him, but his depression, disappointment, and bitterness were lessening. Yet, nothing — not even Kirstin — could ever revive him completely; so what good would a half-dead, disabled man be to a woman like her? Her world was filled with excitement, stimulation, challenges, pleasures. Why would she sacrifice such things for him and a simple ranch life? But, Lordy, it would be wonderful to have her for even a short time . . .

As his gaze roamed her, intense longing and raging desire chewed at him. He realized he'd better talk fast and get the hell out of this steamy room before he forgot about his patient's impending arrival. He went to the bed and sat down, his weight causing her to roll toward him.

"Kirstin," he said in a husky whisper, his

eyes roaming silky flesh. "Kirstin!" he said a little louder when she didn't stir, and gave her arm a gentle shake. He watched her take a deep breath, flutter her lids, and stretch with provocative movements as she made throaty noises. The sensuous material of her nightgown teased at her body and his hands, hands that craved to explore the treasure beneath its rich sapphire color. He twirled a spaghetti strap around his finger and eased it off her shoulder; he leaned forward and dropped several kisses there. His lips traced a stirring path to the hollow of her neck, where he nibbled at soft and warm skin. His lips found her earlobe and toyed with it as he murmured her name once more.

Kirstin sighed, squirmed, and responded by nestling her head to his. She kept her eyes closed as he tantalized her.

He was delighted when he realized she was becoming aroused too. If only . . . "You need to get up now; it's time to eat. Mrs. Dow will be here in a little while," he told her, taking playful nips at her fingers.

"Mrs. Dow?" she asked, still groggy but with eyes open.

"My patient. She's always prompt."

Kirstin sat up, covers falling to her lap. "Are you just getting home?"

The vision of willing loveliness within his

easy reach stormed his control and threatened to steal it. "I came in around three. I just got up and made coffee. It's eight-thirty now."

"I waited up until one. I was worried about you."

"Were you afraid?"

"No, I feel perfectly safe here. At least in the house, away from mad dogs and slithering snakes. Did everything go all right?"

"Mr. Slade had a heart attack. The ornery old cuss wouldn't let the paramedics touch him unless I went in the ambulance with him to the hospital at Clovis. I had a hard time convincing Pete he should go and that I couldn't treat him at home. The only way they could keep him calm and cooperative was to take me along. I couldn't very well say I had other plans for the evening, like a nice dinner with my ravishing house guest."

"The woes of being a doctor? Don't you think it's nice for people to like you and trust you so much?"

"Perhaps I should have awakened you last night to let you know I returned home safely," he said with a hearty chuckle. "It was just so late, and you were snoozing like a log. You need your rest. Did you eat your supper and snack and behave yourself?"

"I obeyed my doctor's orders. Is your patient all right? Do you have to go see him today?"

166

"Did you want to ride along and get a second opinion on your condition and my treatment?"

"I don't need one, Doctor Harrison. I fully agree with your diagnosis and treatment. Are your friends and patients shocked to find a woman staying here with you?"

"I believe John, Frank, and Joe Bob are the only ones who know you're staying here, and none of them are gossips. In answer to your other question, I won't be going to the hospital today, unless he starts giving them fits, which I doubt he will. There's a good cardiologist on the case and I wouldn't want to intrude on his turf. Pete needs bypass surgery, so I wouldn't be of any help." Christopher rushed past that bitter topic. "I'll be riding into Clovis this afternoon. If you'd like to take a breather and make a check on your car, why not come with me?"

"That sounds wonderful. Do you mind me tagging along?"

"If I did, I wouldn't have asked. We'll have lunch in town and maybe see some sights; it'll be fun. You should get dressed, Mrs. Lowrey, before I forget about Mrs. Dow and our outing," he teased, then placed a kiss in the palm of her hand and swirled his tongue there.

She trembled and inhaled at the provocative sensation. "Clear out, Doc, and let me dress before we find ourselves explaining your presence in here with me dressed like this to a nosy patient."

Christopher's eyes observed her agitation and was pleased with his effect on her. "How do steak, baked potato, and wine sound for dinner tonight, with me playing chef and waiter? I might even rustle up some music and candles. Interested?"

Setting the scene for my seduction? Heavens, you make me feel giddy and girlish! She replied, "Sounds great. The coffee's ready?"

He sensed she was grasping at anything to dispel the enticing mood between them. "I'll bring you a cup," he offered.

"Let me dress and come to the kitchen. I wouldn't want coffee spilled all over this carpet if I got the shakes again."

"You can't ruin anything here; it's a bachelor's paradise."

"Have you . . ." She paused.

"Have I what, Kirstin?" he pressed in curiosity.

"Your patient will be here soon; you did say she was punctual. I'd better get showered and dressed. I'll join you in the kitchen." She wanted to avoid any questions he might resent. If or when he wanted to enlighten her about his life, he would. If not . . .

As he trailed his fingers up and down her

bare arms, he queried, "You afraid to ask me something?"

She gripped his biceps to halt the distracting movements. "Yes."

"Ask away. If it's none of your business or too soon, I'll say so."

A surge of daring suffused her. Potent currents passed between them. Maybe she had been spending too much time alone in her condo or in the lab, with only rabbits and mice for company. Perhaps it was time to challenge adventure and real life . . . Summoning her courage, she asked, "Have you ever been . . . Of course you've been married, you have a child. Have you been single long?" She felt the muscles tighten in his arms.

"Yep, years." He released his hold and stood up beside the bed. "You sure you don't want me to bring you some coffee while you're dressing?"

Subject closed, she noted, but he *had* answered. "No, thanks."

"I'll be in the kitchen; call out if you need any help."

"I can manage fine, Doc, even in the dark."

Something about the way she said "in the dark" inspired him to think she wasn't referring to regular light. He stroked her chin and walked out, closing the door behind him. Romancing her was a sheer delight.

169

Kirstin tossed aside the covers and went to shower and dress. She chose a pair of green slacks and a matching shirt. When she was ready, she joined him in the kitchen. "Have you eaten yet?" she asked him.

"I was waiting for you. Milk, toast, and sugar-free jelly, ma'am."

They ate, each aware of the patient's imminent arrival and their approaching "date" for the afternoon and evening.

"Want me to feed you?" he jested at her leisurely pace.

"You're impossible," she charged. "Am I getting jelly everywhere?"

"Only around your mouth. Would you like me to clean it off?"

Before she could reply, he was kissing her. When he leaned back, he ventured, "That was delicious; doesn't need any sugar to make it sweet. Call me when you need my services as a napkin again." He returned to his chair and sipped coffee, grinning each time he lowered his cup.

Kirstin was aroused by his playful behavior. Her blood raced through her body. This man was most persuasive and enticing. Without a doubt he wanted her but he wasn't rushing her into bed. She wanted him, too, but she was relieved he wasn't hurrying her into a sexual relationship. He certainly had a beguiling way

170

of severing her poise and vanquishing her resistance. It felt deliriously exciting to be aroused by his touch and kisses. The scent of Old Spice aftershave had assailed her nostrils when he kissed her—an aroma she found sensual and disturbing, one David had belittled as "old fashioned" and refused to wear no matter how many times he received it as a gift from the children when they were small.

After the kitchen was cleared, he accompanied her to the den. "Want to listen to some music? Rest up for our adventure?"

I'm not an invalid, she wanted to reply, but his last remark halted her words. "How about TV? I can pit my brains against the contestants on game shows."

"Sounds like a good distraction, though I doubt you need more brain power. Medico hires only the smartest and best."

He handed her the remote control. "That should keep you safely occupied until I'm finished. I'll check on you later. If you need anything, call me. Don't take any chances on having another accident."

When he returned, Christopher said, "I want to run a blood series on you in my office, including a glycated hemoglobin test to check your red cells. Your last work-up that

171

Cooper faxed me is old, so I want to make sure there isn't another problem aggravating your condition. I have everything I need for lab work; Uncle Chester did most of his own tests long before the Clovis hospital was built. Plus, I'm faster and cheaper than hospital labs. Is that all right?" She nodded, and he led her to his office.

Kirstin stretched out on the table, and waited. She heard him gathering supplies. Although her arm was touching the side of his leg as he leaned against the table, she didn't move it.

Christopher placed a rubber tie around her upper arm and held up an empty syringe. "This might hurt a little; I'm not good at shots and taking blood, remember?"

She nodded and seemed to brace herself.

Despite a little fumbling, he did it fine with his right hand. He grabbed a sterile cotton ball and dabbed at the afterflow. "Put pressure there until I get a Band-Aid on." After he finished, he leaned over, his grinning face inches above hers. He was ecstatic he had done the procedure so well, without giving away his problem. "Did I hurt you much?"

Kirstin smiled and murmured, "You're very skilled and gentle." As he moved away to put up his supplies and store the sample, without kissing her as she'd half expected, her eager eyes eased over broad shoulders clad in physician's garb. The open throat of a western shirt displayed a hint of a brawny chest with crisply curling black hair. He wore faded denim jeans, snug and revealing; the coat he'd slipped on earlier was unbuttoned. His narrow waist and flat stomach exposed no excess fat, nor did slim hips and firm legs. *Heavens, Christopher Harrison, but you're a handsome hunk.* She flushed at the thought and looked away.

He came back and stood over her, as he had that first day. "I'll run the tests later. Let me take a quick peek in those lovely eyes." He focused the tiny light of the examining instrument on her pupils.

His nose almost touched hers; his fingers on her face delighted her. He moved the occular instrument, away but stayed close to her. His green eyes drilled into her ocean-blue ones. Her breathing became shallow and swift. He smiled, beautiful white teeth gleaming down at her. His head slowly lowered. She waited in anticipation.

His kiss was leisurely and probing, then swift and urgent. Her arms rounded his neck. Her fingers relished the feel of his hair between them. She heard him groan in pleasure as he pulled her into his arms and locked her against his taut body. His mouth devoured hers, as if to savor her surrender, and hers did

173

likewise. He felt good against her. Such a fiery and willing nature called out to be sated. Elaine was correct: her pilot light wasn't out; it ignited her body's long-dormant furnace and put out an enormous heat that surely radiated to him.

He reluctantly pulled away and gazed into her passion-glazed eyes. He wanted to tell her he desired her and she was driving him wild, but let his actions and expressions do his speaking for now. He kissed her again.

She wanted to make the same confession as desire flooded her body. Despite her hunger and eager response, she felt awkward, inexperienced, uncertain about what to do next. Adults should be in control of themselves, but it wasn't easy—if even possible—around Christopher. Dared she be impulsive, bold, adventurous this one time in her life? Would it be wrong to enjoy him to the fullest? Could she try new things? Use this opportunity to learn about men and herself and sex? Discover what she had missed with David? Life and love were about taking chances, bold risks, to find personal and professional happiness, fulfillment, and success. With Christopher, she could sample a safe, passionate, and uncomplicated affair. Surely that was what he wanted, too.

Forcing himself to pull away, he said, "I

want you badly, Kirstin. It's taking everything I have not to pounce on you here and now. When the right moment comes, I'll ask if you feel the same way about me. Until then, just think about it, will you?"

"I'll be ready to answer when you ask." *Heavens, Kirstin, is that you talking? Yes, at last.*

He wanted to ask if there had been other men in her life besides her deceased husband. Since he had slept with lots of women, that question wasn't fair. Unless he was mistaken, and he didn't think so, Kirstin Lowrey wasn't a woman to sleep with any man for whom she didn't have deep feelings and respect. "Let's get you out of here before I forget myself."

"Proceed, Doctor."

"With your exile?" he inquired with a grin.

"For now," she answered with courage. Their hints had been exchanged; now it was only a matter of the right timing, and guts.

He helped her to sit with her legs dangling off the table. He stood between them for a moment, fingers on her thighs. Her hands braced against his chest and noted the thudding of his heart. He leaned over and kissed her again as if to make certain he hadn't misread her signals and words. Her mouth responded and her arms encircled his body to tell him he hadn't. She sighed in contentment and snuggled against his chest when he didn't release her following the heady kiss. She loved being in his embrace, tasting his sweet kisses that would—if real sugar—raise her glucose level to a dangerous high.

"Whew," he said with a loud sigh.

"My thoughts exactly, Doc."

"I think we both need a tranquilizer. Will you settle for fresh air?"

"Whatever my doctor orders. Within reason." *Behave, old girl.*

He scooped her up and swung her around as she giggled. When her feet touched the floor, she swayed against him, lightheaded.

They took the short walk to the house before he reminded, "Get ready to leave soon. All I have to do is saddle up and ride out to tell Frank we'll be gone this afternoon; he's in the south pasture doing chores. Don't forget I'll be doing the cooking and serving tonight."

She murmured, "You're handy in the kitchen, Doc. You would make an excellent chef or waiter if you decided to leave medicine."

"I'm a doctor first and last, Kirstin."

"Did I say something wrong. Christopher?"

"Of course not. I'm just a little edgy today. Probably lack of sleep. And denial of other things." He turned to leave.

"Is that a taboo subject? Every time I mention surgery or medicine, you get tense and moody. Considering my line of work, it *is* a mutual interest." She wished she could see his reaction, but his back was turned.

"I'd rather avoid the subject for now, if you don't mind. I didn't give up surgery willingly, so it's a raw spot. But I wasn't kicked out, either."

"Then I won't discuss it again. I'm sorry," she offered sincerely.

"So am I," he admitted. "I'll be back in thirty minutes or less."

"I'll be ready." From the screen door, she saw him prepare his Appaloosa, mount, and gallop out of sight with an ease that said he was born to the saddle.

She checked her glucose level, freshened up, and fetched her purse for their first outing. Heavens, she fretted, modern dating was so difficult, and especially for adults their ages, newly unattached adults. She knew she'd feel out of place in most bars and clubs because so many of the singles who frequented them, were searching only for sexual partners and good times. The music was not to her taste. Nor were the dances, a few to the point of almost simulating sex. Some contemporary slow-dancing looked like sensuous massaging. She couldn't imagine herself cavorting like that in public, particularly with Christopher. But, in private? Perhaps.

When she was young, there were many safe choices for entertainment: nonthreatening movies, skating, school sports and activities, eating hangouts such as the Pig-N-Whistle or Greene's in Augusta or the Varsity, Harry's, Poss's, and Snack Shack in Athens where she'd attended UGA for years. As for movies, she couldn't imagine sitting next to a casual date while watching such flicks as *Basic Instinct, Fatal Attraction,* or *Wild Orchid.* In mixed company, even some television movies bordered on being embarrassing with their explicit sex scenes.

She went to answer the doorbell, to find a smiling Captain John Two Fists standing there. Kirstin told him Christopher would return soon and invited him inside. After inquiring about her health and car repairs, their talk became more personal. Kirstin told him about her three children and three grandchildren. He told her he had four children and was married to a Mexican-American woman named Maria. He mentioned again how he and Christopher had met as youths and had become close friends. She asked questions about the Native American reservation not far away where he had been born and reared.

Proud of his heritage and at ease with it, John spoke of the *Guulgahende*—"People of the Plains," the Mescalero Apache—and told her

his Indian name: *Kuniiltuude*—"Light Carrier."
"Many Guulgahende believed it was *Ntu'i izee*—
'bad medicine'—to trust and mingle with
whites. I have learned from men like Doc
Harrison, Chris, and others that it is *nzhee*, "It
is good', to have *ch'uunes*—'friends' and 'helpers'—among other peoples."

"That's true, John," she said. "Too many
people misunderstand and refuse to accept
other cultures. When they do, they deny themselves of so much knowledge and happiness.
How can one accept one's self completely if
one refuses to accept others?"

"You have *jei*, Kirstin, a good 'heart'," he explained.

"Do you speak your language frequently?"

"Yes, my grandparents taught me; it keeps
us connected to our roots, as you whites call
them. Did your grandparents do the same for
you?"

"My mother's parents died before I was
born. Mine were older when they met and
married. I'm what's called a late child. We
lived with my father's parents when I was
young. My parents are dead now, too."

"That is too bad; parents and grandparents
have much to teach us. You said you were relocating to San Diego for work?"

"Yes, I'm in medical research at Medico of
America."

179

"Then you and Chris have something special in common."

"In a way. He's well liked around here, isn't he?"

"Everybody loves Doc Harrison. He's a good man; so was his uncle. Don't know what some folks would do if he ever left. Those who hate hospitals would be in a fix. He stepped right into his uncle's shoes and they fit him better than handmade moccasins."

As the conversation shifted, Kirstin noticed how John's speech pattern altered slightly from the Indian style he'd been using to informal English. "From the way he talks about this ranch and his friends, I doubt he ever would leave," she observed. "It's a beautiful place. And so peaceful."

"It made it easier for him to accept being uprooted after that accident ended his operating career back East and drove him here to seek peace. It was a hard and painful time for Chris. He was a world-famous surgeon, one of the best. He flew all over the place to do specialized work. Made him a rich man but he did it because he loved it more than his hide. You're lucky to have a doctor and man of his high caliber treating you."

"An accident debilitated him? That's why he left surgery?"

John went on guard. He had assumed from

his friend's interest in her that Christopher had revealed these things to her by now, and was surprised he he hadn't. "He didn't tell you?"

"He said he had to give up surgery, but gave no reasons. I didn't think I should ask questions. What happened to him, John?"

"I shouldn't talk about his private life to a patient. If he wants you to know about his past, he should be the one to tell you about it."

"Surely he didn't lose his surgical license for doing something wrong," she stated with cunning, hopeful the genial man nearby would defend him with the truth.

"*Shu,* no! He hurt his left wrist and hand in a fight. He can't operate anymore. You don't have to worry; he's still a fine doctor and a good man."

Christopher Harrison in a serious "fight" that cost him full use of one hand and his career? He didn't seem to have a violent temper and fighting streak. If he had been involved in something like that, the reason must have been grave. "I'm sure of that, John. I didn't mean to imply he wasn't either one. He's helpful and kind, and we've become friends. I was lucky you brought me to him. He has taken terrific care of me."

"That's great. How long does Chris think your cure will take?"

She didn't reveal there was no cure for her condition. "Christopher said another week or two. The same is true for my poor car."

They heard her host riding in and John left to speak with him. Kirstin wondered if the officer wanted privacy to check out what she'd told him and to warn his friend of his slip. She deliberated what she'd learned about the handsome physician. No wonder he was bitter and moody on occasion, reluctant to discuss his past, unwilling to talk with her about her own work in animal surgery and research. Was he hiding out in New Mexico to salve his emotional pains, to avoid pity from his colleagues? She needed to learn the reason for the fight and who started it. She needed to know if charges had been made against him, and if a death was involved.

From his work on her, his hand couldn't be totally disabled. It was probably just injured enough to prevent skilled surgery. How sad and tormenting for him. He had worked and studied for years, only to have his dream destroyed. Her heart went out to him. He was proud; he didn't want her pity, either. And perhaps he didn't want her to discover how the disability had occurred. She wouldn't say anything to him about it—hopefully John wouldn't, either. She wanted to pull him into her arms like a hurt child, hug him, kiss him, and help him deal with his lingering anguish. But, like her, he wouldn't want to be babied. And, like her, he had to face a problem that was both incurable and life-controlling.

It was twenty minutes later when Christopher came inside and John drove away. He sent her a mellow smile as he told her he was ready to leave as soon as he washed up in his bathroom.

On the drive into town, Christopher asked, if she would like to go to a barbecue with him Saturday at a neighbor's ranch. "Afterward we can take in a movie with John and Maria. There's an old-fashioned western playing."

"Sounds like fun to me; I'd be delighted."

"Then it's a date. I'll fill you in later about everybody who's coming."

Kirstin wanted to ask if the "date" was his or John's idea, and if John had mentioned his slip about the fight. If the officer *had* disclosed it, Christopher didn't seem annoyed or uneasy. He wanted to show her around, have her meet his friends and neighbors, see the area, and get closer to him, close enough to . . .

They drove past miles of semidesert terrain and grasslands with fences that seemed to stretch from horizon to horizon with cattle and horses and sometimes antelope grazing in them. They saw fields with acres of rows of maize, potatoes, peanuts, corn, sugar beets, and cotton—freshly planted and just sprouting. They were watered by artesian wells, sprays from rotating irrigation equipment, and specially built ponds. Other farms displayed fields of wheat and alfalfa and barley. Grain storage bins were abundant. Railroad tracks ran near the highway to their left.

"If you like, one day we can visit the Hillcrest Park Zoo; it's the second largest in our state. We also have Blackwater Draw Museum near Portales if you're in to seeing anthropological and paleontological exhibits. You might even find our weekly cattle auctions interesting if you've never seen one."

Lots of plans . . . "It all sounds marvelous. You sure it won't interfere with your work at the office and on the ranch?"

"Nope. Fact is, I can use some recreation and diversions."

"It's a deal, Doc; you be the guide and I'll be your follower."

"Even if I have an ulterior motive of leading you astray?" he jested.

"People can be led astray only if they want to be."

He kept his gaze on the highway as he asked, "Do you want to be?"

"Well, there's astray and there's . . . astray. When you start guiding me in a certain direction, I'll know better how to answer and behave."

"A cunning response." As they neared Clovis, Christopher told her it was built across an old Comanche hunting trail, then launched into a short history lesson of the town and its surroundings.

Minutes later, he turned the Jeep Wagoneer off of Highway 70 and onto Mabry Drive. They passed the fair grounds and rodeo arena, then drove by hotels, restaurants, and the RV Sales & Rentals.

Glancing that way, he asked, "Ever been camping?"

"The children took a few trips with clubs but I never chaperoned." *David didn't think it was ladylike or that I could be spared from my duties at home.*

At the Nissan dealership, she met Joe Bob Bridges and they discussed the needed repairs on her car. She felt the mechanic was honest and dependable, as John and Christopher had told her.

Afterward, Christopher pulled into the parking lot of a small cafe down the street. "Janie has the best country cooking around. Plenty for you to choose from to fit your diet. You prepared for emergencies?"

Kirstin grinned as she patted her pants pocket. "Right here, Doc."

He sent her a pleased grin. "Smart woman."

I didn't want any more lectures to spoil our first date. "You've taught me that lesson well."

"That in itself made staying with me worthwhile."

As they ate lunch, Kirstin noticed how many people smiled, waved, or spoke to Christopher. It was obvious he was well liked and respected, and well known in the small town. "Does everybody know everybody here?"

"Just about, especially if you've lived here all your life. The cattle auctions and rodeos bring people close together. Ranchers and farmers have a lot in common; they band together in small towns. Now if you're finished, let's ride. I'll show you a few sights before we head home. I want to run those blood tests before the Master's comes on. You need anything while we're in town?"

"I think you got everything the other day that we'll need for weeks."

Christopher pointed out sights as Kirstin listened and looked from side to side. He noticed how she toyed with the bracelet he had given her. He was glad he had suggested the outing; she was fun and interesting. Each thing he learned about her enticed him to move closer to her.

Kirstin gazed at the high plains landscape that soon engulfed them as they left town. "Is it very hot here in the summer?"

"Nope. We have mild days and nights most of the year because of the high altitude and dry air."

"Year-round tourist weather?"

"Yep. 'Course we do have occasional snows or a blizzard. Harsh weather can be hard on ranchers and cattle, but it also gives time for inside chores and reading—and cuddling before a cozy fire."

Kirstin didn't want to become aroused by envisioning such a scene with him so she said, "We rarely had very bad weather in Augusta; I hope it's the same in San Diego. I know California has trouble with earthquakes sometimes; I'm not looking forward to experiencing my first one. Do you think my health will be balanced enough to see the Caverns and White Sands before I have to leave for work?"

She'd told him she didn't have to begin work for weeks; did her statement mean—

"Will I?" she asked again when he didn't respond.

"I'll be glad to take you if you can hang around long enough for a free day or two in my schedule. It's a bit much for a one-day trip."

Stay overnight in a hotel? Together? "That would be wonderful, Christopher. Actually, I wasn't looking forward to going into that huge cavern alone. I've never seen a cave before. I haven't seen much of anything before. David wasn't into vacationing. He—" *Shut up, you ninny! He isn't interested in your sad excuse for a marriage to a secretive and selfish man.*

"He what, Kirstin? He didn't like traveling?"

She'd opened her big mouth, so it would seem odd not to answer. "David was a workaholic. He loved his job more than anything. He spent too much time out of town and in meetings, and socializing with clients. Because so many people were off on weekends and holidays, he used lots of them to make new contacts or to help out busy clients. If he took the time for a family trip, it was usually a quick and hectic one. Mostly to places for the children, like Disneyland or Six Flags or the beach. I haven't seen much of America; that's why this vacation meant so much to me."

Christopher slowed his speed. "What did he do for a living?"

"He was a top agent, vice-president, and regional manager for a large national insurance company. He had a five-state territory to cover and was based in Augusta. He was in multiline insurance, mostly with clients who had plenty of money. He always took excellent care of them."

Christopher detected bitterness in her last statement and guessed why; though she loved her job, she *had* to work to support herself.

"Insurance and investments are important to one's future. I hope you're vested in Medico's retirement and stock-option plans; you can't go wrong there, Kirstin. I even have Medico stock. I also have a superb financial consultant if you'd like his name. He gives excellent advice on how to protect and invest savings and retirement funds. With the economy as it is, it isn't wise to take chances. Was David always in insurance?"

"Yes. My father got him into it; that's how we met. My parents were thirty-eight and forty-one when I was born. Daddy died five years ago, and Mother eighteen months ago, three months before David was killed in that traffic accident. She'd been a semiinvalid for two years. She had an apartment attached to our home, so I took care of her until the end. Before her stroke, she lived with her sister in Macon. Mother wasn't totally disabled and her mind was clear, so I wanted to keep her at home as long as possible. David allowed me to do so."

Again, Christopher grasped bitterness in her tone.

"To help earn a down payment for our first home, Mother kept Sandi and Steve, which allowed me to work in research—until I got pregnant with Katie and everybody made me quit. My parents adored David and the children, and would have done just about anything for us. We moved into that large and fancy house the minute David could afford it. Image always came first to him. Daddy's insurance job was what took us to Augusta from my grandparents' farm. He was good at it, but he didn't let it consume his life like—" She tugged at her upper lip. "David worked with him the summer before my last year of high school. They got very close; I think Daddy saw him as the son he never had, and David knew how to take advantage of those feelings."

"So they encouraged a romance between you two?"

"Yes. We dated during college and got married just before my senior year. It was my parents' and David's idea; I, being obedient, complied with their wishes. My parents wanted grandchildren before they got older or died. They paid our expenses until we both finished school and went to work."

"What about his parents?"

"They lived in South Carolina. David moved to Augusta to attend a local college his first year. He needed a summer job to earn money for his next year and connected with Daddy. His father had been in the military; he was killed in Vietnam in a helicopter crash. His mother passed away a few years ago. David wasn't close to them, and he was an only child."

"Why didn't he get support or an education loan from the military?"

Kirstin frowned. "His father was dishonorably discharged for protesting the war or something like that and was being sent home. The helicopter he was on was shot down. The Lowreys lost their benefits. Maybe that was why David was obsessed with achieving, to make up for what his father did in the war. I'm sure it's embarrassing and embittering for your father to be dishonorably discharged, almost court-martialed and imprisoned. David didn't talk about it to me, but I overheard him tell Daddy they were almost financially destroyed. Needless to say, that made him tightfisted with money." *And I'd certainly love to know what he did with most of ours. So would Stephen.*

"That was certainly good motivation for him to become obsessed. After David got established, he wanted you to quit work permanently?"

"Yes, so did my parents."

"So after he died, you returned to work?"

"Thirteen months ago. I was lucky to land that job at Medico after being away from research for so long. So much changes in the medical field during that many years. I'm glad they took a chance on me."

"I'm sure it was your skills and personality that landed you the job . . . The kids were gone, so you sold the house and moved?"

"Yes, it was too big, expensive and too time-consuming for me alone."

"I know what you mean. If I didn't have Helen to take care of things for me, my house would be a constant wreck." He chuckled. "New surroundings are best when you make drastic changes in your life."

"Like retirement coaxed you from the big city to a secluded ranch?"

"Yep. So you dumped the mini-van and purchased that fancy sports model. Made new friends. Got a super job. New place. Started going out on the town. And probably left a string of broken hearts back in Georgia."

Kirstin laughed enigmatically. "So, now that you know my life history, tell me about yourself."

He steered the vehicle into his driveway as he said, "Later, woman; we're home and I have work to do. Check your blood sugar; this extra activity might have zapped it." He parked, came around the Wagoneer, opened the door, and held out his hand to assist her. "I'll join you in the den in about two hours for popcorn, Coke, and golf."

"And a little information about my evasive

host and physician?" Kirstin ventured.

"Yep," he said with a grimace. "I'll singe your ears good if you insist on hearing all about me. After you do, I hope you won't regret asking."

Seven

Kirstin was watching the news on CNN when Christopher flopped down beside her on the short sofa rather than taking the recliner. He sighed as if bone-weary as he leaned his head back, closed his eyes, and allowed his body to relax. She stole a glance at him, then returned her gaze to the television. She hoped he hadn't changed his mind about opening up to her.

Christopher turned his head to watch her while he searched for the right words to begin the disclosures about himself. He worried that his revelations would damage her favorable opinion of him when things were going so well between them.

"Are you awake or sleeping with your eyes open?"

She laughed and looked at him. "You finished in the office?"

"Yep, and all of your tests were fine."

"Good, so no other problems to solve."

"Not medical anyway. You didn't have a happy marriage, did you?"

"What?"

Christopher shifted his body to face her and his gaze fused with hers. "You weren't happy with David, were you?"

"I—" Kirstin was unprepared for that question.

"Why did you stay with him so long when you were so miserable? Are you the same woman he married or have you changed since his death?"

Kirstin took a deep breath as she decided how to answer him. "No, I wasn't happy, not after the first few years, but you could say I was blindly content. Never again will I live that way. The strange part is, I didn't know how miserable I was until he died. My life centered around him, our home, and children. With David working so much, I almost reared them single-handedly. I told you I tended my semi-invalid mother for years; I wanted her home as long as possible and as long as I could handle her. David wanted her sent to a nursing home, especially near the end. I didn't think it was necessary or kind and I loved her dearly. That was one of the first and few times I battled him to get my way. Until he and my mother died and the children left home, I gave to everyone except myself. Never again."

After those words came out, Kirstin knew she should explain them. "I don't resent or regret all I did for them; I loved them and my home; I raised good children; I kept my mother happy and well tended; I was a good wife. But looking back, I know I denied myself personal happiness. I wasn't all I could have been, should have been, as a person, as a woman. I admit part of the blame is mine; I should have been stronger; I should have grown while I was helping others to do the same." *Let him know what you like and dislike, what you'll accept and won't tolerate, what you do and don't need.*

Kirstin faced forward as she stared into space before continuing. "David was a demanding person, selfish and stubborn. He had a clever way of making others believe he was always right and you were reckless or stupid to argue or disobey. He had a gift, if you can call it that, of being able to cut anyone down to an inch high with a smile on his face."

Her speech slowed as she remembered what she was relating. "He could do it without raising his voice or chilling his gaze, and usually without you realizing he had sliced you to ribbons. He was insidious and cruel, but never physically abusive. He was so cunningly charming and persuasive that you never knew what hit you or that you could be right and him wrong. He made you feel foolish or ashamed or guilty if you didn't do as he said or if you made a simple mistake. He even made you feel that way if you only thought about defiance. I'm not sure how he worked his wicked magic."

"I've met people like him, Kirstin. They work so subtly and slyly that you fail to realize they're out for blood, your blood. They work on you with fake smiles and sweetness and cunning words so you feel paranoid or silly if you accuse them or defend yourself. They think cutting you down makes them bigger and more important. Was he like that before you married?"

"Yes, but he became more skilled at it over the years. I wasn't the only one blinded by him. Friends and clients were, too. I told you my parents adored him. I was influenced by those Old South beliefs that a woman's place was to marry, have children, and be a full-time wife, mother, and homemaker without a care for her own needs. My, how things have changed for women over the years, mostly for the better."

Kirstin took a deep breath. "I've often wondered what my life would have been like if I'd never met David or never married him.

Maybe I would have changed during my college years—become liberated sooner. From the beginning, David took control and trained me to his liking as if I were his puppet. I never thought about divorcing him and striking out on my own. If I had, my parents would have been disappointed and appalled because David had them blinded to his flaws. To make certain I didn't consider it, he constantly talked about how expensive, complicated, and hard the world was; I thought then that his remarks were used to encourage the children to do their best to prepare themselves for those challenges, but I know now they were aimed at me to keep me down. If I'd left him, I'm sure he would have tried to destroy me." Kirstin grimaced. "Women didn't have the options they have now. I had no money of my own, not even a way to save any and hide it from him; he made certain of that. I had responsibilities to my children and parents; I didn't want them to get hurt. It seemed easier to suffer in silence, to keep up the happy-couple charade."

Kirstin allowed the bitterness to surface. "After the children were grown, I could have gone back to work and left him, but that's when Mother became ill. Daddy left her a nice estate but it was eaten up fast with medical bills. Plus, David, the executor of Daddy's will, paid for the addition to our home and her daily support with Mother's funds. By the time she passed away, David said there wasn't any money left for me to inherit, nothing to use to break away from him. I couldn't even sell her home because it was attached to ours. It was as if David was always outguessing me and blocking my path to freedom. After I recovered from Mother's death and disposed of her possessions, I realized I had to make a fresh start, no matter what anyone said or thought. David died before I had to face that challenge."

Kirstin took a deep breath. "During that time, Katie was the only one who knew what I was planning, and she agreed it was the best thing for me. With a father like David, I'm lucky my children turned out so well. I suppose their friends helped them grow strong enough to not be harmed by his self-centered ways. He used me and the children and my parents to create the image he wanted. I became his property. He considered everything we owned as his. He never let me touch the money; he gave me a monthly allowance, and I had to account for where and how I spent every nickel. Like a fool, I did. Never again."

Christopher heard the tone of her last two words and realized how she'd used them several times.

Kirstin went on as if in a daze. "Since his

199

death, I've discovered that he earned plenty of money, but spent plenty financing his image and career. I've seen the records he kept locked up of how and where some of the money went, wasted on wooing clients and indulging himself while he balked at every cent I squeezed from him. He always wanted and demanded the best of everything; in a way, he had everything it should take to make one happy. But he never knew it; he was too busy looking and reaching higher for more. He made certain his friends and clients were well insured against tragedies and death, but he ignored his family's financial needs. He had no investments, savings, or retirement fund for us. I know," she murmured at his astonishment, "I could hardly believe it myself when I was told that grim news. Where it all went, your guess is as good as mine, or theirs. If women, gambling, or drugs were involved, there was no evidence or clues in any of his records."

"What did you do about the terrible mess he left you in? How could he be so stupid and cruel?" Christopher leaned forward and braced his palms on his thighs to listen to her response.

"I tried to straighten it out without losing everything, which it looked as if I would for a while. His fifty-thousand-dollar life-insurance policy didn't go far after I settled his debts and buried him. Within two weeks, I needed to get away from the house, so I put it up for sale. The girls agreed with that decision, but Steve had a fit. Katie, Sandi, and Cliff helped me convince him I couldn't stay there because it was a financial drain." *The way he acted, you'd think he believed I had all that money hidden away!*

"By then, I'd learned there was a huge balance on our home mortgage that had to paid off; I only cleared six thousand from that transaction. I sold most of the furnishings, bought inexpensive and casual ones, and moved into a smaller place. The car, as I told you, was purchased from Sandi and Cliff before they went overseas. They gave me a good deal; that's how I could afford it. My minivan was paid for, but it needed work and wasn't worth much for trade-in. After the kids were gone, David didn't think I needed a better car for my life—the grocery shopping, beauty salon, errands, et cetera. Sandi, Cliff, and Katie thought the red sports car would lift my spirits and give me confidence." *Not Steve, though. He's still angry about some of my business decisions.*

"Does it?" Christopher asked with a grin to lighten her tension.

Kirstin smiled. "Yes." She had decided not to go into too much detail about her problems with her son tonight.

"Didn't you receive anything from the wreck that killed David?"

"Not much; the other driver was uninsured. He was dirt poor, so there was no point in suing him. He had a wife and kids; I couldn't bring myself to prosecute him. The crash was his fault, Christopher, but it was an under-standable accident. If he'd been drunk or careless, I would have forced the issue. Katie, Sandi, and David's company agreed with my decision to let the matter drop. Steve didn't; he was upset about losing his father and wanted the man punished; I figured he'd change his mind when he settled down and would be sympathetic."

Christopher grasped that hadn't been the case and that there were other strains between them. "So you filed on David's insurance and company?"

Tell him? Why not? "For some crazy reason, David had the bare minimum. UMC: 15/30/ 10. That's irresponsible, especially for a man in the insurance business. The agent who de-livered the bad news couldn't venture a guess as to why a top man in the company didn't have proper coverage. You can bet I have auto policies so my children wouldn't be put in a bind, and thank heavens I took out life and health insurance before I was diagnosed as di-abetic; if not, I couldn't get coverage now, or without a sky-high rider or an exclusion clause."

"What do those initials and numbers mean?"

"Uninsured Motorist's Coverage, fifteen thousand for one person killed or injured, thirty maximum no matter how many people are in a car, and up to ten thousand on the vehicle. His Mercedes was totaled and he still owed the bank twenty thousand on it. I collected the fifteen plus ten, but I had to pay off twenty, so I only had five left. Actually I had forty-seven-fifty after the deductible. As you can see, that left little for daily expenses and to invest in my future or cover any medical needs I might incur. My health insurance won't cover expenses for Type II Diabetes, and, as you know, monthly supplies and routine tests are expensive. I hope the ADA can get that changed; it isn't fair. Some diabetics can't take proper care of themselves because they can't afford the monthly medical bills of three to five hundred dollars, plus the tri-yearly exams and tests."

Christopher hoped she wasn't looking for a wealthy man to support her. He didn't think so, but he had been wrong about Laura. He moved the topic away from her physical condition. "Why would he behave so . . . 'irresponsibly,' as you called it?"

Kirstin shrugged and sighed as she recalled

her exasperation during that arduous time. "I don't know if it was an oversight by David or if he simply assumed he had plenty of time left to get his business affairs in good shape. The worst part is the mystery about where all the money went. Even his checking account had only enough cash to pay for a few months' bills. My lawyer and I couldn't locate any hidden accounts or a safety deposit box. Unless something turns up one day, the money's lost, or it was spent on God knows what. It was just something else David stole from me and the children. Our home should have been almost paid for, would have been if he hadn't refinanced it last year without telling me and done something with the cash. Everything was in his name, so he didn't need my signature for anything. The lawyer and accountant found it just as odd as I did that David left behind such a small estate, and they were astonished that I was so ignorant about our finances. But it's the truth."

Christopher was assured of her honesty.

"I'll never be that stupid again. I was petrified to learn how to manage a budget and deal with all those men and papers. For a while, I feared I might be sent to jail for fraud or tax evasion or such, but the lawyer and accountant explained taxes and inheritance laws to me. Fortunately, David had been honest in those areas. He had a will, but it didn't expose his secrets, just left me everything, including a mess. I was terrified the IRS would be suspicious of my claims and audit me. I didn't know any better. Katie helped with the countless forms and meetings. There's so much to do when someone dies, especially when you've been kept in the dark about finances. It's crazy how your imagination runs wild when you're ignorant and suffering." She shuddered in remembrance of those fears. "I doubt my daughters would wind up in such a predicament; they learned a lot from my situation. When you're married, everything should be owned and decided jointly. There shouldn't be any secrets and selfishness. And a husband should prepare his wife to take over in the event of his illness or death. And she'd better have a skill to help her find work afterward if necessary."

Kirstin frowned. "But that's off the subject. So you see, I always put everyone's needs and wishes above my own. I was Jim and Mary's daughter, then David's wife, then the children's mother. I lost my identity and dreams along the way. You asked if I'd changed. Yes, during my marriage for the worst and since my husband's death for the better. A little over a year ago, I decided it was past time to learn how to take care of myself. I also decided it was my turn to come first for a while; I suppose that sounds silly and selfish and aggressive to a man."

Christopher lifted one hand to caress her flushed cheek with his fingers. "No, Kirstin, it doesn't. I understand what you went through, because I had a sorry and shallow marriage myself."

She came to full alert. "You did?"

"While I was a resident, I met a nurse named Laura who worked her charms on me like magic, like David did with you. I discovered too late she was only trying to capture a promising doctor who would earn lots of money and give her prestige. I divorced her six years ago. She's remarried and living in Maryland with her new husband and kids. The man she dumped me for is a wealthy plastic surgeon, an old friend of mine: Harry Stoker. He gave her everything she wanted, more than I could, including a perfect face and body—he's one of the best in his field."

"I'm sorry, Christopher; that must have hurt you deeply."

"It did, at first. No, I guess it humiliated and angered me more than anything. She was trying to coax Harry into taking her away from me. Being my supposed friend, he was resisting. Laura set it up for me to catch them in bed together so a decision would be forced on him."

Kirstin's gasp of shock halted him a moment. "That's right, I'm positive it was a trap for Harry. I'll admit he loved her, but he married her fast to make sure my pain and his seemed worth what we both endured. I have to admit, I never believed Laura would ever be satisfied, but it appears she is. Unless I'm mistaken, they're blissfully happy together. I made plenty of money and we lived high; I was a busy and noted surgeon; I could heal about anybody, but it wasn't enough for her. Maybe *I* wasn't enough for her. Before you ask, I have no emotional ties to Laura; I realized later, it had been over between us for a long time. Maybe I was as much to blame as she was; maybe I also chose her and used her as the 'perfect wife' to help me on my climb upward."

Where did that crazy remark come from! Yet, it felt genuine to him. He admitted to himself that he'd always put the blame on Laura for their failed marriage, but maybe some of it was his fault. He'd made her out a villainess in his mind when perhaps she'd only been misguided. His ex-wife appeared changed for the better; Laura had matured, softened, become compassionate. She and Harry had been wrong and selfish, but it was past time to forgive them as she'd pleaded in her recent letter and time to stop letting the past hurt him. *Kirstin is really changing you!*

Kirstin wanted to ask if a fight with Harry or Laura had injured his hand. She waited for him to continue.

"I threw myself into my work and I dated countless women, was a party animal for a while. The only thing I'm glad about is that I didn't mislead or intentionally hurt any of those women. My work was fulfilling, but I never met any woman who got to me, until you were dropped in my lap. We have a lot in common, Kirstin, and we enjoy each other. I think we can become good friends. I want to get to know you better."

Tingles raced over her. She tried not to sound tonguetied or to blush as she said, "I've told you all about me, except about my problems with Steve. I'll explain those later. Why don't you continue?"

"Four years ago, there was a traffic pile-up on Interstate-83 near Baltimore where I lived at the time. Some of the victims were brought to Johns Hopkins where I practiced. I wasn't on duty that night, but I *was* at the hospital. I needed to check on a nervous patient I was operating on the next morning and I had to pick up notes for a paper I was writing for a medical journal. They summoned me to Emergency and put me in charge of the woman who had caused the chain reaction of wrecks."

Kirstin watched dark sullenness engulf him. His green gaze narrowed and chilled. His tone was cold and bitter.

"She was cut up badly and bleeding like a stuck pig, but that wasn't the main problem; she was high on a combination of drugs and hysterical with pain and confusion. She was ranting and raving because her boyfriend had dumped her for another woman, after emptying their apartment and bank account. All she wanted to do was get out of there, find him, and rip him to shreds with her fingernails. We couldn't get it through her dazed head that she was hurt and needed treatment or that she couldn't leave because she was under arrest. There was a cop posted outside the door to make certain she didn't get away. She was a wild woman, flooded with adrenaline and strong as an ox. She was beating on the two nurses and fighting with me, but we couldn't sedate her because of the drugs, not until we got a blood sample and its results. We called for an orderly to help subdue her, but he arrived too late. So did the cop when he heard the ruckus. She grabbed a scalpel off the setup tray and sliced the wrist, fingers, and palm of my left hand several times before we got her under control and tied down. What she severed, Kirstin, was my career, the love of my life."

She knew not to say, I'm sorry, so she listened and observed.

He held up his left hand, rolled up his sleeve, and showed her the damage as he talked. "Neuropathy: permanent nerve damage in my wrist, palm, and three of my fingers. She sliced through nerves, tendons, and ligaments, and severed the artery. Most of that was repaired through a series of surgeries over a year's time. I had therapy, too, but it didn't restore the full use of my hand, not to the point of my being able to perform delicate surgery. Valuable time was lost before a surgeon could get to me. I have a permanent loss of feeling and function in some areas, so I can't hold or control instruments; I can't even close my hand completely, and I drop small things all the time. When I realized my career was over and I got tired of the sympathy, I became a rancher and country doctor. Sometimes I can't even stand to hear about or watch anything pertaining to surgery, especially micro and heart surgery. I was in my prime, but that . . . witch stole my life from me. To make it worse, a lawyer got her off on temporary insanity. She ruined lives and cost people a bundle of money, then walked away unpunished, free as a bird. It was the first time I was tempted to take a life instead of saving one, at least beat the hell out of her."

Kirstin fretted over the violent streak in Christopher. He had not dealt with his tragic past, and that worried her. Yet, how could he seem so kind and compassionate if he truly were cruel and vindictive? Wasn't it only natural to be resentful of such losses?

Christopher realized he must be sounding evil to her; he forced a calm tone. "I received a big insurance check, so I had no money worries. 'Preferred Disability,' they called it. Covers eighty percent of lost income until I'm sixty-five. They gave me total disability instead of partial because I can't do my chosen occupation: surgery. But there are some things money can't buy or replace. If I had my way, I'd rather be a poor surgeon than a rich rancher."

"But you're doing wonderful work here as a doctor. The locals need you and love you. The ranch is prosperous. You have a daughter who's doing well for herself, too. You have a lot to be greatful for, Christopher."

"You're right, Kirstin, and I am. But I can't help feeling denied of the thing I loved most, besides my daughter. After I was forced to retire, Peggy wanted to move close to me, but I convinced her that was foolish because she and Phil were already engaged and getting married soon. Her wedding was one of my last public appearances, you might say. Friends, colleagues, and acquaintances were always pitying me and giving me advice. It's amazing how nosy and insensitive or ignorant some people can be when you're down on your luck. I heard, 'You can always teach or do research' so many times that I was turned against both of them."

"Have you ever reconsidered that decision?" She saw him frown.

"I need better control of my left hand to do research; my overworked right one can't do everything that's necessary. I can't hold test tubes, or use instruments, or do animal surgery, and anything similar with only one good hand. If an assistant has to do everything for me, why go into research? It's foolish."

Kirstin was tempted to point out how well he did when he was treating her, and waiting on her, but she knew he wasn't in the mood to hear that, not yet . . . She would love to be his assistant, his other hand. It would be fantastic to share a lab, do experiments together, and—

Christopher cut off her dreamy thoughts about him as he continued. "Nor can I risk causing dangerous lab accidents trying to do things I know I can't manage. The same is true for teaching med students; I can't hold an instrument in the correct position or apply the right amount of pressure needed for making a precise incision. I can do most things with my right, but not delicate surgery, not even on a cadaver whose life wouldn't be in jeopardy with my clumsy attempts. Students would wonder why I was trying to teach them procedures I couldn't demonstrate. And teaching just basic subjects doesn't interest me at all."

Kirstin realized that much as she loved research, if she could no longer do it, she would accept that reality and find another satisfying job. Life was too short and unpredictable, she now believed, for being miserable and unfulfilled. Yet, men were different from women. It seemed as if most women could adjust to changes quicker and easier than the average man and could make the best of them.

"The day before Peggy's wedding I was told nothing else could be done; surgery was my past. It was a hard time because I had to put on a happy face to keep from spoiling her special day. As soon as she was on her honeymoon, I sold everything, packed up, and moved to the ranch. I told myself I had to be content with knowing I'd done great things before the attack: I'd saved or bettered lots of lives."

"So few people can say that, Christopher."

"It's easy and peaceful here. I'm accepted as I am. Local folks think I'm important and

213

special, some think I'm downright perfect. I don't need total use of both hands to be a country doctor or a successful rancher. If I can't be a surgeon elsewhere, I'd rather be in New Mexico. Here, I don't have big social occasions where embarrassing accidents can happen or I'm not introduced as the poor soul who had his career knifed. Peggy's wedding was also the last time I saw Laura and Harry. It didn't improve my sorry mood that day to see them so blasted happy and successful. I received a letter this week from Harry. He wants me to become a surgical consultant on several cases and three new projects he has in mind. I know what he's doing, still trying to make up for the past. He thinks I'm wasting myself here and keeps scheming to get me back into the swing of things."

Kirstin believed there were many important and satisfying things Christopher could do with his skills and knowledge, including research and teaching, if he would accept his limitations and left this secluded area. Though she was empathetic about his disability, he could do something else or learn to be happy doing what he was doing now. But he had to change on his own when he was ready and willing. Maybe she could help point him in that direction before she left . . .

Christopher stretched. "Speaking of swings,

how about watching a little golf for a breather? Let's see who's the big scorer today."

Kirstin watched him switch the channel to the Master's Tournament. She knew he was exhausted by his revelations. She knew now why he could no longer play the sport, and her heart ached for him. "Why don't I get our snack ready? You check the scoreboards while I do."

Kirstin prepared popcorn and drinks, then returned. She warmed to the smile of gratitude he gave her, for more than the service.

They watched the tournament for two hours. They talked about the ones they had attended, past and current golfers, names and descriptions of the course's famous holes, and about the club and town where it was held. At some points, they revealed more about their ex-mates and talked about their children and her grandchildren. They brushed over politics and other topics of mutual interest.

At six, he asked, "Ready for me to cook our steaks?"

She followed him into the kitchen. "What about the baked potatoes?"

"I put them in over an hour ago while you were in the bathroom doing your test. They should be done soon. Care for a glass of wine? . ., Sorry, I forgot for a minute."

"I know, with or after a meal," she agreed.

"You go ahead and have some. I don't mind. I would mind more if you didn't because I can't."

"You make a person feel totally at ease," he complimented as he fetched wine for himself and a diet drink for her.

"Thanks. Anything I can do to help even if it is your turn in here?"

"Just keep me company. You in a hurry to leave after our talk? Afraid I'm too confused to be your friend?"

"Of course not. I would be suspicious if you were perfect. Besides, I'm on vacation and I'm not balanced, remember? And you promised me a ride on one of those Appaloosas and a tour of your ranch."

"So I did," he concurred.

Kirstin wondered at the slight strain between them. How did one behave under such circumstances; their intimate chat seemed to imply an impending affair. Surely the situation and moment would arrive soon. Would she know what to do and say when it was decision time?

"Kirstin?" he hinted, deliberating the same subject. "I don't want to do or say anything to upset you or embarrass you. And I don't want to rush you into anything, even if our time together is limited."

Kirstin's mind was in a whirl: speed things

216

up or slow them down?

Christopher noted her hesitation. "Should I have kept my mouth shut? This kind of situation is new for you, isn't it?"

"Yes. David was the only man in my life, and this nineties style of dating is unfamiliar to me. You're well versed in the rituals, but I'm unsure of how to act and what to say. I know that's silly, but I can't help it."

"It isn't silly at all. If you didn't take the time to get to know me and make certain I'm worthy of your attention and friendship, I wouldn't be interested in you. Just relax and enjoy dinner and my company. Let things happen naturally. If it's right between us, we'll go from there. If you decide it isn't, I'll understand and back off. I admit it's lonely out here, but you're not a passing diversion. I really like you and want you. I won't try to coerce you into anything. But I will make saying no as difficult as possible."

She laughed. "I really like you, too, Christopher. I've never met any man with better qualities."

He took that as permission to pursue her, at a safe speed. He grinned and chuckled. "Let's get started. Those steaks look scrumptious."

Kirstin and Christopher readied the table and salads before grilling the steaks. As the meat cooked, he took a seat beside her on the second step and leaned back against the next one. He stretched out long legs and braced his back against the wood, elbows resting on it and fingers interlocked over a flat stomach. They were quiet for a time as each gazed over the land before them on a balmy evening under a clear sky.

He felt calm and happy, relieved to have the dreaded talk behind him and more relieved by the way she had accepted it — and him. "Feeling all right?"

She smiled and nodded. "It's all so peaceful. It has wild beauty. Did you spend a lot of time here while you were growing up?"

"Yep. I had plenty of great times, and got into plenty of boyish mischief, too. There's a big tree on the pond in the south pasture. When I was twelve, I tied a rope to one limb and would swing into the water. It was going fine until the knot came loose, I smacked the bank hard, and nearly broke my neck. It was back to Scouts and knot-tying lessons."

She laughed. "You'll have to show me when we take our ride."

"It's a promise. I'd better turn the steaks."

Afterward, he came to take a seat between her pants-clad thighs with his back to her. He reached up and pulled her arms over his shoulders and covered them with his across his chest. "This is nice, the best way to end a day."

Kirstin closed her eyes a moment and inhaled his manly scent. She felt the steady beating of his heart beneath her hands. It was more than nice; it was wonderful, stimulating, romantic. She couldn't imagine doing this with David . . . Suddenly she found herself pulled into Christopher's lap with him grinning down at her.

"Now, that's definitely better." He gave her a leisurely kiss. Her head rested against his left shoulder while his hand stroked her amber mane of loose curls and waves. "Your hair looks like ripe wheat beneath the autumn sun." He caressed her cheek as he asked, "Is this shade natural or does this color mean you spend a lot of time outside or in a tanning booth?"

"After David died and I made new friends, I spent as much time at the beach as I could. I have friends who own condos at Hilton Head and the Isle of Palms. We girls slipped off for as many weekends as we could. California is sunny most of the year, so I won't look totally foreign when I get there. I don't tan easy or much because I use gobs of sun block and stay inside during the heat of the day, but I have a little color."

He read between the lines: her life had changed greatly — since her husband died. "You like the beach?"

219

"Yes. It's tranquil and relaxing. I love the sound and feel of the wind and water and sun when they join. Do you like it?"

"In spurts." He realized she was trailing her fingers up and down his right arm as she spoke in an almost dreamy state. He kissed her nose, then set her aside to check the steaks.

Kirstin was reminded of his problem as he held her. There was a long scar on the underside of his left wrist where repair surgery had been performed.

"Ready?" he questioned after removing the meat from the grill.

"Ready," she replied, standing up and swaying slightly.

"You dizzy or weak?"

"Nope. I just got up too fast. A normal reaction, Doc, nothing more."

"Hold my arm," he suggested, and cocked his elbow toward her.

"And risk knocking those steaks out of your hand? No way. I'm fine."

Christopher placed the laden plate on the table while she fetched the potatoes from the oven and salads from the refrigerator. He refilled his wineglass and got her a glass of skim milk. Seated, he made no attempt to conceal the trouble he had cutting up his meat. She noticed how he held the fork between his index and second fingers because he couldn't close the span between his thumb and fingers. He prepared his potato with butter, sour cream, and bacon bits, then selected his dressing and poured it over the salad.

Kirstin tasted the steak first. "It's divine, Christopher. You for hire?"

"You looking for a cook?"

"Maybe. After years of cooking, it would be nice to have someone do it for me after a long, hard day at work."

"Want to be a career woman all the way? A totally liberated female?"

She laughed. "Why not? Meals and taking care of a house are hard work; they require a lot of time and energy if you do them right."

"I see. You want to eat both cakes, freedom and femininity?"

"I like being a woman, but if I do the same job as a man, I should get the same pay and recognition."

"When you compete with men, you run a risk of being forced to act like one," he told her.

"I only compete with men at work. I can do just as well as they can, even better than some. I pay taxes and support myself. Why shouldn't I have the job and life I want if I earn them?"

"Do I hear resentment in those words?"

"No. I personally haven't had problems with men at work, but I have friends who've had bad ones."

"Maybe some men feel threatened or confused by this relatively new independent and aggressive female."

She almost held her breath as she asked, "Do you dislike liberated women? Do you think a woman's place is at home?"

"Plenty of women work these days, but not many love their jobs as much as you do. But you don't strike me as a die-hard feminist. You're intelligent, Kirstin. Obviously you're good at your job and you work hard, otherwise, you wouldn't be at Medico. I respect you for having brains and beauty. That's quite a combination. Plus, you're great company. I think you can do anything you desire. What are your future plans?"

"To remain with Medico in research. It's challenging and fulfilling, and I get a great salary and benefits. My life is nice. But who knows?"

He sipped his wine. "That sounds a bit uncertain."

"Things happen," she murmured. "Life has a way of changing drastically when we least expect it." Kirstin was baiting him to talk about his feelings and opinions, but he reacted differently.

"Such as the accident which killed your husband?"

Her fork stopped in mid-air. She lowered it to her plate. "I was referring to that and to the incident that brought us together. For now I plan to remain where I am, but something could change my mind. If I had been badly injured in *my* accident, I would have been forced to alter my life, as you were. With the state of the economy and world problems, Medico could shut down; I could get fired or laid off; they could transfer me again to another research center; I could become disabled by my condition, or by another illness or accident. In the past eighteen months, I've learned that life can be cruel at times. Haven't you?"

"Absolutely, and change is hard. Downright painful at times."

"I have food in my stomach, so can I have a glass of wine now?" she inquired to get off the topic. She didn't want anything depressing to spoil their evening.

Christopher served her a glass of white zinfandel.

"Do you still have feelings for David?"

She almost strangled on the wine but she answered calmly. "I'm not grieving or pining for him, if that's what you mean. I thought I was clear on what kind of man he was and how I felt about my past."

"Do you see other men? Anybody left behind in Georgia?"

"I've dated, but I haven't met anyone special, and I haven't been looking for a replacement. I like my new life as it is," she said, not wanting him to think she was husband-hunting if that was his worry.

"You don't like bachelors?"

What facts are you searching for, Christopher? "Some are insufferable playboys, or mother's boys, or worse. I met one who was looking for a cover for his gay lifestyle. Another had a violent temper which bordered on dangerous rage. Another's list of conquests would circle this house ten times. Why women dated him more than once I'll never guess. One bachelor couldn't even go to the bathroom without asking his mother's permission. One wanted to get married after two dates because it was time for him 'to settle down and have children.' I've raised mine and I don't care to begin a new family at my age, especially with my health problems. I've met men who only wanted to spite ex-flames or ex-wives and some who wanted mothers for their kids or women to take care of them. I've met all kinds."

"So, you're still looking for the right one?"

"I haven't been looking and I don't intend to start. If and when it happens, great; if not, I'm doing fine. I have children, grandchildren, friends, and work to keep me happy and busy. How about filling me in on *your* lovelife? I'm sure it's more colorful than mine."

"One more question?"

"Spit it out, Doc."

"Did you ever think of doing anything besides research?"

She hesitated before answering. "I wanted to be a surgeon." She saw how he gaped at her. "It's true. But when I was growing up, most women were pediatricians or OBGYNs or nurses in the operating room, not the surgeon. I was still dreaming about it when I went into research. I loved it. It was like finding my niche. I could do research and surgery, on animals of course."

"Ever been sorry you didn't carry out that first dream?"

"No. Several times when an animal nearly died or did die during surgery or afterward, I was relieved it wasn't a person. I don't think I could handle that. It must be terrible to lose a patient and then wonder if you didn't react quickly enough or in the right way. I can't imagine walking out of that room to tell a waiting family that the patient didn't make it. In all honesty, I know now I couldn't do it. I have what I want from life." Kirstin realized how her last sentence must have sounded but she didn't correct her words to mean only the job she wanted.

"Coffee and dessert? I bought sugar-free cookies for you."

"No, thanks. You outdid yourself tonight, Doctor Harrison; that's the best steak I've eaten anywhere." She didn't press when he evaded telling her about his past or current romances. No doubt he found it difficult to expose his feelings to another person. Besides, she didn't want to appear overeager or demanding. Earlier, he had been more open and honest than she had expected. But she would like to make certain she had no rival. Who was the hateful woman on the telephone?

"Thanks, Kirstin, for being you," he murmured. "Good friends are hard to find."

She smiled. "Did I talk too much?"

"Not enough. You're absolutely fascinating." He saw her glow with pleasure. "You amaze me. You're level-headed and perceptive. You've worked hard to create a good life for yourself. I don't think I've ever met anyone like you before."

She cleared her throat. "I don't know what to say. I've never received so many compliments before, at least not sincere ones. I'm glad I met you, Christopher Harrison; you're good for a woman's ego."

"Why don't you go into the den and sit down while I clear the table? Equal rights, remember?"

She laughed. "If you think for one minute I'll demand to help because I'm a woman, you're mistaken, Doctor Harrison. I think I'll freshen up while you take care of the kitchen."

"Cold-hearted feminist," he teased with a broad grin.

"I am not. I'm just sticking to our deal. When it's my turn, I'll whip you up some meals you'll never forget."

"How about eleven of them, one every other day for the next three weeks? That would leave you two days to drive to San Diego and settle in before reporting to work on May fourth?"

He had checked the calendar to see how long I could stay. "Is that an invitation to be a long-time house guest, Doctor Harrison?"

"What better place to spend a vacation? Fresh air, beautiful scenery, romantic dinners, horseback riding, and your own personal physician? I could teach you to hunt and fish. I have two tanks and a pool to swim in. You could even assist me during emergencies when I need a skilled second hand."

That was the first time she had heard him refer to his disability in a light way. "Three weeks of fun and sun sound mighty tempting, Doc."

"Think it over; the invitation will stand for another day or two."

"A deadline?"

"I have my pride, woman. We are two liberated people."

"I'll consider the offer," she murmured with a seductive smile. "But I did make prior plans before . . . being captured by you for a guinea pig."

"Coward," he teased, glancing over his shoulder as he placed dishes in the sink.

"A challenge, too? You sure you're up to deprogramming a feminist? I could be more trouble than I've already been."

"Too bad all trouble isn't packaged like you."

"You are a silvery-tongued charmer, Christopher Harrison."

"Is it working?"

"I'll never tell." She laughed as she left the kitchen and went into the bathroom. *Whatever has gotten into you, Kirstin Lowrey? You're talking and acting like a teenager. But it's so much fun and he's so tempting.* It might be a little obvious, she told herself, but she showered and changed into a skirt and blouse, then brushed her hair and sprayed on perfume. She went into the den and sat down.

Christopher soon joined her, bringing two glasses of wine. He stared at her as he handed her one. "Only half a glass, my lovely patient." He chose five discs and inserted them in the CD player. He pressed the random select button and turned to face her. "Want to dance?" He

228

had to touch her, hold her.

"Why not?" she replied, feeling free-spirited.

He pulled her against him as the music began. The song was perfect. As she listened to Neil Diamond crooning "Until It's Time For You To Go," she wondered if he was giving her a message? When the words said something about "should have stayed outside my heart but in you came" and not to ask for forever but to "love me now," she felt as if her body had melted and would soon flow all over him. They moved in unison to the romantic tune. "You're a good dancer, Christopher."

"Thanks. I don't get much practice. Ever done square dancing?" He asked, needing to distract himself from his increasing desire for her.

"I did in school, but not since. Why?"

"There will be plenty of it at the barbecue at the Thompson Ranch tomorrow. Might be fun and educational. I wasn't planning to accept, but you said you'd go with me."

"Need protection from the local fillies?"

"It's only natural to view a wealthy, available doctor as a good catch. But there's no one around to interest me."

"Want me to discourage those who are chasing you for naught?"

"If you're of a mind to do such a good deed, I won't object."

"Surely my 'personal physician' deserves my unselfish help."

He heard Roger Whittaker singing "Always On My Mind" with those haunting lyrics: "Maybe I didn't . . ." If he didn't go after Kirstin, would he be saying the same thing after she left? "Then you'll stay a while?"

"I'll think it over and tell you tomorrow." It was rash to make such a crucial decision while she was so mesmerized by him. She needed to be alone to weigh the pros and cons.

When Elvis began "You've Lost That Loving Feeling," Christopher asked her if she'd seen Tom Cruise do his rendition of it in *Top Gun*.

"It was wonderful, but I love the Righteous Brothers' version best."

"Me, too. Join me," he coaxed, and they sang it together as they laughed between words and devoured each other with their eyes.

The next selection was slow and romantic, suggestive: Kenny Rogers singing "All My Life." Kirstin quivered as Christopher's warm breath filled her ear as he whisper-sang the words, especially "love me tonight." He released her hand to place both of his arms around her, drawing her closer to him. His chin rested against her temple. His body caressed hers.

"You smell good, Kirstin."

"You, too. I love Old Spice." She realized he had put some on before joining her. Were they heading for a—

A fast song came on and Christopher swung her around as they shagged. They laughed and recalled school dances of long ago when that dance was popular. Then, Kenny Rogers and Sheena Easton started singing "We've Got Tonight" and they snuggled together again, close, intimate.

Her fingers locked behind his neck as they swayed together, their feet hardly moving. His lips drifted over her cheek, then claimed hers, only to travel down her throat, leaving flaming kisses behind. His hands wandered up and down her back. His mouth hesitated at the hollow of her throat as his fingers eased the wide neck of her blouse off one shoulder, seeming to sear the flesh. When they kissed again, their dancing halted and their hands caressed with boldness.

He held her so tightly that breathing was difficult. Their tongues did slow and erotic dancing. Soft groans escaped their throats as desire surged through them. Was there any way either could say no to this intoxicating situation?

Eight

When he lifted her in his arms, Kirstin let herself be carried into her room. No man had ever literally swept her off her feet and she found the action exciting. Christopher lay her on the bed and stretched out half atop her. She responded to his kiss eagerly. His hand cupped a taut breast through her blouse and kneaded the point that already stood at attention, causing her to quiver with passion. He kissed her many times before he rolled over and pulled her to him. His fingers reached beneath her blouse and unfastened her bra, then rolled her on her back again. As he trailed his lips over her throat, he worked up her blouse to expose one lovely mound. His mouth sought the peak and swirled his tongue around it. He kissed it over and over, enticing moans from her parted lips. He pushed the bunched material away from the other breast and savored its pinnacle.

Kirstin was staggered by the flood of powerful emotions. Her fingers laced through his black hair and pressed him closer to her. He shifted to slip the garment over her head and his hands traced over her bare chest and arms, his light caresses stirring her to greater desire. He fondled, teased, and pleasured her breasts until she was thrashing upon the bed with need.

Kirstin's head spun and she felt hot all over. She wanted to be out of her remaining clothes. She wanted him out of his. She wanted their naked bodies making contact. She wanted him completely. David had never made her feel this crazy and fiery way. No man's kiss or touch had made her want to make love in an urgent frenzy. At last he halted his potent siege on her senses to yank off his own clothes. She shifted to help him remove her pants and shoes, wanting to feel the full length of him against her. At last, unclad flesh made contact with unclad flesh. She wanted to feast on his mouth. She wanted his hands caressing her all over. She wanted to do the same to him. She yearned to feel him within her.

Christopher rubbed his chest against her sensitive breasts, which caused Kirstin to almost savagely return his heated kisses. He shifted back and forth, the crisp hair driving her wild as it teased her breasts. He kissed every inch of her flushed face, then traveled down her right arm. He caught her hand and ravished her palm. He nibbled on her fingertips and wanted to taste her everywhere, but that should wait until another time.

Kirstin's mind gave her a last-minute warning and she murmured against his mouth, "I'm not on the pill, Christopher. I don't want to risk getting pregnant. We need . . . protection."

He leaned his head back just enough to lock their gazes. "I'm prepared, Kirstin. I hope you don't mind that I planned for this."

She watched him lean over the side of the bed and saw him withdraw something from his pants pocket, then place a shiny circle on the nightstand. The warmth on her cheeks told her she was blushing but she managed to say, "I'm glad you did. What about . . ."

He smiled. "I saw on your record where you had an AIDS and complete STD test with your last bloodwork and you said you haven't been with anyone."

"I haven't, so I know I'm fine in that area."

"I haven't been with a woman, either, since my last test. Even in my wild days, I practiced safe sex; I always used a condom to prevent any problem."

"Are those . . . condoms safe? I don't want an accident."

"The best, Kirstin. Trust me."

She believed him, as he believed her.

Christopher slipped the condom on, then kissed and caressed her again and soon had their senses whirling and the romantic mood restored. He realized she was feeling a little awkward and insecure, and that endeared her to him. It also implied how deeply she felt about him to make love to him and to respond as she was doing.

His body was sexy and perfect, Kirstin decided. Every part of him felt wonderful and was appealing. His hand slipped between her thighs. She trembled with mounting need. Slowly his fingers fondled and stroked her, his mouth drifting from one breast to the other. She did nothing to protest his intimate actions. Her hands traced every rippling muscle in his back and shoulders. His buttocks were firm and smooth as she massaged them. Even the hair on his arms excited her as her hands wandered over them. He was exquisite. Except for the hall nightlight, darkness encased them. She closed her eyes and called his handsome face, sparkling eyes, and sensual smile to mind. This was more overwhelming than she could have imagined. Of its own volition, her hand closed around his erect manhood. It was hot and sensual, larger than her husband's had been. It excited her to hear him moan and to feel him writhe in pleasure as she stroked him.

She could hardly believe she was being so bold. He was giving her the courage to do so. She craved to feel him driving into her body. "Damn you, Christopher Harrison, what are you doing to me? I want you so badly. Make love to me, now. Please."

Without hesitation, he moved between her parted thighs. He eased into her most secret and sensitive place. He didn't move for an moment as he mastered the urge to end his own hunger at that instant. Her body accepted his sweet invasion and rhythmic thrusts, and she begged for more with words and actions. She was starving and eager to have him. He relished the way she responded so feverishly and freely to him. He set a pattern that tantalized them both.

Everything he did thrilled her to the center of her being. Her legs locked over his. She arched to meet him, sighing and tugging at him each time he pulled back. Never had anything felt this good to her. She strained against the sweet tension that possessed her until spasms shook her to the very core. She murmured his name and clung to him as she rode the powerful waves crashing over her.

Christopher dashed aside his control and went along with her, savoring the almost simultaneous fusion of their release. This woman was a dream come true. What he would give to keep her in his arms and life! He felt her relax in his embrace. He kept kissing her. He eased to his side and took her with him. He inhaled several times to slow his racing heart. "Damn, Kirstin, you're trying to kill me," he teased.

"You're fantastic, Doc. I've never experienced anything like that before. Never, I swear. Is the invitation to stay for a while still open?"

He chuckled and hugged her. "Damn right it is, if I can hold up. You're a greedy and demanding woman. If this is an equal-rights setup, you do the work next time, at least half of it. You were just lying there and enjoying it; that's not fair," he jested playfully, as she indeed had participated.

"I couldn't help it. You were driving me crazy, you sexy devil," she murmured and kissed his shoulder.

"Flattery will get you everywhere and anywhere with me." When she started laughing, he asked, "What's so funny?"

"Me. I can't believe this. I'm lying in bed with a man who's practically a stranger and having the most incredible time in my life. Are you sure you didn't hypnotize me that first day on your examining table?"

"I don't give out trade secrets. If anyone had told me an angel would fly in one spring day and be here like this tonight, I wouldn't have believed him . . . or her. If I'm dreaming, don't wake me up. You're beautiful and special, Kirstin. I don't see how I held out as long as I did."

"Stamina, Doc, and self-control." She caressed his chest. This was something new and astonishing, lying in bed and calmly discussing sex! Yet, she felt totally at ease with him. She liked being relaxed and satisfied, being a sensual woman. Christopher Harrison would make one helluva husband! When he rolled to his other side for a moment and she felt his movements, she knew he was removing the condom and discarding it. He turned back to her. She curled into his arms, beautiful visions of life with him filling her distracted mind.

Christopher pulled the sheet over them and nestled her against him. Yep, he could get used to this setup, fast. But she was liberated and only passing through, he reminded himself. No doubt this quiet country life wouldn't suit her. She had an important career, one she loved and had worked hard to attain. She finally was free of a bad marriage. Would she sacrifice her new life to join his? Somehow, he dreaded to find out.

Kirstin wouldn't fool herself; he had never mentioned love or a possible future together. He liked her and desired her; that was obvious. But he was firmly and stubbornly rooted here, far from Medico. She doubted he was open to another drastic change in his life or ready to confront his lost world again. Could he settle for one woman, her? What about the female who had called twice the other day?

Soon, the sated couple was sleeping in each other's arms.

When Kirstin awoke the next morning, she didn't feel Christopher beside her. She lay there awaiting his return. When some time passed, she realized he must have left early to do ranch chores, as was his custom. She sighed in disappointment and stretched, feeling both lazy and energetic. When she threw the sheet aside and sat up on the side of the bed, she felt light-headed and dizzy. She realized she was weak and shaky, and had forgotten her snack last night. Not eating added to so much exertion with the dancing and lovemaking had caused her body trouble. She stood, to find her equilibrium was off and sat again. She glanced at the nightstand; her tablets weren't there. She needed glucose fast! She was certain she always had a package nearby. Could she make it to the bathroom where her kit held more medicine without fainting. If Christopher came back and found her out cold on the floor, he would be furious.

"Damn, Kirstin! Damn, damn, damn. How could you be so careless?" she scolded herself.

She made it to the bathroom and twisted off the top of the liquid glutose; that would reach her system faster than the hard tablets. She sat on the floor and leaned against the cabinet. Soon she felt fine except for being shaky, sweaty, and queasy, which were normal reactions following an attack of hypoglycemia. A loud buzzer sounded and she realized Christopher had set the alarm clock to prevent her from oversleeping and being tardy with her medical schedule. She mused on how thoughtful he was as she walked naked to push in the button. She was naked, had slept nude! Elaine had coaxed her to have an adventure, she recalled, but had her friend meant for her to behave *this* wantonly? No matter, she had, and she would do so again, as many times as she could work into the days ahead before she left the ranch and her . . . love? "Don't start thinking crazy," she warned herself. "Sex shouldn't make you believe this relationship is more serious than it actually may be. When this fog lifts after you're gone, then see how you feel about him and he feels about you." If it was a temporary enjoyment on either or both of their parts, neither of them should get hurt by expecting more than they'd shared. "Get busy;

240

you have a party to attend. People to meet and impress. Fun and games to enjoy. Secrets to keep."

She returned to the bathroom to monitor her glucose level and smiled at the number the meter gave her. When she had showered, shampooed her hair, and dressed and groomed, she went to the kitchen.

The coffee smelled enticing. She smiled when she noticed that Christopher had set out cups and the sweetener. She filled one cup and wondered if she should eat by herself or wait for his return. Eat to stay on schedule, she decided. She was half finished with her meal when she heard the front door open and close. She set down the cup and waited to see if it was Christopher.

He joined her and chuckled. "That independent streak is showing this morning, Ms. Lowrey. Couldn't wait for service, huh?"

Kirstin laughed. "I didn't know how long you'd be gone and I have a strict regimen to maintain. Chores or a patient?"

"Chores. Too bad you weren't up to help me."

"Is that why you want me to stay? Need an extra ranch hand?"

"I could use one if she looked and behaved like you." He captured her hands, lifted them to his lips, and kissed her fingertips before saying, "But I doubt these important hands would risk injury; it's hard labor out there. Microsurgery might be hard to do with scrapes and blisters."

"How did you know I do microsurgery?" she asked.

"Lucky guess. You're forgetting most doctors go through similar classes and training, especially surgeons? I've done my share of cutting and stitching under a power lens. Lab mice have tiny veins and nerves; makes good practice for us. You've got steady hands; bet you're great at operating."

"The best," she replied with a saucy grin. She jested before thinking, "If you ever have an emergency, I can stitch him up like a French seamstress for you."

"Thanks, but I do my own stitches whenever possible. Thank God I don't get many. Anything bad I refer to the Clovis hospital."

She knew she'd hit a raw nerve. "I was only kidding, Christopher. How about a refill?" she asked to distract him, holding out her cup.

"Sure." He poured her coffee, put in two sweeteners, and stirred it. He kept his eyes glued to hers as he returned the steaming cup.

She wanted to tell him he was too sensitive and defensive in that area, but thought better of reprimanding him. "Thanks. I see you already know my tastes well." she teased to vanquish his tension.

"What do you mean?"

"Two sweeteners. You're very observant and thoughtful. Thanks for setting the alarm so I would stay on schedule."

He mellowed. "I hated to creep out of bed and leave you this morning, but duty called. You're a sexy sight to wake up to, Kirstin."

"Thanks, but I've seen me in the morning; I look a wreck."

"But you make a beautiful and tempting wreck, woman."

Kirstin smiled. This kind of relationship was wonderful and romantic and very good for her self-esteem. Katie and her friends were right: nothing was better than good practice with a good man.

"How was your level this morning?" he asked after fetching himself coffee and sitting down near her.

"Fine."

"Your voice and expression don't agree with that claim. What gives? I am your doctor, too."

With reluctance, she told him about her earlier bout. But she didn't mention not having enough carbohydrates at dinner, another error.

He scowled. "You can't be careless, woman; it's dangerous."

"I was distracted last night, remember?"

Her playful smile and quip failed to calm him. "No excuses. You can't afford to be distracted from your health, not even by me."

"Please don't fuss at me and spoil our day with a lecture."

"I have to scold you when you're wrong or you'll have complications."

His personal and professional concern softened her irritation. "I know, and I promise I'll be more careful."

Scared of a problem taking her from him before they could get closer, he reminded, "You told me that days ago."

"Days ago I didn't have a handsome and sexy doctor stealing my attention. I'm surprised you didn't stop in the middle of our . . . evening and kick me out of bed to check my blood and get me some glucose tablets."

Christopher heard the edge to her tone and realized he was being too stern with her because of his fears. "You're right; it *was* partly my fault. We'll make sure it doesn't happen again. Right?"

"Right." Kirstin returned to eating. *Mighty bossy this morning, Doc. Think I'm under your spell now so you can order me about like David did? I don't want another owner. Next time around, I want a partner. Share with me; don't try to rule me. I don't need a man to protect and take care of me: I can do that myself. I want you to provide only what I can't get elsewhere: a special bond, and great sex.*

Christopher wished he hadn't jumped down her throat. "There was a message on the answering machine. The barbecue is postponed until next Saturday. Okay?"

"Fine." She didn't look up because she wanted to make her point. She was tempted to tell him what she'd been thinking but didn't want to sound foolish and presumptuous this soon in their relationship. Too, he was right in some areas, and his worry was genuine and touching.

"You will be here, won't you?"

"Unless my reservation has been canceled this morning."

"You have one until May fourth and I'll hold you to it. Deal?"

"Deal. So what's on today's agenda now?"

"We'll still go to the movie with John and Maria if that's okay with you."

"Sounds like fun. I like John. I look forward to meeting his wife. I—"

The phone interrupted their talk. It was for her. "Hi, honey. I was going to call you in a few minutes. How's the work going?"

After Katie answered that question, she asked, "How are you doing, Mom? I've been worried."

"Don't worry, honey, I'm fine, no problems. Doctor Harrison is taking excellent care of me." She glanced at Christopher and smiled.

"It sounds as if you're having a super time."

"Yes, I am. I'll be staying a while longer. There's a lot to see in this area and Christopher has been kind enough to become my tour guide."

"Yeah, team. Has the doctor made any passes yet?"

Kirstin hesitated before replying, "Yes, and I'm glad."

"I hope that means romance is in the air?"

"Possibly. It's too soon to tell how I'll respond to the new treatment. Doctor Harrison is an expert in this field. I trust him to do what's best; so far, he has. Thanks to his skills, I'll be leaving here in much better condition than I arrived in; that should make you happy."

Katie laughed. "Can't talk, right?"

"That's right, honey." She put her back to Christopher to muffle her words. "Have you spoken with Steve again? Is he still angry at me? I haven't called but I've sent cards and some small gifts to him and Louise and the kids along the way."

"Don't you dare call him until you finish your vacation and reach San Diego. Besides, they're leaving this morning for the cruise.

May be gone already. He did what he should have done in the beginning; hired a professional sitter to tend those brats."

"Katie, don't say that."

"Oh, Mom, it's true; they're wild, and you know it. If Steve and Louise don't start disciplining them soon, they'll be uncontrollable and nobody will want to be around them. You never let us get away with such behavior."

"Parenting has changed. Times have changed."

"And look what's happened to families. When I have kids, I'm raising them just like you did us. If I don't, whip me. Steve better get his act together and his head straight or he'll be in big trouble."

Kirstin lowered her voice. "He misses your father, Katie."

"Why? Dad was hardly around. And when he was, he might as well have not been. You raised us, not him. Steve's an ungrateful and selfish ass."

"Katie, please don't feel that way."

"I've accepted it, Mom, so has Sandi. It's time Steve realizes Dad wasn't the greatest father alive, like he tries to make him out. I loved him, but he thought only about himself. He left you in terrible shape."

"Maybe that wasn't his fault."

"Yes, Mom, it was, and you know it's true."

"I suppose so."

"I *know* so. I told Steve he needs to see a therapist."

"I wish he would. We'll talk about this when I get there, all right?"

"You forget about work, Steve, and Dad, and just have a good time."

"I will. Thanks, Katie. I'll call you next week."

"I love you, Mom, and I miss you. Please take care of yourself."

"I promise, and I love you, too. Bye."

Kirstin hung up the receiver and leaned against the counter for a moment, her thoughts worried.

"Problems?" Christopher asked as his hands cupped her shoulders.

Kirstin turned and rested her head against his chest, in need of his comfort. She explained the new misunderstanding with her son. "I don't know what to do about him. I love him so much and I hate to see him hurting himself this way. He's so bitter about his father. What he won't admit is how badly David ignored him. He doesn't want to remember I was the one with him most of the time, not David. He's painted this golden image in his head and can't see the truth. Sometimes he sounds as if he blames me for the way David was and even for his death. It's as

248

if he can't bear to see me getting along so well without his father, as if I'm being selfish and traitorous not grieving over David for the rest of my life. Steve thinks I should dedicate myself to him and his children. He knows my work is necessary and important to me, but that doesn't matter to him. He's been so bossy since David died; he's becoming like his father was. I hate to see that happen, but I don't know how to stop it."

"You can't, Kirstin, only Steve can do that. Maybe he'll come to his senses. Katie's right: you did the best thing. If you don't put down your foot, it'll get worse for both of you. He's a grown man; it's time he realizes you're more than his mother and you have needs other than your children and grandchildren. Stick to your guns."

"That sounds simple and logical, but living it isn't. Deep inside, I knew I was going to head right to his home after I visited Carlsbad and White Sands. Highway 25 near there goes straight from Las Cruces to Denver. I was going to tell Steve everything and try to make peace with him. I want to see him and my grandchildren; I love them and I miss them. I was only stalling a visit because I hated to have another fight. Why do I feel guilty for doing the right thing?"

His fingers lifted her chin and cupped it.

"Because you're a kind and gentle person and you hate to hurt or disappoint anyone, especially those close to you. Steve's bitter over what he never had with his father; that's understandable. It's bad enough to lose a father to death or divorce when you're young, but it must be worse to have one at home who's never there for you. David's accident made death a bold reality to Steve; he's probably scared of losing you, too." *I understand that feeling.* "You are a good mother, Kirstin; your girls turned out fine, and Steve isn't really bad."

"But I want my son to be happy, to be free of the past." She rested her head on his broad chest again and snuggled into his embrace.

Christopher's hands stroked her back and his cheek nuzzled the top of her head. "That's up to him, Kirstin. You must accept that reality and not let it worry you so much that it affects your health. I don't think you should tell Steve about your diabetes yet. If he's so afraid of losing you, that could make him even more possessive and demanding. You said he had a recent medical checkup, so you know his health is good. I'd wait a while, give him more time to get his thoughts straight."

Kirstin leaned back and her gaze met his tender one. She savored his compassion, strength, and intelligence. He wasn't the slightest bit annoyed at her troubles. "You're right on both points so I'll follow your good advice. I thought the truth would help him be more understanding, but I suppose it could make things worse."

"Maybe he'll take Katie's advice and get professional help. She has a good head on her shoulders. I know you're proud of her."

"I am." She lowered her gaze. "There's another problem: I'm worried about Steve's children. He's spoiling them terribly; he's afraid of pushing them away from him and being a bad father. They mind me better than they do him, but they're still a handful. They're so used to having their way that they throw terrible temper tantrums if they don't get it. It's so draining for me. I'm scared of getting distracted or passing out and them getting hurt."

"That's possible. You should be extra careful when you keep them. Plus, kids that age get all kinds of infections and childhood diseases that could be harmful to a diabetic. You should stay clear of them, or anyone who's ill. Don't kiss or even shake hands with people who have colds; they're loaded with germs that will spread to you."

"But if Steve doesn't know the real reason, he'll stay angry at me."

"From the way it sounds, Kirstin, if he didn't have that charge against you, he'd find another one. Give him time to wake up and change. Besides, you have yourself to think about — your health, even your survival. This new episode tells us we don't have you balanced yet."

Christopher knew he shouldn't deceive her, but he wanted her dependent upon him so she'd stay around longer. If she got too worried about her son, she might be tempted to leave. He needed time to test this attraction to her, and hers to him. She was changing him, and he *wanted* to be changed. She gave him a new zest for life. She stirred his deepest passions and sated them with bliss. He hadn't felt this important, happy, and needed in years.

Then, there was Kirstin herself. She needed time to get to know him. He was positive now she wouldn't fall prey to a whirlwind romance and another impulsive marriage. They needed to explore their new feelings for each other. If she left now, he might never see her again. If he told her such things this early, she could panic and flee. He was being secretive and manipulative, as David had been in other areas and for other reasons. He had asked Joe Bob to go slow on her car repairs. He knew the diabetic bout this morning was a normal one. But he had to use those opportunities to keep her with him.

"I want you to monitor yourself closely, Kirstin, and I want to see your record daily. We'll work together to get you in perfect control," he told her. The mild deceptions had a nasty taste to him but he was desperate to have something special.

Kirstin sensed his game and hoped she read the real meaning for it: he wanted time to explore their relationship. "You're the doctor, Christopher; I'll follow your advice. Besides, how often does one have such a delightful recovery from an accident?"

"You just like having a man wait on you hand and foot like a doting slave, Kirstin Lowrey. You'd probably be content to have problems for three weeks to get it," he ventured with a playful grin.

She laughed. "Frankly, Doctor Harrison, it isn't half bad. Of course, if it were Doctor Cooper here instead of you, I would be trying harder to recover sooner. But you, you make a splendid nursemaid . . . What time is it?"

"What difference does it make? You promised you aren't going anywhere soon. I'm a captivating doctor, remember? But it's past time for *my* breakfast; I'm starved."

"It's strange, Christopher, but I have no concept of time when I'm with you. To be so distracted is bad for my schedule."

"Yep," he agreed with a cheerful smile. "It also has to do with being in another time zone; your body clock hasn't adjusted to ours yet. Is your watch on the correct time?" He glanced at her wrist and frowned. "Where is it? How can you keep up with your treatment without it?"

She sighed in exasperation. "In my room, tyrant. I wasn't going to put it on until after I did the dishes. You have clocks everywhere."

"But a watch makes you more conscious of time."

"I can take care of myself, Doc."

"Like you did last — Sorry, I wasn't going to mention that again."

"I should be delighted you're so concerned about me, but your constant reminders are annoying. Every mistake teaches me a lesson."

"I just don't want you learning one lesson too many, a bad one."

"I know and I'm grateful. End of subject, okay?"

He nodded and kissed the tip of her nose, then released her to start his breakfast. "You finished or did yours get cold?"

"Finished, and I had everything on my diet. I'll have coffee with you."

As he ate and she sipped, he told her more about some of the people who lived near him and ranching life in general. She listened with interest. She and David had never sat around chatting and having fun, just enjoying each

other's company. Christopher was a complicated and yet a simple person to be with. He
could relax and be himself as her husband had
never been able to do.

Kirstin worried that her impulsive behavior
might be her undoing. After all, she had accepted the research position at Medico and
they were paying for her move to San Diego.
She had a responsibility to them, to herself.
An exciting career awaited her. It was a
chance to grow, to become her own person.
She also had rented an apartment and her
possessions were there. Her feelings and at-
tachment to Christopher had happened too
suddenly to be strong enough to compel her to
change her life for him, and he might not feel
the same way about her. She had been caught
at a weak physical and emotional moment.
Unless she moved slowly and carefully and put
distance between them at least for a while, she
wouldn't know how deep her feelings really
were. If anything was meant to happen between them, time would tell. *For now, Kirstin,
just have fun as Katie and Elaine suggested.*

After breakfast, Kirstin and Christopher did
the dishes, then went to the den to watch
more of the Master's Golf Tournament. They
sat on the sofa and she leaned against his side
with his arm around her shoulder.

At one point, his lips captured Kirstin's and

caused her head to spin. He shifted her body to lie half across his lap and continued to kiss her, which more than suited her. It was as if their lips and bodies were made for each other's. His fingers tangled in her tawny tresses while hers stroked his sable hair. As his mouth drifted over her cheek, hers grazed his jawline. Her gaze touched on the smattering of silver at his temples which reminded her they were both nearing fifty. It didn't matter how old they were, she concluded, passions and desires were ageless, and theirs were strong and alive.

He wondered if she felt his arousal against her hip. The peak of the breast in his cupped hand told her she was sexually affected by him, too. Was she open to a Saturday morning romp in bed? Had David always made love to her in the dark? How could any sane and sighted man not adore this woman and do anything to make her happy? Do anything to win and to keep her? From things she had murmured last night, probably without awareness, he knew she had not previously experienced the kind of lovemaking they had shared. *The things I could teach you and give to you, woman, if you'd let me* . . . "You're so beautiful and sexy, Kirstin. I'm lucky you were dropped in my lap."

As he nuzzled her neck, she wondered if he

noticed how her nipples begged for his hand to continue stroking them, how they craved for his lips to also visit them. How could they and all of her not respond to his touch, especially when he was caressing her in that seductive way with his eyes. He truly made her *feel* beautiful and sexy, and she hoped he believed what he said. If only she knew how to give him the same pleasures he had given to her. She had read and heard about them but she feared she'd be awkward and clumsy. She felt his hardness on her hip and knew he wanted her. Should she encourage him? Was he waiting for her to give him a signal to make love in broad daylight? To hop into bed when a visitor or emergency patient could arrive at any moment? Would she seem wanton to submit again so soon? "I was the lucky one, Christopher, to end up with such a handsome and sexy man."

"I was sorry I had to get up so early, Kirstin. I wish I could have joined you in bed after my chores," he murmured against her lips.

"You should have left a note and told me to stay put, Doc. I was disappointed to find you missing from my side," she confessed.

"I didn't dare wake you at dawn."

"Why not?" she challenged.

He looked at her as his hunger increased.

"You needed your rest; you're my patient and I have to take good care of you."

"Like you did last night? I like your bedside manner, Doc. I hope it's limited to special patients."

His loins twitched. "You're the first to test it. Should I make it a common practice?"

"Don't you dare, Christopher; it wouldn't be special anymore."

"You're a bossy female, aren't you?" he charged with a roguish grin.

"Am I?" she quipped, and kissed him.

He threw back his head and groaned. "You're a cruel one, too."

"Me, cruel? I am not. Why would you say that?"

"I just told you we're going out with John and Maria later, but you're enticing me to carry you off to bed and make passionate love to you. You're getting me all worked up and we don't have time to do it right."

"I didn't start this journey," she said with feigned innocence, and kissed him again. "I was only following your lead, my tempting tour guide. You did volunteer to make my vacation here worthwhile, didn't you?"

"Do you find me tempting, Kirstin?"

She was confused by his odd question; it should have been obvious to him. "I think you proved that last night. Why do you ask?"

"Just curious. The old male ego, I suppose."

His flippant answer didn't satisfy her curiosity, but she didn't probe. "Do you also find me tempting, Doc?"

"As you said, 'you proved that condition last night.' "

"Is this a *male/female* competition to see who has the greater appeal or willpower?" she speculated.

"In my opinion, Kirstin, our chemistries match to perfection. As to willpower, I hope we don't need or want any."

"We could both use some about now. You said we have plans for the day. A most distracting interruption, aren't they?"

Christopher saw how surprised she was at herself at her words and behavior. He relished being the one to give her such courage. "Not for the next twenty to thirty minutes. That would leave us just enough time to eat lunch, shower, dress, and drive in. It isn't much time to devote to . . . enjoying ourselves, but I could lock the doors and try."

"You can?"

"If you're interested . . ." he murmured, his voice low and mellow.

"What woman wouldn't be?"

"I'll take that as a yes. Correct me if I'm wrong."

Kirstin shook her head and returned his

smile. She realized his strength when he came off the sofa with her in his arms and carried her to the guest room. "Do you always sweep women off their feet?" she teased.

As he peeled off his shirt, he said, "It's the macho male in me. I'm a diehard romantic and chauvinist, or haven't you noticed?"

Her fingers trailed over his chest. "Since you obviously hypnotized me at our first meeting, I can't find anything wrong with you." She hoped he comprehended she meant her words in all areas, including his disability.

"You don't say," he jested. When she began fumbling with the buttons on her blouse and her cheeks grew rosy, his gentle hands brushed her fingers aside and he entreated, "Let me do that, please. Unless it rankles to be dominated like this? Make you nervous to have a man in full control?"

"I'm rather enjoying it, for a temporary change. Besides, I call it pampering, not dominating."

"Aha! That scientific mind's showing, Kirstin. Examining the other side of the female liberation coin with your hidden microscope? This isn't some research project with me as the specimen, is it?"

"If it is, Doc, it's a stimulating and challenging one."

"Then I'll try not to disappoint you, Doctor

Lowrey," he murmured against her lips.

He pulled the blouse off her and unfastened her bra without removing it. He unfastened and unzipped her pants and removed them as she lifted one foot at a time to assist him, after kicking off her shoes. He kissed her knees and stroked her thighs. He rose with leisure as his hands trekked up her legs, over her hips and waist, and halted on her shoulders. His fingers drifted up and down her arms as he scrutinized her. "You're an excellent specimen yourself, Kirstin Lowrey."

"I'm glad you approve, Doctor Harrison," she said, unbuttoning and unzipping his snug and faded jeans. She squatted to remove them but couldn't because of his boots. With a laugh, she pushed him to a sitting position on the bed, knelt, and struggled until they were off and cast aside. She did the same with his jeans. "Whew, that was hard work."

Christopher chuckled. "I would have used the boot jack in my room but the view was too good to miss."

Kirstin followed his gaze to where her bra had fallen forward and her breasts were revealed. "You're a dirty old man, Doc." She pulled it off and tossed it atop her clothes. She removed her panties, lay down, and slid over to give him room to join her.

He was out of his underwear with haste and

lying beside her on his stomach. Without delay, he was kissing and caressing her.

Christopher didn't need to heighten his desire; he had been craving her since awakening this morning with her in his embrace. His lips visited her neck and breasts, and she moaned and wriggled in bliss. His fingers worked with devotion, while he only gave hers time and space to stroke his back, arms, and shoulders. It didn't take long to have her fully aroused and squirming beneath him, coaxing him to join their bodies. Soon, his manhood was within her and he was riding her with zeal, and she matched his rhythm. He moved with diligence and delight, knowing time was short. His hips advanced and retreated, and he hoped he read her muffled signals right, that she was ready to be sated.

Colorful lights burst before her closed eyes as the potent release surged through her. Kirstin's flesh tingled and her body burned from scorching desire. The act may have been rushed in his opinion, but it was magnificent, as splendid as he was. Urgent, fast sex was also wonderful. She was relieved to learn it not only was fantastic again, but it was even better than the first time. Surely it couldn't bet even better? she wondered. She would be addicted to him soon!

Snuggled against him as their pounding

hearts and ragged breathing returned to normal, Christopher's right hand teased up and down her left arm. He savored the moment, then with reluctance, he propped on one elbow, gazed down at her, and said, "I have to grab a shower and dress. You, too, woman. Meet you in the kitchen for lunch in fifteen minutes."

She nodded. Suddenly a frightening thought shot through her head. "Did you forget something in our rush?"

"What?"

"Protection," she murmured with pinkening cheeks.

"Nope. I took care of it while you were jumping into bed."

She let out a sign of relief. "I didn't notice. I just thought about it." She sent him a strange look as she asked, "Do you go around prepared for . . . emergencies?"

He chuckled. "Nope. I just thought it wise to do so around you. I can't ever tell when . . . something will come up and I wouldn't want to spoil the mood by rushing to my room to rummage through my drawer."

"What if someone sees them? What will they think?"

"Who's going to see inside my pocket?"

"As tight as your jeans are, doesn't it make a telltale circle?"

"Are you saying I need to buy a larger pair? Are mine indecent?"

She frowned at him. "Stop teasing, Christopher! I'm serious."

"Don't worry about your reputation, Mrs. Lowrey; I'll protect it also."

"Yours, too, Doctor Harrison. You don't want friends and neighbors thinking you're an unethical letch who takes advantage of his patients."

"Nope, I certainly don't, because it wouldn't be true. I'll be careful."

Kirstin believed his implied promise to prevent complications. After he was gone, she left the bed to get ready for their double date, wanting to look her best. She did a blood-sugar check and dropped some glucose tablets into a pocket. As she took a last peek in the mirror, she prayed his friends would like her, then wondered if that was what Christopher was testing this afternoon. She'd soon see . . .

Nine

As they left John and Maria Two-Fists' driveway, Kirstin sat sideways in the car seat to chat with them. "Your children are precious, Maria, so well mannered and cheerful. I enjoyed spending time with them."

The Mexican-American woman tucked straight, shoulder-length hair behind her ears and laughed. "They can be very rowdy when the mood strikes them. I'm glad they were on their best behavior for you. Ask Chris; he's seen them wild as bucks."

"Only when John and I get them overexcited with backrides and teasing. They're great kids. The oldest boy and girl are already rodeo stars in their age category. If you come back to visit, you can see them perform."

Kirstin's heart fluttered. "Let me know the dates and I'll try my best, if it's on a weekend or a holiday. I can't take time off from work so soon after beginning a new job."

Maria's dark eyes twinkled with mischief and humor as she murmured, "Sometimes I wish I had a job, for the rest. A house and kids, and husband," she added with a laugh, "work me to exhaustion."

"You wouldn't go to work if a job was tossed in your lap, Tsine."

Maria grinned at John, winked, and concurred, "I know, but I have to remind you once in a while how valuable I am."

"I know how priceless you are, Tsine."

"Is that her nickname?" Kirstin asked the officer, whose eyes glowed every time he looked at his lovely wife.

"It's Apache for *love* or *sweetheart*."

Kirstin liked how John explained the word without embarrassment. She enjoyed watching Christopher interact with other people, with friends, with his *best* friend as far as she could tell.

"You said you have children and grandchildren?" Maria hinted.

For a time, the women talked about families and Kirstin's work. Then, the four chatted easily about local and national happenings, the sights nearby, and possible plans for future outings.

They purchased tickets, popcorn, and drinks at the theater located in the North Plains Mall. They took their seats only minutes before the movie began and silenced their conversation for two hours, except for brief whispers.

As they were leaving, they commented enthusiastically on the picture, all agreeing it was an excellent and authentic western.

"The cinematography and costumes were fantastic," Kirstin remarked to Maria, whom she had learned was a bundle of energy and fun.

"Wait until you see the get-ups at the barbecue next Saturday. Chris said you're staying over and going with us. We'll have a great time."

"I don't have anything western to wear. Will I look out of place?"

Maria suggested, "Why don't we find you an outfit now? They have a great store here."

"I doubt the men want to hang around while we shop."

"We don't mind," the two males said simultaneously.

The dark-haired woman pulled on Kirstin's arm. "Come on, let's do it. I can use something new and fancy, too."

Maria guided them through the mall to the store she had in mind. The men sat on wooden benches outside to wait and chat while the women shopped.

It took only thirty minutes for them to find

what they wanted and rejoin the men. Maria related information about their choices. "With luck, we'll make a country-western woman out of her before she leaves."

"I'll get Christopher to teach me the Texas two-step before next weekend so I won't embarrass him on the dance floor. If I don't learn it, he'll be dancing with every woman there except me."

"I doubt that." Maria tapped Kirstin's shopping bag. "With this outfit on, he won't notice anyone else. Of course, every man there will be breaking in on him to take a whirl with you. When the women see how Chris looks at you, none of them would dare break in except—How about an ice cream?" she asked in a rush to cover the near slip, licking her lips as they neared the specialty store and pretending that had distracted her.

Christopher shook his head. "Kirstin can't have sugar; she's diabetic. Why don't we get a bite to eat? It's time for her to refuel."

Kirstin refuted, "You all can get an ice cream first; I don't mind."

"Supper can't wait for you, woman," Christopher protested.

"I can pop a glucose tablet or two so we can wait longer to eat."

"No need. I'm starved. What sounds good to you guys?"

"Fred's Barbecue?" John suggested.

"Too much protein and not enough carbohydrates there for her."

Kirstin was embarrassed at being discussed this way and controlling their plans. "Not if I use bread to substitute for milk and fruit. They have cole slaw for a vegetable, don't they?"

"Eat four pieces?" he pointed out. "You also need two starches."

"I can fill in with glucose tables this one time, Doctor Harrison. Don't make such a big deal of it."

"It *is* a big deal, Kirstin, especially when you've been having trouble. That's why you're staying with me, remember? To get you balanced."

While the two mildly argued, John and Maria went to a store window and looked inside and pretended to be interested in the items displayed.

"Please, Christopher, don't spoil our day. We're making John and Maria uncomfortable. My books and instructors told me exchanges are fine on rare occasions. Please."

He saw that he was making her unhappy. "All right; we'll do it your way this one time."

She sent him a smile of gratitude. "Thanks."

"Let's go to Fred's," Christopher told the other couple.

As they passed the Nissan dealership, John asked Kirstin questions about her car repairs. In front of the RV Sales & Rentals, the policeman asked if she liked camping and Kirstin told him she'd never been.

"We love it and do it a lot. Ninety percent of the time, we take the kids with us. We have plenty of scenic spots nearby. I've got a great idea. I have Monday, the twentieth, off. Why don't you rent a motor home, Chris, and we'll take ours and go see Carlsbad and White Sands? That's where Kirstin was headed before her accident. We might even tour the Mescalero Reservation if that sounds interesting to her. We could head out early Sunday morning after the Saturday barbecue."

Stopped at a traffic light, Christopher looked at Kirstin and asked, "How does that sound? You game for roughing it for two days?"

Kirstin kept her face forward to prevent the couple in the backseat from seeing her expression. Travel and sleep together in a camper, she mused, with another couple along? What would they think of her?

As if reading the reason for her surprise and hesitation, Christopher added, "Most have a private bedroom plus a sofa bed in the sitting area. You can take one and me the other."

"Say yes, Kirstin. We'll have a wonderful

time," Maria coaxed.

"I . . . It's sounds like fun, but . . ."

"If you're worried about your reputation, you and Maria can use one camper and John and I will use the other at night. Okay?"

"I suppose that would be all right."

"Of course it will be," Maria concluded. "We'll do it."

Kirstin was sitting on the bed, a bottle of lotion in her hand, when Christopher entered the room that evening after his chores and checking his office answering machine. He flopped down beside her. She kept a bare foot propped over one knee but stopped spreading cream on its heel.

"I didn't coerce you into accepting their invitation, did I?"

"No, I was just worried about what they'd think if we stayed together."

"Always the lady, Mrs. Lowrey?" he teased.

She had straightened the bed, which had been left rumpled after their morning activity there and rush to leave the house. They hadn't even taken time to pull down the covers, only leapt upon them and made urgent love. "Apparently not, considering our relationship."

Christopher had noticed her expression and tone of voice during the day whenever she talked about her work and move: pride, joy, and love. He comprehended her need for independence, yet, that need would take her away from him soon. "Why do you think what we're doing destroys that image?"

"I know times and people have changed, but I wasn't reared to behave this way. Doing so takes some adjusting."

"Do you think we're wrong? Do you regret what we've done?"

"No, but that doesn't mean I want to flaunt it before others. Something private and personal has happened between us. I wouldn't want them to think I do this all the time, because I don't."

"I understand that, Kirstin. I'll behave around them." He took the bottle from her and looked at it.

She explained, "Dry skin; it goes with my condition, remember?"

He grinned. "Lie back and let me do this for you."

She reached for the bottle, but he held it out of her arm's length. "Christopher, you don't want to touch my feet."

"Afraid I have a foot fetish I want to sate on my guinea pig?"

"Don't be silly. I just can't imagine you wanting to grease my scaly smelly feet."

"Will it make it easier if I grease you all

over, sneaking in the feet?"

"Sometimes I don't know what to think about you, Doc."

"I know what I want you to think."

"And what's that?" she asked, trying not to sound as breathless and aroused as she felt.

"That I'm irresistible and you can't say no to me about anything. Now strip, woman, and lie back."

Her eyes widened in surprise at his command. "What?"

"I can't give you a proper massage with your clothes on."

"Excuse me? Just strip and stretch out naked?"

"Yep."

Kirstin eyed him as erotic thoughts raced through her mind; her body seemed to overheat and quiver. Could she be that daring?

"Well? Do you or don't you want the massage of your life?"

When her expression said yes but her modesty caused her to hesitate, he said, "I'll fetch me a drink while you get undressed and covered with a towel." He stood, tossed the bottle on the bed, and headed for the door. "A *small* towel," he flung over his shoulder with a seductive grin.

"How about giving me time to run through the shower first?"

"Don't want to put dirty, sweaty feet into these skilled hands?"

"That's right, Doc. Give me fifteen minutes."

"You've got 'em." He left the room whistling.

After the quick shower, Kirstin sprayed on perfume, and returned to the bed. She was tempted to don the sexy black nightgown her friends had given to her but that might look as if she had seduction in mind. Of course, she hoped that was exactly what he was planning. She lay on her stomach and pulled the bath towel over her body from breasts to buttocks. The realization she was naked beneath it was stimulating.

Christopher strolled into the room, freshly bathed and shaved, and clad only in a towel around his hips. He eyed the stirring sight of her. He could wait no longer to get his hands on her. He lifted the bottle and began his provocative task at her feet, evoking sounds and wriggles of delight from her within moments. He teased fingers in and out between her toes, then worked her ankles.

"That feels wonderful. Don't stop. You have magical hands, Doc. You can do that all night."

"This is only the beginning," Christopher promised. He trailed his way up and down both legs in turn, halting each time just short of touching her in an intimate manner. He gave special attention to her sleek calves. As with her ankles, he occasionally dropped kisses on the inner surface of her knees. He straddled her thighs, lifted the towel a bit, and massaged her firm derriere, careful not to press too hard or be too rough.

As he labored with gentleness at her lower back at the waist, she murmured, "Sheer heaven, Doc. How can I ever afford such service?"

"I'll think of something for repayment," he replied in a husky voice.

As she felt his aroused manhood brush over her legs, she knew how she wanted to reward him, and herself at the same time. The hairs on his legs tickled her flesh. His rocking pattern titillated her senses. David would never have done this in a thousand years!

Christopher shifted to one side to tend to her right arm and hand. Once more, his fingers roved in and out between hers and his thumbs stroked her palms in playful circles. As he journeyed her arm, he brushed his lips over her elbow, them climbed over her to minister to the left ones. When they also were silky from nourishment and limp with relaxation, he straddled her again to caress and lotion her upper back, shoulders, and neck with his cream-softened and deft hands. He trekked her spine from end to end several times, his fingers going up and down as they passed over vertebrae. When no muscle or area on that side was left untended, he said, "Roll over; time to do the front."

Kirstin obeyed, adjusting the towel to keep herself covered, for now. Her eyes remained closed to allow her senses to absorb every glorious moment and touch. She moaned and signed dreamily as he lotioned her neck and upper chest and nibbled here and there. He straddled her hips and pulled the towel to her waist. As he spread cream over her breasts, he kneaded and fondled them, taking extra care to entice her nipples to tighten with pleasure. "Um-m-m," she sighed deep in her throat when his teeth and tongue assisted his task. "Sheer ecstasy."

Christopher's slippery fingers drifted over her rib cage and stomach, and he felt the latter tighten at his touch. He shifted to kneel between her thighs, which his knees spread with gentle nudgings so his exploring hands could journey across her abdomen. With sensual motions and deliberate leisure, he covered her inner thighs with satiny rapture, allowing the edges of his hands to barely enter her center of her desire and graze its secret peak. Soon, he was caressing her there with skill and intensity, and Kirstin could no longer lie still or quiet.

276

Just when she could wait no longer, he slid his manhood within her. He lay atop her and kissed her lips. He could hardly restrain himself when she responded with unleashed eagerness. His sinuous body undulated against hers and enticed Kirstin's to do the same with his. It didn't take long for her to achieve her goal, or for him to do the same.

He almost collapsed beside her in breathless splendor after his spasms ceased. "You drain me every time, woman. You're the best, Kirstin."

She hugged him and beamed with joy to hear he got such pleasure from their union. She cuddled into his embrace. It was hard not to confess her feelings for him, which were much stronger than desire or infatuation. They had so much in common and had such good rapport. She had never felt free and open like this with David. She had never enjoyed and craved her husband almost every minute of every day as she did Christopher. But there were obstacles between them. He was firmly lodged on this ranch and she needed to be elsewhere for a time. Nor was there a place close by where she could work at her chosen occupation; on the other hand, he could practice medicine in almost any area.

Why should it be the woman's place to stay with the man? Kirstin reasoned. Why couldn't he go with her to a place where they could both work and have a meaningful career? Why did men think a woman's job wasn't as important as theirs? Or a woman's wishes as important as theirs? She had given her word to Medico and cost them a lot of money with her transfer. She feared it wouldn't mean anything to him, and was afraid to ask and hear his answer.

It was foolish and impulsive to even think of throwing away all she had worked for and accomplished. How could she sacrifice her new-found independence for an affair with a man she'd known less than a week? Though she couldn't, mustn't, allow him to sweep her off her feet, she couldn't stop her fantasies. She should not convince herself that love was all-consuming, the most important facet of her life. So many challenges and pleasures awaited her in San Diego. She couldn't give them up to become only a rancher's wife in a near-wilderness. Christopher was still plagued by his past, she fretted, and needed time to deal with it. But after sharing so much with him, how could she be totally happy and complete without him? Why couldn't all of her dreams come true? Because, she believed, he wouldn't agree to sell the ranch and move with her. He would never head for—

"Up, woman, and get your snack before you

fall asleep."

"Yes, Doctor. Do you want anything?"

"I've had all the treats I need tonight."

Kirstin wondered if that was all she was to him, a "treat," a passing fancy, a diversion. Maybe that was all he wanted or expected. After she was gone, she'd see if he missed her, if he came after her. He hadn't mentioned love, or even any deep feelings for her. But he did keep mentioning "friendship" and the dates she was to leave and be at work, May first and fourth, as if fearing she might forget or think he'd changed his mind. When she returned to bed, he was fast asleep. Troubled in heart, it was a long time before she did the same.

Sunday afternoon, they watched the final round of the Master's Golf Tournament. As the winner was given his Green Jacket award, Christopher stood and stretched and said he had chores to do and would return later.

Kirstin wished he'd asked her to ride with him and was curious as to why he hadn't. He had been quiet this morning. Had she said something in the "throes of passion" that scared him? If so, she couldn't recall it. She ate her snack, then went to the phone and called Elaine, her best friend.

"I don't know what to do, Elaine; he has me thinking crazy." Kirstin didn't go into intimate details but explained her worry.

"Grab him, old girl, fast. He's a real catch."

"I don't know if he wants to be caught; that's the problem, among others." She clarified for her friend.

"For once, forget about what Steve will think. Listen to your heart. How often does a perfect man come along, Kirstin? I should know. I've gone through dozens of them and haven't found a single one who comes close."

"What about Medico?"

"Would they confer with *you* before making a decision in their best interest? No. Pay back their expenses from your next check."

"I think I owe it to them to work there for a while. Besides, I've only known Christopher for such a short time and he hasn't given me any indication he feels the same way about me."

There was silence on the other end for a time. "Well, Elaine? What?"

"You're right; go on to San Diego and let him come after you. That would be more romantic and would clear up your doubts about him. But don't let him forget you after you leave. Call him. Write him. Visit him. Be irresistible."

Sometimes it surprised Kirstin that she was

MORE PASSION AND ADVENTURE AWAIT... YOUR TRIP TO A BIG ADVENTUROUS WORLD BEGINS WHEN YOU ACCEPT YOUR FIRST 4 NOVELS ABSOLUTELY *FREE*
(AN $18.00 VALUE)

Accept your Free gift and start to experience more of the passion and adventure you like in a historical romance novel. Each Zebra novel is filled with proud men, spirited women and tempestuous love that you'll remember long after you turn the last page.

Zebra Historical Romances are the finest novels of their kind. They are written by authors who really know how to weave tales of romance and adventure in the historical settings you love. You'll feel like you've actually gone back in time with the thrilling stories that each Zebra novel offers.

GET YOUR FREE GIFT WITH THE START OF YOUR HOME SUBSCRIPTION

Our readers tell us that these books sell out very fast in book stores and often they miss the newest titles. So Zebra has made arrangements for you to receive the four newest novels published each month.

You'll be guaranteed that you'll never miss a title, and home delivery is so convenient. And to show you just how easy it is to get Zebra Historical Romances, we'll send you your first 4 books absolutely FREE! Our gift to you just for trying our home subscription service.

BIG SAVINGS AND FREE HOME DELIVERY

Each month, you'll receive the four newest titles as soon as they are published. You'll probably receive them even before the bookstores do. What's more, you may preview these exciting novels free for 10 days. If you like them as much as we think you will, just pay the low preferred subscriber's price of just $3.75 each. *You'll save $3.00 each month off the publisher's price.* AND, your savings are even greater because there are never any shipping, handling or other hidden charges—FREE Home Delivery. Of course you can return any shipment within 10 days for full credit, no questions asked. There is no minimum number of books you must buy.

4 FREE BOOKS

TO GET YOUR 4 FREE BOOKS WORTH $18.00 —MAIL IN THE FREE BOOK CERTIFICATE T O D A Y

Fill in the Free Book Certificate below, and we'll send your FREE BOOKS to you as soon as we receive it.

If the certificate is missing below, write to: Zebra Home Subscription Service, Inc., P.O. Box 5214, 120 Brighton Road, Clifton, New Jersey 07015-5214.

FREE BOOK CERTIFICATE
4 FREE BOOKS
ZEBRA HOME SUBSCRIPTION SERVICE, INC.

YES! Please start my subscription to Zebra Historical Romances and send me my first 4 books absolutely FREE. I understand that each month I may preview four new Zebra Historical Romances free for 10 days. If I'm not satisfied with them, I may return the four books within 10 days and owe nothing. Otherwise, I will pay the low preferred subscriber's price of just $3.75 each; a total of $15.00, *a savings off the publisher's price of $3.00*. I may return any shipment and I may cancel this subscription at any time. There is no obligation to buy any shipment and there are no shipping, handling or other hidden charges. Regardless of what I decide, the four free books are mine to keep.

NAME

ADDRESS _____ APT _____

CITY _____ STATE ____ ZIP _____

TELEPHONE ( )

SIGNATURE _____ (if under 18, parent or guardian must sign)

Terms, offer and prices subject to change without notice. Subscription subject to acceptance by Zebra Books. Zebra Books reserves the right to reject any order or cancel any subscription.

ZB0893

GET
FOUR
FREE
BOOKS
(AN $18.00 VALUE)

ZEBRA HOME SUBSCRIPTION
SERVICE, INC.
120 BRIGHTON ROAD
P.O. Box 5214
CLIFTON, NEW JERSEY 07015-5214

so friendly with Elaine, since they were so different. If Elaine wanted a man, she chased him until he dumped her. Yet, Elaine was a good person, a fun person, one who'd do anything for a friend. "Wouldn't that be presumptuous? Forward?"

"Not if you love him and want him. Do you?"

"I think so. It's just that it happened so fast and out of the blue."

"Don't act until you're certain. You don't want another bad marriage."

"You're right; don't get out of one trap and fall into another." She changed the topic. "How's Betty? I tried calling, but she doesn't answer."

"She and her hubby are out-of-town for two weeks."

"Do I detect a hint of envy?"

"Damn right! He's a jewel; our friend is one lucky creature. If only we can be as fortunate our next time around." Elaine sighed dramatically. "Seriously, Kirstin, don't let a romantic interlude and wild sex fool you. Lord knows I've made that mistake plenty of times when I took 'pillow talk' to heart, so I'm not the best one to give you advice. Whispering sweet nothings in our ears while our eyes are crossed in ecstasy and our wits are out to lunch makes us do crazy things, old girl, makes us

281

think the men care for us far more than they do. Enjoy him and have fun, but be careful, Kirstin; make sure he's what you want. Make sure he's worthy of you. I've been misled so many times I can't count them. We're just too gullible and trusting. We think men's actions match their feelings; they rarely do, I'm sorry to say. He's nothing like David, is he?"

"Heavens, no, the opposite. He's wonderful."

"Maybe that's the reason you're so attracted to him. Go with your gut feelings. Use that smart brain, not that tender heart of yours. I don't want you to get hurt."

"That's all I needed to hear to make certain I wasn't being foolish, or overly cautious. I'd better get off the phone before he returns. Tell Betty I said hello and I'll call her in a few weeks."

"Bye, Kirstin. Lordy, I miss you. It just isn't the same without you."

"I miss you, too. You'll have to come out and visit me this summer."

"I will, if you'll help me land a good catch," she teased.

"I'll see what I can do. As soon as I learn my way around and get to know people there, I'll get some prospects lined up before you arrive—only good ones, though. Bye."

It wasn't long before the phone rang again. Kirstin saw that the button of the house line lit up. She wondered if she should answer it. He had told her it was all right to do so if it wasn't his office line, which the machine or service handled. With indecision but thinking it might be Katie, she lifted the receiver and said, "Hello."

"Who is this? Did I dial the wrong number?"

The female caller gave the number she wanted and Kirstin said, "This is Doctor Harrison's home. He's doing chores outside. May I take a message for him?"

"Who are you?"

Oh, no, not another jealous rival, she fretted. "A friend of his. Would you like to leave a message?"

"Tell him Peggy phoned and to call me back."

"You're Peggy Beattie, Christopher's daughter?"

"Yes . . . Who is this?"

That time, the tone was almost demanding. "Kirstin Lowrey. I'm visiting your father. He should be back soon. I'll tell him to call you."

"Why are you there alone?"

Kirstin felt as if she were experiencing déjà vu and wasn't sure how to answer. This time the caller was his daughter, so she couldn't be impolite. "Christopher asked me to wait for him here," she white-lied. "He shouldn't be gone much longer. He—"

"Is that for me, Kirstin?" Christopher asked as he entered the room.

"Just a minute, Peggy; he's here now." She handed him the phone and noticed his brief scowl. "I'll take a walk so you can have privacy."

"Hello, squirt. I was going to call you later."

"Who is that woman, Father?"

"Uh-oh she's calling me father! A patient."

"She said she was a friend."

"She is."

"What's going on? You sound strange. What's she doing there alone?"

"She's visiting a while. She—"

"Visiting? As in staying there with you?"

"Yes."

"Father, I know how you men are! Why would you let a woman, a patient to boot, shack up with you?"

His voice was stern but kind when he scolded, "Don't use that tone with me, young lady. I'm a grown man, your *father.*"

"I bet she's a gold digger. You're a fine catch, Father, a rich one."

"She isn't out to get me, so don't worry. We're just friends."

"I bet. What's she like? How did you meet? When? Where?"

"Mighty nosy, aren't you, Squirt?"

"Why not? I love you. I don't want a woman taking advantage of you."

"She won't. She isn't like that. She's nice and kind and a lot of fun. You do want your old man to have some fun in his life, don't you?"

"There's fun and there's fun. What kind of *fun* are you two having?"

"I'm holding her captive here so I can ravish her day and night. I don't dare let her escape or she'll sic the authorities on me."

"Stop teasing me, Father."

"Then stop being silly. I can take care of myself."

"Are you going to tell me anything about her or not?"

"She's in research at Medico in San Diego. She had an accident nearby and John brought her to me. I liked her so I asked her to stay here while her car is being repaired."

"You took in a stranger? She could be dangerous. She could sue."

"Give it a rest, Squirt. I'm doing fine. How's Phil?"

"He's fine. Work's fine, too. How long is she staying?"

"As long as she can," he replied with a chuckle.

"Father! Be serious. I bet she has designs on you already."

He chuckled again to conceal his feelings. "I hope so."

"Will I get a chance to meet her?"

"Perhaps. You'll know after I do."

"I don't like this."

"You don't like any woman getting her hooks into me."

"You haven't let one do so since you and Mother got divorced."

"Haven't met one I'd want to get to know better than superficially. And I'm not going to answer any more questions. Remember how you fussed and fumed when I questioned you about Phil? You told me, if I recall accurately, to mind my own business."

Peggy dropped the subject and they chatted about other things for a while. Before hanging up, she warned in a motherly tone of concern, "If she's still there in a few weeks, I'm coming for a visit to check her out."

"She'll be gone soon; I promise."

"Does that disappoint you?"

"I haven't decided."

"Men!" she muttered in exasperation.

"Daughters," he retorted with more chuckles. "I'll be fine."

Kirstin sneaked down the back porch steps, away from the screen door where she'd been eavesdropping on his end of the conversation. She walked to the swing and sat down but kept it motionless as his words raced back and forth across her mind. Obviously his daughter was curious, worried, suspicious, and possibly jealous of her being there.

Inside the house, Christopher finished his conversation.

Peggy told him, "Bye, Dad. I love you and miss you."

"I love you and miss you, too, Squirt. But you stay put in Oregon, understand?"

He hung up and went to look for Kirstin. "How about we take a picnic supper to the pond? We can enjoy the sunset better there."

They packed a meal, then went horseback riding on Christopher's sprawling land. She rode behind him on his favorite Appaloosa. With fingers interlocked around his narrow waist, she mused on the unnecessary caution. Evidently her state of health had nothing to do with his persistence; she felt fine and could ride alone. She smiled to herself; she didn't mind their contact at all.

He reined in the mottled animal near the pond, threw his leg over the horse's neck, and hopped to the ground. He reached up to grasp her by the waist to help her down, again an unnecessary action. She placed her hands on either shoulder and surrendered to his strength. As her feet touched the grassy earth, her hands slipped down to his chest and lingered there. He gazed into her upturned face before sighing and pulling her against his hard, lean body. His arms encircled her and snuggled her to him. His head bent forward to allow his lips to drop a kiss on her silky head and to inhale the freshness of her hair.

Kirstin molded her slender frame into his arms, laying her face against his shoulder. "It's so lovely, Christopher," she murmured. "Do you come here often?"

"When I need to relax. Want to swim?"

"Without a suit?" she teased.

"Why not?" he jested. "This is private property."

"You have men working for you, remember? And it's too cool."

"I forgot about them. I'm used to swimming in the buff. You chicken?" he challenged, his green eyes glittering with daring.

"Puck, puck," Kirstin imitated the real thing as she placed hands under her arms and flapped them like wings.

His chest rumbled with laughter. "At least you're honest, and still a bit modest," he added and cuffed her chin with a playful gesture.

"I don't care for your friends and workers seeing me *au naturel*. I'm surprised that you would be willing to share your private view, either."

"I'm not. You want to eat now? We should

to keep you on schedule. You did test your blood and are carrying enough emergency tablets?"

"Yes, and I'm starved."

He lifted the basket they had brought with them, took out a blanket from it, spread it beneath a solitary tree, then pulled out sandwiches, chips, carrot strips, fruit, and drinks—a diet one for her. He finished unpacking a bottle of Chablis, two wineglasses, some napkins and paper plates. "For later," he said, nodding at the bottle.

As he opened the wine to let it breathe, she remarked, "I see you're well prepared, Doc. Does that mean you do this frequently?"

"Is that jealousy in your voice?"

She giggled like a young girl on a first date.

He handed her a glass, tapped his to hers, and murmured, "Only a sip for now. To good times which are flying by swiftly, Kirstin."

"To the best vacation of my life," she added, tapping his glass again. She could only take a sip on her empty stomach, and set the wine aside for later.

They enjoyed the light meal. Afterward, they lay down to rest and talk some more. They covered casual subjects, avoiding the one which was foremost in both their thoughts: each other.

Christopher rolled to his stomach and

propped up his chin with folded arms. He reached out and snapped off a blade of grass to chew. His gaze traveled before him as he sank into deep thought.

Kirstin turned her head to observe him. A breeze lifted wisps of his ebony hair and played with them. Slivers of fading sunlight filtered through the leaves as wind moved them with gentle fingers. The lulling sound of cattle and horses in the distance drifted across the almost flat landscape. Every so often, a fish flicked its tail, made a splashing sound, and rippled the water's surface. The taller grasses swayed to and fro, wildflowers sent forth sweet scents, and the Appaloosa munched on grass beneath its hooves. The setting was serene and romantic.

Kirstin looked toward the vanishing sun and the colors it created on the horizon, then closed her eyes. She inhaled the variety of scents surrounding them, and let her body go limp. How long would this simple life and cozy arrangement satisfy her before boredom and a hunger for her career and family set in? She frowned, knowing she wasn't ready to accept this uncomplicated lifestyle.

Christopher witnessed the mixture of emotions that played over her face. He sensed what she was feeling and thinking, and grimaced. Eventually she would be miserable.

Living here was fine for a short time, but permanently wouldn't please her. He wasn't insensitive to her needs. How could he ask her to give up her life in San Diego and move here? Give up her work and become only a housewife again? That wasn't right or fair. Trouble was, he needed her and wanted her with him all the time. If she hated her work or could enjoy this rustic existence permanently, he would ask her to marry him today!

That thought shocked him; yet, he admitted, it was true. He wouldn't even mind them having a child together; that thought gave him a greater shock. Kirstin had already reared her children and made it clear, with many good reasons, that she didn't want to begin another family. How would she feel about settling down with him? Would he push her away in panic, if he pressed her this soon? How would he feel if she rejected his proposal? He almost laughed at himself for having impulsive and premature ideas; she hadn't mentioned love, not even during their most passionate moments. Too, she hadn't even hinted at a future together; she just kept implying this was a vacation. Her desire and affection were apparent, but did they go deeper? Could she fall in love with him, given time and opportunity? Encouragement? Marry him?

Her eyes opened and she glanced at him.

Her gaze clouded with puzzlement at his grave look. "What are you thinking about, Christopher? You look so solemn."

He leaned forward to nip at her mouth and nose. He grinned and said in a deceptive tone, "I was trying to decide if you were asleep. And if you were, should I awaken you and make passionate love to you."

She laughed. "Not here, Doctor Harrison. Some things shouldn't be done in public."

"I want you, Kirstin Lowrey," he vowed in a husky tone, his words carrying a deeper meaning than she realized. His mouth captured hers with an urgency he felt soul deep. As his body moved over hers, he groaned with passion and spread kisses over her face and neck. His hands roamed her prone body.

Kirstin returned his kisses and caresses as her mind warned of the sheer madness of their actions. What if, she fretted, someone rode up on them? She struggled to master the fire that raged within her. "Christopher," she called to him. He didn't answer, just continued his heady assault on her senses. "Christopher!" she repeated sharply, pushing back his head.

His eyes glittered with desire and his voice was hoarsened by it. "I need you, woman. You make me feel crazy with hunger."

"I need you and want you, too, but not here in the open like this."

"Hell, Kirstin, my men knocked off work on the east side long ago. I'm burning for you. Make love to me," he entreated, as if her submission would prove something important to him.

"Then let's go home right now. Any time and any place at home, Christopher, but not here. I'm sorry, but I can't. It isn't even dark yet."

"I promise no one will come by."

"I couldn't relax worrying you might be wrong."

He studied her, then smiled. "I'm sorry if I sounded demanding and selfish. If it wouldn't be good for you, it wouldn't be good for me. We should get back; the sun's almost set and we'll have to ride slowly. Let's get this stuff gathered and packed."

"You aren't angry, are you?"

He kissed her forehead. "Of course not. Disappointed and aroused, but not angry."

"Thank you." How unlike David you are! He would have thrown a fit if he'd wanted sex and I'd refused—which she'd wanted to do many times!

After Christopher left for town the next morning, Kirstin changed the sheets on both beds and washed the linens. While they were drying, she made his bed, then hers. She reflected on their lovemaking last night. Breath-stealing and rapturous as always.

Suddenly the phone rang. It was Joe Bob at the Nissan dealership in Clovis; he had called to say her car was ready whenever she wanted to get it.

Kirstin hung up the receiver and frowned. She was doing fine with her medical condition. Her car was repaired. Did she have a logical reason to stay at the ranch longer? She fretted over that question during lunch. Before returning to her household chores, she put on a roast with vegetables to cook for dinner.

Several hours passed in steady labor and distracting thought. Kirstin began her final cleaning project at three-thirty, unaware something terrible was about to happen.

Ten

Kirstin dusted items on the built-in bookcase unit in the den. It made her feel warm and serene to do simple tasks for Christopher and to be a part of his life, if only for a while. She wished the house and furnishings reflected his tastes more than its past owner's, because she wanted to know and understand him better. She assumed these familiar surroundings had been soothing to Christopher after he fled his other world, so he hadn't redecorated. Apparently he felt comfortable and protected in the old-fashioned but cozy setting. Would he object to any colorful and modernizing changes if she ever came to live—"What's this?" she muttered to herself and frowned.

Kirstin stared at an engraved plate on the back of an eight-inch-high pewter—trimmed in 24K gold no less!—statue of a physician: "I'll never forget last night . . ." The signature showed it was from Carla Thompson—that hateful woman who called last week—and was dated March eighteenth, less than a month ago! Hadn't Christopher told her or implied that he hadn't been with a woman in *months?* What was so special about that "night" that she'd rewarded him for it with a suggestive reminder? Had they slept together? Many times? Used safe sex as Christopher had vowed was his practice?

Yet, there could be an innocent meaning behind those alarming words. She shouldn't jump to wild conclusions until Christopher gave an explanation. But if nothing special happened, why keep the memento and why had Carla been so angry to find another woman with him? She was sure she would glean some enlightening clues when she saw them together at the barbecue.

In vexation, Kirstin leaned too far to the left to replace the disturbing statue; her head spun like a toy top, her vision blurred, and she lost her balance. Her fingers grabbed a shelf to prevent a fall but failed to get a grip. The stool teetered and flipped to its side, tossing Kirstin off its worn leather seat. Her hands tried to lessen the force of contact with the floor. She screamed as she crashed downward. Her right wrist took the brunt of her weight; pains shot up her forearm; two fingernails snapped off near the quick and bled.

Christopher dropped an armful of packages on the kitchen floor and came running to her side. He dropped to his knees. "Kirstin, are you all right? What on earth were you doing up there?"

She moaned and grabbed her left ankle. "Damn!" she squealed as she released it to cradle her wrist. She couldn't decide which hurt the most, or if she should tell Christopher about her other problem. Before lunch, she had skipped her glucose monitoring. She had begun the procedure, but the meter had flashed the insufficient sample message: "NOT ENOUGH BLOOD. RETEST." On the second try, the meter had warned: "ERROR 1. RETEST." On the third attempt, it had said: "CLEAN TEST AREA." Each time required a new prick for fresh, first-drawn blood and she couldn't bring herself to stick a fourth finger as all were sore from the numerous daily checks Christopher demanded. The extra exertions with housework had devoured the glucose in her bloodstream and she hadn't replaced the spent fuel in an adequate amount to prevent hypoglycemia. If she admitted her oversight, it would evoke another lecture, which she didn't need in her anguish.

"Let me check that hand."

"Ouch!" she screamed as his fingers tested for trouble.

"Sorry," he murmured. "I don't think it's broken, just sprained."

"My ankle," she shrieked as he pulled her to a standing position. With haste, she took her weight from that leg and swayed against him.

He dropped back to his knees and she braced herself with hands atop his shoulders. Through a series of finger probings, questions, and responses, he concluded the ankle wasn't broken either, to his relief. "It's tender and swelling. What the hell happened?" he snapped.

With reluctance, Kirstin related what she'd been doing. "I'm not an invalid. I was working slowly and carefully. I slipped."

He scowled and motioned to her throbbing ankle and wrist as he asked, "This is a result of being careful? How many times do I have to tell you, woman, you can't take risks?"

"I can't live in a vacuum, Christopher. I have things to do."

He made sure he softened his tone. "I can handle any necessary household chores. Just tell me what needs doing."

"I have to learn to take care of myself; I'll be alone soon."

"But while you're recuperating, let me do everything. Please. This is your second fall in a week. I don't want you getting hurt again. Broken bones or a cracked skull aren't any fun. Damnation, woman, you could have struck your head on the bookcase and been killed."

"Don't be such a worrywart; accidents happen."

"Too often," he muttered. "I'm taking you to the hospital." Dreading to lose her from any complications, he carried her to the car.

Kirstin protested, "This isn't necessary. Just get some ice bags and elastic bandages. We can—"

"With my bum hand I can't wrap them correctly. We have to halt the swelling and prevent further injury. Besides, we need x-rays, too."

She was rigid with discomfort and tension. Her face was pale and her expression was tight. "You win," she responded in a strained voice.

He caressed her cheek. "It isn't a contest of who's right or wrong or the strongest willed, Kirstin. This precaution is for your benefit."

"I know. It's just that I'm being so much trouble."

"Would it be selfish and impolite to say I like this kind of trouble? Any help with keeping you around longer is appreciated."

Was he jesting, she wondered, or did he believe this was a trick? "I wasn't trying to create another reason to hold me here."

"I'll be damned," he quipped with a mischievous grin and twinkling eyes. "I'm not worth a little pain and feminine wiles?"

Kirstin couldn't help but laugh. "Well, this does give me a good excuse to hang around without risking gossip; now your neighbors can see an excellent explanation for my continued presence here. Joe Bob called while you were out to say my car is ready. It's a shame I can't drive with an injured hand and foot. Despite the temptation, it really was an accident."

He grinned. "I know. You need anything before we leave?"

"A sugar fix; I'm feeling a little low and light-headed. That's normal."

He didn't retort that stress usually raised glucose levels, as he was certain she knew that fact. He suspected a low had caused or contributed to her fall. Eventually she would accept and follow the rules. He didn't want to fuss at her now. "I'll put you in the car, then get it for you. You can snack on the way to Clovis. Anything else you'll need?"

"My purse." After he nodded, she relaxed in his strong arms.

Kirstin settled on the sofa with her left foot propped on an ottoman. "It's feeling better. You're certainly living up to your promise of being a personal physician," she teased to coax Christopher from his moody state. The hospital x-rays and treatment had proven his diagnosis of simple sprains and his suggestions of bindings and rest to be accurate. Yet, the incident had called attention to his tormenting inability to handle what he must consider a simple medical procedure. His pride as a man and physician were stung. "I promise, no more recklessness and accidents, even to earn TLC."

"I'll hold you to that vow, woman. Some vacation, isn't it?"

"The best I've ever had."

"Is the pain bad?"

"Not if I baby them." The staff doctor didn't want her to take any medication unless it was necessary because she was diabetic. "How about dinner? My tummy says it's past time. Your surprise is ready by now."

"You're a relentless slave driver. Coming right up. I smelled my treat when we walked in the door, and my mouth's watering to sample it."

"If you need any help, I have those crutches you insisted on getting. But in this sorry condition, it looks as if I'll have trouble repaying you properly for services rendered as we agreed."

"You heard the doctor's orders: rest those injuries as much as possible for a few days. I'll watch them closely and decide when you can return to duty. No hurry to be up and around too soon," he murmured.

Kirstin cherished the beguiling and heart-tugging grin he sent her. "You aren't tired of playing nursemaid yet?"

"Nope. It's a nice habit I'll hate to break."

After they ate and he cleaned the kitchen, they returned to the sofa. Christopher placed his arm around her shoulders and drew her to him. She half turned to nestle her head against his chest, her hand lying across his muscled thigh. She sighed in dreamy contentment, then she closed her eyes and allowed her body to go lax in his embrace. It felt wonderful to sit cuddled together.

On the CD player, Kenny Rogers crooned the words to a stirring love song. Christopher wriggled down on the sofa, lay his head back, and closed his eyes. His hand caressed her arm, then her thigh. She was soft and firm, and she fit perfectly in his arms and lonely life. His other hand played in her silky tresses, admiring the texture and vitality. He cocked his head to look at her. She was beautiful and desirable. If only she would accept him, they could share a wonderful life here. He wanted to beg her to stay forever but that had to be her decision. He had to be patient.

Kirstin lifted her head. Her bright sapphire gaze fused with his sparkling emerald one. His hand left her thigh to trace over her cheeks and parted lips; the action made her quiver.

His finger trailed over her nose, around her eyes, and poised on her chin. His hand was like an explorer, branding each area it discovered as his property. Even if she possessed the will to break his visual hold over her, she didn't want to. She was lost in his eyes. Her hand drifted up to stroke his chest. She eased her fingers between his shirt buttons to make contact with his warm flesh; they toyed with the curly hair there as they traveled in tiny circles. She was aware of the heavy thudding of his heart and that of her own. Her fingertips made contact with his nipples and a guttural moan escaped his throat. He was just as stimulated and intoxicated as she was, which thrilled her to the core. "Are you going to kiss me or not?" she murmured. She didn't wait for him to respond before reaching up to bring his lips down to hers.

Kirstin had never felt freer or more confident to behave as she pleased. This man was what she wanted and needed tonight. She would accept and take whatever he was willing to give, and for as long as he was willing to share anything with her. She felt comfortable and safe with him, desirable and special, feminine and powerful, happy and alive again; no, for the first time. She feasted on his lips and kisses. When his hand slipped beneath her top and inside her bra to fondle her breasts, she

303

didn't protest. She wanted to murmur *yes* a thousand times.

Kirstin was delighted her bra unfastened in the front, and he managed to free her straining breasts with ease and quickness. She sighed and moaned in beckoning bliss as his fingers, lips, teeth, and tongue went to heady work on the two rosy-brown points. She had the wild urge to yank off the remainder of her clothes and shout for him to take her, any time and any way he desired. She was breathless with sensuous anticipation as his skilled hand made its way past the elasticized waist of her sweat pants. Her heat and arousal heightened as his fingers slid lower to reach and tantalize the pulsing peak between her thighs. With eyes closed and pleasures abounding, she thrashed her head on the back of the couch, squirmed in ecstasy, and surrendered her all to him.

Kirstin felt steamier than boiling water. She bravely suggested, "Let's get undressed. I want to feel you against me. Inside me, Christopher."

He hated to pull his mouth from her chest and his hand from between her thighs for even a second, but her entreaty was too irresistible to refuse. He came up on one knee to pull the top over her head. His shaky fingers removed her bra, then her pants and panties. His greedy eyes savored her naked body as he stripped with speed and tossed his garments on the floor along with hers. His heart lurched in joy when she reached for him. He settled his blazing frame over hers and pressed her body into the cushiony sofa. He yearned to make unhurried love to her, but they were too aroused to postpone full contact of hard flesh within soft flesh. After a minute or two of thrusting and deep kissing, he halted and took several ragged breaths. Careful not to pull her hair, he propped his elbows on either side of her head, gazed down at her, and murmured, "Kirstin, you have me hot enough to explode. Damn but you're too tempting for me to stay in control. You make me feel like a green teenager who hasn't learned to control himself. Lordy, I want to love you like crazy. When I look at you, I almost go wild."

She encouraged, "Go wild and crazy, Christopher, you have me burning up, too." Her injuries forgotten, she greedily sampled his talents. She propped her left foot atop the sofa back and rested the other on the floor, open fully to him. "Get busy, Doc; I want more of you."

He fastened his mouth to hers and obeyed her last order.

How, Kirstin pondered afterward when she lay cradled in his arms, had this man remained single for so long? He was handsome, virile, fun, charming, intelligent, hard-working, dependable, and self-assured. Her admiration and intrigue were exposed in her smoldering eyes.

"What are you thinking about?" he asked, stormed by curiosity.

"You. I was just mentally listing your good qualities."

A look of skeptical surprise flashed over his face. "Do I have any?"

"Too many."

"I didn't know that was possible. What about bad ones? Lots of 'em."

"I haven't noticed, but . . . You seemed so cool when I arrived."

"Was I?"

"Stop grinning. You know you were, Christopher Harrison."

"For the life of me, Kirstin, I can't imagine why. Unless . . ." He leaned over and stole a hasty kiss.

"Unless what?" she prompted as she traced a finger over his thick brows, sun-kissed nose, and cleft chin.

"Unless I instantly recognized you for the dangerous temptation you are. It's hard for a doctor these days, woman. A ravishing female trapped alone with me? I could forget my ethics and seduce a helpless victim. Then I'd find myself sued for conduct unbecoming a doctor. Maybe I should get a nurse to protect my reputation and prevent malpractice suits."

She knew he was jesting, and his mood was contagious. "Not a soul around to protect me from a lecherous and determined sex fiend. What's it worth for me not to press charges against you, Doc?"

"Let's see . . . I could forget the debt against you for medical treatment, room and board, and . . . entertainment."

"A bribe, Doctor Harrison?"

"Blackmail, Mrs. Lowrey."

Their gazes fused; they burst into laughter. "A deal?"

She sent him a provocative smile and echoed, "A deal."

"What should I list under entertainment?"

His husky tone aroused her. "You," she replied, laughing at the glimmer of astonishment in his eyes.

"You liberated women certainly don't beat around the bush. When you want something, you speak right up."

"You have only yourself to blame, Doctor Harrison. It has nothing to do with independence or liberation. Since I'm on vacation and time is short, I can't be coy or conservative. As you said, we're consenting adults and we have no commitments to other people. If it's wrong for me to desire you, then it's just as wrong for you to feel and act the same way. Right?"

"You don't have to lecture me on women's

rights, Kirstin. I fully agree with you. I was just surprised to hear you voice such feelings aloud. It's my guess you're normally modest and reserved, always the perfect lady."

"You're most perceptive, Doc. I don't know why, but I never feel that way around you." She laughed. "I can't believe it's actually me, here naked beneath a near stranger and making love on his sofa in daylight when anyone could drop in. I think I'm as stunned as you are."

"I feel as if we've known each other for a long time. We're very compatible. You're easy and fun to be with, Kirstin. I'm going to miss you."

Stabs of loneliness pierced her. "I'm going to miss you, too. Think we can get together in the future? Is that being presumptuous?"

"Not in the least. How about, as often as we can pull it off? How many days do you get each month?"

"Only weekends and holidays. I'm having my vacation now. I couldn't ask for more time off from a new job and boss."

"That'll do, for starters. How are you set for traveling expenses?" he asked.

"What?"

"M-o-n-e-y," he spelled it out. "You want me to come to San Diego, or do you want to come here, or should we meet somewhere in between?" he specified his thoughts. "I have plenty of money, but I wasn't sure if you could afford to see me as often as I would like to see you."

"Whatever you decide. I make a good salary and I'm not a spendthrift."

"Then a little of each?"

"Terrific. Just let me know when and where and we'll work out the details by phone."

"You can bet on that, Kirstin."

I will.

Later that night, Christopher was awakened to Kirstin's tossing and turning. "You're mighty restless. Any pain?"

"Sorry, Christopher, just uncomfortable. The bindings are snug."

"Let me get you something to help you sleep. I know what's safe for someone in your condition. What about it? Just tonight while the discomfort is at its worst. It'll be better tomorrow."

Assuming she was disturbing his own sleep, she agreed. Christopher brought her a mild sedative and some water. Kirstin swallowed the tablet, then he drew her into his arms and held her tenderly until both were fast asleep.

* * *

The next day, the foreman stopped by the house to leave a package for his boss while Christopher was away seeing a patient.

"Chris told me 'bout yore new accident. Sorry to hear yore having such a run of bad luck; it always seems to come in bunches. If you need anything while he's gone, just leave a message on my answering machine. I check it a few times a day."

She liked the nice and friendly man. "Thank you, Mr. Graham; that's very kind. You really enjoy this ranch, don't you?"

He twirled the right edge of a thick brown mustache that was tinged with gray. "I love it, and call me Frank. I've told Chris a thousand times, if he ever wants to sell it, he has a deal with me. I've been here a long time, know every inch of her like the back of my hand."

Kirstin saw the twinkle in his eyes and glow on his sun-darkened face that attested to his feelings. "Christopher told me you have five children and lots of grandchildren. I'm looking forward to meeting your wife. He's told me many good things about you two. When's she due home?"

"Chris told her there weren't any hurry, that he's doing fine, so she's coming back May fourth. I guess he told you she's helping our daughter with the new baby. A long visit will do 'em both good. 'Course, I miss her."

Kirstin felt a little embarrassed that Christopher had requested time alone with her until the date she was due to report for work in San Diego. Yet, if Frank thought she was terrible for living like this with a near stranger, it didn't show. "As soon as this wrist and ankle heal, I'll be able to drive. My car's repaired, but I can't manage the gears and clutch like this." She saw him look over her bound injuries and crutches for support.

"I know what you mean. Hurt my hand once and it gave me fits. I'm glad Chris has you for company. I've never seen him so relaxed and happy. Thanks, Kirstin. He's a good man and deserves a good life." When she blushed, he smiled and said, "I best git back to work. Got lots of chores to do. Just sing out if you need anything."

"Thanks. See you later."

You sly devil, Christopher Harrison, talking about me to others and making sure we have privacy. You must be enjoying me as much as I'm enjoying you. But do I fill more than physical needs?

Kirstin decided to test him later that day. She told him about part of her chat with the foreman. "Frank really loves this ranch. I can't blame him; it's beautiful and prosperous. Have you ever considered selling it and moving

311

somewhere to practice medicine? Perhaps teach?" She kept silent and attentive as he took a deep breath before responding.

"I gave teaching a try; I hated it. It was like being an alcoholic with an unreachable bottle in sight. When I was stuffed with my students' and colleagues' sympathy and pity, I came here to avoid them. I suppose I'm lucky, all things considered; I'm still in medicine and I have a good life."

"You're very bitter, aren't you?"

"Hell, Kirstin! That's only natural. I had a brilliant career and future in surgery. It was my food and air. Damn, it was like cutting out my heart to leave it! I've tried settling for second best, teaching or research; it isn't enough. End of confession and topic, all right?"

Kirstin knew pity or sympathy from her was the wrong emotion to show. She responded simply, "You seem to be doing great here."

"I suppose so," he moodily agreed and left to take a cold shower.

When they made love that night, Kirstin realized he was still brooding. She hoped it wasn't his way of emphasizing the point that she wasn't to discuss his troubles again. How could he get rid of them—and of his resentment—if he refused to deal with them? He was always telling her to accept her condition and make the best of it. Well, he should take a little of his own advice! Until he did, she couldn't consider becoming a part of his sullen and secluded existence. She'd endured enough misery with David not to put herself in a similar position again. *We'd make a marvelous team. We could tackle diabetes research. We could be good for each other, be happy. First, physician, heal thyself.*

The following evening after his chores, Christopher rushed to the house from his office to tell her, "I've got to go to the Carlisles'. There's trouble. You want to stay here or come along?"

Before she could respond, he picked up the receiver and called Jenny Carlisle who was in premature labor with her first child. Thankfully, the message had just come in on his recorder. He talked to Bob for a few minutes, asking questions and giving orders. He grabbed his medical bag and turned to Kirstin.

"Will they mind if I come?" she questioned in uncertainty.

"We're ten minutes away and the ambulance is thirty, after it returns from another call. The other one is having mechanical problems. With this bum hand, I may need help over there, and Bob's in a panic. Coming?"

"Yes." She retrieved her purse and followed him. She moved as fast as she could on the crutches. She was tempted to cast them aside but she couldn't because putting her weight on the sprained ankle hurt too much.

He sped over winding dirt roads with Kirstin stiff in her seat, belted for safety. When they arrived at the small, wood-framed house, Bob rushed out to meet them. He was terrified; the baby was coming out! Kirstin hobbled behind the two men.

Christopher held the door open for her. "I wasn't kidding, Kirstin; I may need your assistance."

Christopher surged forward to follow Bob Carlisle into the bedroom, where Jenny was twisting and turning in anguish and fear, her eyes wide in anxiety and her face dampened by it. Kirstin halted just inside the door. This delivery was a first for her, as she hadn't had her babies by natural childbirth, nor had Sandi. She knew what happened but had not experienced it firsthand. Surely an ambulance was on the way by now!

There had been many times during animal surgery when the dedicated, skilled technician's hands had been covered with bright red blood. Why, she fretted, should the sight of *human* blood be any different? For heaven's sake, she had once planned to become a surgeon! During tricky experiments, she had proved herself capable and resourceful when things seemed to be going awry. She was well versed in anatomy and first aid. All three people in the room needed her help, so why was she stalling?

Kirstin tossed her purse onto a chair and made her way into the room. Christopher was working frantically to calm both Jenny and Bob. Kirstin took the initiative, and tugged at Bob's arm. When he turned to her, she empathized with the look of alarm on his face.

"Listen to me carefully, Bob," she began, inserting firmness and calmness into her voice, hoping it concealed her own panic. "We'll need a bucket of hot water, some towels, and some coffee. You go and get them while I assist Doctor Harrison."

When Christopher glanced up at her, she winked at him and smiled conspiratorially. He grinned in understanding and returned to his examination. Bob left the room in a hurry to obey her. Kirstin maneuvered herself next to the bed. "What can I do to help?" she questioned, almost afraid to look down at the writhing young woman.

Christopher flashed her a quick smile of encouragement and appreciation. "You're doing it now. Thanks."

Jenny was in too much discomfort to be embarrassed by her half-nude body or her splayed position. Kirstin was shocked when she glanced down and saw a tiny dark head peeking through. Kirstin helped Christopher ease two folded sheets beneath the lower half of the expectant mother's body to protect the bed. "Put on surgical gloves, Kirstin. In my bag. We can't risk infection," he ordered in a voice tight with concentration.

Kirstin obeyed, then held Jenny's hand and spoke soothing words while Christopher called the hospital to update them on the emergency. He was told the ambulance should arrive within twenty minutes, thirty at the most. Christopher informed them it was a premature birth and some precautions would be mandatory to safeguard the baby. He told them the infant was delivering at present, and prayed he was capable of preventing any injuries and of saving both lives if things worsened.

It was too late to give Jenny anything for the pain or to relax her. In a gentle tone, Christopher coaxed her along with instructions. Minutes seemed like hours as the difficult labor continued. Though the baby was small, Jenny required an incision to assist its birth. Christopher gave her a local anesthetic and performed an episiotomy with a shaky right hand, cursing the loss of use of his left one. He was relieved and overjoyed he did the procedure without error.

At last, the baby's head was in full view. Jenny squeezed Kirstin's hands when the shoulders made their way out next. Kirstin spoke in a soft but firm voice to the patient. She stressed Christopher's instructions, encouraging Jenny to do as he ordered as the wonder of bringing a new life into the world seized her. She was warmed by his bedside manner and proud of Christopher's skills, which weren't as lacking as he seemed to believe. No doctor, she concluded, could be doing a better job. Kirstin's ears rang when Jenny sent forth one last scream as the rest of the baby's body seemingly surged out of her fatigued body.

Jenny collapsed against the bed, her sweaty hands releasing Kirstin's aching ones. Kirstin's injured wrist throbbed, but she didn't complain. Christopher cleared the baby boy's nose and mouth, then smacked his rump to compel him to inhale rapidly to fill his lungs with air. The baby loudly complied, but his breathing wasn't normal. Kirstin wrapped the infant in a clean blanket. As Christopher waited for the cord and afterbirth to be delivered, Kirstin knew something was wrong with the tiny infant. She didn't say anything aloud, fearing to panic the new parents.

Jenny was being comforted by her relieved husband at that moment, her hands held between his. Kirstin inched toward Christopher and nudged his arm. He glanced up from his work, his expression inquisitive. She nodded to the baby she was holding against her breasts, inhaling suggestively to alert him to her discovery.

He caught her implication and took a look at the baby who was now struggling to breathe. A worried frown creased his brow. "Do you know mouth-to-mouth resuscitation?" he asked, his voice low and guarded.

She nodded, but looked uncertain.

"Cover the entire nose and mouth. Four times a minute. Not too much or too hard," he cautioned. "I'll take over as soon as I finish here."

Kirstin lay the endangered infant on the dresser and began to assist the baby's battle for air and life. Christopher explained to Jenny and Bob that the child was small and premature, that it needed help learning to breathe. He made his voice reassuring, as if this was normal in such cases.

Bob came over to watch her and to see his firstborn son. He realized something wasn't normal. "What's wrong?" he demanded of Kirstin.

She glared at him in warning, shaking her head and cutting her eyes toward the bed. Bob understood she was trying to keep Jenny calm and in the dark. He watched in mounting alarm as Kirstin labored over his son. He noticed her injured hand and foot and the swelling above and below the elastic bandage on her right wrist and suspected she was in pain herself. He waited quietly, and prayed.

The ambulance arrived. Bob rushed outside to show them the way. Two paramedics entered the room, one taking Kirstin's place with the baby. The other assisted Christopher as he completed his work. A small oxygen mask was secured over the infant's nose and mouth. Jenny and the baby were loaded onto stretchers and transported to the ambulance.

The paramedics were well trained, so there was no need for Christopher to go along with them. However, Bob was in no condition to drive and would need a way home later. Christopher asked Kirstin if she minded waiting there for him while he drove the new father to the hospital in Bob's car. "I'll get John to meet us there and bring me back here for you and my Jeep."

Knowing she couldn't drive his Wagoneer since it had dual foot pedals, she agreed. The ambulance pulled out of the driveway with Bob and Christopher behind it. Kirstin collapsed wearily into a nearby chair. She hadn't mentioned her aching wrist to Christopher, but pains were shooting up her forearm. Maybe she should have gone along and had it checked; but she didn't want to upset Jenny or worry Christopher, or get in the way during the hectic journey and check-in at the Clovis hospital. Tears clouded her eyes. She was mentally and physically exhausted.

She fetched a cup of coffee and sat down to relax while she sipped it. To give her wrist and ankle relief, she propped one on an ottoman and the other on the chair arm. At last, the discomfort lessened. It felt odd to be sitting in a strange house, alone.

As time passed at a snail's pace, Kirstin decided to make herself helpful. She went to the bedroom, located clean linens, and changed the bed for Bob. She washed the soiled sheets in cold water to remove the blood. When the laundry was done and the house was neat for the new mother's return, she sat down to sip another cup of coffee and watch television, an old rerun featuring John Wayne.

As she shifted her position, her head whirled and tiny lights filled her vision. She realized she felt weak and clammy, and it was way past eating time. She hadn't thought to bring along her test kit, but she didn't need it to recognize hypoglycemic symptoms. Nor had Christopher thought to remind her of the monitor during his frantic rush. *Food, glucose tablets!* her mind shouted. She grabbed her purse, fumbled for what she needed, and twisted off the top of a liquid glucose tube. She squeezed it into her mouth and got it down quickly. She waited a few minutes for it to take effect, then went to the kitchen where she made a sandwich, poured a glass of milk, took an apple, peeled two carrots, and sat at the table to devour it all. She hated the queasiness and tremors that went along with an attack and prayed for them to be gone soon. As she settled down, she was relieved the cupboards hadn't been bare or she'd have been in big trouble. And Christopher would have blamed himself for her dilemma when he returned and found her out cold.

Kirstin smiled as she realized how well she had handled this one. She hadn't exactly panicked, and she was fine now. Yes, she was getting a grip on her condition. Every day and with each incident, she was learning better control and conquering her fears. She would have this beast tamed before she reached California. Confidence and pride surged through her as she assured herself that the diabetes wouldn't hold her down.

After she finished eating and the kitchen was clean, Kirstin went to the medicine cabinet for some aspirin to ease the discomfort of her injuries. To reduce their swelling, she filled plastic baggies with ice and fetched two towels, which she spread on the chair arm and the ottoman.

She placed her ankle on one towel, positioned ice bags on either side of it, and encircled her foot with the cloth to prevent dripping water on the furniture and floor. She did the same with her wrist. She leaned back and waited for relief. In the middle of the late movie, she fell asleep.

"Kirstin?" Christopher's voice and gentle nudging pulled her from her dreams. "Kirstin, it's time to go home."

Her lids fluttered and opened. Groggy, she rubbed her eyes and yawned. The television was off. Bob stood nearby, waiting to thank her for her help, which he did. Christopher sat on the edge of the couch near her. "I thought John was bringing you after me and the car. What happened?"

"It wasn't necessary; the doctors sent Bob home. Jenny and the baby are fine." He unwrapped the towel, checked her wrist, then her ankle. He eyed her with an added respect and increased affection. In the beginning, he had irrationally resented her strength and talents. Now, he didn't begrudge them in the least. He smiled in satisfaction. "I'm proud of you, Kirstin, and grateful. I couldn't have managed alone tonight. You constantly amaze me, woman," he admitted, even though Bob was standing there listening.

Kirstin was aware of the other man. "You said they're fine?"

"In excellent condition and hands. The baby's a shave over five pounds. How're the sprains?" He guessed they must be hurting like hell, or had been.

"Better. I used some aspirin and ate a snack, Bob; I hope you don't mind. Does he have a name yet?"

Bob grinned from ear to ear. "Christopher Lowery Carlisle. Jenny and I thought Kirstin sounded too girlish. She asked me to thank you for what you did for us tonight. I was too scared to be any help. I was out of my wits when I called the doc and he didn't answer. Sorry about your hand. I know Jenny must have squeezed it something fierce."

Kirstin was touched by his concern and her eyes filled with tears. "I hope you didn't tell her. It's fine now," she alleged as she flexed her fingers to prove her false claim. "We'd better get going, Christopher, so Bob can get some rest; he'll need it soon."

The three chatted while Kirstin and Christopher prepared to depart. Bob noticed the chores Kirstin had done and thanked her for being so helpful.

On the drive home, Kirstin rested her head against the car seat. She didn't mention the baby's name, which locked both of theirs together for the child's lifetime. She thought about Christopher; he was such a complex man. Each day, she discovered more about him. So many men were resentful of successful, intelligent women. It was wonderful to have the freedom to be herself. He appeared to accept her as she was, which was rare these turbulent days when females were making their skills and ambitions known loudly, to many men's dismay. What a delightful situa—

"Sleepy?" He thrust himself into her thoughtful silence.

"Yes, but pleasantly so. That was some experience, Doc." The lights from the dashboard and the moon mingled to outline certain angles of his handsome face, while shadows concealed other pleasing contours.

"You were scared, weren't you?" he asked.

"At first. Weren't you, the first time you worked on a human patient?"

"Terrified," he admitted with an amused chuckle. "Frankly, I was tonight, too. If you hadn't been there, Kirstin, one of them might not have made it. I'm really grateful to you." *We made a good team tonight. If only I could lure you into staying here as my assistant.*

She studied him for a time, suspecting the confession was difficult, but from the heart. *We work well together. What a team we'd make in the lab*

if you'd just give up the ranch and come with me . . .
"You're a great doctor, Christopher. These people are fortunate to have you around."

"Flattery so early in the morning?" he murmured.

"No flattery intended, Doctor Harrison. Do you have many emergencies like that?"

"Very few. Mostly just routine check-ups, sickness, and minor accidents. Only once in a blue moon do I require help." *Damnation, Chris, you're supposed to convince her you need her! But don't point out your blunder by trying to explain it.*

"Lucky for you I was around when your 'blue moon' rose tonight."

He chuckled. "Conceited little snip, aren't you?"

She laughed. "Yep, it's one of my bad habits. I'll have to work on it. Criticism noted and applied."

"I wasn't criticizing you, Kirstin. Just kidding."

"I know. I guess I'm feeling a little heady with pride right now. I really didn't think I could help much. Sometimes I surprise even myself."

He threw back his head and laughed. He asked, "How's the blood sugar level?"

"Fine. I ate at Bob's. And I was prepared for emergencies, thank you."

"Smart woman." He pulled into his driveway

and parked the car. He came around, helped her out, and lifted her to carry her inside.

"This isn't necessary; I have my crutches."

"It *is* necessary. I have to remind you constantly that I'm the male and you're the female. Men are expected to be domineering in some situations; this is one."

As they mounted the steps with her arms clasped around his neck, she challenged, "How so, Doctor Harrison?"

He gazed into her face and mischievously warned, "I'm taking you straight to bed, and not to sleep, either, exhaustion and swollen head to boot! Not to mention a swollen wrist and ankle," he added.

"I see," she murmured in a mellow tone. "You intend to make love whether or not I'm willing or in the mood?"

"Are you?"

"Am I what?" she questioned.

"In the mood? Willing?"

"Both, but you could ask me first. This is a fifty-fifty partnership."

He propped her on the porch as he unlocked the door, then held her by the shoulders as he murmured, "Mrs. Lowrey, will you do me the honor of sharing my lonely bed and affections this evening?"

Assuming a heavy southern drawl, she responded, "Why, sir, do these delicate ears deceive me? Are you implying that I should fall into your arms and bed like some brazen hussy? Wherever would you get such an insulting idea? I do believe you have gotten the wrong impression about me. I'm a lady, sir, but you're no gentleman. The door unlocked yet?" she asked in her normal voice. "We're wasting time; it's almost daylight."

Hearty chuckles rumbled in his chest. "You are a fetching tart, Kirstin Lowrey," he accused playfully.

"Then I pray you love sweets, Doc."

"Indeed I do."

He kicked the door shut and locked it with the hand under her knees. "Would you like to join me for a shower first?"

A grin crossed her face. Perhaps this was a night for many new firsts. "Why not?"

"An adventuress after my own heart."

Eleven

"That tickles, Christopher!" Kirstin shrieked, squeezing her arms to her sides as he trailed soapy hands up and down her ribs, her back to him in the shower.

His hands found another target to tantalize. They approved of what they encountered as they moved over her ivory buttocks. He remarked. "You have a cute fanny, Kirstin. Nice legs, too."

"Your rump isn't bad, either," she tossed over a shoulder, grinning.

He leaned forward to gaze over it. "Not a bad looking front, either."

Kirstin turned to face him and eased her lathered hands over his chest. She twirled wisps of sudsy hair around her fingertips. Flattening her palms against the firm and furry chest, she moved them upward to caress his shoulders and to slide with leisure down his powerful arms. The physical labor on the ranch had honed his body into hard, bronzed flesh. It was apparent he often worked without his shirt, since his upper torso was cinnamon-shaded, while his lower half was pale.

Her gaze walked his towering length. His legs were firm and shapely. The hair on his husky chest tapered as it traveled downward to fan out around his navel and manhood. Her admiring gaze had an instant effect upon him there.

Her sparkling eyes came up to fuse with his as his finger beneath her chin lifted it. "You're a tease, woman," he murmured hoarsely.

"A tease doesn't deliver, Doc," Kirstin corrected him.

Christopher drew a ragged breath, then grinned. His hands reached out to play in the bubbles on her breasts. With stimulating slowness, he passed his hands over her shoulders, down her arms, and grasped her hands. He lifted them to wash each one at a sensuous pace, slipping his forefinger between each of her fingers, then drawing soapy circles in her palms. His hands touched beneath her arms, then made their way down her sides, over her hips, and around her buttocks, to grasp them and pull her body forward, crushing it against his.

Christopher's head bent forward to sear his

lips over hers. Her arms went around his neck, to hold his mouth to hers as he explored it. He nibbled along her neck toward its hollow, jerking backward and spitting out soapsuds. As Kirstin laughed, he turned to the water to rinse his mouth and face of the white lather.

"Damn, I thought you tasted better than that," he jested, her laughter spilling forth in unleashed amusement to fuse with his chuckles.

Christopher twisted to rinse soap from his body, then maneuvered her under the gushing flow to do the same. He stepped out on the mat and towel dried himself.

When she left the shower, Christopher began to dry her off, too. Kirstin reached for the towel. "I can do that myself."

"I prefer to do it," he protested, holding the cloth behind him.

Seeing he was not to be dissuaded, she held out her arms and commanded, "Then get busy, my dashing slave."

He squinted his eyes and creased his forehead as he rubbed his upper lip with the side of his forefinger. "Maybe I should let you drip dry."

Kirstin reached forward to fondle his manhood, flashing him a smug smile. "I don't think you have the time, Doc. Someone's talking loudly and strongly about going to bed."

He dried her off in haste. "Sit," he ordered, pointing to the toilet seat. "Let's get that foot and hand unwrapped and checked now."

After the protective baggies were removed, he lifted her naked body and carried her to his bed. Kirstin wondered why he wanted to sleep in his room tonight, but didn't ask him to explain. He dropped her on the bed and hopped in beside her. "Eager, are we?" she challenged.

"Starved," he admitted.

"Shall I fix you something to eat?" she purred.

"I can think of a much better way to sate this lusty appetite," he declared, rolling over on her and assailing her neck with countless kisses. He halted a moment to ask, "You need a snack before we get engrossed?"

"Nope. I ate at the Carlisles'. Continue, please."

"Um-um-um, you feel good," he murmured, caressing all the places his hands touched and letting his lips trail close behind them.

He didn't seem in a hurry to take her. He was like an explorer—seeking, mapping, documenting, and collecting rare treasures.

Kirstin's fingers were just as inquisitive, roaming freely over his sturdy physique. It was strange how his toughened hands could fondle her so gently to such ecstasy. When his teeth nipped at her breasts, it was as if tiny surges of electricity sparked through her body. She was alive with feeling, her nerves sensitive to his every touch. She thrilled to the blissful sensation of their naked bodies pressed together. Her smooth legs eased over his; the coarse hair tickled. The stubble on his jaw and chin excited her as the rancher brushed it over her taut nipples.

As he devoured her breasts ravenously, she placed feathery kisses on his head and her fingers wandered through hair the color of coal in the dazzling sunlight. He had a way of making her feel intensely aware of being a woman, a desirable woman. He brought to life sensations and feelings she had never questioned or known before.

Kirstin knew she would never be the same after knowing him. At this moment, she was willing to sacrifice all just to have him for herself, but knew that would be reckless and impulsive. She tried to shut out such upsetting thoughts. She refused to think about her work or ambitions, even her family, particularly her son. Her life was in San Diego and his was here. Besides, he hadn't mentioned love or permanence, only desire and affection, and only for a few weeks.

Christopher couldn't seem to touch Kirstin

enough. Each time his greedy hands and lips left one delicious delicacy, they came away starving for more. Her body was sleek and supple, her skin flawless and silky, her mood as sultry as an August day. He thought he knew every inch and taste of it by now, but he constantly found a new feeling or flavor as his hands and mouth roved over her time and time again. Pleasure flooded him as his hands caressed her vital, warm skin. She seemed aroused by his every touch. No woman had ever responded with such feverish and honest abandonment as Kirstin did.

Her responses encouraged him to continue his heady and stimulating assault upon her luscious body. He delayed entering her as long as possible, knowing how quickly their mutual desires would take over and demand release from this heavenly hell they were enduring. But his manhood was aching to feel her haven surrounding it. She was driving him mad the way she was slowly and lovingly stroking him. Soon he was unable to wait any longer and he entered her with a groan of delight.

Kirstin arched to match his rhythm, straining to feel every inch of him. His lips plundered hers. He drove with purpose as she writhed and moaned in rapture. He wished he was spilling forth into her body to mingle his release with hers. That one remaining pleasure would come true soon, he hoped. But she'd need to get on the pill.

Afterward, he was breathing hard and heavy from his exertions as he held her close. She sighed in contentment and nestled to him, bringing a smile to his face. He rolled to his back and placed one hand beneath his head. Kirstin curled against his side, lay hers on his shoulder, and rested a leg over his thigh. His arm eased around her. "You know something weird, Kirstin?" he asked through the darkness surrounding them. "I've known lots of women, but none like you. You demand a great deal, but you give more than any other female I've known. The way you sate a man only makes him greedy for more. I can't take enough of you, I can't touch you enough. Does that sound crazy?"

"Not at all, and thank you very much. Of course, I don't have your countless experiences for making comparisons, but I would bet you're the best lover and teacher available. I can't imagine any man being better at this than you are. One thing I've learned with you, amongst lots of others, sex and lovemaking aren't the same thing. You don't 'have sex,' Christopher; you 'make *love.*' *Everything* is good and different and exciting with you. After I reach San Diego and start work there, I'll be looking forward to weekends and holidays. My heavens, listen to me. Kirstin Lowrey planning secret rendezvous."

Christopher urged himself to be cautious. It was too soon to make demands on her about giving up her career to move here. Would she if he asked her? Would she turn and walk away from her life in San Diego to marry him, a country doctor living in the middle of nowhere? He was afraid to find out. Now that he had found a woman who was perfect for him, what would he do if she didn't feel the same? If he spoke too soon, she might panic and leave. She hadn't even hinted at love or wanting a prolonged relationship. *Let her go to California and fulfill any feelings of responsibility and loyalty to Medico and herself. Let her miss you and see what a wonderful life she could have here with you. Once she's there and craving you, confess your love and propose; by then, maybe she'll be ready and eager to take a chance with you. But before she leaves, show her what you have to offer in exchange for her challenging life. Show her the good things about this area and these people. Let her see how much fun it is to work together. Captivate her subconscious; then, let it work on her conscious mind after her departure.*

By five o'clock in the morning, they were asleep in each other's arms, each plotting how to win the other without revealing too much too soon, and without giving up what each

335

presently possessed.

When Kirstin finally awoke, it was almost noon. The house was quiet, and Christopher was gone. Lying on his pillow was a glucose tube for a quick fix if necessary. Her gaze roamed his tidy bedroom. He'd put away their rumpled clothing and straightened up as she slept. She smiled as she approved of his cleanliness and thoughtfulness. After years of picking up after David, it was wonderful to meet a man who not only did his share of chores but sometimes did hers. Christopher often went out of his way to do extra things to help her or please her, and even seemed to enjoy doing them. But would he and his behavior alter later? Would he take her for granted, forget she was a woman and attempt to make her his shadow? Men could be so kind and generous, during the wooing stage, then become old-fashioned husbands as soon as the vows were exchanged.

Kirstin went into the guest room to shower and scrub her tawny hair. She dried off and removed the baggies that covered her bandages. She checked her wrist and ankle to find both looked better. She gelled and scrunch-curled her hair, using a diffusor and fingers to arrange it as her beautician had instructed.

After she applied the light makeup as the cosmetologist had taught her, she looked into the mirror a final time. *Not bad for a forty-five-year-old. God, woman, you're nearing fifty! Over half of your life is gone. How much time do you have left to fulfill your dreams?*

Kirstin put aside those dreary thoughts and gathered her dirty clothes to wash this afternoon. After breakfast, she made the bed and straightened the house. The crutches were a nuisance, but they kept weight and stress off her ankle. Her laundry and chores completed, she started wondering what was keeping Christopher away so long. It was almost three o'clock. He could have left a note or phoned her by now.

She called Elaine and they chatted a few minutes, her friend teasing her about her exciting situation. For some inexplicable reason, Kirstin didn't tell her about the new injuries or how far the relationship had gone.

Kirstin wondered what the future would bring. She knew she could be happy in San Diego with her daughter nearby. She would be free and independent.

If she married the good doctor, what would her life be like here? What would she do all day? Housework and ranch chores. Christopher had his medical practice and the ranch to occupy him. Did she want to labor by his side in all kinds of weather? What would his patients say if she became his assistant and was underfoot all the time? Cooking and cleaning for hours every day for the rest of her life certainly weren't for her. She would become restless and dissatisfied; she would make both of them miserable. Life wasn't an endless romantic fling. Would Christopher be enough? Was *love* enough to fulfill her, especially now that she had tasted the alternatives? Too, there were their children to consider. And what if he wanted more kids? She was too old for babies and all they entailed. And, when *they* were grown, other duties were added when the grandchildren arrived.

She had been a wife and mother. One whose existence had been a full-time devotion to others' needs and schedules. But what about her needs and desires? If only Christopher lived in San Diego. If only he was still a surgeon in a large city that also contained research facilities. If only he didn't live in the middle of nowhere. Would a man like Christopher love a woman enough to move to a large city? If he did, would he be just as misplaced as she would be here? Was it fair to ask?

Kirstin walked to the sink and gazed out the window over it. There was little to do here, except make love and take care of herself

and Christopher. To shop or eat out would require a lengthy drive into Clovis or Portales or
Roswell. If she surrendered to her strong emotions and pursued Christopher, she could en-
trap herself.

She looked outside. No one was in sight,
not even any animals. The solitude sent pangs
of loneliness into her heart. Could she live like
this? Christopher was almost fifty; he was accustomed to freedom. If she tagged along
every day, he would feel confined. She shook
her head in sadness. There were no easy answers for them. Perhaps in time . . .

Aren't you jumping the gun a bit, Kirstin? she
asked herself. *Here you are thinking about marriage
and sacrifices when he hasn't even mentioned love! Idiot! He's a carefree bachelor, has a bad experience
under his belt. What makes you think he would even
be interested in marrying you?*

Annoyed with herself, she picked up the
crutches and went outside to the swing. She
flopped down and propped the wooden arms
against the seat. Soon she became tense and
bored and left the noisy swing to hobble
around and give the place a twice-over. The
house on the large ranch was a spacious and
lovely one. The yard, with a nice but small
pool, was half landscaped and half natural,
growing wilder as it moved outward. The
other structures were neat. Everything ap-

peared to be in good condition. She was irrationally annoyed by the perfection that surrounded her, as nothing appeared to need a woman's touch. If he'd wanted changes inside the house, he would have made them by now, and he'd probably balk at her wanting to do so.

Her gaze roved the vast deserty terrain. The ranch was secluded, with neighbors at a far distance. How would she make friends? Could she ever feel at home here? To the north, she noted dark clouds lowering themselves on the horizon. A storm was brewing. It was muggy and oppressive; perspiration formed on her face and trickled a path between her breasts. Where was Christopher, she mused again, and what was keeping him? His vehicle was in the driveway and his Appaloosa was standing near the fence. Perhaps Frank had fetched him in the truck to assist with a chore.

Kirstin hobbled to the corral to watch the horses. She decided to check out the barn. There, too, everything was clean and in top shape. Why not? He had plenty of time and energy! What else was there to do? How could he live such a lonely life? He was a doctor, a damn good one. No, an excellent one! He could easily set up a practice anywhere. Why did he hide out here salving his wounds?

Kirstin's fingers trailed over the saddles,

gear, and tools. Their scents assailed her. She smelled hay, leather, polish, sweet feed, horse sweat on their blankets and pads, soil, oil and gas, dust, and a few foreign odors she didn't recognize. Even the aged wood of the barn had its own peculiar fragrance.

She stiffened and jumped as thunder boomed loud and ominous over the barn; the noise lessened as its echoes moved farther and farther away. Another span of rolling thunder rent the still air and even vibrated the enclosure. It was time to return to the house. As she reached the doorway, a torrent of water started. It was as if a flood gate had been opened wide. The violent thunderstorm lashed rain into the opening. Dazzling streaks of lightning danced around the barn; some seemed to strike the earth. With her injured ankle and crutches, she would be sopping wet within two feet. Nor did she want to get zapped by the lightning streaks that were clawing the air. It was best to wait out the storm there.

Kirstin put aside the crutches and shoved the doors together. With the dark clouds and heavy rains outside, the barn was shrouded in dimness. The doors rattled as brisk winds pushed and tugged at them. One flew open before she was a few feet away, allowing rain to pour inside and soak the dirt floor in seconds. She dropped the crutches and closed it, making sure it was secured. Mud attacked and glued itself to the treads of her tennis shoes; she knew it was useless to try to remove it until it dried. The incident reminded her of the many times her children, especially her son, had done the same. *Oh, Steve, how will you feel if I marry again?*

Kirstin couldn't torment herself with what might be. She was missing her snack, so she withdrew two glucose tablets from her pocket and chewed them. She noticed the apples on the grain crib which Christopher intended to feed his horses. She ate one as she sat on the saddle blanket she'd spread on a pile of straw. She rubbed her underarms where the crutches had chafed the flesh. She waited and tried to relax. The interior smells became stronger as dampness sneaked through the cracks. Pungent odors from areas where horses had been stabled soon grew noticeable with the absence of a fresh air flow.

The storm increased its furor. The barn door flew open again. Kirstin heard the noise and gritted her teeth in annoyance. Before she could rise, Christopher slammed it and stalked forward. He halted, standing with his feet apart. His jaw was clenched, his clothes and hair soaked. He mopped the water from his face.

"What the hell are you doing?" he asked.

His face was lined with anger and his body taut with it. "Excuse me?" she murmured, bewildered.

"I've been calling you for hours. I was crazy with worry when you didn't answer the phone. I looked everywhere in the house for you. I was afraid you'd gone riding alone and had been caught in this storm."

"I was walking around and got trapped in here. I was waiting for the rain to let up. I wouldn't borrow a horse without permission. Where have *you* been all day? You could have left me a note."

"I didn't think about it; I'm not used to answering to anyone. I tried to phone lots of times. My errands took longer than I expected. I figured you'd sleep late and I'd probably return before you were awake. Joe Bob came by for me so I picked up your car. I almost got a speeding ticket hurrying home. Damnit, woman, you scared the life out of me!"

"Why? I'm not a baby. I can take care of myself."

"I can see that. Next time, answer the damn phone, will you?"

Did you get my car so I can leave? "Would you please stop yelling and settle down? I told you, I was waiting here until the rain stopped because I didn't want to get drenched. Do you mind?" she asked in a tone as snippy as his.

He sighed and dropped down beside her. "I'm sorry, Kirstin. I should have known you'd be all right. I was just so worried about you. I was afraid you'd had another accident or attack. Do you have your pills with you? Did you eat before you got trapped in here?"

"Yes, to both. I had two tablets at four. See, I have my watch on. I even stole one of your horse's apples. Old, but good." He didn't smile.

"You shouldn't eat anything without washing it first. Germs."

To shut him up, she white-lied. "I held it in the rain."

"You need soap to remove any chemicals and germs."

That time, she told part of the truth. "I washed them before I put them in the fruit basket, remember? That's a habit of mine. It was only a little dusty, and that rinsed off. Drop all the talk about my diet and health, will you?"

Christopher realized she sounded as unsettled as he felt. He had panicked when he couldn't locate her. He should have realized she was too level-headed to go riding alone. And too considerate to go with Frank without leaving a note. He propped his arms on his knees and cupped his jaw. He'd made a mountain out of a molehill, and annoyed her royally in the process!

Kirstin studied his profile. He had been worried, really worried . . . She warmed. "You're drowned, Christopher." She caressed his wet back and toyed with his wet hair. "I'm sorry I panicked you for nothing. You won't have to put up with me much longer. Thanks for getting my car. When this foul weather clears, we'll get you dried off and fed."

He glanced at her and scowled. *Ready to desert me now?* "I'm not a baby, either. Don't go mothering me, woman."

"But you could catch a chill. But then I could doctor you for a change."

Christopher's eyes locked with hers. "You don't need another excuse to hang around, do you?"

She returned his smile. "Do I?"

"Nope. I guess that run-in with Thompson's daughter put me in a foul mood. Sorry. I just wish she'd leave me alone. Carla's a persistent woman when she wants something and she has her sights set on me. I can't seem to get it through her thick skull I'm not interested and never will be. I suppose I should explain to you. I dated her a few times, but I haven't seen her in months. She still calls, sends invitations, and drops by on occasion."

"I noticed the little trinket she gave you."

"What trinket?"

"The doctor's statue in the den. I saw it while I was dusting."

"Oh, that. She had a flat tire once and I was the unfortunate one who happened along to fix it for her. She made a big deal out of it. She left that toy with Helen while I was doing chores one day. I should have returned it or tossed it in the trash, but it's expensive and I'm not rude. I figured she'd get the point when I failed to acknowledge it."

"Did she?"

"You took a call from her. Do you think she's moved to greener pastures?"

"No." *And who can blame her?*

"Let's go inside. We have groceries to put away."

Kirstin noticed the silence and realized the storm had ceased. She reached for her crutches and struggled to get up. Oddly, he didn't pick her up and whisk her inside the house or even assist her. He stood and started walking away. She glared at his back. Taking her for granted already? Or only distracted? At least she knew about Carla now.

He propped the doors aside. He headed for the house, thinking she might resent his assistance after she'd claimed she could take care of herself. She'd also gotten miffed with his reminders about her health. Sometimes that independent streak annoyed and frustrated him. She had broken free of her past and she was liking that freedom too much to suit him.

Kirstin followed him, her own mood suffering. Why did men have to behave so ridiculously when they didn't get their own way or problems arose! Why did they have to resent a woman for being strong and standing on her own two feet?

The sky had cleared to a cobalt shade, leaving almost no trace there had been a violent thunderstorm. Water dripped from the buildings, bushes, and vegetation, absorbed into the thirsty earth. At the porch, Kirstin sat down and removed her shoes to prevent tracking dirt into the house.

Christopher halted to shuck his boots, observing her from the corner of his eye. He opened the screen door and they went inside together. Sacks of groceries were on the table and counter. Kirstin began to unload then: fresh milk, bread, fruit, and vegetables.

"You sit and rest that ankle while I put them away."

She didn't argue. She sipped the sugar-free cola he handed her.

As he worked, Christopher explained his absence. "I looked at some fine horseflesh today and a feisty bull for breeding. If I decide to buy them, I'm to close the deal tomorrow. First, I want Frank to check them over; he knows more about stock than I do." He glanced over his shoulder as he told her, "I had lunch with John; he sent a hello."

"You had a busy day after an exhausting night."

He chatted on. "I did a little banking business, stopped at the hospital to check on two patients, and picked up a few other things I was out of."

"You should have awakened me to write Joe Bob a check for my car."

"I paid him, so don't worry."

"I'll get my purse and write you a check."

"Don't bother, Kirstin. Let it be my treat."

"I can't do that, Christopher. You're already furnishing room and board, medical treatment, and entertainment."

"That women's lib streak is showing again. Have to pay your own way even when you're somebody's guest?"

"Car repairs are a different matter. That's my expense, not yours."

"Get settled into your new home and send me the check later. You could have some unexpected bills awaiting you there. No rush to pay me."

"I insist. But I will wait until I reach San Diego, if you don't mind. That way, I can transfer funds from my savings to checking account without lowering my balance too much and having to pay a monthly fee."

"That's fine. I got you some postcards to send your family. They're in that little bag on the table. Is the barbecue Saturday still OK?"

"Why do you ask?"

"After what I told you about Carla."

"You said you needed me to discourage her. I'm still game. It's the least I can do to repay you. And I don't want her pestering you again after I'm gone."

Christopher realized his earlier rudeness to her. It wasn't her fault that she hadn't answered the phone, or that he had been frantic with concern, or that she had gotten trapped in the barn by the storm . . . or that she would be leaving in two weeks. Maybe sooner because of his assinine behavior. This wasn't the way to persuade her to stay! Damn, he was stupid sometimes!

Twelve

"It's time for you to eat, Kirstin."

"Let's wait a while. I'm not hungry." *Not for food.*

"That isn't a good idea. You have to get your belly on western time."

"I know and I will. I'll pop a tablet for now."

"They're no substitute for food."

"Thirty minutes or so won't hurt me. I realize I'm your patient, but can't you go off duty tonight? We need to calm down before we eat."

"Lost your appetite because I made you mad? I'm sorry I acted like an idiot, Kirstin. I had things on my mind. When I couldn't reach you, I was worried; it's the doctor in me. Besides, I wouldn't be a man if I weren't a fool occasionally. It's expected, isn't it?" he teased. He noticed her foot was resting on a chair. "The ankle giving you trouble today?"

"You said to keep it propped up as much as possible. Just obeying instructions, Doc. Trying to get well in all areas."

Christopher leaned against the counter. "Was my offense unforgivable, Kirstin? You seem so distant." He had apologized and explained; what more did she want from him?

"Like you, I just have things on my mind. Sorry if I seem crabby."

"Just unusually quiet. Want another drink?"

"I haven't finished this one, but thanks. Why don't *you* get something to eat if you're hungry?" She smiled at him to calm his anxiety. It was hard to get to know another person, open up, change, decide what they wanted.

He returned the smile. "How about a snack to tide us over? I have cheese and crackers," he offered.

"Perfect," she agreed. "I'll help. What would you like?"

"You, later. Scotch with a splash of water and a snack right now."

She looked at him and grinned. "Excellent choices, Doc."

"I'll get everything ready. I want you in the den with that ankle propped up. It's got to be mended by Saturday so we can kick up our heels." He lifted her and took her there. He

351

fetched the crackers and cheese and returned. "Here you are, ma'am. Anything else?"

"Later."

Their gazes fused and they burst into laughter.

They snacked and chatted while they watched several television shows. One had a segment that featured a dramatization of open-heart surgery. Kirstin glanced at Christopher. His gaze was narrowed, his forehead furrowed, and his body taut.

"Christopher, do you mind if we change the channel? A bloody operation while we're eating doesn't appeal to me."

He changed the channel quickly. For a while, he was quiet. Then a comedy came on. Kirstin kept pointing out funny things until he was concentrating on the show and laughing merrily. She didn't realize how grateful and touched he was for her generous kindness.

At eight, he said, "Time for supper. I'll get it ready. You stay here."

As if fate were determined to spoil their evening, a *Mash* rerun came on after their meal. Christopher stiffened again. He stood up and flexed his body. "I think I'll turn in, Kirstin. I got very little sleep last night and this has been a hectic day for both of us." He couldn't sit there and observe the action, but neither would he embarrass himself by switching the channel again. How could she understand what he was feeling? Every time he watched anything relating to surgery, his palms sweated and he was consumed with bitterness. Would this yearning and emptiness ever leave him? Could she help end his misery? "Don't stay up too long. You need your rest, too."

He took a long, hot shower. He yanked the sheets aside and lay down, punching the pillow beneath his head. Moonlight drifted into the room to produce a dim glow. He waited and hoped for Kirstin to join him. The house was silent; she had turned off the television. Except for the hall nightlight, it was dark beyond his room. Time passed; she didn't come to his bed. He waited a while longer before throwing the sheet aside to check on her. He needed her. He wanted her. Knowing her, she wouldn't be so bold as to pay him a visit after how he'd behaved earlier. Her room was dark but for the sifted moonlight. He stood in the doorway, gazing over the small mound in the guest bed. She was curled into a ball on her right side. Had she fallen asleep that fast? Would she mind being disturbed?

"Did you want something?" she called out as he turned to leave.

"I wondered if you'd gotten to bed okay. I

thought . . . Goodnight."

"I assumed you were exhausted and wanted to be left alone."

"No, I didn't. Do you?"

"No," she confessed.

"Do you mind coming to my room? I sleep better in my own bed."

Kirstin tossed the covers aside and sat up, clad in a cherry satin gown. Christopher helped her to her feet and captured her head between his hands, his lips fastening to hers. She swayed against him and returned the almost urgent kiss in like manner. He lifted her and carried her into his room, gently depositing her on his bed. He lay down beside her.

For the first time, Kirstin noticed he was nude. She sat up, pulled the gown over her head, and dropped it to the floor. She leaned forward, lying half over him. "You could market this taut elastic in your neck and shoulders. Relax, Christopher; I don't bite," she teased. "Turn over," she suggested. "You're the one who needs a massage tonight."

He rolled to his stomach. Kirstin straddled him, lightly and firmly kneading his neck and shoulder muscles. With persistence, she had them relaxing within a short time. She moved to his powerful biceps and labored there. She shifted to sit beside him, ministering first to one hand and then the other. She continued the pleasing treatment down to his calves, up his thighs, then provocatively over his taut buttocks. She finished at his waist.

He rolled to his back and challenged, "What about the front?"

Kirstin grinned to herself, reaching for the only part that needed caressing on that side. He groaned and undulated his hips. When she halted her movements, he asked her to continue.

"I have an injured wrist, remember? Besides, I think you're enjoying this too much. If I continue, I'll forfeit my reward."

"You're right, Kirstin; you do have me primed to explode soon."

She reached for the foil packet on the nightstand. The waxing moon and sheer curtains offered enough light for her eyes to see what she was doing. "Let me see how this works," she murmured as she opened it.

"You're going to put it on for me?"

"Why not? It might me fun for both of us. Just make sure I don't make any mistakes. Know what I mean?"

"I'll be certain it's secure."

Christopher guided her, and with stimulating leisure, Kirstin completed the task.

"If I don't get busy, you'll be left in the cold," he teased. He devoured her breasts until she quivered with longing. He ravished her mouth as his hand slipped between her thighs to play for a while. When he eased into her, she moaned and told him how good it felt.

This was sheer bliss, they both decided. Together, they climbed the spiral road to heights of pleasure that left them sated and happy in each other's arms.

Christopher covered her face with kisses. When he withdrew from her sated body and disposed of the condom, he rested one leg over hers and lay an arm over her chest. His lips dropped little kisses on her shoulder. "You're really something special, woman."

Kirstin sighed in tranquility. Her hand caressed the strong arm over her chest. "You, too." Her eyes closed and she was soon asleep, as he was.

The following morning at dawn he made passionate love to her again before leaving to do his chores. He told her to go back to sleep until he returned, which she did for another hour.

When Christopher came back at eight-thirty, breakfast was in progress and Kirstin was drinking coffee. The smell of cooked bacon filled the kitchen. The table was set and eggs were in a bowl, ready to be scrambled. He glanced around and smiled. "This is a pleasant surprise," he commented and came forward to drop a kiss on her neck. "You're going to spoil me if you aren't careful. I get used to things fast."

"I bet you thought I'd become a stranger in the kitchen. I've been negligent with my part of our bargain. Sorry. I'll do better."

"I doubt there's little you can't do, Mrs. Lowrey, when you set that keen mind to it," he remarked, his voice husky.

"Is that a back-door compliment, Doctor Harrison?"

"Just an observation from my research."

"And how is this liberated specimen making out?"

"Not bad at all, Mrs. Lowrey, not bad at all."

She laughed. "Coffee?"

"Love some. I'll wash up and help," he said, and headed for the bathroom.

When he returned, she smiled at him. "Just about ready," she said, knowing by now how he liked his eggs cooked.

Afterward, they joined forces to clean the kitchen. "Come to the office now and let me check those injuries," he suggested.

She followed him on the crutches and submitted to his examination. He grinned at her. "Wrist's doing fine. It may be a little sore for another day or two. Leave housework alone;

that's an order. Save all your energy and strength for me. Don't put any pressure or strain on it," he advised. "And no driving. You aren't ready for that."

"You mean, do nothing with it besides give massages?"

"Besides massages. You see, I'm a selfish man. The ankle should stay wrapped until tomorrow. Keep your weight off of it as much as possible."

"Stay in bed?" Her eyes twinkled.

"Only when I'm there to take care of you from head to foot."

"Conceited, selfish person," she accused, tugging on a lock of ebony hair.

"Guilty as charged, Mrs. Lowrey. I have a few patients this morning. Want to go riding this afternoon? Horseback," he clarified.

"I thought you said not to put any pressure on my wrist?"

"Riding with me, double-back," he clarified again, a sensual smile creating little creases near his eyes and mouth.

"Who could pass up an invitation like that? Not me."

"Oh, yes, I rented a camper yesterday while I was in town. Still interested in going with John and Maria?"

"I wouldn't miss it."

* * *

While Christopher pulled patient charts and set up for appointments, Kirstin made the beds and straightened the house to get her needed exercise; because of her injury she couldn't use the treadmill or take vigorous walks, part of her treatment plan. She also wanted no evidence of their affair to be visible in case company arrived. She checked the freezer to plan the evening meal and pulled out a package of ground beef. She would decide later what to prepare with it. She heard a car pull into the driveway, telling her Christopher's first patient had arrived.

Kirstin sat in the den to write cards and letters to family and friends. Christopher said he would mail them for her, along with the toys he had purchased on her behalf to give her grandchildren. He hadn't shown them to her until this morning or mentioned the rented camper yesterday during their disagreement. She thought he was clever and helpful; this was a way she could keep in touch with her son's family without getting trapped in a nasty conversation with Steve on the telephone.

Kirstin called Katie to tell her daughter news of the barbecue, the Carlisle baby, the double-date with John and Maria, and the imminent camping trip.

"That's fantastic, Mom. I'm so glad you're

having fun and relaxing. It sounds as if you're achieving a lot there. Are your arrival plans the same?"

"Yes. If anything serious comes of this, honey, it can't be rushed."

"That's smart, Mom."

"I'm improving in that area every day, I hope."

"You're doing okay healthwise?"

"Fine, Katie, just fine." Kirstin felt a little deceitful not telling her daughter about her current injuries, but she didn't want to worry the girl. Later, she would reveal the incident and they'd laugh about it. "Heard from Steve or Sandi?"

"Steve's basking in the sun or scuba diving about now. Sandi called since I talked with you. She's doing fine. I hinted about your adventures and she's as excited and pleased as I am. She said for you to call her as soon as you get here. Not before. Wait until all the facts are in."

"There might not be anything more to report."

"And there might be. We have our fingers crossed for you two. Shall I keep them that way?"

"For now," Kirstin replied.

They chatted a while longer before saying their good-byes.

Kirstin was about to coat her dry and brittle nails with a moisturizing and strengthening treatment when she heard a child's terrified scream. The piercing sound came again through the open office window and kitchen screen door. She glanced up as Christopher rushed inside.

"I need a distracting treat, and fast." As he searched cabinets, he explained, "I have a five-year-old over there who needs a shot and his mother refuses to watch or help. She has him panicked and wiggling and crying. I've tried everything to settle him down. No wonder they can't get med students to go into pediatrics!"

"Mind if I assist you again?" she asked. "A woman can sometimes have a calming effect on children. I don't mind shots, at least watching them. In fact, I'd rather have a shot than my countless finger pricks. My fingers are so sore they bother me every time I use them."

"Come on, woman; I can use any help I can find. Name's Timmy."

Kirstin followed him to the office. She gazed at the boy with teary eyes and pale face. He looked so small and vulnerable sitting in a big leather chair with his hands clenched in his lap. Obviously he'd leapt off the table the mo-

361

ment Christopher left. His shorts exposed legs scuffed from normal play. One tennis shoe was untied. Kirstin went forward and smiled at him. It reminded her of the many times she'd soothed her son's pains and fears. If only Steve was that sweet, unselfish, and obedient child again . . .

"Hi, Timmy," she said, going down on one knee before him. She lifted his foot and placed it on her thigh. "Let's get this lace tied before you trip over it and skin your nose. See my bandaged foot and wrist?" She pointed at them. "I fell and hurt them the other day. Doctor Harrison fixed them for me. They feel better now. He's a very good doctor. Did you know that?"

He nodded, but his eyes revealed his skepticism. "Doctor Harrison gave me a checkup just like you're about to have. It didn't hurt at all. Think you can be a brave soldier and let him check you out, too?"

"I'm scared. He wants to give . . . me . . . a shot," he wailed, his dark eyes wide and misty.

"I was scared, too," she whispered to him. "But don't tell him. Big girls aren't supposed to be scared of anything. I even cried. I shouldn't have; it didn't hurt at all. Have you ever been bitten by a big mosquito?" she asked, dramatically holding her hands apart, creating a space large enough for a basketball to fit between them.

Timmy nodded as he tugged at his upper lip with his teeth, eyes wide with attention.

"A shot is sort of like a mosquito bite." She playacted as she said in a humorous tone, "It's an ooou—chy stick, but it's fast. If you hold out your arm and close your eyes, it will be over before you can say, That hurts, Doc."

He looked at her, clearly questioning her story. "If I tell you how the zebra got his stripes from Santa Claus, will you let Doctor Harrison examine you?" She deviously attempted another ploy.

"Did Santa give him stripes?" he asked, excited by the promise of a story, "How?" he demanded.

"While I tell you the story, let Doctor Harrison check your ears and throat. A deal?" she offered.

He nodded, eager to hear the tale. He let her put him on the table.

"Once upon a time, all zebras were solid white. But zebras didn't like being all white and looking like horses. Other animals had lots of colors and patterns to make them look pretty and different. Turn your head, Timmy," she told him as Christopher checked his ears.

"The zebras were very jealous of the other animals. When Christmas was near, the zebras knew what they wanted Santa to bring them.

Open your mouth, Timmy," she inserted, the child's eyes and concentration staying on her as he obeyed without thinking.

"The big zebra who was their leader told Santa's elves the zebras wanted a colorful pattern all their own. When the elves returned to the North Pole with the zebras' message, Santa gave the problem deep thought. Lean your head back a little, Timmy," she said to allow Christopher to check his nose.

"Santa wondered what he could do for the zebras. The lions had a fluffy mane and gold tail. The peacocks had beautiful feathers with eyes on them. The birds had used up the red and blue colors. The horses and cows had been colored brown and white and black. There were so many elephants and they were so large, there wasn't any gray color left. The giraffes with their long necks and legs had used up the yellow paint. Take a deep breath, Timmy. 'What about pink or brown?' Santa asked his elves . . . Take another deep breath, Timmy, and let it out real slow." As Christopher listened to the boy's heart and lungs, she continued. "The elves told Santa the pink was used up on flamingoes and the brown on monkeys because God had made so many of them. Santa had worked hard giving snakes, butterflies, and bugs different colors and decorations. What could he do, Santa wondered, for the white zebras? 'How much black do we have in the pails?' Santa asked his little helpers. 'Not much,' one told him, 'Bears, and dogs, and other animals used up most of it.' Santa was worried."

Christopher checked Timmy's reflexes and enjoyed the story along with Kirstin's gestures, and exuberance.

"Santa flew to the jungle in his sled. He checked the zebras over, just like Doctor Harrison is doing with you, Timmy. He looked in their ears and eyes. He studied them from end to end. He decided he couldn't change their ears; zebras needed ears like horses so they could hear any danger that came near them. He couldn't change their eyes; they needed sharp eyes to see where they were going. He couldn't change their legs; zebras needed strong legs to run away from hungry lions and tigers. Santa checked their tails. He shook his head; zebras needed fluffy tails to sweep away flies. Santa was confused. How could he decorate the zebras?"

When she paused, Timmy asked, "What did he do?"

"Santa told the zebras they needed a shot to make them strong enough to be painted. The zebras didn't want a shot; they were afraid it would hurt. The lion came over and told the zebras he wasn't afraid of a shot. He was the king of the jungle, and kings were never afraid. You know what, Timmy? The lion was scared inside, but he didn't want the other animals to know he was. He pretended to be very brave. He held up his front leg and told Santa to give him a shot to make him even stronger than he was. Santa gave the lion a shot. The big lion laughed and pranced about; 'The shot didn't hurt very much,' he said, which was true. He looked at the zebras and asked, 'Who's next? If you want to be strong and brave, come and let Santa give you a shot. Then, he'll give you a pretty color as a prize.' The zebra leader looked at his friends to see who would step forward."

"I bet none of them did," Timmy asserted with confidence.

Christopher had the syringe ready and out of the child's sight, but suspected Timmy wouldn't fall for her ruse.

Kirstin looked at the physician and winked. "Let's play a game. I'll be the lion, Timmy, and you be the leader of the zebras. Doctor Harrison can be Santa. I'm ready for my saline shot, Santa," she gave her clue. "I'm a lion, king of the jungle. I'll take a saline shot to make me brave and strong."

Christopher prepared a syringe of sterile saline solution with a small needle. He took her arm to give her the harmless injection. "Ready,

Mr. Lion?"

Kirstin nodded and forced herself to smile and remain still. "Now, I'll be even stronger and braver. Zebra leader, will you be next? Will you show the other zebras they shouldn't be afraid?"

Kirstin waited for Timmy to decide if he would play along with the game. Timmy nodded and held out his arm to the doctor. Kirstin hurried on with the story to distract him. The needle was small and Christopher was gentle. He had given Timmy the shot almost before the boy realized it. "When all the zebras had their shots, Santa revealed how he would reward them. He had told the elves to get the remaining magical black paint. The elves worked a long time painting black stripes on white zebras. When they finished, not a single drop was left in the buckets. The zebras pranced around, showing all the animals their beautiful patterns; every one was different and special. Santa told them not to forget to bathe in the river because the magic paint wouldn't come off in the water. From that day on, zebras have worn black stripes on their white coats. Now, how about if we reward Timmy with some cookies and milk?" she tempted.

The boy cocked his arm to look at the spot where Christopher had given him the injection. He grinned and stuck out his chest in pride. "Now I'll be brave and strong, won't I, Doc Harrison?"

"Yes, you will, son." He watched Kirstin lead Timmy away to fetch a treat while he spoke with the child's mother.

When Kirstin and Timmy joined them, his mother couldn't believe the smile on her son's face and his bubbly chatter. He gave Kirstin a timid and appreciative smile.

She knelt and hugged him. "This is the bravest little boy I've ever met," she told the mother. "He'll grow up to be big and strong and brave just like the king of the jungle. Right, Timmy?"

"Right, Kirstin," he agreed, then placed his small arms around her neck to hug her. "Will you be here next time, Kirstin?"

"It's Mrs. Lowrey, Timmy," the mother corrected.

"She said I could call her Kirstin, Mom," the child explained. "We're friends. Will you be here next time?"

"Doctor Harrison almost has me healed. I have to go home and get back to work. I'll be leaving in two weeks," she told the disappointed child, unaware of the matching look on Christopher's face.

"Will you come back soon?" he pressed.

Kirstin glanced at Christopher and smiled. "If Doctor Harrison invites me to visit him again, I will."

"Can she, Doc Harrison?" The boy's eyes pleaded with him.

Christopher grinned and nodded. "She can visit anytime she likes."

Timmy's mother took his hand and left. Christopher and Kirstin stood in the office doorway and watched their departure, returning Timmy's waves until the car was out of sight.

Christopher eyed Kirstin. "Will you never cease to amaze me, woman?"

"I hope not, Christopher Harrison; I surely hope not. You see, all liberated, career-minded women aren't cold-hearted."

He didn't want to think or talk about the obstacle between them. "Don't forget we have the barbecue tomorrow, then camping Sunday."

"I won't. I have a wonderful escort and tour guide lined up for those events so they're certain to be fun and interesting."

"I hope so."

Kirstin thought his tone and expression were odd. *Worried about gossip, Doc?* Afraid that by dating her she would get the wrong idea that his feelings were deeper than they were? If so, she'd relieve his tension. "You'd better enjoy yourself because your guinea pig will be gone soon."

"Don't remind me; superior ones are hard to

find and replace."

"Thank you, kind sir. Here comes your next patient up the road so I'll get out of your hair. See you later. Thanks for the diversion."

"You're welcome, and thanks for the help." As he watched her return to the house, his mind replied, *Just so you don't get out of my life.*

Kirstin sat down to watch television while she rested her ankle and waited for him to finish. Her gaze widened as she noticed Carla's statue was gone. She fiddled with the medical alert bracelet he had given to her as she tried to determine his motive.

When he came in for lunch, she didn't mention the curious matter. She did ask, "Who does your billing for you?"

"I do it myself. It isn't much work. I have it set up on my computer; I make the entries at the end of the day. Most patients pay with checks after their visits."

"What if someone doesn't pay while they're here?"

"I send a statement at the end of the month. My program kicks them and envelopes out in a hurry. I stamp 'em and mail 'em. It's simple, quick."

"What about insurance claims?"

"I do them as time allows."

"And if a patient or company still doesn't pay?"

"If there's a good reason and the amount isn't much, I let it slide. That's happened only a few times. Why? You applying for a book-keeper's job?"

"No, I just wondered how your business ran because you're busier than I realized. You're doctor, nurse, receptionist, secretary, janitor, office manager, and bill collector. That's a lot of hats to wear. All those jobs in addition to being a rancher and head of household keeps your schedule crammed full. Some retirement, Christopher. Now I can see why you wanted me to hang around and give you a rest."

"If you weren't laid up with injuries, I'd be coaxing you to wear some of those hats for me while you're here."

"Ah ha! So that's how you planned for me to repay my debt to you."

"Oh, no, my captive patient; you're more than repaying it. I didn't realize I was so overworked until you pointed it out. If I let you do much, you'd be too tired and busy and grouchy to . . . entertain me."

Kirstin laughed. "You lecherous sneak, I think I've been tricked."

"Will you call foul?"

"No way, because I'm also taking advantage of you and the situation."

A horn beeped and halted their playful banter. "Damn. I shouldn't have scheduled so many patients in one day. I did it before you arrived. I bunch them up to get my doctoring done in spurts. I'd better go."

After he left, Kirstin cuddled on the sofa. Could she be satisfied, she mused, as his assistant? No, those other jobs couldn't replace fascinating research. Some people loved those positions, but her interests and skills didn't lie in those directions. No doubt Christopher would be delighted to turn all except doctoring and ranching over to her, and would probably try to do so if they—*Stop it, Kirstin, or you'll irritate yourself.*

It was three o'clock when Christopher returned after seeing his last patient.

Kirstin was dressed in jeans. "I'm ready to go riding," she told him.

"Sorry, Kirstin, but Jerry called and has another offer on that stock I mentioned yesterday. Frank and I have to go check them over and see if I can make a deal with him. Frank has a keen eye for good horseflesh and breeding bulls. I don't know what I'd do without him. Ranching is like a science of its own. Mix the wrong chemicals and you have a mess. I know he's getting anxious for his own place. I surely would hate to find a replacement if that happens. I try to make it worth his while to stay on with me, but when a man wants something badly, he goes after it. He's picking me up in fifteen minutes so I have time to grab a quick shower and change. You can fetch my clothes for me: jeans and a blue shirt, and my best boots. They're in the closet."

Kirstin followed him to the bedroom. While he bathed, she took out the requested items. She saw Carla's gift lying on its side on a shelf. So, he hadn't tossed it in the trash, only removed it from her sight. She decided that he probably didn't know what to do with the expensive statue.

Christopher entered the bedroom and yanked on his briefs and jeans. As he sat down to pull on his boots, he asked, "Toss me an undershirt, would you? Top drawer on the left."

Kirstin gaped at the sight that greeted her eyes: condoms, lots of them! "Heavens, Christopher, this is a year's supply."

"Oh, sorry. I forgot they were in there. I bought them yesterday. I was hoping we'd need at least half that many. I can go back for more."

She flung the shirt at him. "Stop teasing. Where did you buy them? Who saw you? Do they know I'm here? Oh, my heavens, this is so humiliating."

"Hold your horses, woman. I drove all the

way to Texico to buy them. I visited several stores where nobody knows me. Our reputations are safe. I wouldn't do anything to hurt or embarrass you, Kirstin. Honest."

She calmed down. "But so many?"

"We have been rather active in that area and I hope we continue to be."

She grinned. "You're right, Doc; we'll use all of them, eventually."

"Were you on the pill before . . . David died?"

"Yes. Why?"

"Would you be interested in going back on it, if your doctor says it's all right, safe in your condition? Sex is better without condoms, much better."

"When I see the new gynecologist, I'll get prepared for our weekends together. Of course I'll have to keep them hidden from my children and grandkids when they visit."

"That would be a tough explanation to make. When I get back, if—" Frank's horn interrupted a moment. "If it isn't too late, we'll go riding."

Christopher hurried out the door and jumped into Frank's truck. She returned to his room to clean up the mess he'd made in his rush. She didn't mind picking up after him, as it was a rare task.

When the phone rang later, Kirstin got off the sofa to answer it. Expecting the caller to be Christopher, she gave a cheerful, "Hello."

"Oh, hi, Carla. Is my dad there?"

Kirstin recovered her wits fast and replied in a polite tone. "No, he isn't, Peggy. He's in town on an errand, buying stock, and this is Kirstin."

"Oops. Sorry, Mrs. Lowrey, I just assumed you were Carla Thompson. I didn't realize you'd still be there."

You little brat, you recognized my voice. "I know you don't want to embarrass yourself in the future, so I'll tell you that your father no longer sees Carla and hasn't in quite a while."

"Really? That's surprising. What happened between them?"

Want to play games, eh? "Why would he tell me that?"

"For the same reason he told you they weren't dating anymore."

"If he mentioned the reason, it would have been in confidence. He should be back soon. I'll tell him you called."

"I'm surprised you're still there."

"I hurt my ankle and wrist and couldn't drive. I'll be leaving soon."

"Another accident? I hope you won't sue my father."

"Of course not. It was my fault and no damage was done."

"Only enough so you can't drive, right?"

Kirstin stayed pleasant and alert. "There's no permanent injury."

"That's good. My father told me you're in medical research?"

"In San Diego with Medico of America. I'm relocating from Georgia."

"There aren't any research facilities near the ranch, are there?"

"None, that I know of. Nothing close by, I'm sure."

"Did you and Dad check?"

Worried, are you? "No, but we've never heard of any."

"I had a friend who wanted to become a med tech, but it didn't pay enough so she switched to nursing."

"She must have checked with small companies or medical schools. Big and important ones pay well, especially after you work your way up the ladder. I'm at the top."

"So, you earn a nice living. That's good."

I'm not after your father's money.

Peggy barraged Kirstin with questions pertaining to her marital status, then asked her age. When she responded with the figure, the younger woman paused before commenting snidely. "My father usually dates women under thirty-five, mostly in their twenties. I suppose it's nice to find someone near his age as a friend."

"We have a lot in common."

"How close are you two?"

Uh-oh, here it comes. "I beg your pardon?"

"I was wondering how close you are. With so much in common, I assume you're very close."

End this conversation fast! "We've become good friends. I have to go."

"How good?"

She's going to be trouble, but be nice. "I know you love your father and are concerned about him, but don't you think our relationship is private?"

"Are you sleeping with him?"

My heavens, you're rude! "Excuse me?"

"Are you sleeping with my father?"

"If I were, Peggy, I wouldn't discuss that with you or my children. I have to go now; Frank is taking me riding. I'll tell Christopher you called."

"One caution, Mrs. Lowrey, if you hurt my father, I'll claw out your eyes."

Kirstin was shocked, but she held her poise and rebuke. "You needn't worry, Peggy, we're adults. I hate to rush, but Frank is waiting. Goodbye, Peggy. It was interesting to chat with you. I hope we can meet one day."

You dislike any woman who gets close to your father. How does one win over a selfish and hateful brat? If you got your manners and personality from Laura, no wonder Christopher dumped her!

Christopher returned too late for their horseback ride. He was all smiles about the deal he made on the stock. Kirstin wasn't; it meant he was digging himself in deeper and deeper here. There was no way, she concluded, he would ever sell out and move.

At they neared the end of their dinner, Kirstin asked, "Does Peggy know Carla? Have they met in person?"

"That's an odd subject. Where did it come from?"

Kirstin put aside her empty plate and met his inquisitive gaze. "Does she know her? Did they like each other? Did you tell her about the break-up?"

"Is there a point to this line of questioning?"

"Yes, your daughter called today and we had an interesting chat."

Christopher came to full alert, stopped eating, and asked, "About what?"

She repeated the conversation. He gaped at her. "Well, what's true and what isn't?"

Christopher dropped his fork into his plate. "That little devil. Just wait until I get my hands on her. She knows I can't stand Carla and dumped her. Peggy didn't like her, either. They *did* meet during one of her trips here. She was delighted when I told her Carla was history. Daughter or not, how dare she have the gall and bad manners to talk to a patient and guest of mine like that! She was pulling your leg, Kirstin, I don't rob the cradle, never have. And to think she threatened you! When I see her next, I'll take a belt to her fanny for the first time!"

Kirstin mellowed a little as she didn't want to cause problems between father and daughter like she was experiencing with Steve, or have Peggy hate her for being a snitch. "She's just possessive and worried about you because she loves you so much and doesn't want to see you get hurt. That's natural for a daughter. Don't be overly hard on her."

"There's no excuse for what she said to you. It won't happen again. I'm going to my office to call her and straighten her out right now."

She called out to him to delay his exit. "Calm down first or you might say something you'll regret. Once you create a breach, it's hard to build a span. I know from my trouble with Steve. Besides, if I ever get the chance to meet her, I don't want her to hate me. Be gentle during your scolding, okay?"

"That's good advice, and I'll take it. I'll be back soon."

Christopher leaned back in his desk chair and gave the situation some thought before dialing his daughter's number. Phil answered, and the two men chatted a few minutes before Peggy was put on the line. "Kirstin said you phoned this afternoon." He waited a minute. When he continued, he kept his tone and mood unreadable. "She said you two had quite a talk."

"We were . . . getting acquainted. I hope she didn't mind."

"Why should she?"

"I was my usual nosy self and asked lots of questions."

"That sounds like you. I raised my daughter to be kind and polite, so what happened? When did you become a snoop, squirt?" He chuckled to put her off guard.

"I . . . How is she feeling?"

"Why, did she say she was having more problems?"

"No, but she's still a patient of yours. Right?"

"That's right, and I hope you don't say or do anything to upset her. She's diabetic and doesn't need any extra stress."

"Diabetic?"

"Yes, and you know what that's like."

"Yes. Phil's mother. She didn't mention it to me this afternoon."

"That's how we met, squirt. I thought I told you she had a hypoglycemia attack and wrecked her car nearby. She's had a few others; one caused her to fall the other day. I'm trying to get her balanced and healed so she can head on to San Diego. She's a good woman, squirt, the best I've met so far. You'd like her daughter, Katie." He related interests the two young women had in common. "You'd like Kirstin, too. She's smart, fun, well mannered, and tender-hearted."

"Not a gold digger or femme fatale?"

"Neither, thank goodness."

"You really like her, don't you?"

"Yep, she's a very likable person."

"What are you planning to do about it?"

"Nothing any time soon. We're still getting to know each other, but time is short. I hope we can visit each other after she leaves. We're going to the Thompson ranch for a barbecue tomorrow."

"You're going to introduce her to Carla? That'll be interesting."

"Why?"

"Because Carla's a bitch, Dad. I told you that a thousand times."

By then, he realized he had kept her ignorant about her talk with Kirstin, and he'd try to keep it that way. That should make Peggy grateful to Kirstin for keeping silent. "I agree.

That's why I stopped seeing her. I told you about that decision."

"I remember, and I'm glad she's out of the picture."

"Just do your old man a favor and don't help push Kirstin out of it before I make a decision about her. Okay, squirt? Please."

"I get the point, Dad."

"And don't worry; she isn't chasing *me*. If I decide to make a play for her, I'll be lucky if I can catch her. She's open, honest, good with people. I wouldn't mind having her as my nurse."

"And new wife?"

"Whoa, squirt, that's jumping the gun. Don't put that idea into her head before I'm ready to let my feelings be known."

After a few more minutes of cunning and partly deceitful talk, they hung up. Christopher relaxed in his chair before rejoining Kirstin. He smiled and said, "Mission accomplished, and I was terrific." Leaving out the sections about love and marriage, he related their talk to Kirstin.

Kirstin smiled. "You were terrific, and very wise. I'm glad."

"Now, let's see if it works, see if she obeys her old man."

I hope so; I don't think I can deal with trouble with two kids.

Following a passionate night in each other's arms and a morning "quickie," the new day hit a snag, the first of many.

Thirteen

While checking his answering machine and service, Christopher took Carla's call on the business line in his office.

"I knew I'd catch you in there; always the dedicated and compassionate doctor. I wanted to make certain you're coming to the barbecue. Everyone, including me, is eager to meet your . . . new friend. We're all curious about that mystery house guest of yours. You *are* bringing her along, aren't you?"

"Yes, Carla, I'm coming, and so is Kirstin. Your father said it's okay."

"Of course, it is, silly man. I'll be looking for you two, early."

Christopher and Kirstin were watching a golf tournament in the den. She was baffled by the odd mood he had been in since working in his

384

office after breakfast. She knew the phone had rung, so a call must have annoyed him. Surely Peggy hadn't phoned back and started a fuss . . . She also thought it odd that he wasn't making any preparations to leave for their entertainment for the afternoon, which included a late lunch. When she couldn't endure the strained silence or stingy conversation any longer, she asked him if something was wrong.

"That damn barbecue," he grumbled. On top of Peggy's meddling yesterday, he was worried their day at the Thompsons might do harm to their relationship, pushing her away from him.

"What do you mean?"

He was positive Carla had phoned on his medical line to make sure she reached him and not Kirstin. He couldn't imagine how Carla or the other guests would treat Kirstin. He shouldn't be surprised that idle gossip was making its rounds by now. "I don't want to go, but I should. My friends and patients expect it. What do you think?"

"Me? They're your friends and neighbors, not mine. If it will make you miserable, why go?" she questioned, bewildered.

Before he knew it, he blurted out, "I'm not concerned about me."

She studied him. "If you prefer I stay home, I don't mind. Does everyone here have a low opinion of me? Is that it?"

"They have no right to form any opinion about you."

"I see, gossip is circulating. Someone phoned and dropped hints?" His scowl told her she had guessed right. "Why don't you go alone? I'll be fine here. Anyway, I need to wash clothes and pack for our camping trip. You said we're leaving early. It's no big deal for me, honest. I'll be gone soon, so I don't matter. Your reputation in the community does."

"If you don't go, I don't go. And you do matter; you're my guest."

"That wouldn't be fair or wise, Christopher. I can't go where I'll make people uncomfortable, including myself," she protested. "But I think it will appear rude if you refuse to make an appearance. I know how small towns are: everybody gets into everybody else's business. It's no secret I'm staying here, but we don't have to flaunt it in their faces. You should go; these are your friends and patients," she stressed.

"Damnit, Kirstin, I want you to meet them!" he snapped.

"If they don't care to meet me, I can't inflict my company on anyone, Christopher. *Anyone,*" she emphasized. "Who called and what was said?"

"Carla, that bitch. My friends and neighbors aren't the problem; it's Thompson's daughter and people like her. Knowing her, she'll do her best to give you a hard time." He related the contents of the call. "I don't want to put you through that stress. I don't need you to discourage her or any local woman for me; that was a joke. Let's take a picnic lunch to the pond. We can relax, eat, and ride all afternoon. It'll be more fun."

"You should go alone. At least, visit for a little while," she coaxed. "It isn't a good idea to alienate neighbors and patients."

She was right, he decided; why allow Carla or anyone else to control him? Yet, he wanted to share the day with Kirstin. He wanted her to get acquainted with his friends and way of life, and see how it affected her. "Then, come with me and I'll do my best to control Carla's behavior. I want you to meet the others; they're good people and they'll like you. You'll like most of them, too, I promise."

Kirstin had endured plenty of unpleasant evenings with David and his circle. Why should she put herself through a possibly nasty episode with Christopher's crowd? Even if she won them over, what difference did it make? Still, he wanted her to go. "All right, Doctor Harrison, you win. But we leave early. Agreed?"

"Are you open to changing that if we're having a good time? John and Maria will be there. So will Joe Bob, his wife, and Frank. And Timmy's mother and Henry. Not everyone will be a stranger to you."

"If *we're* having fun, we can stay longer."

He grinned at her compromise. "Let's get dressed and head over, woman. I'm starved for some great barbecue."

When Kirstin was ready, Christopher joined her in the den. Her tawny hair was an array of loose curls and fringed bangs that framed her beautiful face. She wore just a hint of makeup and perfume. The cornflower shadow on her lids caused her sea-water eyes to appear even bluer and lovelier. A tinge of blush provided a healthy glow and look of vitality to her complexion. Her lashes lay against her golden face like tiny black feathers, a striking contrast to her wheatish hair. Her mouth was soft and full, colored a soft mauve. His gut tightened and his loins ignited simply from looking at her. He concluded that no one present would be fooled by their relationship. Would they give her, and him, a difficult time? An idea came to mind. "Take off your left boot," he instructed. "I'll be back in a minute."

Kirstin sat on the sofa and did as he asked, pondering his intention. His jeans were snug and enticing. His blue denim shirt fit him close to a second skin. The shirt was embroidered with several designs in colorful threads; cactus, a Plains sunset, and an eagle in flight. He wore black snakeskin boots, expensive and tasteful. There was a large leather belt around his waist, a bronze buckle near hear his navel. He appeared ruggedly handsome and virile. Her heart raced as she watched him walk toward her.

Her brow lifted. "What are those for?"

"Self-defense," he replied, chuckling. "The way you look, we'll need a visible excuse for you still being here. No need to fuel the gossip furnace before they get to know you."

"This is absurd, Christopher. I just got rid of those crutches this morning. How can I have any fun if I'm hobbling around on them? If you think such a deception is necessary, I'd rather not go."

"All right." He thought a minute. "Then, we'll say we're old friends."

"No, the truth or nothing. Well, part of the truth. We don't have to tell them more than the bare facts. If they're 'good' people as you claim, no matter what they suspect, they won't say anything cruel to us; I'm sure of it."

"You win, woman. I want you to meet them. Get a firsthand look at my lifestyle. Except for Carla, they'll all be nice."

His insinuation intrigued her. What other way could she discover how it would be to live here? "On second thought, Doc, make me a hobbler today who can't drive yet. No need to encourage problems."

With her assistance, he wrapped her left ankle and right wrist in elastic bandages, then handed her the crutches. As he flexed his partially disabled hand, he said, "They wouldn't serve you well if you really needed them, but they're perfect for our ruse." He congratulated his keen idea."

"This means no Texas two-stepping or square dancing. At least for me." She purred and sent him a feigned accusing look. "I bet you just want me out of circulation, or out of your way."

He shook his head as his glowing eyes swept over her. "Neither. Besides, all the men around here are either married or nastily divorced or too old or too young to catch your eye."

"What about the females and *your* eye, Doctor Harrison?"

"With you there, who could notice any other woman?" he asked, his hands easing around her waist to draw her into his embrace. His lips covered hers and savored their sweetness. When the stimulating kiss ended, he leaned back his head and gazed into her eyes. "We best leave before I can't."

"Will I be carried? Or must I struggle with these wooden arms?"

"To the car, yes. At the barbecue, you're on

your own. Sorry."

The Thompson Ranch appeared immense to Kirstin; surely every person in town was present. Cars, jeeps, and pickup trucks were parked along the driveway and in the huge yard in front of an enormous house. To the right of the mansion were lovely gardens, walkways, countless tables and chairs, and an olympic-size pool with rocks, a waterfall, and greenery decorating it. Tantalizing smells filled her nose from roasting meat and other delicacies. The area was noisy with chatter, laughter, and music from a live band, positioned behind a moveable dance floor. The warm spring day was perfect; the blue sky clear. She glanced at Christopher. "I suppose this couldn't be described as an intimate patio party."

"You might say the Thompsons are the wealthiest folks in this part of the state. Almost everyone gets invited to their barbecues. Carla insists and Daddy obeys."

Christopher helped Kirstin out of the car; she felt silly and tense about their deception. He shortened his lengthy strides to allow her to keep up with him on the crutches. As they approached the edge of the crowd, many faces turned to study them, curiosity and surprise filling some of them. Most of the people smiled, nodded, waved, or shouted greetings to Christopher.

John Two Fists came forward to join them. "What's this?" he asked, pointing to her crutches.

"Kirstin sprained her wrist and ankle Monday. I had to take her to the hospital for x-rays and treatment. Her car's repaired and she's doing fine, but she can't drive with the gearshift and clutch," he explained in a loud voice he knew would be overheard and passed around the large group.

"That's terrible, Kirstin, but it keeps you around a while longer in our beautiful area. I'm glad. Maybe you'll get a nice view of it yet."

"I'll be leaving when I can drive without screaming in pain or risking another highway accident. Some vacation," she jested.

"One you'll remember for life."

"That's for certain, John. I've made good friends here. Everyone I've met has been so nice and helpful, and it's so lovely here. I—" she halted as a woman nearby turned to speak with them and cut into her sentence.

"Hello, Chris; I'm glad you could make it. I was hoping you'd come early so we could have a private chat before all the commotion began. You're late. I was getting worried. It isn't like you to be tardy for anything, you bad boy, unless it's an emergency."

The woman's cool hazel eyes swept over Kirstin as she spoke her last words. Thompson's daughter was clad in a red western dress with glittering silver fringe and embroidered designs on the bodice. The garment — no doubt custom-made and expensive — was snug enough to reveal a stunning figure. Her matching boots were planted close to her male target whose arm she had captured. A no-doubt-real silver belt cinched a small waistline. Her cloying perfume pervaded the area. Silver hearts dangled from pierced ears and danced with her movements. Kirstin decided this was a woman who knew how to take center stage.

"Is this your latest emergency, the one we've heard so much about?"

Christopher disentangled himself and stepped to Kirstin's other side. "Kirstin Lowrey, our hostess, Carla Thompson."

"It's a pleasure to meet you, Carla. Thank you for including me in your invitation. It was gracious of you and your father." She watched her would-be rival tuck long and silky hair behind her ears and tip back a western hat to make her lovely face more noticeable.

"It's a shame about your accidents, Kirstin, but I can see you're making the best of them. You're a smart and fortunate woman. I know from experience that Doctor Harrison has skilled hands and a marvelous bedside manner. All of his patients and friends adore him."

Kirstin hoped she wouldn't blush or stammer at the bold innuendos. "I've seen him with children and others," she replied carefully. "He is a wonderful physician. I was fortunate John took me to him."

"You're even luckier your accidents didn't require hospitalization. How long will you be laid up at Chris's?"

Kirstin caught the naughty implications but pretended she didn't. She was positive others grasped the double entendres, too. She smiled and answered, "He says a few more days; then, he'll see if I'm ready to leave."

The doctor put in, "Her injuries will be sensitive for a while. She doesn't want to risk more trouble by putting too much pressure on them too soon."

Carla said, "If you will all excuse me, I must see to my other guests. Please, have fun and eat plenty. Ask for anything that's missing. Perhaps you and I will have a chance to talk again, Kirstin, before you leave."

Kirstin smiled and nodded and watched the woman retreat.

Frank Graham strolled over and handed Christopher a cold draft beer from one of the numerous kegs. The Harrison foreman asked Kirstin what she would like to drink. She smiled, thanked him, and asked for a diet anything. He went to get it for her.

Henry Williams and his wife came over to them. He asked Kirstin if she had gotten over her confrontation with his doberman pinscher. Everyone in the growing group listened to the tale. Kirstin entreated the older man not to worry, that the dog had been just as shocked and terrified as she had been. Even so, Henry apologized once more.

Fred Haskell and his wife joined them. The men talked for a short time, while Kirstin observed. *So far so good,* she decided.

Christopher suggested Kirstin sit and rest her foot, the ploy working too well to foil. She settled into a wooden chair which the half-Apache man had fetched.

"Thank you, John. That's better. Where's Maria?"

The officer leaned over to whisper, "She'll join us soon. Tom's wife has her cornered asking about some Mexican recipes. She's a great cook. If I didn't stay active and push back from the table, she'd have me fat as a hog."

The men continued their conversation about planting and harvesting, the dry weather, and politics—local, state and national.

After David Carson, Bill Hainsley, and their wives joined the group, the conversation switched to the impending cattle and horse auction. Kirstin was aware of the way they—ranchers all—kept stealing furtive looks at her as Christopher answered questions about how they met.

"What kind of work do you do, Kirstin?" Bill's wife asked.

"I'm a technologist at Medico of America in San Diego."

"You're in medicine, too?" Bill sought more information.

"Yes, in the research end."

"Kirstin's good at her work; Medico hires only the best," Christopher added.

"Are you married?" David asked.

Would I be staying at your friend's ranch if I were? "A widow."

"Do you have kids?" David's wife inquired.

Kirstin answered politely; everyone in the group seemed to be having fun. While the genial conversation was still in progress, a lone man arrived. He had to ask Christopher to introduce them.

Kirstin soon discovered why Christopher made the intentional oversight and complied with seeming reluctance. She was unnerved by the lustful look in Lance Reynold's eyes when he reached for her hand to shake it, then held it much too tight and too long. She finally was compelled to pull it from his firm grasp.

"You didn't tell us the other day at Joe Bob's, that your patient and house guest is so beautiful and charming, Chris," he chided.

"Lance is our local Don Juan," he explained to Kirstin. "Recently divorced for the third time, so beware of his suave manner and silver tongue."

"Aw, hell, Chris, don't bad mouth me to our ravishing guest."

Christopher chuckled. "I was only kidding. Lance owns a stockyard in Clovis and runs some of our biggest and best auctions. He'd be worth a fortune if he didn't have so many ex-wives and kids to support," the doctor added.

"How long will you be staying in these parts, Kirstin"

"Until I'm healed and Doctor Harrison releases me from his care."

"If I were the doctor, I'd find excuses to keep you around a mighty long time. Chris is slipping if he's letting you leave so soon."

"I'm a working woman, Mr. Reynolds. I prefer for my injuries to heal fast so I can drive and get around better. I'd hate to be forced to leave my car here or pay an outrageous amount of money to have it hauled to California. It was kind and generous of Christopher to let me stay at his ranch. His place is far nicer than a hotel room or hospital room. It appears westerners are as gracious as we southerners are alleged to be."

"Call me Lance, please," he coaxed in a husky voice. "If you're in a rush and need a ride home, I have some time off next week and I'd be happy to chauffeur you. I swear I'll be more than kind and gracious."

"That won't be necessary. Mr. Reynolds. I have friends and family who can pick me up if I can't drive soon. My schedule isn't that rushed. I was on holiday when this series of unfortunate events happened, and my vacation isn't used up yet. But thank you for the offer."

Christopher was delighted that Kirstin declined Lance's offer of transportation and refused to call him by his first name, probably with the hopes of putting the egotistical flirt in his place.

"I'm starved," Bill interjected. "Let's get some chow. Chris, you and Kirstin want to come along and join us?"

"I'll fetch Kirstin's food and drink, but thanks anyhow."

The group headed for the food-laden tables, all except Lance who lingered behind.

"You having fun at Chris's?" he asked Kirstin.

"One could hardly call suffering three painful injuries having fun."

"Chris is a good man. I guess he's lonely over there. I bet he's enjoying your injuries. I mean, your company and mutual interests."

Considering the number of people she'd come into contact with on and off the ranch, her presence there was no secret. Many must suspect she was sleeping with Christopher. She was proud of herself for how she was handling herself. "He doesn't appear to be a lonely man. He's a fine doctor and a perfect gentleman. It's a shame more men aren't like him. The world could certainly use them."

"What do you do all day with a hurt foot? You have to lie around a lot?"

"The hospital doctor ordered me to stay off of it as much as possible, which I do," she responded, feigning ignorance of his insinuation. "Anyone with intelligence can entertain himself."

"What sort of games and entertainment do you like, Kirstin? I'm sure we could have a good time together. I promise you wouldn't be bored."

Kirstin couldn't believe his forwardness. The vile creature lacked all manners and tact. She struggled to her feet. "If you'll excuse me, Mr. Reynolds, I'll go tell Christopher what to put on my plate. Goodbye." She hobbled away.

Just as she located her companion, Carla rushed over to him, hugged him, and spoke loud enough for others—including her—to hear every word.

"Chris, darling, you naughty boy, where have you been keeping yourself? Work and your company can't be taking up all of your time."

Kirstin saw Carla cling to him. Feeling out

of place, Kirstin glanced around and brightened when she saw Jenny Carlisle sitting near the oversize swimming pool and joined her. "Hi, Jenny. How are you feeling? Should you be out already?"

Jenny smiled at Kirstin. "They don't keep new mothers down long these days. Afraid they'll spoil us. I made Bob bring me along. The baby's still in the hospital. They won't release him until he gains more weight and gets stronger." She held out a picture for Kirstin to view. "He's beautiful, isn't he?" she murmured in love and pride.

"Yes, he is. And you're looking great. How do you feel?"

"Still a little weak, but I was restless. Never been a couch potato. This is my first day out. How's the hand and foot?"

"Getting better every day."

Jenny motioned for Bob to bring Kirstin a chair. He thanked her again for helping out the night the baby was born. They chatted for a short time before Bob left to get the couple's meals. Kirstin realized Carla kept glancing her way. Evidently they were discussing her. The tiny visual daggers Carla sent into her face and body made it obvious she wanted and planned to get Christopher Harrison.

Jenny noticed their hostess's behavior and frowned. "You'll have to overlook Carla's misconduct. I bet she feels like a wet hen with you here."

"Why?" Kirstin asked as if ignorant of the past situation.

"Need you ask? See the way she's clinging to Doctor Harrison?" Jenny hinted. "If Carla had her way they'd be a twosome. I doubt Doctor Harrison's interested, though. You'd think she owns this whole state the way she carries on. If she sets her sights on a man, he'd better watch out and run for cover."

"You don't like her?" Kirstin whispered to prevent being overheard.

"Like Carla? People endure or avoid or brown-nose Carla, not *like* her. If she weren't rich and single and an only child who'll get all of this one day, half these men wouldn't be here today. You and Christopher look great together. You like him, don't you?"

Kirstin flushed, but nodded her head. "He's a fine man."

Jenny smiled in undisguised pleasure. "Carla plays the Queen Bee. She buzzes around lots of men, but she wants to light on him the most."

"I see," Kirstin murmured.

"Don't worry. With you around, what man would notice her?"

"I'll be leaving soon. Once I'm all right, it'll look strange for me to hang around. I'm already getting funny looks from some people for staying at his ranch."

"Don't pay any attention to old busybodies and prudes. I think Christopher's quite taken with you, and he needs a good woman. Why not let him know you feel the same?" Jenny reasoned.

"We haven't known each other very long, and time is running out."

"You could always fake an accident. Say, fall off a horse and break the other leg?" Jenny conspired.

"I couldn't do that, Jenny. Anyway, I have to get to work soon."

"Then you better work fast," Jenny pressured her.

She and Jenny laughed, then began talking about the baby and their joint adventure and Kirstin's family.

Linda, Timmy's mother, joined them. "Kirstin, I want to thank you again for helping my son the other day. He's still raving about you. I've told everyone how wonderful you are with kids."

Kirstin smiled. "He's a wonderful little boy, Mrs. Shaw, and I've had plenty of practice like that with my own children."

"Please call me Linda. I couldn't believe you actually took a shot yourself just to calm him down," she said in appreciation.

"It was only saline solution. Thank goodness I'm not Doctor Harrison's assistant. That job would get painful fast."

The three women laughed. "I can't even watch them. I faint every time I have one myself," Linda admitted. "Your story worked like a charm; Timmy adores you. Too bad you *aren't* Christopher's assistant."

Christopher arrived just then with her meal: corn on the cob, potato salad, barbecue, roll, and raw vegetables. As Bob set up two folding tables, Christopher told Kirstin, "I'll bring you a bowl of fruit after you finish this. That'll cover everything you need. I'll fetch you a drink and join you after I get my chow."

She looked at the plate. "Must I eat everything?"

"Every bite, Mrs. Lowrey. Doctor's orders." He turned to Linda and Jenny. "Can I get you ladies something to eat?" he offered.

"Bob's getting mine," Jenny responded, smiling.

"I'm joining Lance," the divorced Linda told them.

Kirstin masked an unfavorable reaction to that news; an alert Christopher caught it before leaving to fill his plate. Bob returned, and Linda excused herself. He pulled a chair over and sat down next to his wife, balancing a plate on his knees. The three chatted until Christopher joined them, deciding he would ask for an explanation later about Lance's behavior.

When the dancing started later, Christopher—to thwart Carla and Lance's pursuits of both of them—initiated their departure. They edged their way through the crowd toward his vehicle. Christopher told the people that Kirstin needed to get back to the ranch to soak her foot. Everyone expressed pleasure at meeting her and voiced hopes of seeing her again. Their final words were with John and Maria, who canceled the camping trip because John had just gotten the word that another officer had taken ill and prevented John's days off on Sunday and Monday. To make up for the change in plans, the New Mexico couple invited them to dinner Thursday night, and Christopher accepted for them.

Kirstin was astonished by their hostess's conduct. Carla didn't come over to speak with her again. Nor did Lance come to say goodbye, but she and Christopher were cognizant of the flirt's occasional stares. The party was over, Kirstin mused, and no major problem had occurred.

Christopher helped Kirstin into his Wagoneer and drove away. On the way home, he asked, "Was it okay to tell John and Maria we'd come over for supper Thursday? I should have asked you first. But with them standing there and waiting for an answer, it seemed best to accept. You did say you enjoy their company."

"No, it was fine. I'd love to go. They're fun. Nice people."

"How was the barbecue itself?"

"It was fun, too. I like your friends and neighbors, most of them. I can get rid of these now," she said, unwrapping her healed limbs. "Do you have socials like that often around here? Had any at your ranch?"

"We have 'em a few times a year, here and there, but I've never given one. The Thompsons is the biggest; they invite almost everyone."

"The entire population of Clovis and Portales wasn't there, was it?"

"Oh," he murmured as he grasped her meaning. "I meant, everyone they like and know, and whoever else has a reason to be asked."

"Ulterior motives to include them?"

"You catch on fast, woman. Mix business with pleasure."

"It's like that everywhere, isn't it? I had to attend plenty of functions and parties and a few conventions with David when I'd rather have been home. As a *housewife*. I wasn't considered very interesting or important in a group of career people and socialites."

"That's hard to believe, Kirstin. I've never found you boring. Neither did the folks at the barbecue today. You must have been a big asset to David."

"Thanks. I tried to be one but it didn't work many times, not that I could see. The moment we arrived anywhere, he was off socializing or enticing clients and I was left to fend for myself. I used to be shy and uneasy in those settings. I've changed a lot since his death; I've had to. I have my own friends and niche in the world. I'm Kirstin Lowrey now, not Mrs. David Lowrey. It's wonderful to be a person again."

Christopher nodded in respect. "Actually, I remember Laura practically shunning housewives when we went places. I guess she didn't want to be considered and treated as one. She didn't have an outside job after I went into practice but she was involved with clubs and organizations and board memberships. But she always had an ulterior motive for any charity work she did. The more publicity it got, the better she liked it. Laura viewed herself above others but I'm glad to say that seems to have changed in recent years; I think both marriage to Harry and time have had a positive effect on her. They keep extending the olive branch; I guess I should accept it. I was a culprit, too, before I moved here. I didn't talk or listen much to wives of colleagues, unless they were professionals. Now I do, and I enjoy it.

Women like Jenny and Maria are interesting. I suppose we all have our shortcomings . . ."

They laughed and exchanged nods of agreement.

"You still on for camping?" Christopher asked. "We're supposed to pick up the RV at eight in the morning. I can cancel if you don't feel right about going without John and Maria."

"Miss Carlsbad and White Sands? No way. Besides, if people are going to talk about us, they'll find something else as fuel for their gossip, so why miss a great time and marvelous sights?" Kirstin laughed. "If we're careful, we won't get caught."

"Excellent suggestion. I've already told the answering service to take my calls and refer any emergencies to a colleague or the Clovis hospital."

"All we have to do is pack tonight and leave tomorrow."

"You have everything you'll need?"

"Absolutely. And I told Katie where I'll be so she won't worry."

"What did she say?"

"To have fun. She's a great kid, Christopher. The best. I hope you can meet her one day. You will if you come to visit one weekend."

"I accept your invitation. We'll work out the details later."

"Did you tell Peggy about our trip?"

"No."

"If she calls, she might worry when you don't answer or respond."

"I'll check my machine with my little gismo while we're gone."

"I wouldn't want her annoyed at me again."

"I think she's over her initial shock and bad behavior. I hope so. Hey, I have a great idea; why don't we throw our stuff together and leave now? Carlsbad is only a few hours away; we could be there long before dark. It stays light in these parts until nine. I can leave a note at the rental place. They won't mind us heading out today."

Before five, the camper was loaded and they pulled out of the parking lot, leaving his vehicle around back and out of sight.

Kirstin gazed at the high plains-enclosed road before them and wondered what would happen during their cozy trip alone.

Fourteen

"Tell me about New Mexico and this section of it," she coaxed, *in case I ever come to live here.*

Christopher enjoyed her smile and interest in the state where he resided. "We have whites from countless ethnic groups, including Spanish and Mexican. We've got a large Indian population: Apache, Navajo, and Pueblos. Seventy percent sunshine year round. Some thunderstorms in July and August, but mostly great weather. We've got deserts, forests, and mountains. About the only thing we don't have is a beach; sorry about that."

Christopher continued his enlightening lesson for a while, then asked, "What did Lance say to you?" as if just recalling the curious scene he had witnessed from a distance, even though it had been preying on his mind.

"Say to me?" she echoed, wondering about his motive and feelings.

"At the barbecue. From the look on both your faces, he was making a pass at you, not a welcome one, either."

"Is that jealousy I hear, Doc?" she murmured.

"I doubt he's your type."

"He definitely *isn't* my type," she vowed. "He was just being nosy about us and our . . . living arrangements."

"Why, that low-down snake," he snarled. "Did he insult you?"

"Let's just say I found his remarks embarrassing and repulsive. He's a conceited bore, so you have nothing to worry about where he's concerned. I ignored him and pretended to be the innocent female. It was obvious he suspects what's going on between us, but I didn't tell him anything. I can't vouch for my guilty look, however."

"I hope you told him off," he growled.

"With the sweetest expression and voice and words I could muster, under the circumstances."

"Did he ask you out?" he pressed.

"No, but he was leading up to it. I didn't give him the chance. I was almost rude; I made it crystal clear I didn't like him or his behavior."

"Good for you. He deserved a put-down. He thinks he's God's gift to women. Other than that misconception, he's a fine fellow and good businessman. When he's not on the make, he's good company. Too bad those are rare times. I only tolerate him and his antics then because I have business dealings with him. With his history, you'd think women would see through him and avoid him, but they don't. He's got a charming and persuasive way with females. I hope Linda doesn't get tangled up with him. She and her little boy don't deserve the trouble such a selfish and destructive man can bring them."

"If I were Linda, I wouldn't trust Lance Reynolds as far as I could toss him. And I would be very cautious about a second marriage. She doesn't need to repeat mistakes from her first one. She seems to be doing fine on her own."

"Don't jump out of a frying pan into a fire, right?"

"Absolutely. Look, Christopher! What is that?"

It was clear to him that she wanted to drop the disturbing topic, so he did. "Bottomless Lakes is sixteen miles southwest of Roswell. I wish we had time to stop by; maybe we'll come back another day. It was a major stop on the Goodnight-Loving cattle trail. It's something special to see. You'd also like the museum and art center."

Kirstin wondered if the area was as quiet and secluded as it seemed on the surface. She asked, "What do you all do for entertainment year round when you aren't ranching or farming or doctoring?"

"Lots of things: rodeos, stock auctions, livestock shows, street dances, barbecues, chili cookings and contests, hayrides, horseshoes, county fairs. Some towns even have armadillo or mule races; they're a riot. We have festivals of all types: heritage, ranching, pioneer. Portales has a Peanut Valley Festival that's fun. It's not a big town, but it has plenty of business: grain distilling plants, soft drink canners, grain storage and shipping, and lots of trucking. You've probably noticed how many trucks there are on the highway. When they pass us, I have to hold this steering wheel hard right to keep from being blown off the pavement. I hope I'll be used to driving this big boy soon."

"I think you're handling the RV just fine."

During the forty-minute drive to Carlsbad, Christopher explained some of the aforementioned events to a lively and amused Kirstin.

"Let's take in the Living Desert Park before we settle in our campsite."

"Suits me. You're the tour guide."

"Just make sure we don't overlook your eating schedule."

"I'll keep one eye on my watch, Doc. And I

412

had my snack."

"Yep, and I'll have mine later."

Kirstin grinned as she was warmed by his smoldering look. Alone and snuggled together in the bed behind them . . . she'd never had sex with David anywhere except in their bedroom, not even in hotels during the few trips away from it.

In the Ocotillo Hills overlooking the town, they visited the park with its numerous examples of native plant and animal life in their natural habitats. They savored the scenery and information about the Chihauhuan Desert and each other's company. Hand in hand, laughing and chatting, they strolled around the cacti, and mountain lions, the roadrunners, elk, deer, and bobcats, the javelina, prairie dogs, foxes, snakes, birds, and other creatures.

"This is great, woman, but it's getting late. It'll be dark soon. Let's get moving to our campground. I have some juicy steaks to cook."

"My mouth's watering in anticipation."

"I hope for more than food."

"There's food and there's . . . food, Doctor Harrison."

The RV was set up and meat was on the grill. Christopher relaxed in a chair and sipped a beer. Kirstin had the folding table ready for their meal and was drinking a diet cola. They talked about their plans for the next two days. After the steaks were done, they ate and continued their chat. When everything was put away, they strolled around the picturesque area. The moon was almost full; it lighted their path and bathed them in a romantic glow. They passed many campers of various sizes, a few with amusing name tags on them. Some were adorned with colorful lanterns; others had all sorts of items around for the comfort or entertainment of the occupants. Genial folks nodded, waved, or spoke a few words to the couple. It became a game to see who could spot the funniest or most creative tag.

"Check it out, Christopher: 'Old but not over the hill, agewise that is, just this rig.' There's another cute one: 'Roughing it smoothly.' "

"This certainly isn't like old-time camping. I like it. What about you?"

"I could get used to it fast, Doc. Sort of like taking a minivacation."

"No wonder John and Maria enjoy it so much. They keep their RV ready to pull out at a moment's notice. I'll have to consider buying one. There's a lot to see in America. Some of the boys go on fishing and hunting trips around the state and northward. And some groups have rallies that John says are loads of fun. They travel to all different places and do all kinds of fun things. They meet interesting people from everywhere, even foreign countries. Most of my travels in the past were medical trips, so I didn't see much. Of course it wouldn't be much fun alone. Maybe I can persuade you to tag along."

"Sounds great to me. As I told you, I haven't seen or done much, either, around the country. This is a good way to travel."

"Maybe you should go with me to select which size and model to buy. We'd want all the comforts of home like this rented one has. I could even earn expense money doctoring along the way when folks have accidents."

Kirstin realized how excited he appeared about the unexpected idea, which included her. She was surprised by his mention of doctoring without a glance at his disabled hand or hint about it. Was he viewing them as a couple? She decided not to comment about his statements, in case they were just slips because of his relaxed mood. "Look: 'Retired before the kids used up all our money.'" She spotted two more side by side: "I bet 'Rebel Rouser' is from the Deep South. The 'Eagle has flown' on that American Eagle is cunning. I bet those cost plenty; they're huge and sleek.

Probably loaded with extras. My kind of camping."

Christopher noticed she didn't respond to his remarks. "Those next two aren't shabby, either: 'Big Bucks' and 'Southern Comfort.' I bet it cost them some big bucks. Yep, I could get into this easy-going lifestyle."

"We'd be spoiled in a week and hate to return to work. Those two say it all: 'Retired: home is where I am.' 'Lost but I don't care.' "

"That's nothing, look at that one: 'If I'm rocking, don't come knocking.' I wonder what it means?" he asked with a grin and chuckle.

"I wouldn't have the vaguest idea," she laughed. "There's mine, 'Sweet Time.' How cute, 'Peters Perch' on a Blue Bird."

The owners of it, setting up for the night, rounded the recreational vehicle at that moment, smiled, and greeted them.

"Hi, we're the Peters, Larry and Corky, from St. Louis. This is some location, isn't it?"

"Yes, it's lovely. I'm Kirstin and this is Christopher. We were just reading all the signs and tags. They're adorable. This is our first trip."

"What kind of camper do you have?" Larry asked Christopher.

The men chatted about RV's and sites while Kirstin and Corky got acquainted. When Kirstin mentioned the tag next door, the redhead told her she was a diabetic.

"So am I," Kirstin revealed. "How long have you been diabetic?"

"Nearly all my life. I'm an old hand at it. What about you?"

"Only a few months. I'm still learning and adjusting. It's hard sometimes because our society seems built around eating events: food, drink, and those infernal sweets to tempt even the strongest person."

"I know what you mean," Corky replied, "You can't pick up a woman's magazine or watch TV without being inundated with pictures and recipes for no-no's. I finally stopped looking at them. When I see something sinfully delicious, I keep telling myself what the eater will have to do to work off all that sugar and fat."

Kirstin laughed. "Does it help?"

Corky pushed windblown fiery curls from her eyes. "Are you kidding? No. But sometimes I fool myself long enough to get beyond the temptation. I lecture myself about how fast simple sugar dumps into the body and how one candy bar or piece of pie could land me in the hospital. I have too much to do and too much to see to waste time lying around in a white room."

Kirstin liked the vivacious woman. "If only

we could live in a vacuum and not be tempted at every turn. We need to enjoy holidays and special events, too. Planning strategies with doctors and dieticians gets tiring, doesn't it?"

"Yep, but we can occasionally splurge or cheat by rearranging our diet, medication, and exercise. If you're interested, Kirstin, I can give you lots of tips I've learned over the years."

"You've had more practice than I have; I'd appreciate it. I don't come into contact with many people I know well enough to get down to brass tacks about the condition. It seems to make some people uneasy and others think you're dying before their eyes."

"It gets easier; I promise. You can't let it make you feel helpless, because you aren't; you're in control of your health and life."

"It's just so intrusive on my life and work. Few people have to almost stop in their tracks to eat on schedule or suffer the consequences. It's hard on people around you, too."

"No matter how much family and friends love you, worry about you, and want to help, the responsibility is yours. But they have to adjust to our moods and insulin reaction problems. Why don't we get together tomorrow and I'll give you those tips I mentioned? Larry and I had a long drive and we're starving. Are you two staying around for a while?"

"Just tomorrow until we visit the caverns. Then we're heading for White Sands. We only have until Monday night to take in the sights."

"That matches our plans until Monday. Then, we're on to Arizona for the sixth time; there's so much to see there." She nodded toward her husband, chatting a short distance away. "Larry works for the postal service and has a month off. We take advantage of every day."

"Christopher is a semiretired physician. He has a ranch about three hours from here. I work in medical research and I'm finishing a vacation. I would like to chat with you. I need help."

"What about if we see the caverns and have lunch in the underground restaurant together?"

"That sounds wonderful. Thank you. We'd better get moving, Christopher. Corky and Larry had a long drive today and they have chores."

"We'll meet here at nine. Okay?"

"See you then," Kirstin replied without asking her companion.

As they continued their stroll, she said, "I hope you don't mind my making plans without consulting you first." She related the reason.

"Both things sound perfect to me. I liked the Peters. I can learn plenty about RV's and places to go from Larry. They've done this for years. Besides, we men made plans to cook out and play cards together tomorrow night."

"Wonderful. But I thought we were heading for White Sands after we tour the cavern."

"We are; so are they. Larry suggested we visit the space center at Alamogordo and spend the night at Oliver Lee State Park, then do White Sands on Monday. He says if we pack too much into one day, we won't get the full benefits of each sight. What do you think? Want them along?"

"Sounds fine to me; they'll make good tour guides for us greenhorns."

"Learning western lingo already. I hope you don't mind my telling him we're married. I thought that would make you feel more at ease around them and others we meet. You didn't tell Corky otherwise, did you?"

"No. She didn't ask and I didn't offer any personal information," she said, then related the tiny exception to her statement. "But what if somebody you know comes around tomorrow and contradicts you?"

"I doubt it. And I figured we'd never see the Peters again."

"It's fine, really. I'm sure lots of couples do the same when traveling."

Following a passionate night and morning,

Kirstin and Christopher joined the Peters at their camper at nine. If any questions were asked about them, they had their "wed three months ago story" ready. The Peters towed a car with them for sightseeing, and the four got inside and drove to Walnut Canyon.

After listening to the ranger's talk, they approached the cave's entrance, a gaping hole in the earth that was surrounded by rocks and gray-green vegetation and a multitude of colorful cacti in varying species. As they toured America's largest underground chamber of beautiful and breathtaking formations, the two women chatted almost nonstop, as did the men, to Kirstin's surprise. They worked their way through the remarkable honeycombs and admired the awesome sights of draperies, crystals, domes, soda straws, helictites, stalagmites, and stalactites.

Kirstin was glad she was wearing a light jacket and comfortable tennis shoes, as the air was cool and the path rugged. She also was relieved they could tour at their own pace to help regulate fuel-sapping exertions for her and her new friend. Even so, she had an ample supply of glucose tablets in her pocket for emergencies, as did Christopher and Corky.

The couples talked about the legendary bat flights at dusk, something they would miss this time because the migratory creatures had not returned from their winter location. The guide told them that about three hundred thousand came each year around mid-May and remained until October and gave visitors a memorable and stimulating sight.

Everyone nodded when the redhead quipped, "Well, I guess that gives us an excuse to come here again during the right season."

As hours passed, Corky filled Kirstin's head with information about diabetes: safe ways to alter a rigid schedule, facts on "sugarless" treats, calling ahead about restaurant menus and parties, how to pretreat before special events to avoid problems, when and how many glucose tablets to use to forestall trouble during rushed or inconvenient times, discount places for ordering supplies, charts and lists to make and post inside kitchen cabinets for quick reference, reduction of her instruction book to a carry-along purse size, heating hands under warm water in the winter to aid taking blood samples when they were cold and stubborn, how and when to exercise without encountering hypoglycemic attacks, and ways she could test herself to ward off complications.

"I've read countless books and brochures on diabetes, but you've told me things I didn't know. All of this will be a big help, Corky; thanks."

"Somebody who's been there a long time learns lots of tricks. If at all possible, Kirstin, you want to stay off insulin injections. Take good care of yourself and you might accomplish that."

"I'm doing my best. With all this knowledge, it'll be even easier." For the first time since her diagnosis, Kirstin felt in control of the situation; she experienced hope of staying well; she felt resentment fading. Some of the terror was lessened or gone. The highway episode and its aftermath was a godsend. Now, all she had to do was deal with the two men in her life: her son and Christopher. Everything she was learning improved her courage and gave her strength.

When their drinks were delivered in the underground lunchroom, Corky pulled out a bottle of strips and told Kirstin, "Keep some of these in your purse for testing your sugar. We ordered diet drinks, but busy waiters and waitresses can forget and serve regular ones. Sometimes it's hard to tell with fountain types. One cola has nine spoons of sugar, and we know what that can do to us. The strips are good for checking sauces, too. If you can't get enough liquid to pool, just add a smidgen of water and stir and dip. It only takes thirty seconds to be certain something's safe for us. Don't ever be embarrassed or reluctant to special order, like duck without a sugar-loaded cherry sauce. Chefs don't mind, and don't let waiters con you into thinking it's too much trouble for them. Protect yourself at all times."

"Kirstin's smart; she'll take your good advice," Christopher assured Corky.

"She's lucky she has you for a husband, Doctor Harrison. You can understand what she's going through and how to help."

Christopher chuckled. "Sometimes I'm too much of a nag."

"So is Larry. But even when we frown and fuss, we appreciate you two caring so much about us. Don't we, Kirstin?"

"Yes, we do."

The talk halted a time while they finished their meals.

While the men waited, the women purchased souvenirs. Kirstin bought a picture of the landscape to hang in her apartment as a reminder of the lovely day. It was one she'd never forget because of Christopher and Corky. She hoped they could see each other again after this trip, meet at other places. She had observed Christopher with the other man; they seemed to have struck up a good rapport and friendship. Once, to her amazement, she had overheard Christopher telling Larry why he had retired, and she hadn't detected the usual enormous bitterness in his voice.

As they were leaving the cavern, Kirstin chatted with Larry about children, as the Peters had one in high school and one in college. Corky used the few private minutes to talk with Christopher about "his wife's" health and how not to take her mood swings to heart. Christopher was delighted by the woman's caring and generous manner.

On the return drive, they drove the loop along the Guadalupe ridge. They stopped several times to look at the splendid terrain of wild beauty: sweeping hills, arroyos, rolling dunes, with a wild variety of plant and animal life. They reached the campground and separated to prepare for departure.

As Kirstin readied herself for travel to their next location, she mused on the day. She felt wonderful, happy and relaxed. Christopher appeared the same. He was so cuddly and sweet and attentive that he almost made her suspicious. If she didn't know better, she would think he was convinced of their marital tale or he was trying to tell her something without using words.

He grinned and quipped, "I'm fast, woman. 'On the road again.' "

"That isn't fair, Doc; the engine isn't running yet, so it doesn't count. You can't win a treat by being first to say it if you cheat."

"You wound me to the core, woman: me, a

cheater?" he jested, one hand held over his heart and a feigned grimace on his face. "I'm going to win this contest more times than you because I'm going to stay alert; I need all the treats I can get before you go."

"Just so you share those treats, Doc. I don't mind you winning them."

"Or mind playing Kirstin Harrison on the trail? Oh, yes, 'On the road again,' and I win. I gave you time after I cranked up to leave."

"Cheater! You had me distracted. I'll have to watch you closely."

"I hope so; I truly hope so, woman." Whistling, he put the gear in drive and pulled out of the assigned slot behind Larry Peters's rig.

The two couples drove through the southern Rockies and national forest, the desert heat and landscape left behind. They passed Cloudcroft and its fine resorts high in the mountains and woods.

"Do you snow ski?"

"No, do you?" she asked.

"Not anymore, and I didn't do it much in the past. Don't miss it, either. But I miss golf and racquetball. I never could get them down with my right hand, so I gave them up and stopped aggravating myself."

Kirstin glanced at him from the corner of her eye; she couldn't read his true feelings. To avoid a mood change in him, she ignored that

426

topic. "I would be terrified to fly down a slope at such a pace and without control; I don't have the slightest interest in trying that sport. I water-skied some when I was in high school and college. I'm too old for it now."

"No you aren't, but you don't want to risk breaking bones."

She jested, "Just adapt to a rocking chair and Granniehood to protect my health?"

"I wouldn't go that far. You've had fun hiking and camping, and you've taken proper care of yourself during them. Horseback riding doesn't zap your sugar and lots of other activities wouldn't, either. I'm glad we met the Peters; Corky is teaching you a lot."

"You seem to have hit it off with Larry, too. I overheard some of the information he's been stuffing inside your head about campers. You'll be prepared for anything after you purchase yours."

"You'll trust me better during trips after I'm well trained, right?"

"I trust you on this one. You're doing fine; no, great. You look born to that RV seat just like you do to the saddle."

"Ranching isn't my career by choice, but I like it." He fibbed because he didn't want her to think he hated his life and was consumed by bitterness. Besides, he had no choice but to accept his existence.

Once more, Kirstin steered the subject away from the loss of his career and his torment by asking, "What's in this area?"

As they rolled past the turn-off for Sunspot Christopher related facts about the solar observatory built there and the annual Futurity at nearby Ruidoso Downs; he suggested they make the last one a future adventure. He talked about the first A-Bomb site at Trinity.

The couples reached Alamogordo where the International Space Hall of Fame and Space Center were located. They parked side-by-side at a complex that was backed by the picturesque cliffs of the Sacramento Mountains and overlooked White Sands Missile Range. The awesome structure—a huge golden glass tube—was outlined in glorious splendor against a blue sky and had been built in honor of men who had dared to take chances on and beyond Earth. They got out of the vehicles to visit the outdoor displays, theater, and planetarium.

They ended the exciting day at the Oliver Lee State Park, south of town. There was enough light left to tour the visitor's center and historic exhibits, many of them having to do with ranching and Indian battles. It was a cool evening, and their jackets felt good during their stroll.

Following pork chops on the grill and several games of cards, the two couples separated for the night, to meet at nine to head for White Sands.

"You're enjoying yourself, aren't you?" Christopher asked Kirstin.

Kirstin replied, "Very much. The scenery was so beautiful and varied: caves and desert to mountains and sand dunes. I can hardly wait to see the view tomorrow. The boys will like those little rockets I bought them today; I'll mail them from the ranch."

"White Sands will be different from how it looks on TV when the shuttle lands. I wish John and Maria were with us. You would have liked seeing the Mescalero Reservation. We can go there another time, okay?"

"I hope so." *Let's see if you keep your promises.*

Christopher's lips and hands roamed Kirstin. She sighed in contentment. *If only I weren't so afraid of telling you how I feel about you, afraid you aren't as serious about me as I am about you.*

Within moments, neither one could think of anything except each other and their fiery lovemaking.

Kirstin stared at the setting before her. "It looks as if the ground is covered with snow as far as you can see," she murmured. "The bro-

429

chure says it's a two-hundred-seventy square-mile ocean of gypsum crystals and borders alkali flats."

The tawny-and-green landscape halted suddenly and became a blanket of stark white stretching beyond visual capacity. A mountain range in a bluish haze created a magnificent backdrop on one side. They left their RVs at the visitor's center to drive in the Peters's car to the Heart of Sands Loop and Big Dune Trail. Undulating dunes glittered beneath the sun, occasionally too brilliant to look at without sunglasses. Some areas were flat; others rose and fell in wondrous beauty, a few at great heights. Some were barren; some were dotted with tenacious greenery: saltbush, yucca, iodine bush, squawbush, and soaptree. Many places lay in waves like a pristine beach or an ebbing tide.

As the two couples stood atop one dune and gazed over the rugged terrain, they saw round ones, short ones, tall ones, and some with lumpy ridges and sharp crests. They noticed the countless footprints of visitors that would soon be concealed by blasts of wind.

When their tour was over, they snacked at the visitor's center and chatted before parting for what might be the last time. They exchanged addresses and hopes of getting together again in the future.

Kirstin wished she could tell the perky red-head the truth, that she'd be heading for her home in San Diego soon. She liked Corky Peters and wanted to deepen their friendship, but that wouldn't be possible without a confession of her deceit. Corky had a glow about her that had nothing to do with health, a smile that was genuine and warm, and an outgoing personality. She wanted this genial relationship to continue and was dismayed that would be denied her.

Corky gave one last piece of advice: "Don't kid yourself, Kirstin: you'll have bad times and feelings, but anger and frustration and upsets are normal for us. Stay positive and confident and don't let anything or anyone get you down."

The women embraced and said another farewell. The two rigs pulled out of the parking lot, one heading southwest and one northeast.

Christopher and Kirstin crossed the Apache reservation, rode through the national forest, passed Roswell, and in less than four hours arrived back at the ranch. During the drive, they chatted about the trip, their new friends, the sights they passed, and plans for the next nine days before Kirstin was to depart for San Diego.

Christopher unloaded their belongings and checked his answering machine and medical service before he returned the rented camper and retrieved his vehicle. He took the precaution of going alone in case men were around who might tease them and embarrass Kirstin.

During his absence, Kirstin phoned Katie. Her daughter was out, so she left a message announcing their safe return. She then unpacked their food and possessions, and put supper on to cook.

While Christopher was checking on his elderly heart patient at the Clovis hospital the next day, Kirstin wrote Sandi and Steve, but only the letter to the girl revealed news about Christopher. Her son's enlightenment should come in conversation when the time was right. She also sent letters to her two best friends in Augusta, as she couldn't phone them during working hours or at night while the major subject of interest was present; she told them she would call when she reached California. She wrapped the children and grandchildren's gifts to mail the next day. Then, she did some light house tasks. She knew Christopher had called Peggy from his office last night, but he hadn't shared their talk with her. She hoped no new trouble had arisen with his daughter. She dreaded the thought that if things worked out between her and Christopher they would have problems with Peggy and Steve.

It was after five when Christopher arrived home. He told her he'd stopped to chat with John and they'd discussed camping and RVs. Again, he suggested they look at recreational vehicles before her departure. Kirstin smiled and agreed.

Wednesday, Christopher saw several patients. After the last one left, Kirstin went to ask if there was anything she could do to help with charts and clean-up chores. The well-oiled storm door didn't make noise when she opened it and entered the front room. She heard his voice, but knew it was on a recorder. She peeked into his office and saw him sitting at his computer, his back to her.

Kirstin observed him and realized what he was doing. He had joked days ago about his writing with his right hand being illegible and the task impossible with his disabled one. The few times she'd assisted with patients, she had seen him dictate notes about them into a small machine which he kept in his pocket. He played and replayed the information unit so he could type it into his computer, mostly using a single-handed pecking. Following each entry, he printed out the sheet, placed it in a patient's chart, and put it in the file cabinet nearby.

Kirstin's heart was panged by the extra work created by his problem. She was tempted to offer to do the typing and filing for him, then decided it wasn't wise to cast additional light on his disability. He could use a secretary to do typing, billing, and insurance filing, a nurse to assist with patients, set up for them, sterilize instruments afterward, give shots, and help with treatments he couldn't perform. He seemed to have adjusted to her assistance but was reluctant and too proud to display his troubles before others.

She sneaked from the small building. *Why must you hide out in this wilderness and refuse to heal, refuse to accept your loss, refuse help from others? You aren't the only one who's lost a career, a spouse, or a dream. You have to find replacements, as I'm doing. Your medical problem isn't any more frustrating, angering, or debilitating, than mine is. You can have a wonderful life if you'll only let go of the bitterness. If you can't have all of a dream, take what part of it you can or find a new goal. Don't bury yourself here in self-pity. Don't be less than you can be. I've seen those scrapbooks hidden in your closet; you have so much to give to medicine and surgery. Don't be selfish with your skills and knowledge. Come with me, Christopher; build and share a new dream with me. Don't ask me to go into hiding here with you.*

Christopher suddenly called her name.

"I'm over here near the barn!" she yelled back to him.

After he joined her, Kirstin started to tell him what she'd been thinking, but decided she didn't have the right to intrude in such a personal matter since he hadn't revealed matching feelings. Perhaps when he was confronted with losing her, it would open his eyes. Then, she resolved she would speak the truth.

Christopher stepped behind her and wrapped his arms around her waist. His heart and body warmed when she placed her hands over his and leaned against his chest. It wouldn't hurt, he decided, to give hints about his feelings. "Have I told you how special you are, woman? You've come to mean a lot to me. I hate to see you leave when we're getting along so well, but I know you must. I hope things can continue for us after you go. Good women are hard to find."

Kirstin was disappointed by some of his words: "continue *like this*" and "Good *women*." He didn't even hint about her staying. "I feel the same way, Christopher. You've been a big help to me. I've had a wonderful time here with you. I want our friendship to stay strong."

"If we don't let obstacles get in the way, it will. As soon as you're settled in San Diego, we'll make plans for our next camping trip.

435

Okay?"

"Perfect." She freed herself and turned to him. "Time to eat," she said.

He drew her into his embrace and nibbled at her ear. "Supper isn't the food I had in mind right now."

She laughed and teased, "Aren't you the one who harps about me sticking to my regimen?"

"You're doing fine, thanks to Corky's help. You no longer need a full-time doctor at your beck and call. With the reduction in medication and fill-in tablets, you've had no more problems with hypoglycemia."

"Thanks to your help, too, Doc; I wouldn't be better without it. Am I being released?"

"Only medically." He kissed her forehead. "I still need you for other things."

"Like this?" she murmured as she nuzzled his neck and rubbed a flattened palm over the hardness in his jeans.

He grinned. "You've become a bold creature, Kirstin Lowrey."

"You're to blame, or due the credit." She continued to stroke his maleness and thrilled to her effect on him.

Kirstin worried that someone might drive up or the foreman might ride over and catch them being intimate, outside and in daylight. "Why don't we go inside?" she suggested.

A chuckling Christopher scooped her up and

headed for the house. "I'm going to rush you to bed before you change your mind or we're interrupted."

"How do you know that's what I had in mind?"

"What else? You have to stock up on me before you leave."

"What if I'm insatiable, Doc?"

"Where I'm concerned, I truly hope so."

He used her thigh to close the kitchen door, then fumbled with the lock to shut out anyone who might disturb them. He carried her to his bed and laid her there. Soon, they were out of their clothes and consumed by passion's delights.

A full moon shone overhead as they returned home from John and Maria's the following night. Kirstin said, "I feel light-headed and bubbly. That Mexican food was delicious, and the sugar-free cookies were out of this world. If I hung around much longer, I'd be fat and sassy, and my doctor would kill us both. You have nice friends, Christopher. I'm going to miss those two."

"Only if you never return for visits. You promised you would."

"I did, and I will, as many times as you invite me."

"You have a standing invitation, woman, so don't wait for a spoken word."

"What if you're entertaining when I make a surprise arrival?"

"If you're not with me, I won't be."

"Doctor Harrison, I've gotten very accustomed and attached to you. I'm looking forward to carrying out all of our plans."

So am I, my love, so am I.

As they cuddled in bed together, Christopher told her, "I usually play poker with friends every fourth Friday night of the month. Would you like me to cancel so we can eat out or take in a movie or something?"

"No, you keep your regular schedule. You need to see your friends. I don't want everyone to think I'm hogging you. I can't make a good impression on them if they believe I'm stealing you away from your life here, much as I enjoy your company."

Christopher almost took her provocative bait, but held his revealing reply. *Not yet, old boy. Wait until it's closer to her leaving time to declare your love and propose marriage. If she loves you and you're worth more to her than a research career, she'll accept and stay. Six more days to convince her, here with me is where she belongs.*

Fifteen

After Christopher left, Kirstin realized eighteen mostly glorious days had passed on the Harrison Ranch; her departure date loomed on the near horizon. She settled on the den sofa to watch television. She felt strange in the house tonight, out of place and alone, an intruder. Even with a noisy program on the set, a curious silence plagued her. Maybe it was because nothing here was hers. She phoned Elaine in Augusta.

"Hi, I thought you weren't going to call again until you reached San Diego. I just got your letter today and it was oozing with happiness, you lucky thing. I'm jealous . . . Is something wrong, Kirstin?"

"I'm not sure. Are you busy?"

"I'm not going out until nine, so talk. What's up? Where's the sexy doctor?"

"Out with the boys, a monthly poker game."

"He left you alone on a Friday night? Is he neglecting you already, the cad? What fills your days on that ranch?"

Kirstin didn't take offense to the query, which was similar to Lance's; Elaine cared, was worried about her, and was helping her begin a difficult conversation. "We cook and eat most meals together, and he helps with washing dishes and other chores. He runs his errands and buys the groceries; he's good at it, too. I tidy up the house or do laundry while he does ranch chores or sees patients. I've assisted him a few times with a difficult or frightened one, or when he can't do what's needed because of his injured hand. I told you about those in my letter."

"He sounds like a jewel, a liberated male. So, what else keeps you two occupied?"

"We go riding. He has some beautiful horses. He's given me tours of his land and the surrounding area. It's nothing like Georgia, almost like a desert. I tag along sometimes when he tends the horses. We talk about everything—except us. We've gone out alone or double-dated with his best friends. That camping trip I mentioned and meeting the Peters was wonderful. Some nights we play games or watch TV; others, we listen to music or walk in the moonlight."

Kirstin gave more details about the things

she had mentioned earlier or in past letters. "It's almost as if we're a true couple and this is our home."

"So, what's wrong with that setup? You've captured a real prize, nut. Go with the flow and enjoy him."

"That's what I've been doing. I suppose I'm floundering because I've never done anything like this before. Christopher seems to like things the way they are, but I'm scared and nervous. I don't know where this thing is leading, if anywhere. Marriage is such a serious commitment."

"Marriage? Has he proposed to you?"

"No, but I think he's trying to show me he cares without using words; I could be misreading his signals. I have so many questions. Should I reveal my love and take a chance he feels the same way? Take a risk on being happy as a housewife? Take a bigger one on Steve and Peggy not objecting?" She related the girl's telephone call and his reaction. "How can I know what I'll be missing at Medico if I don't work there for a while? Besides, I gave them my word, Elaine, and I've cost them a bundle. Will things work out if Christopher never accepts the loss of his surgical career? Would I only become his shadow and make him more determined to stay rooted on his ranch?"

"How is he acting? What's he saying?"

Kirstin related some of the hints he had made about his feelings and plans. "Yesterday at John and Maria's, he was so relaxed and cheerful that they commented on my good effect on him and coaxed me to return often to make sure it continued. I watched him play with their children and I could picture him tussling with my three grandsons. I wish he could play golf with Steve and Cliff, but he can't because of his hand. I want my family to meet him, and for him to meet them. I need to see how they get along. I need to meet Peggy and win her over. I want him to discuss and consider working elsewhere. I need those things to happen and to get answers before I can make a decision about a life with him."

"I see your dilemma. But you two seem to get along fantastically."

"Yes. Sometimes we tease each other like kids. But having a good time and great sex aren't all there is to a permanent relationship. There'll be hard times in marriage, too. How will he deal with those? Run and hide again? Become bitter and miserable? Make us both miserable?"

"I think you're right about him dealing with his troubles first. You don't want him bringing excess baggage into your relationship. Do you like it well enough there to settle in and be happy, really happy, Kirstin?"

"I'm not sure. Some things bother me. I wish people like Carla and Lance would mind their own affairs and not begrudge us this little time together. Christopher hasn't said anything, but I sense he's annoyed by the rumors that are going around this tight-knit community. Surely he realized he couldn't keep my extended presence a secret when he coaxed me to stay! Five remaining days . . . Should I stay until next Thursday or leave early?"

"That's a decision only you can make, Kirstin. And Christopher."

Christopher got home from his poker game at two in the morning. Kirstin was asleep in the guest bed. He had uncharacteristically drunk a great deal of liquor, and he didn't want to talk; he wasn't even in the mood to make love to her. Tonight, he had become aware of the rampant gossip about him and Kirstin. He mentally fluctuated between not giving a damn what anyone thought and fury over being the subject of rumor. Several times during the evening it had been impossible to control his temper when some of the men had made crude jokes about Kirstin and their intimate relationship. He wasn't accustomed to boyish teasing and it rankled. He yanked off his clothes and fell into bed.

The incident returned to plague him and deny him sleep. He had almost slugged Lance Reynolds when the divorced man asked Kirstin's measurements and how much pleasure she gave on the examining table, then jested about the advantage of having a female patient with her looks and figure. When Christopher alleged he was still observing her, Bill Hainsley had remarked he would like to observe a woman like that if he weren't married. The five men had laughed. Then, David Carson had asked how long she would "hang around being observed."

Christopher gritted his teeth and snarled, "Until I say she's ready to leave. Does anyone have a problem with that diagnosis or doubt my ethics?"

The men went silent until David spoke up to say they were only kidding around. Bill asked if Christopher was falling in love with her.

Christopher choked on his drink and stared at the nosy rancher. His gaze traveled around the table as they waited in suspense to hear his answer. He finally growled, "That's none of your damn business."

The men exchanged curious looks, then grinned in assumption. Lance couldn't resist asking if "the lovely patient" felt the same way.

Christopher slammed his fist on the table, causing full glasses to slosh liquid on it. He told them to change the subject or he was leaving, that his private life was his own business.

"This is a small town, Chris," Tom had pointed out. "Frolicking might go on without notice in big cities but not around here. Natural curiosity."

"Then maybe I don't belong around here," he thundered. "If a man can't have privacy in his own home, he needs to move on where he can." That statement ended the distressing conversation.

The men played cards—in near silence—for another hour. Christopher drove home at a slow and cautious pace to allow himself time to think and settle down, and to scold himself for drinking so heavily. If he refused to take Kirstin anywhere again, he worried, would she be angry? If he did, would someone offend her, drive her away from here and him? *Damn people and their nosy ways!* The only good thing to come from the evening was news that Lance wasn't seeing Linda Shaw anymore and risking the destruction of her and Timmy's lives; the Don Juan was hooked onto Carla Thompson now, who seemed to be reciprocating his interest. That, he decided, was a perfect match!

445

In the morning Kirstin noticed Christopher's strange mood. She chatted and pretended to ignore it, assuming he had drunk too much and perhaps lost too much money last night. As they ate lunch, she worried over his continued near silence and preoccupied expression. If it wasn't a hangover, she fretted, what was wrong with him today? When she questioned if he was feeling all right, he claimed only to be tired.

For the next three days, Kirstin was surprised each time Christopher asked for her assistance in his office with patients or secretarial work, and when he asked for help or her company during his ranch chores. She wondered if it was meant to entice her to stay there with him, as he didn't verbalize his thoughts and feelings. He was eager to make love to her as many times, places, and ways as she would allow.

Kirstin stayed in a good mood, as things with Christopher were glorious though a little guarded at times. She was doing well with her health, avoiding hypoglycemic attacks with extra snacks and glucose tablets when additional exertions drained her energy between meals.

446

She chatted with Katie about her imminent arrival, and was eager to see her daughter.

Christopher suggested a private farewell picnic before her departure. They rode off on horseback to the pond. She was delighted when he unpacked a delicious meal he'd purchased that morning in town: fried chicken, potato salad, rolls, carrot sticks, and diet drinks. They laughed and chatted while they ate or fed each other.

After they finished the main course, he removed the last item from the basket: a sugar-free cake he'd had baked for the special event.

"Christopher, it's too pretty to eat. You're so thoughtful and clever." With misty eyes, she kissed him, long and deep. "What did the cook say when you ordered one with a wrecked red car on it?"

He caressed her cheek and stroked her tawny hair. "She didn't ask. I thought it appropriate since it symbolizes how we met." He picked a decorative headlight from the cake and popped it into her mouth. "It's also low fat, so you can stuff yourself with as much of it as you want. Shall I be your slave and feed you?"

She scooped icing onto a finger and slipped it into his mouth. "Be my royal taster instead

447

and make sure it isn't loaded with aphrodisiac," she said. "Of course, I could use some lately to keep up with you. You have a powerful appetite, Doc."

Christopher held her finger in his mouth and licked on it. "I have to stay busy to stock up on you before tomorrow. Besides, you wouldn't want to risk leaving me with such a large and tempting supply of little balloons."

She punched him in playfulness.

"You better not sleep with anyone but me!"

Christopher grasped her hands and pulled her down atop him. "I'd like to smear that icing all over you and lick it off, slow and easy." His hand went behind her head to pull her lips within reach. He sealed their mouths and kissed her with longing. He rolled her to her back on the blanket and began to caress her with urgency. "I want you, woman," he murmured amidst groans of desire.

The kissing and stroking continued for a short time until Kirstin realized they were both becoming too passionate for the outdoor setting. "Whew, we'd better stop while we still can."

As he nibbled on her earlobe and trekked down her neck, he said, "I don't want to stop. Let's shuck these clothes. I want to feel you against me. I want to be inside you, now."

"This isn't the time or place. Stop that," she

told him when he tried to unbutton her shirt. "Let's eat some of the cake."

"What I want to feast on is you, woman, and I'm ravenous."

"Later, Christopher."

To Kirstin's dismay, he tried to make love to her. "I told you last time, Christopher, I can't do that here in the open in daylight. Frank or your other workers could catch us. I'm sorry, but I can't."

To her surprise, he announced that a dip in the cold water would soothe his fiery body and improve his spirit. He stripped and dove into the pond.

Kirstin drew up her knees to her chest and encircled them with her arms. She watched him swim back and forth, analyzing his odd behavior. Suddenly the thudding of horse's hooves caught her attention. She turned to see Frank Graham riding toward the pond. Without thinking how this situation would appear to him, she sighed in relief that they weren't making love. Then, realizing that Christopher was frolicking in the nude, she flushed. She couldn't face the foreman in that risqué situation, so she stood and began walking toward the low hill that partially hid the house.

Frank spotted her and veered his horse in that direction. When he reined in, Kirstin shielded her eyes from the sun and looked up at him. She laughed and explained her hasty departure, "Christopher wanted to swim for a while, so I thought I should give him privacy."

Frank glanced toward the pond. "My boss needs some manners, Kirstin. He's so used to doin' as he pleases, he forgets 'em sometimes. On the other hand, he probably ain't thinking straight with you leaving tomorrow, probably needs to clear his head. I've never seen him so happy an' unbent since he moved here. We all hate to see you pull out. I hope you'll come back for lots of visits."

"Thank you, Frank, that's very kind of you."

"You'll get to meet Helen next time; you two will get along well. I've told her all about you an' what you've done for Chris. You've brought a lot of sunshine to the boss's life; he's gonna miss you sumpthin' fierce. He loves this place, but Doc ain't no rancher at heart. What he needs is to get back into that other doctoring where he belongs. 'Course he's stubborn and won't admit it, not after such foul luck with his hand. Ever' time we're doin' chores, all he can talk about is you. Won't be the same around here without you."

"I've enjoyed my stay, and I hope to see you again soon. Please tell Helen I'm sorry I missed meeting her. She keeps a fine house for Christopher."

"Yore mighty kind-hearted, Kirstin, a good

450

match for Chris. I'm headin' to the barn to fetch some tools we need for repairs. Want a ride home? It's too far an' hot for a long walk this time of day."

Kirstin smiled in appreciation and nodded. He moved his boot for her to step up and offered his hand for assistance. Nimble, Kirstin placed her foot in the stirrup, grasped his hand, and swung up behind him. She was amazed by the things he had revealed to her and tucked them away in her heart.

The foreman yelled, "Chris, I'm givin' Kirstin a lift to the house. We'll see you later." After Christopher waved to show he'd heard, they galloped away.

Christopher realized her worries had been proven accurate. Once more, he'd behaved like a fool! What had gotten into him? He almost had insisted she surrender to him! Kirstin wasn't an object; she was a person, the woman he loved and wanted. It was crazy to treat her like that and was evident she was annoyed with him, enough to leave the pond and his company. She was probably heading home to pack and run. *Pack and run?* his mind repeated and panic seized him.

He left the pond and yanked on his clothes, struggling and cursing as his wet body resisted his urgency. He didn't bother to load the basket and take it home, just leapt into the saddle and kneed the horse into a swift pace. If she was hurt and angry, she might toss her stuff in the car and leave before he could stop her and apologize. At the corral, he jumped off the horse, removed the saddle, and turned the Appaloosa free. The ride had been short, so the animal could go without a curry. He covered the distance between the barn and house as fast as possible.

Kirstin was in the kitchen. He halted inside the doorway and watched her as he asked what she was doing.

Without turning, she replied, "Putting on a meatloaf for supper. Does that suit you? Or do you hate them like Steve does? I should have asked first."

"Everything you cook is delicious. You've spoiled me. Even Helen can't hold a candle to you . . . Kirstin, about before, I'm sorry. I don't know what got into me."

"I think you're taking me and our situation for granted. I didn't refuse you because I didn't want you. Since Frank did show up, you must admit my point was valid. It would have been wonderful to make love out there; it's a very romantic spot. But it isn't private. You should have seen me trying to explain why you were swimming in the nude with a *lady* present."

"What did he say?" Christopher asked, set-

452

tling down because it seemed she wasn't rushing to escape him prematurely.

She revealed the excuse she'd used with the foreman. "I just don't want things spoiled between us, especially on our last day together for now."

Thank you, Lord, for those last two words. "Did I spoil them?"

"Not exactly. But you will if you start acting like that every time we're together and we can't make love when the mood strikes you."

"But you wanted me, too; I could feel it."

She put the pan into the oven, set the controls, and turned to face him. "Don't be stubborn. You were wrong. Why can't you admit it?"

"I *can* admit it; I was selfish, inconsiderate, and wrong. Not wrong to want you, but wrong to press you like that. Satisfied?"

"Your words are fine, but your attitude's not. It has been strange, off and on, since the poker game. You can talk to me. What's really bothering you?" she asked as she came to stand beside him. "Please, talk to me."

He cupped her face between his hands. "I don't want you to leave tomorrow, Kirstin. I want more time with you."

She stared at him. "But I have to go to work Monday and I need time to settle into my apartment. I can't ask for more time off from a new job. Why don't you come to visit on my first weekend there? We could have fun exploring San Diego together."

"It won't be the same here after you leave. I've gotten very attached to you and used to having you around. Meeting in between here and there every few weeks doesn't give us enough time together. I want you to stay."

No vow of love or proposal of marriage, just move in with me? "I can't, Christopher," she responded, more to her thoughts than his words.

"Why? Because you don't feel the same way about me?"

"I don't know how you feel, Christopher; you haven't told me."

"I love you and want you to stay."

"You love me?"

"I thought you realized that by now."

"I'm not a mind reader."

"Neither am I," he hinted.

"I love you, too, and I wish I could move here. But it wouldn't be right."

"If we're married, it will be, won't it?"

"You're proposing to me?"

"Yes. Will you marry me, Kirstin Lowrey? Tomorrow?"

"I . . . Oh, heavens, this is so sudden, two revelations in almost the same breath. We've only known each other for three weeks; we need time to make sure this isn't just infatuation. We need time to get to know each other better. Besides, I'm moving to San Diego. Would you come with me and work there?"

"What?"

"Move to San Diego and work there."

"I can't do that."

"Why not?"

"If you really love me, you'll stay here and marry me."

"If you really love *me*, you'll come with me. We can both make a fresh start in a new place, away from our losses. Make a place of our own, Christopher, a place without bad memories or ties to the past. Why must I prove my love by staying? Why can't you prove yours by going? Why is my career and life less important than yours? If I thought you were truly happy and fulfilled here, I wouldn't ask this of you. In San Diego, I'll have my work and you can have yours. Here in New Mexico, I can't."

His hands dropped from her face. "I can't work there, Kirstin. Nobody wants a doctor or a researcher or teacher with a near useless hand."

"You've proven that isn't true, to me and to the people here."

"It isn't the same in a big city; the competition is fierce; patients want the best. I'm no longer the best; I'm barely competent in some areas."

455

"You're strong, intelligent, skilled, and brave; you can make things work there just as you did here. Give it a try."

"I don't belong out there anymore."

"You belong where you want to belong, where you carve out a place for yourself, for us. You aren't the only one with a problem and challenge. When will you learn," she reasoned in a gentle tone, "that your loss isn't the end of the world and it isn't humiliating to ask for and receive help from others? It isn't a defeat to go into teaching or research or to become a GP elsewhere. Why must you hide out here, refusing to heal, refusing help from others?"

"You don't understand what I've been through, what I've lost."

"Your medical problem isn't any more frustrating, angering, debilitating, or life-controlling than mine is."

He balled one fist at his side, but the left one wouldn't close, as usual. His fingers teased over numb areas. "You have the use of both hands."

"Yes, but my body is like my enemy, my challenge, my loss."

"But you can still practice your chosen career with diabetes."

"I can in San Diego. Not here. Your condition can't cost you that limb or your vision or your life. At any time, serious complications could—"

"Don't say that!"

"Not saying it or thinking it doesn't change what's true. But you can change and control your destiny. You, we, can have a wonderful future if you'll only let go of the bitterness and accept your limitation. If you can't have all of a dream, take what part of it you can. Find a new goal and challenge. Don't keep burying yourself. Don't be less than you can be. Come with me; build and share a new life with me. Don't ask me to come into seclusion with you where I'll be denied my other love. We could work together in research; I can be your other hand when you need one. I can help you learn to use your right one better."

"I've had the best in known surgery and therapy, more than once. Neuropathy doesn't go away and it can't even be improved. Why can't you resign and just be happy being my wife?"

"If I were asking you to give up surgery to become a house husband, would you?"

"Can't you at least take a leave and try it? Take a chance on me?"

"Can't you at least come to San Diego and explore the possibilities there?"

"I can't, not yet, if ever. I have to be honest with you."

457

"See, we do need time and distance to test our feelings. If what we have is true and strong, things will work out for us; we'll find a fair compromise. Let's do as we planned while we continue to explore and deepen our relationship."

"If you leave, I'll lose you. You'll find a better man, a whole man, one who can give you what I can't, and you'll forget about me."

She didn't say, Like you think Laura did? She was certain he had no emotional bonds to his ex-wife, but her betrayal—and especially with a friend—had scarred him. "You're the only man I want, Christopher; that won't happen. Unless you push me away. Not everything I need is here, in the place you refuse to leave."

"Swear it, Kirstin, swear you won't stop loving me."

"I swear it, Christopher."

"If only I knew for certain you can keep your promise."

"We need time away from each other for additional reasons: I don't want to make another mistake with a man. I have to be sure our marriage will work, especially with the stipulations you're putting on it. I'm terrified to go through what I did before, terrified of losing myself again. That happens so often with housewives. How can you understand something you've never experienced? You've always been number one with yourself and others, important, in charge. You did as you pleased. You don't know what it's like to be only a wife, a mother, or a daughter. It was a long and tough struggle to become Kirstin. I'm afraid she'll vanish again if I become Mrs. Christopher Harrison and give up a big part of myself."

"You're too strong now for that to happen again."

"Am I? No other man has made me feel as you do. Maybe your power over me scares me the most."

"Well, I'm scared, too, Kirstin, scared of losing you if you leave here. I haven't felt alive like this in a long time, not since I was forced from surgery. I'm hurt you can't just say and feel that all that matters to you is me. You're right, I *am* selfish and near-sighted. I know what I want and I'm losing it."

"No, my love, you aren't. Give us time. Who knows, once I live and work there a while, I might decide to return here?"

"Once you leave, you'll get busy with your work and forget me. You'll see other men. What we've shared won't seem as important to you in your new life. Your panic about marriage will dull it; distance will help you ignore or deny it. I don't want you to go."

"I must; it's the best way to test our feelings. If we rush a decision, we can both get hurt." She stepped to him. "I had to change my whole life after David's death. Changing it all again just to have you is frightening. I can't be impulsive."

"I'm willing to take a chance with you."

"Only if I make sacrifices and you don't have to give up anything."

"I already have: all I studied, trained, worked for, and loved."

"None of that was for me. You aren't willing to give up your life here to come with me so we can have more time to get closer, but you expect me to do that for you. Why is that responsibility mine alone?"

"I can't leave the ranch and move in with you. What would I do while you're at work? Here, I have the ranch and my patients."

"You can work there, too, in research or teaching or general practice. You have plenty to offer the medical field."

"I can't go. I tried it once; I've finally given up that foolish idea." He related some of his past embittering episodes. "Besides, it's too painful being around a life that I'm being denied."

"You're practicing medicine here, so what's the difference?"

"It isn't the same. I know from experience."

"If you can ask me to give up my career for you, why can't you do the same for me? We could have a wonderful life there," she stressed.

"We can have one here."

"No, *we* can't. You can continue as before with all you have now, but I'd become your shadow. I love you, Christopher Harrison, and want to marry you, but I need more than you and a family. I need other things, things I never had before, things important to me now. Is that wrong?"

He had to shake his head and respond with a sad, "But I don't know where that leaves us in our dilemma."

That night, they made love with a mixture of melancholy and urgency, knowing what morning would bring: separation, a kind of tiny death with its own period of grief and loneliness and adjustment. As they snuggled together afterward, each hoped and prayed the other would have a change of mind before the moment of Kirstin's departure arrived.

Sixteen

The disheartened couple stood beside Kirstin's loaded car and gazed into each other's eyes.

He asked softly, "Do you have everything you'll need?"

She caressed his strong jawline, then lowered her hand to his chest. "Except for you, Christopher. Join me soon, please."

He lowered his troubled gaze to the ground and took a deep breath. "I don't know if I can turn my life upside down again."

"This time, I will be there to help you straighten it."

He wondered if that were possible, even with her love and patience and support. Take a chance on things being different, better, than they were last time when he faced the challenge of trying to work in a large city with a disabled hand? Endure colleagues' pity and people's curiosity or hurtful remarks? Have embarrassing accidents in social settings or at work that call attention to his helplessness? Constantly ask assistants for help with simple tasks he could no longer perform? Place himself in a location that revolves around surgery? "All I can say is, I'll think about it seriously, but don't get your hopes up. I can't imagine changing my mind about a decision forced on me long ago. Contrary to what you think, Kirstin, I *have* accepted my limitation, and this is the best way to deal with it in the least painful manner. I'm just sorry it has to come between us, but I do understand your needs, too. I never thought I'd find a woman like you, or find true love. Maybe you'll retire early and choose New Mexico as your home. I hope so. Until then, I'll be waiting, and we'll go on as we have been for the last month."

She realized nothing she could say would influence him today. "I best get going; it's a long drive and I don't want to be in the middle of nowhere after dark. I love you and I'll miss you terribly."

"The same here. Be careful and stay alert for any problems. I don't want you falling into the hands of another lonely and miserable doctor."

His attempt at humor failed on both of them.

"Call me when you stop this evening. I have to be assured you're all right. Until I know you're off the road and safe, I won't rest."

"I will, and don't worry. I'm doing fine now, thanks to a wonderful doctor, friend, and man."

"Keep alert and keep your emergency supplies at hand."

"They're on the front seat, and I'm wearing the bracelet you gave me." She held up her wrist. "Take care of yourself. I'll see you soon."

"Goodbye, Kirstin."

She hated the sound of that first word. *Please, God, let it become* hello *soon.* He was going to let her leave, but at least she had given him—and herself—plenty to think about and time in which to do it. "So long for a short while, Christopher."

They shared a bittersweet kiss and tight embrace.

Kirstin got into her car and turned the ignition key. She almost wished it wouldn't start, but it did. She asked herself a final time if she was doing the right thing? *For now,* her mind responded. *No,* her aching heart refuted, *but you must go for a while.*

Christopher propped his elbows on the window, leaned inward, and kissed her. He retreated so fast afterward that he bumped the back of his head on the door. He gave a forced smile and ordered, "Go, woman, before I drag you out of that car and lock you in my house."

"See ya, Doc." *Come join me soon, my love, please.*

"See ya, guinea pig." *Return soon, my precious angel, please.*

Kirstin guided her vehicle out of the concrete driveway and down the parallel gravel road. At the highway, she halted to take in the ranch setting again. She stuck her arm out the window and waved to a watching and motionless Christopher. She pulled onto the recently paved asphalt road, blew her horn, and raised the window. *I'm not going to lose you, Christopher Harrison, even if I have to move here. I'll give Medico their due, but if you don't change your mind within a month or so, I'll give up my career. But, heavens, I hate to do that. I love research. It's so exciting and challenging. It makes me feel important and confident, downright independent.*

Kirstin's gaze took in the almost-flat high plains landscape and seemingly endless horizon of few trees and miles of telephone and utility poles that detracted from the green-and-cobalt view. *Blast it all, I don't want to live in a near desert without a research facility close by. If you love me and need me, why can't you come to San Diego and work? Stop it, Kirstin, or you'll get resentful! His decision was as difficult to make as yours was.*

465

After driving three hundred and ninety-five miles that day, she checked into a motel in Wilcox, Arizona, and phoned Christopher before eating. The state was not on Daylight Savings Time, something her love had pressed into her mind for her strict regimen. His answering machine took her call. She gave her location, the time, the hotel and room number, and a report on her health. "I'll be in my room if you want to call back after you get home. I miss you and love you. And I hope you're alone when you hear this message or you'll get teased again. Talk to you later. Bye."

She also placed a message on Katie's answering machine. Afterward, to prevent missing Christopher's call, she ordered room service. She hated to get into the shower but did so. The first thing she did after drying off was check the red light on the phone to see if he'd called; he hadn't.

Where are you, Christopher? Out celebrating your freedom or dulling your misery with a few drinks or just refusing to answer or phone back?

Kirstin watched television until ten, and tried not to worry. She forced herself to get to bed to prepare for the long drive tomorrow. *Don't get paranoid, Kirstin. He's probably out on an emergency or at John and Maria's.*

* * *

466

Kirstin stretched and yawned. She glanced at the silent phone and saw the red light flashing. She called the hotel operator for the message, which was from Christopher. He'd gotten in too late from an emergency and didn't want to disturb her. She dialed his number, but he was out again. She left another message, ate breakfast, and departed.

Past Tucson, she took Interstate-8 to Yuma for her second night, over three hundred miles and enough stops to prevent health problems. She phoned Christopher and found his home line was busy. She phoned his medical line but didn't leave a personal message with the answering service. The next time she called, he wasn't home. Could it be possible, she mused in excitement, that he was en route to San Diego to join her?

She teased, "I hope keeping in touch via machines doesn't become a habit for us. I'm doing fine. I have about three hours to drive tomorrow. I'll call you from there. Sorry we missed talking both times. I love you. Bye."

Upon rising on Saturday morning, she was miffed there was no response to her call last night. In her agitated state, Kirstin didn't realize she had forgotten to tell him where she was and to leave the number. By nine, she was on the road for the last leg of her trip.

At the California state line, she remembered to change her watch and car clock to the new time zone.

Traffic got heavier and heavier as she neared the large city. She paid close attention to the signs. Soon, tired and tense, she reached her apartment, her new home. She eyed the complex of ivory stucco buildings, all single-story units. She liked having no one above or below her for the quiet and privacy. The landscaping was lovely: green grass, palms, flowers, shrubs, pebblestone walkways, and decorative entrances with porticoes to get out of the rain.

Kirstin unlocked the door with keys her daughter had mailed to her before leaving Georgia. Her gaze widened and her mouth went agape.

"Surprise! Welcome home, Mom. God, how I've missed you."

Amidst tears, hugs, and laughter, Kirstin and Katie embraced. When they parted, the mother glanced around the living room.

"It's beautiful, honey; I couldn't have chosen better. And you have everything arranged, even pictures and knickknacks in place."

"I wanted you to have time to rest and enjoy your new apartment this weekend. Besides, we have lots to catch up on, right?"

As Kirstin stroked her daughter's long, curly

hair whose color matched her own, she replied, "Yes, we do. The balloons and flowers are wonderful. You're such a special girl, Katie. I love you so much."

"I love you, too, Mom, and you deserve the best. So, how was it to leave him behind?"

Kirstin's gaze met Katie's. Since the girl was five-nine, she had to look up. "Harder than I imagined. I love him, honey."

"I know; I could tell. Don't worry; things will work out, you'll see."

"I don't know. I couldn't reach him a single time along the way. Well, he did leave a message during my first night on the road."

"Maybe he's hurting too much right now to talk. Men are such funny creatures, Mom, all that pride and ego. He's probably still suffering from the shock of your actually leaving; he probably never believed you would. You have to accept you did the right thing for both of you."

Kirstin related their last two serious talks.

"As I said, Mom, infernal male pride and ego. Give him time."

"Should I call him and let him know I've arrived safely?"

"Natch. I'll get us something ready to eat. Phone's over there." Katie overheard her mother placing another message on his answering machine.

Kirstin entered the kitchen. "Out again, I suppose."

"People do take showers, use the toilet, and run errands. And doctors like him make house calls, you said. Try again later."

"I think I'll wait until he calls, if he does."

"Don't become a Doubting Thomas, as you used to call us."

"I'm scared, honey, scared it will all fall apart."

"It's just as easy and reasonable for him to move here as for you to move there."

"And just as hard. Let's talk about something else while you give me the grand tour. This kitchen and eating area are fantastic, and so roomy. I love the color scheme. Somebody used a talented decorator."

"We're lucky they chose some of your favorite colors: ivory and mauve. There's a skylight in here, the master bath, and over the bed. All the better for seeing the stars and moon on a romantic night . . ." Katie glanced at her mother, and smiled. "Why, Mom, I do believe you're blushing like a teenager. I love it! I'm so happy for you. I'm dying to ask a thousand questions, but I won't give you the third degree, yet. Tomorrow I will, so be prepared to tell all."

"You're a nosy little twerp," she teased.

"Natch. Until you're ready to use that starry

470

view, you can plunk him before a cozy fire on that lush carpet. Get a good supply of huge toss pillows! And better keep a coverlet at hand; you don't want to get carpet burns while you're having fun there."

"Kathryn Lowrey!"

"Oh, Mom, I'm teasing. Maybe," she added with a twinkle in her eye and a mirthful grin on her face. "Look at the bedroom and master bath."

As they headed in that direction, the vivacious Katie pointed out the guest room, half-bath, and other amenities. "The walls are off-white and the carpet's light tan throughout so they'll go with anything. Voilà, your suite, madame. A bay window and sitting area for relaxing after a hard day. The lounger is a housewarming present from me and Sandi. It's very sturdy and comfy, so don't mind using it for anything." Katie giggled as she guided her mother into the adjoining bathroom. "Garden tub with a heavenly view, dressing area, huge walk-in closet, and a toilet behind this half-wall; that's nice for privacy when someone's shaving nearby and you hafta go."

Kirstin ignored her last remark. "My goodness, honey, you have towels and the accessories out already. This wallpaper is beautiful; I like this swirl of blue, green, mauve, and ivory. It's almost as if they knew my tastes

471

and favorite color scheme. I'm so glad you found this one for me; thanks."

After receiving a hug and kiss, Katie chatted, "I looked at countless apartments. When I saw this one, I knew it was you. The location is perfect: you're two miles from work. There's a shopping center a few blocks to the right that has a grocery store, dry cleaners, and just about anything you'll need. Three miles to the left are the offices of your two new doctors. I've written down their addresses and directions, and marked them on a city map in your desk drawer. Plus, I'll show you around tomorrow. Most of your stuff is unpacked, but you may want to make some changes. I tried to remember how you set things up at home; you were always so organized. I know you're going to love it here."

"How did you get all of this done and work, too?"

"I did it between assignments. It was fun."

"Everything is perfect."

"It is, isn't it?"

They shared merry laughter before Kirstin said, "You've done a marvelous job of making this move easy for me, honey."

"You were always there for me, for all of us, when we needed you for anything. You're my best friend, Mom. It's going to be so wonderful having you close by. I'll teach you all

I've learned about sunny California. Let's get your suitcases and get you unpacked so we can have our sandwiches and milk. Oh, yes, the fridge and cupboards are stocked. Anything I missed, we can pick up tomorrow while were sightseeing."

Tears ran down Kirstin's cheeks.

"What's wrong, Mom? Are you feeling sick?"

"No, just happy and proud and lucky. You're a jewel, Katie girl."

"Because of you, Mom, because of how you raised me."

"That's the nicest thing you could ever say to me, honey. I just wish Sandi and Steve . . ."

"He'll come around, Mom. Just give him time. He's supposed to phone tonight." *If he does as I told him.* "The balloons are from me, the flowers are from him."

"They are?" Kirstin smiled and perked up.

"Yep. The card's still attached. Just says, 'Welcome home.' "

"I'll call him and thank him."

Katie grasped her arm and halted her. "Later, in case he's vintage Steve today. Don't risk spoiling your big event. Please."

"Since you did all this work for me, the least I can do is obey."

"That's a good girl," Katie echoed Kirstin's words from the past. "Sandi's going to call to-night, too. I talked to her yesterday and she wishes she could be here. I'll fetch your suit-cases. Gimme the keys, and no arguments, young lady."

"Yes, ma'am."

Kirstin strolled around and admired her new home. It was large enough for two people, and she had a king-size bed and lots of closet space. She wished Christopher was there to share this moment, and the rest of her life. Where was he? Why hadn't he spoken to her by now? *Please, God, don't let it be the worst.*

After Katie returned, they joined forces to unpack and prepare lunch, then savored it in the eating area. They sat on the sofa and chatted for hours about Katie's work, Kirstin's adventures, future plans, the past, and the men in their lives.

"Playing the field, isn't that what it's called?"

"Yep. Maybe one day I'll find somebody special, too. Until then, I'll keep looking and trying out the merchandise."

"Do your old mom one tiny favor, just make sure he's special and deserving before sharing yourself with him in such a manner. Dating is so different from when I was young."

"You're still young."

"I'm nearing fifty, Katie girl."

"That isn't ancient, Mom, and you look ten years younger than that."

"Only ten years, a ripe forty?"

"Your math's off, thirty-five if mine's accurate."

"You always were a top student, just like Sandi. Poor Steve, some subjects gave him fits."

"Only because he hated to study and speak up in class. I had a couple with him that one year we were both at UGA. Steve has a bad habit of wanting everything to come easy and quick. Remember how he almost screwed up his first promotion at the bank? You can't put pressure on a boss for a raise or a promotion until you've earned them."

"I see you've learned a lot about work since moving here."

"It's the only way to succeed. I love doing commercials and modeling and movies, even if most parts have been tiny ones. The worst thing is the competition; there's so much of it. I have to watch every bite that goes into my mouth and exercise every day, and never go to bed with makeup on."

Kirstin laughed. "All that nagging was to stop stains on pillowcases and to keep that lovely complexion clear."

"It worked, thank goodness. You'll be amazed how great I've become in the kitchen. I eat balanced meals, exercise, and get enough sleep. I've become a real health nut."

"It shows; you're a beautiful and vital young

woman, Katie."

"You're biased. Out here, there are thousands of girls with better faces and figures, with more credits under their belts, too. But I have courage, determination, and confidence: things my mother taught me."

"Things my daughter helped me learn. I—"

"I'll get it," Katie offered after the doorbell chimed. "Maybe it's the neighborhood welcome wagon, so you should answer it, Mom."

Kirstin looked through the peephole, then opened the door. "My heavens, what's this?"

"Flowers for Kirstin Lowrey. Sign here, please."

As soon as she did so, Katie passed a tip for the delivery man over her mother's shoulder. The girl closed the door and Kirstin carried the large arrangement to the kitchen to check the water level.

"There must be two dozen of them."

"Try three dozen, Mom. Here's the card. Who's the sender?"

Kirstin opened the small envelope and smiled. "Christopher . . ."

"Well, what's the message? Or is it private?"

Kirstin handed the card to her daughter, too full of emotion to speak.

"Wow, 'I love you and miss you like crazy. My proposal is still on the examining table.' That's pretty clear to me, Mom; he's nuts

476

about you."

Kirstin smelled the fragrance of the numerous red roses nestled amidst feathery ferns and baby's breath. "Was I a fool to leave, Katie?"

"No, Mom, so don't beat yourself. You've always been the one to do and sacrifice for others. It's time for you to think about you and your needs."

"I need him, honey."

"You also need research, don't you?"

"Yes, but . . ."

"Trust me, Mom, you'll have both. These say you're on his mind. As soon as he gets to missing you and . . . all you shared, he'll come running."

"What about that male pride and ego you mentioned?"

"Loneliness and an empty house will dissolve them."

"It won't be empty after Monday; his housekeeper's returning then."

"That isn't the same as having you there day and . . . night."

"Do you really think he'll change his mind?"

"Natch. What man in his right senses would risk losing you?"

They chatted again for a time. Then, Katie suggested, "Why don't you give the good doctor a thank-you call while I drive real slow to fetch us Chinese food from down the street? I know what you need. I've been reading up on diabetes. I even talked with your new doctor and he gave me a copy of your diet plan. We'll have a toast after you get a full belly and it's safe. When you're relaxed and calm, you can talk with Steve."

Katie left and Kirstin picked up the phone. She almost held her breath until he answered. "Hello, stranger. I got the roses, Christopher; they're beautiful. You know how to get to a woman's heart, don't you?"

"I'm trying every trick I can think of. I'm sorry we kept missing each other. Emergencies, a shower, and chores got in the way. You didn't leave your number at your last stop, so I couldn't call back. Lordy, I miss you. This place is like a tomb with you gone. It's already a mess and my cooking's lousy. How are things on your end?"

"Good and bad. It seems like a month since I've seen you, but Katie has done wonders with the apartment." She related details about her new home and all her daughter had accomplished.

"Damn, I was *afraid* it would be too much competition for me."

"No more than the ranch is my rival. So, when are you coming to visit? Is next weekend too soon?"

"Not soon enough to suit me, but it'll have

to do."

I'll get you here and change your mind, you stubborn devil. "Make sure you don't run into any emergencies to stop you."

"I've already asked a friend to be on call for me."

"Good. I'll have a special meal waiting for you."

"All I want and need is you waiting for me."

"I have been since I left the ranch." *No, no, Kirstin.* "I went through some beautiful country that would be ideal for camping trips. Arizona is loaded with beautiful views."

"We didn't pick out an RV while you were here. I'll take John and Maria with me next week and let them help select one."

"Or we can do it during one of my visits there, unless you're in a rush."

"No hurry; we'll do it later. It's a short plane flight between us."

"You're flying?"

"Yep, to save time. I want every minute I can have with you."

"That suits me perfectly, Doc."

"You been taking good care of yourself?"

"Following doctor's orders and having no problems. You healed me fine, in more than body, Christopher. I hope . . ."

"You hope what, Kirstin?"

"I hope I helped you, too."

479

"You solved a few problems but you created a bigger one."

"Like what?"

"Like getting me addicted to you then taking away my drug supply."

"You did the same thing to me."

"I wasn't the one who left."

"That isn't fair, Christopher."

"I know, and I'm sorry. It's just that I miss you."

"I miss you, too. I love you, Christopher, please believe that."

"I do but it doesn't make being separated any easier."

"Have you . . . considered what I said?"

"I've thought of little else except you and our situation."

There was a short silence. "Has Jenny's baby been released from the hospital yet?"

Making small talk to change the subject? "Some time next week; he's doing fine, just needs a little more weight. Frank said to tell you hello."

Don't press him anymore tonight. "I like him; you're lucky to have such a good man working for you. How are John and Maria?"

"Haven't seen them; they went camping this weekend."

"Making up for missing our trip together?"

"Yep."

The door opened and Katie entered. She shrugged, Sorry.

"Katie's here. She went for Chinese food. She says hello."

"Go eat while it's hot. I'll talk to you in a few days. Bye, Kirstin."

He hung up before she could say goodbye. She gazed at the receiver for a moment before replacing it.

"Did I interrupt at a bad time?"

"No, honey. It was a little strained, but that's natural. We sort of danced around words and tried to avoid touchy topics."

"Don't worry; it'll get better soon. When's he coming to visit?"

"Next weekend."

"Give him the royal treatment and he won't want to leave."

"I don't know, Katie; it didn't sound encouraging in that area."

"Stop fretting and come eat. Strict schedule, remember?"

"If I forget it, this blasted condition reminds me fast!"

"Mom, take your test now. You look a little pale and shaky."

Kirstin focused on herself for a moment and realized what those symptoms meant: add fuel now. "You're right. When I see the doctor, I'm hoping he'll take me off my medication. I think I can control this with diet and exercise. I'm having to eat extra snacks or pop glucose tablets to prevent lows. That won't be good for my weight, and weight is a big factor."

"I'll set the table while you do your thing," Katie offered.

"Thanks, honey. I'll need a clear head and stamina when I talk to your brother." *Lord, how I dread this first talk in a month.*

"Don't take any nonsense from him, Mom. By the way, your mail's in the desk drawer, too. You have a package from Medic Alert."

"Probably my identification bracelet. Christopher bought me this one." She held up her wrist to show Katie. "He was always doing nice and thoughtful things for me. I feel like such a traitor for leaving him. Blast it all, I shouldn't feel guilty for being myself and being honest!"

"Mom, your blood test and food," Katie prompted.

"You're right; I am getting moody and feisty, aren't I? Glucose coming in, and I need a fix badly."

Kirstin stood at the door with Katie. "I hate to see you leave, honey. Are you sure it's safe to drive back this time of evening?"

"It isn't far, about two hours. I just zip up

Interstate-5. There's plenty of traffic around on Saturday night. I'm sorry I can't stay as planned and show you around; a sleepover would have been fun. That's the peril of leaving your number with the service. With that modeling assignment tomorrow, I need to look my best. You rest. Take a bubble bath and check out where I put everything. I'll call you Monday night to check on your job. Stop worrying and enjoy this fresh start, Mom." She hugged Kirstin, kissed her cheek, and left.

Her son hadn't called by nine. Kirstin took a deep breath and lifted the receiver. "Hi, Steve. I'm in San Diego now; I arrived this afternoon. Katie's been helping me settle in but she had to leave for home; a last-minute job came up. Thanks for the flowers. It was a nice surprise."

"It was Louise's idea; she sent them."

Kirstin heard and felt the chill in his voice. "How was the cruise? Did you have a wonderful time and good weather?"

"Yes. I hired a stranger to take care of your grandsons."

Kirstin continued to try to sound light. "How did they like her?"

"Fine. You've been out of touch a long time, Mother."

"Didn't you and the children get my letters and presents?"

"Yes, they came while you were sneaking across the country."

"Are you trying to make me feel guilty because I didn't babysit?"

"If you don't want to spend time with my kids, you don't have to."

"That isn't true, Stephen Lowrey, and you know it. I've kept those boys plenty of times for you and Louise, and I love them, just as I love you."

"You have a strange way of showing it, Mother."

That's enough. "So do you, son. Every time we talk, you seem to be intentionally cruel and hateful to me. I don't understand what's gotten into you, Steve. I want to spend time with the twins, but not become their fill-in mother or on-call sitter. You expect me to drop everything and come running when you call. I have a life, too, Steve. I have to work and support myself. I was always there for you children. What have I done to hurt you and create such bitterness? Why do you have this need to manipulate me?"

"You call asking a favor of my own mother being manipulative?"

"It's the way you do it, Steve, and how you behave if I don't jump."

484

"I've never forced you to do anything for us."

"Not physically, but you work on my emotions. I'm not up to that, and I wasn't up to babysitting for ten days."

"Oh, yes, you wanted a nice vacation alone, right?"

"I needed it, Steve. I have a problem that could have made keeping the twins dangerous for all of us." She revealed news of her diabetes and past problems, but left out Christopher for now; she didn't feel it would be to her benefit to give him two shocks at once.

"So you had the health and energy to travel the country for a month but not enough to rest here for ten days?"

She hoped and prayed his insensitivity stemmed from his ignorance about the disease. Either he wasn't hearing what she said, or was ignoring it in fear, or he didn't believe her. She would send him a booklet to enlighten him. "How much rest could I get while chasing two active boys?"

"Louise doesn't have a problem with that, so why would you?"

"I'm not Louise; I'm much older and I'm diabetic now."

"You're right; you've become a much different mother since Dad died. The boys' and Louise's feelings were hurt when I told them

485

you didn't want to come and visit, before, during, or after your long holiday."

"If you truly believe I'm that selfish and unfeeling, you don't know me at all. I'm hurt and disappointed that you would even think such wicked thoughts and say such cruel things to me. You weren't like this before your father died, and it isn't my fault he was killed, or that he didn't give you and the girls the time and attention you deserved. But to use your children to punish me by telling them such lies is cruel. I've tried to do everything I could for you, but no matter how much I do or give, it never seems enough for you. I only have so much time and energy to spend. Until you do some serious thinking and accept me as a person, a parent to respect, we shouldn't talk for a while. Goodbye, Steve, and I do love you."

Kirstin wiped tears away with a tissue and tried to tell herself things would improve one day. She was tempted to call Christopher, but she didn't want to cry on his shoulder and turn him against her son before they even met. If Steve didn't come around within a few weeks, she would tell him about her marriage plans and let him deal with it as best he could.

The phone rang. Kirstin cleared her throat and answered it.

"Hi, Mom. It's great to hear your voice."

"Sandi! I'm so glad you called. It must be some godawful hour there."

"Yes, but you're worth it. How is the place? Katie said it's a dream."

"It is. She was going to spend the night, but they called her about a job tomorrow in Los Angeles. The other model is sick and the shoot, as she called it, is set up and can't be cancelled without costing the company a lot of money. They asked her to fill in." She and her oldest daughter talked about the apartment, Kirstin's new job, her vacation, and Christopher.

"That's wonderful news, Mom. I'm so happy for you. Katie filled me in yesterday. She's mighty impressed by the sound of him. So am I."

"You'll like him, Sandi. I wish you could meet him soon."

"Maybe I will. I'm coming for a visit the last week of the month. Is that okay? Got room for me and the little tyke?"

"Yes. Oh, I can't wait. How is he doing? How is Cliff?"

Sandi gave all the news about her son and husband. She talked about their plans to return to America next year.

"Where are you two planning to settle?"

"Texas . . . or California. Actually, California

is our first choice."

"Here?"

"That's right. That'll put us all close together again. Steve won't be too far for reunions and holidays. How is my baby brother and his family? He doesn't write much."

"He's doing fine with his new job. They like Denver. They—"

"Mom, what's wrong? Are you crying?"

Kirstin struggled to get her emotions under control.

"Mom, what is it?"

"It's Steve; right now, he hates me, Sandi, and I don't know what to do about it. I haven't told him about Christopher. He would think I'm betraying your father. We just had an argument over the phone, so I'm a little upset, that's all. I'll be fine."

"What did he say? What's he done to you?"

"This is long distance, Sandi, costing you a fortune."

"I can afford it. Spill the beans now, Mom, all of them."

"I don't want to burden you with this when you're so far away. I didn't mean to upset you, too. It just hurts so much."

Kirstin related the sad story, pausing a few times to master her tears.

"That sorry snake! How dare he treat you like that! Overlook him, Mom; he's being a fool. You've done nothing wrong, so don't feel guilty."

"He has a way of making me feel that way, like I'm the enemy."

"You aren't selfish. Nobody could have been a better mother than you. He's the selfish and self-centered one, not you. That babysitting business is pure crap. He shouldn't take advantage of you, and he should have understood after you explained. He knows what diabetes is; it's in our family, and he dated a girl with it for a long time. You remember Doris; he had to rush her to the hospital once when she passed out on him. As for kids, I only have one and he runs me ragged."

"He's just so bitter about your father. I'm not even sure he realizes that's his problem. It's going to eat him alive if he doesn't accept it. If only he'd get counseling."

Kirstin didn't want to cause hard feelings between her children. She hadn't wanted to involve the girls in her problem with Steve. But it was wrong to keep it from them, and Steve probably wouldn't keep silent, either. "I'll talk to him again after we've both had time to calm down."

They chatted a while longer, then said goodbye. Kirstin hung up feeling better. After all, two out of three children loved and appreciated her, understood her, and wanted her to be happy. What she didn't know, because Sandi didn't tell her, was that Steve was going to receive a long and serious talk from her as soon as she could dial his number. Nor did Kirstin suspect it would come on top of the one he'd just received from Katie, who raked him over the coals after he revealed his conversation with their mother and made some nasty remarks.

Exhausted from the busy day and expenditure of emotion, Kirstin took a hot shower and went to bed.

At the ranch on Sunday evening, Christopher answered a call from his daughter.

"How are things going, Dad? I haven't heard from you this week. I guess you've been busy."

"Kirstin's gone, if that's what you mean. She left Thursday morning, bright and early."

"You sound in the dumps, Dad. That's only been a few days."

"It feels like ages. This blasted house is too quiet without her."

"So, when's she coming back to visit?"

"I don't know. I asked her to stay but she wouldn't."

"What do you mean, 'asked her to stay'?"

"I asked her to marry me, Peg. I love her.

She's the woman I want to spend my life with."

"She refused?"

"Not exactly." Christopher gave the highlights of their problem.

"Her career means more to her than you do and you still want her?"

"Kirstin has her first taste of freedom and independence in over twenty years. She loves research, as much as I love surgery. I can't blame her for wanting both of us."

"If she has to make a choice, Dad, it should be you, if she loves you."

"I don't doubt that fact for a moment, squirt. Neither should you."

"Have you considered moving to California?"

"A thousand times since she left. I don't know if I can face that again. We were perfect together while she was here. We work well together. She walked in and gave my miserable life a good shaking. She made me feel happy and come alive. She made this house feel like a home. We had fun, Peg. We have a lot in common. It will never be the same here without her. I feel like she ripped out my heart and soul and took them with her. I know you don't like her or trust her, squirt, but she's the best thing that ever happened to me besides you and surgery. She's special, Peg, very special in every way."

"Sounds as if you have it bad for her. Are you sure, Dad? You've only known her for a short time."

"How long did you know Phil before you knew he was the one for you?"

Peggy laughed. "I get your point; the first time I laid eyes on him. We were engaged in a month. But we didn't marry for a year; we had time to test our feelings."

"Would you give her a hard time if I married her? I'm aware your conversation with her was more than you told me. I have to know some of the things you said to her."

Embarrassed, Peggy related the talk with Kirstin. "I'm sorry, Dad, if I did anything to spoil things between you two. I'll phone her and apologize."

"Let it go for now. She has two daughters so she probably guessed your intentions were good."

"They were. I love you and only want what's best for you."

"Kirstin is what's best for me, Peg."

"If you don't change your feelings about her soon, go after her."

"What do you mean?"

"Compromise, Dad. At least check out San Diego. How do you know it won't work if you don't research it? You've been stuck out there for three years. Maybe it's time to get back into the mainstream. You're not a rancher; you're a doctor; you should be working full-time in some branch of the medical field. And you aren't a cripple, so stop seeing yourself as one. You always told me to do the best I could in every situation. Take your own advice."

"That's easy to say, but not easy to do."

"Life and love aren't easy, Dad; they're challenges."

"I'll give it more thought."

"Don't think too long; she's out there among a lot of competition. She might get the idea you were only having fun with her and look elsewhere. If she's who you want, don't take a chance on losing her."

Kirstin talked with Elaine and Betty, who gave her much the same advice as her daughters had yesterday. She wandered around the apartment, then went for a brisk walk.

Preparing for a shower, she removed the bracelet Christopher had given her and put on the one from Medic Alert with all the information about her engraved on the underside. She dangled Christopher's in the air and gazed at it. "I love you, Doctor Harrison. What shall I do about you?" She dropped the inexpensive but precious gift into her jewelry box and headed for the bathroom.

She needed a long and soothing soak in the large tub. Tomorrow, she would begin a new job. So many changes and adjustments, so many decisions to make. What the future would bring, she didn't know. For now, she would concentrate on her work and hope there wouldn't be any problems at Medico.

Seventeen

On the Harrison Ranch, Christopher told his best friend, "She's gone, John. I tried everything to get her to stay, but she wouldn't. Her job means too much to her, maybe more than I do. It's been a long five days for me, but she's having a ball out there. Hell, we've only talked once!"

"*Bi'niiya*, Chris, it's more than a mere job, and she had to get settled in. Think, old boy: remember how you felt when you were forced to give up surgery? I do." The sullen physician frowned at the officer but he was not deterred from saying what he thought was needed. "But you want to force Kirstin to give up research; you expect her to do it. Where does it say she loves and needs her career any less than you do, any less than you did?"

"Maria would move or stay with you at the drop of a hat. And she wouldn't even consider a transfer like this one. She'd quit work first."

"Kirstin isn't like Maria. Kirstin's fought hard to get where she is. She's special, *ch'unne'*; that's why you want her so much. Am I wrong?"

"I've never known any female who didn't quit her job to transfer with her husband, or any man who left his work behind for a wife to relocate."

"You two aren't married, Chris, not even engaged. Couples with a longtime history have a marriage bond compromise. You don't have that with Kirstin; you have known each other only a few weeks. Asking her to make sacrifices and take a risk moving here when you aren't willing to do the same isn't fair, *ch'unne'*. She didn't even know you loved her and wanted to marry her until she was ready to leave and her plans were already in motion. Your revelations must have come as surprises, maybe shocks, to her. I suspect she needs time to consider such an important decision. I would also think she feels she has responsibilities and a loyalty to Medico."

"Women quit work all the time to get married, relocate, or have babies. Aren't those things more important than a career?"

"It should be the same with a man, Chris. Besides, you two haven't even met each other's children; they have a part in this matter, too.

Also, both of you came out of bad marriages; don't you think she's just as scared as you are about changing her life so drastically? Maybe she needs to make certain this love is for real, not just passion talking. It did happen mighty fast. Swept in like a twister if you asked me and spun you both around until you're dizzy. You love her, don't you?" The troubled doctor nodded. "She's worth a compromise, a move, isn't she?" Christopher grimaced. "I know you like your friends and neighbors, the ranch your uncle left you, and this peaceful area, but do you truly love them above all else, and is this really how you want to spend the rest of your life?" John saw his friend's pensive look. "I know you, Chris, you're no rancher bone deep and a small practice isn't enough for you, not after the road you've traveled. It's like you've been biding your time until this golden chance came along. Grab it and take it, *ch'unne'*. Don't you realize, nothing will satisfy you any more without Kirstin to share it?"

"Kirstin must be lonesome and miserable, too," he surmised. "I'll wait a while to see if she likes it there. San Diego is mighty different from a small Georgia town. That part of Medico may be nothing like the one where she worked in Augusta. Kirstin didn't strike me as a big-city lover: the noise, traffic, pollution, crime, expense. She might hate her new

497

boss and have no interest in his projects. After being here, she might decide she prefers me, the ranch, and a quiet life. How do I know research and independence will mean as much to her if she thinks she'll lose me so she can have them? I'll let her have the thinking time she wants. If she refuses to move in with me, a decision this big on my part will take time and deep thought."

"Don't count on her tossing it away and returning here, Chris. Frank would snap up this place in a minute. You can turn your practice over to Niles. You can find a position or create a partnership in San Diego. Remember what you told me happened at the poker game? Are you sure your love and loyalty belong here more than with Kirstin?"

"I just throw in the towel and chase after her?"

John grinned and chuckled. "Why not? I would if it were Maria."

But Kirstin isn't Maria and I'm not Captain John Two Fists.

Kirstin's first day at work seemed to evaporate faster than pool water on a hot and dry day. Afterward, she talked with Katie, who told her the wonderful news that Steve had seen a therapist. Then, Katie gave the other side of the coin: her brother hadn't decided if he was going to continue. Katie finished the chat with other good news: she had a bit part for a week, maybe two, in a television soap opera. That meant she couldn't make up the cut-short visit last weekend by returning on this one.

"Don't worry, nosy, you can meet Christopher another time."

They chatted a while longer before Katie had to leave for a date.

Kirstin called Elaine in Augusta. "Still up, stranger? Are you alone?"

"Yes to both. You sound in a terrific mood. What's the cause?"

"What and who," Kirstin replied and laughed again. "The what is work, my friend. I wish you were here to share this new challenge. You'd love it, too. Medico is fantastic, exciting; it's huge, Elaine, and a little intimidating; no, a *lot* intimidating. The who is my new boss; Dr. Charles Summeraul is wonderful. We got acquainted while he was giving me a tour of the complex; heavens, it's enormous and it has high-tech security: cameras, guards, checkpoints, badges, the works. They issued me a clearance badge and a card key to wear around my neck for admittance to private and/or hazardous locations: both of them are marked with my name, fingerprint, and photo so no one else can use them. They're real sticklers for secrecy and defense, nothing like how it was there. At first, I was almost afraid to breathe wrong. I got a new nuclear medicine badge, too," she related, referring to a two-part badge—one permanent card and one to be changed monthly which tested for radioactive contamination—to be worn at all times for protection. She knew how many microcuries she was allowed to have on her badge readings before being treated for radiation poisoning and becoming dangerous to herself and others. She also knew that a spill of a "hot" material could have a laboratory put off limits for a specified—if clean-up was possible—or permanent time period, if it wasn't. She knew it was critical to use caution with perilous products and procedures and know how to dispose of contaminated waste properly. "He showed which facilities and areas I'll use in our work and which ones are forbidden to my med-tech level. I met other Medico researchers, assistants, and various staff members. Everybody seems nice and helpful; I got a real southern welcome.

"My visit to the human resources office took quite a while. I had to put my name on so many papers that I almost felt as if I were signing my life away. You should see the size of the Benefits and Regulations manual they gave me. They filled my head with tons of instructions and rules. I'm officially employed, Elaine; it's done."

"Any problems when you told them about the diabetes?"

"I didn't, not yet. But I will. We ate lunch in an adjacent building in a lovely cafeteria. The food was delicious and I had no trouble getting the food I need. To be on the safe side, I had an ample supply of glucose tablets in my pocket. I'm going to stick to my original plan and reveal my news later, soon. I'm only two miles from my apartment, so I can go home for lunch if I like."

"Did you and the new boss get down to any business today?"

"After lunch, we sat in his office to discuss the first project and future ones."

"I'm proud of you, Kirstin. I know it's exciting to be in such a stimulating and prestigious place."

"It is," she concurred. "I must have glowed with pride over the way they treated me, like I was valuable and indispensable."

"You are. That's why they were so eager to keep you. What's the new boss like? Good-looking? Any chance he isn't married? I bet he's pleased to have you as his assistant and he has to be impressed by your record. I mean, your last two bosses listed you in the medical journals as their research assistant. What did that last one say?"

"I believe, 'Research done by Kirstin Lowrey.' "

"Believe?" Elaine echoed amidst laughter. "I thought we framed the entire article. If not, it was an oversight. So, what's the old boy like?"

"I liked him on sight; I'm going to enjoy working with him. He has gentle brown eyes and a pleasant manner. Neat and attractive, even his mustache and short beard. Remember the old TV show, *Marcus Welby, M.D.?* That's who came to mind, but he favors Welby's assistant more than him. He has a grandfatherly aura."

"How old is he?"

"Two years older than I am. He seemed impressed by my experiment suggestions. He wrote them down and we discussed them. We talked about families, past projects, and common interests. He seems happily married and he didn't make the slightest pass at me."

"So you spent the first day touring, signing, and chatting?"

"Nope, we donned white lab coats and dug in to the first experiment. It's going to be a long and well-funded project. I'm so excited about it. I can hardly wait to get back to work on it tomorrow."

"Sounds as if you made wise choices. Both

the relocation from Augusta and not staying in New Mexico. How is the sexy doctor taking your absence?"

"I'm not sure. But he's coming to visit me this weekend and I can hardly wait."

"You want them both, don't you?"

"Yes, with all my heart. Cross your fingers for me."

"I wish you luck, Kirstin, both at Medico and with Christopher. I'm downright jealous, pea-green with envy. But I do have some good news."

"What? Tell me, you devil. I know that tone. Who is he?"

"Remember Bob Martin?"

"The one we met at the gym before I left?"

"The same. We've been out three times and he seems to be really interested in me. Believe it or not, I'm taking it slow this time. I don't want to scare him off or give him a bad impression. He's old-fashioned."

"They still have those kind around? How lucky can we both get?"

They joined in laughter, then chatted about Elaine's new romance and job at the Medical College of Georgia.

After they hung up, Kirstin smiled. She was going to enjoy working with Charles Summeraul in his laboratory, and at the Medico complex. In a good mood, she phoned Christopher, half expecting not to get him.

"Kirstin, glad you called and I was home this time."

"So am I. How are things going?"

"About the same. What about with you? First-day jitters over yet?"

"Almost." She told him many, most, of the same things she had related to Elaine. She added, "Our next project is one dear to my heart: effect of diabetes on vision — causes, cures, and preventions. Our current project is dear to yours: it involves new heart medications: one is hoped to be an aid during open-heart surgery and transplants, your specialty."

"My *former* specialty. So, you love everything there; that's good for you, bad for me. It means you won't be tempted to ditch it all and return to me."

"I don't need to throw it away, not if you move here. You could be a valuable asset to this project and others. Doctor Summeraul said he needs the assistance of a skilled heart surgeon; that's you, Doc. The three of us would make a super team."

"No, Kirstin, it isn't me. Research is your interest, not mine."

"You don't have to become a researcher to provide information and suggestions and evaluate our findings and —"

"Can we change the subject? Talking about

surgery depresses me."

"Okay. How are the ranch and your patients? Had any emergencies or made any changes lately?"

"Neither, and all's fine on my end."

"Looked at motor homes yet?"

"Nope. Couldn't get in the mood without you here."

"How are Frank and Helen?"

"Fine. She's glad to be home and he's just as delighted."

I'm running out of small talk, my love. "How is Peggy?"

"Doing fine, too. We had a long talk yesterday. How are your kids?"

No details about that chat with your daughter? Uh-oh. "Katie's on cloud nine," she said, and told him why. "Sandi's great. She's coming to visit in a few weeks. I can hardly wait to see her and my grandson. I bet he's grown like a weed. She says he's walking and trying to talk. I plan to get a supply of toys for his visit."

"From how you described the place, you have plenty of room for them."

"For you, too. You can check it out this weekend. Heavens, I miss you. I'll prepare my finest meal for you Friday night."

"I'll make sure I arrive hungry. Heard from your son?"

"Yes, and Katie just told me he's in therapy.

505

For now. I hope he sticks with it and it works. Lord knows, we both can profit from his treatment. Estrangement is torment. That's why I didn't want to create any problems between you and Peggy. I hope I didn't."

"You didn't. I told her I love you and proposed."

"You did?"

"Why does that surprise you?"

"I just didn't expect you to do it so soon."

"Was I premature? Are you going to reject me?"

"I haven't and I won't, Christopher. I love you. I want to marry you."

"So, come back and honor your word."

"I am honoring it, to Medico and myself at present. I don't know how long it will take."

"Is there anything I can say or do to speed up the process?"

"That's something I have to work out for myself."

"I'm trying to understand. I love you, woman, and I'm waiting for you."

"And I'm waiting for you. Please reconsider your decision."

"I'm hoping, with time, you'll reconsider yours. And I hope time brings you home to me."

"I'll talk to you later this week and see you this weekend. I love you."

506

"I love you, too. Bye, Kirstin. Stay well and safe, love."

"You, too. Bye." *Darn, I forgot to ask what Peggy said about us. It couldn't have been too bad; she didn't talk you out of your visit.*

Kirstin started to phone her son but decided not to intrude on Steve yet. *Please, God, let him see the light. Help Christopher see it, too.*

Her second workday, Kirstin joined two other research technicians for lunch. Both women were at her same professional level and also were involved in exciting projects. Talk of past and current work, families, Medico, San Diego, and other topics consumed their midday break with speed and ease. Before separating, they invited Kirstin to go shopping and have lunch on Saturday while their men were enjoying spring sports. She told them she expected company for the weekend, but promised to join them another time.

Kirstin returned to Doctor Summeraul's laboratory in a cheery mood. There was a note from him on her desk to inform her that he was in a meeting and to start today's experiment without him. She donned a lab coat and went over his instructions. She made notes to use for quick reference later when her hands were occupied, then began the challenging

507

task. She assembled the needed instruments and beakers and put out surgical and anesthesia supplies. She weighed tiny amounts of chemicals on a delicate scale which was encased in glass to prevent moisture in the air from affecting its weight. She used graduated cylinders and syringes to measure solutions and liquids, as the slightest error altered and voided the test results. She calibrated medical equipment that read and recorded responses, and made certain the units had sufficient ink and paper. She prepared the oxygenator and blood-flow tubes to keep tissue and organ samples alive and healthy. When everything was ready, she pressed a button to indicate an experiment was in progress; it illuminated a red light outside the laboratory door and sent a message to the switchboard operator that any disturbance until otherwise notified should be considered an emergency.

As she wriggled her hands into latex gloves, she murmured, "Okay, Kirstin, let's see how you do by yourself this afternoon. For all you know, the doctor might be testing you."

She drew blood samples from a specimen and marked the small tubes. Two "controls" were stored in a tray in a refrigeration unit, a third was to be used for treatment, and a fourth was placed inside the centrifuge. Its motor whirled fast as cellular elements were separated from plasma. Using a syringe, she extracted the liquid and added more markings to those tubes. She sat at the surgical table and wished Christopher was there to assist her. Soon, the experiment was in progress and her full attention was on it.

"How is it going?"

Kirstin jumped and squealed, then glanced at her watchful boss. "Just about finished, sir. I didn't hear you come in."

"Sorry I startled you; you have some concentration." He lifted sections of the readouts and studied them. A broad smile made creases near his large nose and chocolate eyes and on his tanned cheeks. "Excellent, Kirstin. You've accomplished a great deal this afternoon. I bet you're a neat housekeeper." His gaze slipped around the large room as he explained, "The lab's so clean and uncluttered. My last tech was messy and, a few times, careless."

"Thank you. My last boss was a stickler for everything having its place, so I'm in the habit of straightening up as I go along. Let me know if it gets on your nerves."

"It won't; it's a constructive use of time. Most technicians and assistants just sit around or goof off while experiments are running; then, they fuss about having to stay late to clean up their labs. As I told you, I'm not one for overtime unless it's a dire emergency. I love my work, but I have a family and life outside this lab."

Kirstin was delighted at that nonrestrictive schedule. "I've completed the instructions you left. Do you want to check anything or do any repeats before I shut down for today?"

"No, everything looks in order. I couldn't have done better myself. I'll have no qualms about leaving you in charge. Now, I understand why Medico was so eager to keep you aboard; you're good, very good. I'll have to thank my last tech for quitting and the company for assigning you to me."

"That's kind, Doctor Summeraul."

"Charles, please. We'll be working together for a long time, I hope."

"So do I, Charles. I love this project and I love research."

"It shows, Kirstin, in your work and in your expression."

"Will you be here tomorrow or do you have my instructions?"

"I'll be here, eight o'clock. Let's get this place cleared now."

Kirstin was surprised and pleased when he pitched in to help. In fifteen minutes, they were in the elevator and heading for the parking level.

* * *

The following day, it was much the same, out by five-thirty. Kirstin was glad because she had the last doctor's appointment of the day at six. When she reached home, she called Katie in Los Angeles.

"Hi, Mom, glad you called. How's it going there?"

"Wonderful. Doctor Summeraul let me run the experiment alone yesterday and, I might add, I was splendid." Kirstin laughed.

"I expect only the best from my mother. I love hearing you sound so happy and confident."

"Me, too, honey. How do you like doing the soap? I taped it to watch during supper. You were so good yesterday and today. I can't wait to see tomorrow's episode. If I'm not careful, you'll hook me on that program."

"If viewership rises, they might want to keep me on."

"Would you like that, Katie? Will it interfere with your other jobs?"

"It's fun and I get plenty of exposure, but it does cramp my schedule. It's surprising how much time and work each episode takes. I'll wait and see. What did the new doctor say? You did see him after work?"

"I did, and I received a fantastic report.

When he checked my record book and learned how many lows I was having and how many tablets and snacks it was taking to prevent others, he took me off my pills altogether. He thinks I can control my diabetes with diet and exercise."

"That's wonderful news, Mom. Make sure you stick to your routine. Just because you're off medication, don't forget to take care of yourself or you'll start running highs again, and they're worse for you than lows."

Kirstin was overjoyed that her daughter had educated herself on her condition. "I'll be careful, honey. No more hypoglycemic attacks will be a relief for me. I was so scared I was going to overexert or lose track of time and have an attack in the lab, I popped extra glucose tablets just to make certain I didn't. I'll be so good, honey, Doctor Johnson will think he has an angel for a patient."

"You'd better, or I'll move in with you and play tyrannical nursemaid."

"That won't be necessary; I promise."

"Need privacy for your company this weekend, eh?"

"Don't tease me, Kathryn Lowrey. This visit is important."

"Think you can persuade him to stay?"

"I hope so. I love him and miss him so. I sent him a sneaky letter yesterday. I raved about research, Medico, the apartment, San Diego, my new friends, my boss. If only I can spark his interest in them, maybe . . . Am I being foolish and selfish?"

"No, Mom; keep working on him to change his mind."

"Have you heard from Steve again?"

"No."

"What if he didn't go back after his first visit?"

"As you always say, 'Let's be optimistic.' Now, tell me all about your victory yesterday, every juicy and exciting detail."

Thursday evening, Christopher phoned Kirstin. "I got your letter and check today, woman. I told you not to repay me for those car repairs!"

"I had to; you spent so much money on me."

"You might as well add it back to your bank balance because I'm not cashing it. That accident brought us together; it's worth every penny to me."

"To me, too, Christopher, so please let me repay that debt."

"Repay me in another way."

"You have anything special in mind?"

"I'll think of something before we get together. It seems like ages since I've seen you and touched you. I hate rambling around this house by myself and sleeping alone. Phone calls aren't enough, Kirstin. I need you with me, all the time. Damn research for stealing you away"

You can call or join me any time you like, my love. "I wish you were here. I miss you so much. I want to wake up every morning with you beside me. I want to cuddle up with you on the sofa, share another shower where I can lather and massage you thoroughly." She heard him groan in rising desire as she refreshed those sensuous moments in his mind and implied more pleasure in the future. "I miss your smile and laughter, and even your nagging. I miss talking to you countless times a day. We had so much fun together. I'd settle for being near you in the same room. Of course, I couldn't promise to keep my hands and lips off you for very long. I just might throw you on the floor and ravish you on my new carpet. Did I tell you I have skylights over my tub and bed? We can make love under a starry heaven in both locations. I can give you a bath like you've never had before. Oh, yes, there's a skylight in the eating area, too, if we can find anything to feast on. Is seven tomorrow night the soonest you can get here?"

"Afraid so, Kirstin."

"Is that your only response to my erotic inducements? What do I have to do or say to get you as hot and bothered as I am?"

"I stay that way where you're concerned. I miss you like crazy, too, woman, but it can't be helped, can it? Are you taking care of yourself?"

Caught on to my trick, did you, and you're foiling me? "Doctor Johnson took me off my medication. I'm doing fine, no lows and very few highs, all in the diabetic safety range."

"That's great news, Kirstin; you're doing fine on your own."

"In the work and health departments, but not in the emotional one. It's harder being separated from you than I imagined."

"I've been tempted to fly over there every day."

"Why haven't you?"

"I knew it wouldn't do any good, not this soon."

"Is that also why you haven't phoned every night? Want me to pine and suffer so I'll change my mind and rush to the ranch?"

"You have a telephone, too, woman, and you're liberated."

"I thought you needed time to think about our problem."

"Is there really anything to think about, Kirstin? We've made our decisions and they don't

515

mesh, not yet. We'll have to do the best we can with visits and phone calls and letters until something changes."

You mean, until I change my mind. "I guess so. But if you're here when I get off work, we'll have another two hours together. Why not stay over until Monday morning so we can have Sunday night?"

"There weren't any plane seats available any time on Monday."

"Stay until Tuesday or Wednesday then."

"I can't; I have patients and chores. Kirstin, I was hungry for you the instant you left my driveway. It's gotten worse every day and night. I should have locked you in the house and refused to release you."

"Being your captive and love slave sounds interesting."

"But not as much as your career in research, right?"

"Those are different needs, Christopher. I want both. I need both. It would be the same for you if it were surgery involved."

"You're right, but knowing it doesn't make losing you any easier."

"You haven't lost me and you won't; I love you. Neither of us knows what the future holds. We'll find a compromise." She abruptly changed the subject. "What do you think of the project I mentioned in my letter? Think it will work to help heart patients during surgery?"

"The doctor's ideas sound logical and he's going about his experiments right. He may want to check out some of Alquist's past work on beta receptors."

Kirstin didn't reveal she had made that same suggestion during her initial talk with Charles. Both being from Augusta and he a past staff member at Medical College of Georgia, she was familiar with Alquist's prize-winning and important work. "Thanks, I'll tell Doctor Summeraul. Do you have a suggestion for a surgeon to test our findings later?"

"No, but he shouldn't have trouble locating one there. What do you do when you aren't working? I bet your evenings aren't as lonely as mine are."

"Will discussion of our careers, such vital parts of us, always be off-limits?" she asked in frustration.

"Surgery isn't my career and will never be again, and yours took you from me; both are painful topics, Kirstin."

"Doesn't talking about them ease any of the anguish? Ignoring them won't make them disappear. I want to share everything with you."

"Maybe later. Maybe soon. Not tonight, okay?"

"Okay. So, how's the ranch, all your patients

517

and friends doing? Any more snakes or attack dogs on the loose? Did you get your new bull? Been dipping in that cold pond again?"

Christopher caught her up on all the local news. After they hung up, he rested his head against the recliner and sank into deep thought. He wondered why he had silenced her when he was really eager to hear about her stimulating work, when he had read her descriptive letter several times and had experienced surges of anticipation and a flood of ideas for the project. He hadn't even told her how he'd been poring over old medical journals on the subject. He hadn't revealed the minor surgery he'd done with his right hand, even if it was only on an injured animal; the procedure had worked. He hadn't mentioned a call to a colleague about a new nerve replacement technique that was still in the research stage, nor that he was doing hand therapy again on his own.

Afraid none of them will work and your disappointment will increase, Chris? Afraid you can't get better with practice and with therapy because they both failed in the past? Afraid your news will only encourage her to push harder for you to move there?

Christopher closed his eyes and calmed himself. Kirstin didn't treat him as somebody to discard. She made him feel alive, proud, as if he could accomplish anything. He wondered if he was hurting both of them by staying on the ranch. Was he denying others his skills and knowledge, his experience? Could he help more people if he moved? Would research or teaching or private general practice be so terrible in San Diego with Kirstin at his side? Was he denying them a chance at a happy future together?

Friday around noon, Christopher answered a knock at his office door. His gaze widened and he stared at his daughter. "What are you doing here, squirt? You didn't tell me you were coming to visit."

"I wanted to surprise you. I was worried about you, Dad. I thought you could use some company. We haven't shared a visit in ages. We need special time together. But do you have other plans? I can catch the next plane home and come another time. I just miss you so much. I just had to see for myself if you're all right. I love you, Dad."

As they embraced, Christopher said, "Your timing's fine, squirt. Why don't you go prepare us some lunch while I finish up here? It won't take long, ten minutes max. We can begin our visit while we eat. I skipped breakfast and I'm starved," he white-lied to obtain some time alone.

"That's a great idea. See you inside. I'm

glad to be here, Dad."

He hugged her. "I'm glad to see you, squirt. I'll be there soon."

After Peggy left, Christopher canceled his plane reservations and tried to phone Kirstin; the Medico operator said she couldn't put through the call unless it was an emergency because an experiment was in progress and the no-disturb signal was in force. He didn't insist because it was an emergency only to him and Kirstin, and he didn't want to put her in the position of having to explain the intrusion to her boss. He realized he might not have a private moment later to try her again, so he put a message on Kirstin's home answering machine. He hated for her to get the bad news in that manner, but it couldn't be helped. He headed for the house to learn what had really brought his daughter to see him.

Eighteen

Kirstin rushed home from work, showered, and dressed for the long-awaited evening. She did a blood sugar test and ate a snack to tide her over to dinner, a meal she hoped was delayed by a visit to the candlelit bedroom. She wished she could meet Christopher at the airport, but he had said it was best if he took a taxi to her apartment because he didn't want her out in the heavy traffic.

She paced and looked out the window numerous times. Twice, she checked her makeup and tawny tresses to see if there was any repair needed or room for improvement. Her blue gaze scanned the large walk-in closet to make certain she was wearing the most appealing casual outfit she owned. At seven-thirty, she called the airport to see if his plane had been delayed; it had arrived on schedule, plenty of time for him to be there by now.

She asked if he had missed the flight, but the woman said she couldn't give out information on a passenger, not even when Kirstin claimed he was her fiancé.

Kirstin fretted in annoyance and apprehension, and started pacing again. She examined the apartment to make sure it was perfect. The flowers Christopher and Steve had sent were gone by now, but rose petals were drying in a basket in the pantry. Delectable smells filled her nostrils. The meat and vegetables she had put in the crock pot this morning to simmer all day were ready, as was the fresh salad stored in the refrigerator. Wine was chilled and rolls were wrapped in foil to be warmed in the oven later. All she needed to begin the romantic evening was her missing lover. Her concern increased.

At eight, she phoned Christopher's two numbers; his personal answering machine responded at home and his professional service took the office call. She didn't leave a private message with either in case he had asked someone to check them during his absence. She didn't want anybody to discover he was visiting her for the weekend and gossip.

Kirstin turned on the television to see if there was any news about a traffic problem; nothing. Nor about an accident. She tried to force herself not to think about losing Christopher in the same manner she'd lost David: That would be too cruel to endure.

Much as she loved and needed her family and career, they weren't enough to complete her life; only Christopher at her side could do that. Research couldn't smile, laugh, talk, cuddle, embrace, kiss, touch, love. It couldn't share joys and sadness, successes and failures, good and bad times, strong and weak moments. It couldn't give advice, provide a shoulder to lean on, offer a kind ear. It couldn't have fun with her. It couldn't provide the peace and security she felt when simply snuggled in his arms on the sofa while watching television. She should re-examine her priorities. She should reassess working and living on the ranch as his wife and assistant.

Yes, you should, but don't be hasty or impulsive and don't do serious thinking while you're being influenced by worries over his safety.

Kirstin wondered if she should check with the local police and hospitals to see if—*No. That can't happen to you twice. Oh my God, keep Christopher safe and well.*

She glanced at the answering machine; the red light wasn't blinking, which she would have noticed earlier. The near-frantic and distracted woman remembered setting the microwave clock because four bright dashes had exposed a power disruption of nine minutes.

Too, the television had displayed slashes when she'd turned it on, revealing its memory was erased today. Those recalls of interrupted electricity while she was at work told her there could be a message from Christopher on the tape!

Kirstin pressed the repeat button and listened:

"It's me, love. Peggy came for a surprise visit at noon so I have to cancel our plans. She seems to need this time with me and I guess I need it with her, too. If I get a private minute, I'll call you. I don't want her to catch me and think she's spoiled my weekend. I promise to come next Friday and make it up to you. I'm sorry. I love you and miss you. Bye. Oh, yes, I read about a new blood monitor yesterday. It works by a light beam, right through the flesh, and should be on the market within eighteen to twenty-four months. No more pricks and sore fingers and blood spots everywhere. I'll check on it and keep you posted. I've also been collecting everything I can find relating to your next project with Summeraul on diabetes and vision. It'll impress him if you're knowledgeable and prepared in advance. There's a fascinating article on treatment with laser surgery. I'll bring everything with me next week. Peg and I are eating supper with John and Maria tonight.

Talk to you later."

Kirstin pressed the repeat button and frowned as she listened to his message again. He wasn't coming. It would be a whole week before she saw him. *Well, get into a cozy nightgown and eat. You have the weekend alone. Or . . .*

Kirstin phoned Janet and asked, "Is it too late to join you and Franci tomorrow for shopping and lunch? My visitor just cancelled on me."

"Not at all. We'll pick you up about ten."

After their pleasant chat, Kirstin ate dinner and changed clothes. She flopped on the sofa and half-watched a movie that had been shown several times before, but so had everything else on the other channels. She'd read every magazine nearby, and wished she had a new book. She decided to write letters to Sandi and Steve and listen to music. First, she glanced at the answering machine as certain statements registered belatedly in her mind. He had talked about surgery and research. He was studying them! He wanted to discuss them with her! What, she mused, had changed his mind overnight?

Saturday evening, Kirstin curled up on the sofa to relax and rest after an enjoyable day with her new friends. She made a few short phone calls. She chatted with Katie before her daughter's date arrived for dinner and a movie. She learned Steve was still in therapy, and both hoped he would continue. She spoke with Betty for only a brief time, too, because the Augusta friend was leaving to eat out with her husband. She talked with Elaine for five minutes; the divorcee was preparing for a date with her new flame. There was nothing on television, and she'd forgotten to purchase a book or magazine. She yearned to speak with Christopher, but it seemed unwise to intrude on his special time with Peggy.

Work, family, and friends were enough for me before I met you, Doctor Harrison. Heavens, I miss you and want to be with you. Oh, Christopher, what are we going to do? I'm half happy and half fulfilled both there and here. Which half is more important to me? Love or career? Perhaps Medico will make that decision for me when I . . .

Kirstin recorded her findings and removed a glass slide from the microscope. She put away marked petri dishes with samples in them. She checked the in vitro experiment in progress. She stored chemicals in their places. She washed beakers and cylinders in special solutions. She tensed in anxiety when her boss returned to the laboratory. "Charles, there's something I need to tell you, something I should have already told you. While we're waiting for this step to finish, may I talk to you?"

After Kirstin related news of her medical condition and her motives for withholding it, Charles smiled and said, "If that's the only secret you kept from me, Kirstin, nothing's changed. You have your diabetes under control and you're smart enough to keep it that way. It won't interfere with your position with me or Medico. Just make sure you stick to you regimen. A manageable health problem won't take away the best assistant I've had. In fact, you'll be perfect for the next project."

"Diabetes isn't always a minor problem, Charles."

"I know, my son is on insulin shots every day. You could say I'm an expert on the disease. That's how I know you'll be fine in the lab."

"Thank you, Charles, for being understanding and generous."

"Thank you for trusting me enough to confide in me, and for moving across country to work with me. We'll be a great team."

"Christopher, it's me, Kirstin."

"As if I wouldn't know your voice anywhere or anytime," he jested.

"Is Peggy still there? Can you talk?"

"It must be good news the way you're jabbering. What's up, woman? Did you earn a raise and promotion this fast? I wouldn't be surprised."

"Of course not, but thanks for the confidence in me. Are you alone?"

"Yes, Peggy left last night. She's a career woman like you."

"Why didn't you call me after she left?"

"It was too late when I got back from Lubbock. Their airport is bigger than ours. She caught the last flight. I figured you were asleep."

"You could have awakened me."

"You need your rest, woman, remember?"

"I forgot you just retired from being my personal physician and know all of my secrets. I have good news: I told Charles about my diabetes, and it won't be a problem. His son is diabetic, so he understands. I also saw my gynecologist after work. I started the pill."

"Birth control pills?"

"Yes. Isn't that what we agreed I'd do?"

"Yes, but I didn't realize you'd handle the matter so promptly. We'll still need to be careful for a while."

"That's what she said, to use condoms for the next two weeks until I'm sure I'm protected by the pill. I told her I didn't want to get pregnant at my age. So, what's wrong? You sound . . . odd."

"You sound so downright independent, getting everything done by yourself. What did you give as a reason for wanting to go on the pill?"

"I told the doctor I was getting married in a few months and wanted to be ready for my honeymoon. As I recall, you did propose to me."

"But you rejected it and left."

She was silent for a minute. "Does that mean the proposal is withdrawn?"

"Never. What did Summeraul say about your condition?"

She related that news before she asked, "What about your talk with Peggy?"

"We had a good visit. I'll give you the particulars this weekend, but there's nothing to worry your pretty head about."

She waited for him to broach other topics of mutual interest or dispute, but he didn't. "It's getting late, so I'd better get off the phone, take a bath, and go to bed," she said regretfully.

"Too bad I'm not there to give you a soothing scrub and massage."

"I wish you were, Christopher, and I'd return the favor."

"Let's put it on our calendars for this weekend."

"If nothing and no one comes up to make you cancel again. It seems like forever since I left the ranch."

"To me, too. Friday will be here before we know it."

"It's four nights and almost four days until then."

"Will it help if I call every night at eight?"

"Yes."

"Wherever I am, I'll stop to call you on time."

"I'll be here, Christopher, ready and waiting."

He chuckled. "That's one way to make certain you're not out on a date with somebody else."

"If I didn't know you were teasing, I'd give you a kick in the . . . rump."

"I'll do more than that to you if you step out on me, woman," he jested. "Good night, Kirstin. Sleep well. I'll call tomorrow."

"Good night, Christopher, and you'd better phone. I love you."

"I love you, too."

True to his word, he called on time the next two nights. Then, Thursday at seven, Peggy Harrison Beattie took Kirstin by surprise when

530

she phoned.

"Before I tell you why I called, Mrs. Lowrey, my father doesn't know about this conversation and he'd be annoyed if he learned I meddled in his business. What we say must be held in confidence between us. Agreed?"

Intrigued, Kirstin said, "Agreed, Peggy."

"First, I need to apologize for our last conversation. I was rude and nosy. I hope I didn't do any damage to your relationship. I love my father very much and I don't want to see him hurt or used. Second, I want to see if there's anything I can do or say to either of you to help you and my father get together."

"How much did he tell you about us?"

"I know he proposed and you mostly accepted. I understand there are some obstacles between you two, but I don't want to be one of them. I want Dad to be happy. I spent this past weekend with him and it was a real eye-opener. He's very much in love with you, Mrs. Lowrey, and he's miserable without you. I'm hoping you feel the same way about him. I saw how you've changed my father, for the better, I should add."

"Thank you, Peggy. It means a lot to hear you say that. I never expected to meet anyone like him; he's unique and special, the most wonderful and handsome man in the world. Leaving him was one of the hardest things I've done in my life, but I felt as if we needed time and distance to make our decisions with clear heads. I know we love each other and I believe we're perfect for each other. But we do have career and location conflicts. Naturally, both of us thinks it's best for the other to yield. Change and risks are scary for people our age, especially when we have other loved ones to consider and when we've both suffered losses in the past. Frankly, it's been difficult to get Christopher to even talk about his disability and starting fresh here. I've seen him and helped him with patients, Peggy; he has more skill and dexterity than he realizes. And there are ways to work around the things he can't do. He has to accept the fact that major surgery is out, but minor surgery or research surgery is possible. He just has some limitations. There's no shame or humiliation in asking for assistance when he needs it. He still has his keen mind, and he can do almost anything he wants if he only tries. It isn't a defeat to change careers—to teach, to do research, to go into general practice. I don't want to push or put pressure on him, just love him and help him, be his partner."

"I was prepared to dislike you, Mrs. Lowrey, and to do everything I could to get you out of my father's life. But after listening to him and talking with you, I'm convinced I was wrong and you two should be married. I overheard John and Maria working on him, too. So are Mr. and Mrs. Graham. I think his stubbornness is weakening, either from being apart from you or because he's afraid he'll lose you altogether. Until this weekend, he hasn't mentioned surgery in years or been tempted to do something else with his life. I never thought I'd see the day when he'd consider selling the ranch, changing occupations again, and remarrying. We talked until our mouths were dry and our jaws ached. He needs you, Mrs. Lowrey."

"He actually told you he might sell the ranch and move here?"

"He said he was considering it, and I think it's a real possibility; but when, I don't know. He explained your dilemma to me, and I agree with what you did. I like the ranch for visits, but I can't imagine living there, being a rancher's wife and losing my career. I'd also love to see him back in the mainstream of medicine. He's too good to be running such a small practice. He has too much to offer. I tried to convince him you're right."

"That's very kind, Peggy. I do love him and want to marry him. I honestly believe the best place for us is here. If I let him persuade me to move there, he'd always feel guilty about what I'd have to give up, and he'd probably think I was resentful inside. I doubt it would help either of us for me to become a rancher's wife. But if he doesn't change his mind within a few months, a year at the most, I will move there. I love and need my work, but not at the price of losing Christopher."

"I doubt you ever will, Mrs. Lowrey. He's crazy about you. Every time he talks about you, he's like a kid at Christmas. He lights up like a tree and acts as if he's gotten the best present of all time. He's so alive again, so proud, so happy and miserable combined. He's got it bad for you."

"I have it bad for him. So, woman to woman, what should I do?"

"Exactly what you're doing now: entice him to come to you. Get him more involved in medicine and the outside world. You seem to have ignited his interest in research, heart research to be specific. He chattered away about it. I think he'd enjoy working at Medico, especially with you."

"First, I have to get him here and prove to him he can do it."

"If all else fails, make him jealous and afraid he's going to lose you. Once he's where he belongs, he'll be glad you coaxed him out of hiding. I've said and done all I can think of to point him in your direction."

"Thank you, Peggy. You don't know how

much it means to me to have you on my side, on *our* side. I promise you, I'll do my best to make him happy and to never hurt him in any way."

"If I didn't believe that, I wouldn't have called you."

When Christopher phoned, Kirstin didn't reveal — as promised — that she had just gotten off the line from Oregon with his daughter. She hoped and prayed Peggy was right about her father leaning toward moving to San Diego.

"John and Maria send hellos and hugs. They think I'm loco for letting you live out there alone amidst all those tempting men."

"Nobody is tempting except you, Christopher."

"You'll never guess who I talked to this afternoon, Harry and Laura Stoker, my ex-wife and my ex-best friend. A friend of Harry's told him I was checking into a research project on neuropathy and nerve replacements. It seems that Harry's an adviser and surgeon on the team involved, sort of like what you asked me to do on your project with Summeraul. Anyhow, he filled me in on the work. It sounds great, but it'll be years before they're ready to try anything with a human specimen. By then, I'll be too old for it to matter."

"No, you won't. There are plenty of doctors and surgeons in their fifties and older still practicing. You were one of the best, Christopher. I bet you've forgotten more than the med students are learning these days. Heavens, you could teach them so much."

"Maybe. Who knows, I might check into teaching one day."

Don't push and mess it up. Let him work it out in his own time and manner. "What did Laura have to say?"

"She apologized for taking my dog years ago; isn't that funny?"

"What made her think of that?"

"Harry gave her a new boxer for her birthday last week. She asked if I wanted a puppy after he was bred."

"What did you tell her? You have plenty of room for one on the ranch."

"Yeah, but . . . I don't want to be tied down to a pet. I have traveling to do. You did promise to go camping with me."

Were you about to say something like, No dog in an apartment? "I'll be settled enough by June to take off to places unknown."

"I can think of one special trip I'd like to take."

Anticipation shot through her like tiny electrical sparks. "Where?"

"I'll tell you about it later, tomorrow night

when I see you."

"You sound in a good mood for someone who talked to two people who were enemies."

"We got things pretty well settled between us. I guess we were all to blame for what happened. It's over and done with. I have to admit I think they're perfect for each other, and they seem genuinely sorry about the way they got together. They're happy, Kirstin, really happy. I want the same thing for us. I hope you don't mind my telling them about you and my proposal."

"Of course not. I bet Frank's excited about running the ranch for you while you're gone, sort of like being boss and owner for a time."

"Yep. Nobody, not even me, does a better job. There's John's horn. He's coming by to talk. I'll see you tomorrow."

"Bye," she rushed out the word as he terminated their conversation and a noisy dial tone filled her ear. She stared at the phone as she murmured, "You're acting mighty strange, my love."

Friday afternoon, Kirstin's front tires bumped the curb as she pulled into the assigned space in front of her apartment. She stared over the steering wheel. Sitting on the step of her portico was Doctor Christopher

Harrison with a bouquet of multi-colored roses in his hand. He stood as she stepped out of her Nissan, locked the door, and hurried to join him.

He set down the flowers for a quick embrace and a brief kiss. "If we weren't in public, Kirstin Lowrey, I'd give you a better greeting. I've been so eager to see you, I'm as strung out as tight barbwire. I thought you'd never get home."

She held his hands as she smiled. "I'm early, in case you forgot to change your watch to our time. Where's your luggage?"

"In the trunk of a rented car over there. We'll sneak it in after dark."

"That isn't necessary. I don't care what my neighbors might think."

"They'll have plenty to gossip about if we don't get inside fast. You're getting to me in a visible manner. I'm just burning for you."

"Let's go cool both of us off," she whispered. "We'll fetch your luggage later."

Inside, he glanced around as she placed the flowers in a vase. "I chose these flowers very carefully. Red's for love and passion, pink's to show loneliness, and yellow is for happiness and friendship. The language of flowers says it all. I have all of those things with you, Kirstin, but I want more, much more."

"Then you're in luck, Doc, because I'm in a

generous mood today. You can have anything and everything you want from me."

"How about I start collecting with this?" he murmured and nibbled at her earlobe, then let his lips roam her throat.

Kirstin leaned back her head to give him ample working room. It felt good to feel his touch and lips again, to hear his voice, to see his smile, to be with him.

He embraced her with tender possessiveness as his mouth tantalized her parted lips. He lifted her into his arms. "Which way to your room?" he asked as he nuzzled her neck.

"*Our* room," she corrected with a glowing smile.

"*Our*, what a beautiful word. As beautiful as you are, woman."

They were out of their clothes with haste and lying on the bed. Passion's flames burned brighter and higher as they kissed and caressed each other eagerly, neither able to wait an extra minute for this special joining.

Laughter filled the room as they lay on their backs side-by-side and gazed at the blue sky filtering through the skylight.

"Whew, woman, that was magnificent. You drive me crazy and I can't go slow enough with you sometimes, not after being apart for so long. I'll do better next time."

"If it gets any better, I'll melt into the bed

like butter under the sun."

He rolled to his side and propped his head with a balled fist. He gazed down at her. "We are good together, aren't we?"

"Yes, my love, we are." Kirstin's fingers lifted to play with his hair, but he captured them and kissed the tip of each one.

"Let's get you fed, woman; you're too far off schedule. I want you well nourished and strong to keep up with me this weekend."

"Now that I'm off my medication, my routine isn't as strict."

"That's no excuse to take advantage of it, and I know you won't."

"Especially with my personal physician in residence."

They joined forces to clear the table after dinner.

He said, "I'm hoping everything can work out for us soon. I hate being separated from you."

Ready to relent, Kirstin answered, "It doesn't have to be that way."

He watched her refrigerate the last of the leftovers and step to the sink. "I'm not blind or deaf, Kirstin; I realize you wouldn't be totally happy at the ranch. You have everything you want and need here."

She stopped loading the dishwasher to look at him. "I don't have you with me all the time. I love you, Christopher Harrison. I need you. I want to be your partner. We're so compatible, but it's hard and painful to get closer with so much distance between us. We can't lose this glorious second chance. We have to take any risk necessary to capture it and hold it, even if it means I must retire and return to the ranch."

He was afraid to trust his hearing. Was she saying she would—

"I love you," she said again. "I'll move to the ranch as soon as I can finish the current project with Charles and work out a decent notice."

"You aren't kidding, are you?"

"No. I think I fell in love with you the moment I saw you leaning over me and heard your voice. I can't imagine not sharing a life with you. I'll miss research, but living with you is more important to me. Who knows, maybe I'll be just as happy being your assistant?"

He pulled her into his arms and kissed her. "Well, I guess we have only two choices: either I move to San Diego, or we find a city that offers us both what we need. The ranch isn't for either of us."

Her still wet hands stroked his cheek. "You

would do that for me?"

"For *us,* Kirstin. Now that I've found you, I'll move heaven and hell to keep you. I can't ask you to move to the ranch and sacrifice your career."

"But what will happen to the ranch?" she asked as she toyed with his sable hair.

"I'll sell it to Frank and Helen; he'll do great things with it. My uncle would approve, if he were still alive."

She felt as if she were laughing and crying at the same time. "You amaze me, Christopher Harrison. What other man would give up his home and life for a woman?"

"If a woman can do it for her man, why can't he do the same for her? As you've pointed out there's no research there for you, but I can start a practice anywhere. It's the logical and fair solution. That is, if you'll marry me, Kirstin Lowrey."

"Are you sure about this, Christopher? It's a big change for you."

"I'm sure, Kirstin. I didn't realize how much I was missing and how miserable I was until you showed up. I thought if I couldn't do surgery, I couldn't be around it. That doesn't matter anymore. Now that I have you, things will be fine. Fact is, if I hadn't left surgery and moved there, I wouldn't have met you. Fate has a way of putting us where we should

542

be. I have no regrets, Kirstin. Being with you makes everything wonderful."

"If you don't like San Diego, we'll look for another place to work. A compromise, Doc; wherever we settle, we must both agree on it. How long will it take to pack and close your practice and make a deal with the Grahams?"

"We can get married soon and live in your apartment. It's big enough for both of us. I'll look around next week for a new position. I have a few ideas to check on; if one of them works out, we'll stay here. A new career will be fun and challenging, spark the old gray matter to life again," he teased as he tapped his head. "I've been hiding for too long; it's past time to get back where I belong, where I can do the most good for myself and others. Not that what I do in New Mexico isn't important, but I can benefit more people in another line of medicine or in a general practice with more patients. I'll even hire a nurse and secretary if I go that route. I have too much knowledge and too many skills not being used to their fullest. Frankly, you've gotten me excited about research. There's so much happening in that field, so many discoveries waiting to be made. I've been doing a lot of reading and studying and collecting information on projects in progress. If Medico has any openings and are interested in me, I could settle there."

"Your intelligence and generosity are astounding, my love. I always knew you were smarter and braver than you let on," she jested.

"How about a nice reward for my opening my eyes to the truth?"

She turned off the water in the sink and dried her hands; the rest of the dishes and chores could wait. Something more important was at hand: love and their future. "What do you have in mind as payment?"

"After I do a better job of what I started earlier, to make you Kirstin Harrison ASAP," he murmured. "Not a bad note in that new song."

"You're right, Doctor and Mrs. Christopher Harrison. Um-m-m, nice, a very nice ring to it."

"Speaking of ring, John helped me select this one for you. That's why I had to rush off the phone. Mr. Gibbs was keeping the store open late for me to come in." He held up a diamond solitaire.

"Oh, Christopher, it's beautiful. Put it on quickly before you change your mind." She held out her left hand and almost vibrated with excitement.

"I'll never change my mind about you, woman."

After he slipped it on her finger, she held

544

up her hand and gazed at it. "This makes it official; we're engaged. We're going to be married. I love you, Christopher." She kissed him with feelings to match her words.

He chuckled and flipped off the kitchen light. He lifted her and headed for the bedroom with Kirstin snuggled in his arms, this time to make love slowly and blissfully.

As they nestled together, both thought that changes and taking risks had their rewards after all; and this was only one of them.

Tuesday evening, Kirstin phoned her son. She dreaded the news she was about to tell him, feared how he would take it and might try to spoil her happiness. She had made up her mind; either he accepted her love and marriage or she would proceed without his blessing. "Steve, you and I need to have a serious talk. I have some important things to tell you."

Nineteen

"I'm glad you called, Mother. I was going to phone you tomorrow night. How are you feeling? Are you taking good care of yourself? Are the job and move working out for you?"

He sounds in a sunny mood. "I'm doing fine, Steve." She related news about her health, position at Medico, and apartment.

"That's wonderful; I'm happy for you and proud of you, Mother."

"You are?" *What's the catch? When does the mask come off?*

"Yes, you've accomplished quite a lot on your own. Not many women would have had the courage to do what you've done. You're very special."

I despise being so suspicious, but he's been treating me so cruelly for ages. "Thank you, Steve; that's a much appreciated compliment."

"I guess you're wondering what's gotten into me?"

You bet your britches, son. "You do sound different tonight."

"I am, Mother. I've been seeing a therapist and he's helped me understand how much trouble I was having dealing with Dad's death, and the past. You, Katie, Sandi, and Louise were right; I had a lot of bitterness and resentment bottled up inside and was taking some of it out on you. They've given me needed lectures and advice which I've taken to heart, and shouldn't have waited so long to do it. I'm sorry for the terrible way I've been treating you since his death. I've been mean and selfish and demanding and manipulative, the very things I resented my father for being. I hope it won't happen again. Forgive me, Mother, please. I love you and I never meant to intentionally hurt you."

Kirstin was almost too overcome by relief and emotion to respond. It took her a few moments to be able to speak; her son waited until she could. "I understand, Steve. It was hard for you. I'm sure David never meant to hurt any of us. He just didn't know how to show his love and share himself. I've been worried about you, I hated the breach between us. We were always so close. It was hard to step back and be seemingly cruel."

"It was for my own good, Mother; I understand that now. I've made a lot of improvement and changes, but I'm not finished in therapy yet. By the time I am, I'll be a better father, husband, son, and brother."

"I love you, Steve, and I'm happy you're taking this step. If anyone knows how difficult change is, I do."

For a while, they talked about the past, David, and other things.

When Kirstin thought the moment was right, she said, "Steve, there's something else I need to tell you. I've met someone, someone very special. He's asked me to marry him. I love him, Steve. I said yes. We want to get married on May thirtieth. Can you come for the wedding?"

The young man paused before asking, "You've already met someone and it's that serious? Isn't this rather fast?"

Kirstin related how, where, and when she met Christopher and the time they spent together getting acquainted and falling in love. She talked about the now-removed obstacle between them and she explained why she didn't tell Steve sooner about the accident and new relationship.

"You were right to keep them a secret, Mother; I would have been a bastard about them. I suppose a whirlwind romance doesn't have to mean something bad. You're both adults, so you know what you want. Congratulations. I hope you'll be happy, really happy this time. Tell me more about him."

Kirstin gave mosts of the details and a description of Christopher. "He signed on at Medico yesterday. First thing in the morning, he met with the board and presented his ideas. He wrote up such good and valuable proposals, they accepted them immediately, before lunch. They would have been crazy not to grab him fast, and Medico's smart; they realized what an asset he would be to them. Before five, he had his own lab, research assistant, and a big budget. His projects are so important and timely, and he's the perfect one to do them. I'm so proud of him, Steve, and he's so excited about his ideas and new career. He's like a kid in a candy store."

"That's fantastic, Mother. Will you two be working together?"

"We don't work in the same lab, but we'll be doing joint projects in the future. He's agreed to become an adviser on our current heart research. Doctor Summeraul is thrilled to get him; he already knew Christopher by past reputation. We have so much in common, Steve, and we get along so well. He was a brilliant and famous surgeon and he'll make history in research, too. I can hardly wait for you to meet him."

"Neither can I. So, what are the plans?"

"We're getting the license and blood tests to-morrow evening, then going to New Mexico for the weekend to handle the ranch sale and all the packing. Sandi is coming to visit on the twenty-ninth. I haven't called her about the wedding; I will after we finish our talk. I'll phone Katie, too. Does this news upset you, Steve? Do you think I'm being foolish and impulsive? Are you angry with me for keeping secrets? Will this cause another breach between us? I know it's fast, but we do love each other. At our ages, we need to take advantage of every day we have left."

"It comes as a shock, Mother, but it's fine with me. I truly want you to be happy. I'm eager to meet him, and of course I will come for the wedding. Louise won't be able to travel; the doctor's told her to be careful for a while and to rest. Nothing serious, just a precaution."

"Thank you, Steve; Christopher's acceptance by my children means so much to me and to him. He's a good man, Steve; honest and kind and generous, fun and thoughtful and compassionate. I'm sure you'll like him and respect him." She told him about Peggy, then added, "We're making out our wills and doing a prenuptial agreement to protect our children's rightful shares of their inheritances. He's also taking out a large insurance policy for my

550

support if anything should happen to him."

"I think that's wise, Mother, to prevent any future problems with his daughter, if he is a wealthy man. From what you say, he sounds like a good choice for you. And he's damn lucky to get my mother."

"We're both lucky we found each other. I haven't met Peggy, but we've talked several times. We get along fine. She knows I'm not after her father's money and she knows I'm not a threat to her bond with him or her inheritance. My estate is small, but it's only right for my children to get it. Christopher doesn't need or want my holdings. I do have a nice insurance policy, so you children won't be caught in a bind as I was."

"That's something I need to tell you about, Mother; you have more money than you realize. Dad's lawyer contacted me last week with some wild news because he didn't know how to reach you. I was planning to visit you to discuss it in person rather than doing it by phone."

"What are you talking about, Steve?"

"Dad had money hidden away, and it's turned up."

"He what?"

"He had a variable insurance annuity with another company and kept the policy a secret, kept the record and statements in a lock-box

551

in another city. He paid for it with a check made out to cash; that's why it wasn't traceable. Ed was tipped off when a bill arrived for the lock-box. I flew over and checked it out; he had paid for two years' rent in advance and it just expired. He didn't have to report interest income on his taxes because he kept reinvesting it and it's tax deferred. I guess he did it that way because of his fear of being broke, of being poor again. He figured we would discover it if he died and cash it in when needed."

"If it was hidden, how did David expect us to learn about it?"

"By the annual statement sent to his office or notice of payment due on the lock-box."

"Why didn't we receive a statement this past January?"

"I don't know. Mail does get lost and mishandled. There was a letter to us in the lock box with an apology and explanation. Dad did love us, as you said, but he made mistakes. That letter and money for our support helped me forgive him and continue therapy. I have everything here with me. You'll need to decide what to do with the money; it's over two hundred thousand dollars."

"I'll invest it and divide it between you kids in my will."

After they completed their conversation, Kirstin phoned Katie, Sandi, Elaine, and Betty to give them the good news about her marriage. Both daughters promised to be present at the church ceremony and party afterward, but the two Augusta friends couldn't make the trip.

When she finished her calls, Christopher made one to Peggy, who was ecstatic and delighted to make the flight next weekend.

As they sat on the sofa and snuggled, Christopher told Kirstin, "I'm giving John my Appaloosa and Helen most of the furniture in the house, if that's agreeable with you." She nodded it was. "Helen and Frank are coming to the wedding, so are John and Maria. We should be able to close out everything there and pack in two days since I'm not bringing much here."

"There's a lot of space in the hall closet. What about your patients and practice? Have you made arrangements for them?"

"I've already talked to a friend there about taking them for me. It's all in motion, woman. Soon, we'll be married and settled here. I can hardly believe how my life has changed in such a short time. Makes my head spin and my heart race."

"Mine, too, Doc. I love you, and our life is going to be wonderful."

"Maybe we can get that RV and go camping this summer. We'll contact the Peters and give them our new address. It'll be fun to go some place with them. Next time, we won't have to deceive them."

"That's a great idea. We can include John and Maria, too."

Kirstin revealed her talk with Steve about David's hidden assets. In view of all he'd learned about the deceased man, it didn't surprise him. Nor did it alter the financial and legal decisions they had made.

On Saturday, May thirtieth, Christopher Harrison and Kirstin Lowrey stood before the minister in the new church they were attending. Their children and friends sat in pews behind them, ready to observe the sight of two people deeply in love getting married. Katie was with Steve, since the pregnant Louise couldn't fly at that time. Peggy held hands with her husband Phil and beamed with joy. Cliff, who couldn't miss the occasion, had his arm around his wife, Sandi, and their son on his lap. John and Maria were all smiles, as were Frank and Helen. Janet was there with her husband and Franci with her fiancé. Charles Summeraul prayed he wouldn't lose his assistant over this stirring experience, then smiled at his wife.

The couple and their children had shared

dinner and a long talk last night. Christopher and Kirstin planned to visit with their families this weekend and to honeymoon later when things settled down.

The music ceased and the ceremony began. "Family and friends, we are gathered here in God's house to witness the uniting of this couple in holy matrimony." The minister read several appropriate Scriptures and made remarks that warmed the lover's hearts.

The vows came next: "Do you Christopher Harrison take Kirstin Lowrey to be your wedded wife, to love, honor, and cherish her in all things and in all ways until death do you part?"

The physician smiled at his woman and said, "I do."

"Do you Kirstin Lowrey take Christopher Harrison to be your wedded husband, to love, honor, and cherish him in all things and in all ways until death do you part?"

"I do," she replied as her blue gaze seemed to melt into his green one.

The minister asked them to repeat other vows and promises, which they did with love shining in their eyes and audible in their voices. He asked for the rings and blessed the bands of gold before handing one to Christopher and saying, "Place it on her finger and repeat after me, With this ring I thee wed until death do us part."

"With this ring I thee wed until death do us part," the doctor echoed.

Kirstin did the same, and didn't release his hand afterward.

The minister said, "By the power given to me by God and the state of California, I now pronounce you man and wife. What God has joined, let no man put asunder without just cause. Let us pray."

Kirstin and Christopher listened to the meaningful words which blessed their union, sought guidance and protection for them, and gave thanks to the Heavenly Father for bringing them together as one.

"You may kiss the bride."

Kirstin and Christopher gazed at each other for an instant, then shared a brief and bonding kiss. Within moments, the newlyweds were being hugged, kissed, and congratulated by family members and friends. Tears of joy would have spilled onto Kirstin's pale-blue suit if not for the tissue an exuberant Katie handed to her to absorb them.

Everyone traveled to the hotel a mile away for the reception. A table was piled with gifts from friends far and near; they would join the collection at home, accumulated from a surprise party they had been given in New Mexico last weekend. There was even a present from Laura and Harry Stoker: silver champagne goblets, engraved with their names and wedding date.

The couple danced together and with others. They ate delicious snacks and sipped champagne, as they had worked the treats into Kirstin's diet plan. They laughed and talked; both sides of the family got along with perfection. Katie and Peggy struck up a quick and easy friendship, enjoying the fact they had much in common. Phil, Steve, and Cliff seemed to have plenty of interesting topics to discuss as they huddled together like a small football team, laughing, joking, and chatting like old friends.

As Kirstin danced with her son, they exchanged smiles; both knew their differences were in the past.

"I love you, Steve; I'm so happy you're with me today to share this."

"So am I, Mother. You're absolutely radiant. I like him. Peggy, too. I think our families will blend nicely."

"I'm glad, Steve. He likes you, too. Maybe with a special club to compensate for his hand problem, you two can play golf together."

"I'll check into it. I know a man who does excellent work. He could have something ready before summer's over."

"Wonderful. Thanks. Make sure you give Louise and the boys hugs and kisses for me.

We'll try to get to Denver soon for a visit. I want Christopher to meet them. As soon as the twins get a little older, we'll take them camping with us. Sandi's son, too, when she returns home. She did tell you they plan to settle here?"

"Yes, and she's getting eager to get back to the old USA."

"The experience overseas was fun and profitable for them, but I'm ready to have her home again. Things get so crazy and dangerous over there so fast."

"They'll be fine for the little time they have left there. We'll all be fine."

Kirstin looked at her son, smiled, then glanced at her two daughters who were watching them with misty eyes and smiles. Yes, she decided in happiness and gratitude, they would all be fine now. *Thank you, God.*

Cuddled together in the bed in their apartment, Christopher and Kirstin Harrison began their first night as man and wife in glorious splendor.

"I love you, Kirstin."

"I love you, too, Christopher. What do you say about a little game of switch tonight? I'll be the doctor and you be the patient."

He teased, "A captive patient or a guinea pig for a researcher?"

"Neither, just a willing partner who'll let me operate on him."

As she stimulated him, he chuckled and said, "I love your technique, Mrs. Doctor Harrison. Examine me and treat me all you like."

"You've already healed yourself and me."

"We healed each other, Kirstin. We're both whole again."

"No, we're halves, my love, of a perfect whole."

"You're right. Now, get back to work; you were having a big success."

As her hand grasped him again, she quipped, "Yes, I was, wasn't I?"

They laughed, kissed, and hugged, and a passionate night began. They made love beneath the skylight that revealed a starry heaven and lovely moon. Both realized how magical and special it was to find true love, to be given a second opportunity for a glorious life, and how dull and unrewarding that life— and they—would be without taking chances.